Cameron Johnston

FIRST MAGE ON THE MOON

ANGRY ROBOT
An imprint of Watkins Media Ltd

Unit 11, Shepperton House
89-93 Shepperton Road
London N1 3DF
UK

angryrobotbooks.com
10, 9, 8, 7, 6, 5, 4, 3, Incantation, 2, 1, Lift Off!

An Angry Robot paperback original, 2026

Edited by Simon Spanton Walker and Kevin Eddy
Cover illustrated by Jörg Asselborn
Cover designed by Alice Claire Coleman
Set in Meridien

ISBN 978 1 91599 806 4
Ebook ISBN 978 1 91599 807 1

Printed and bound in the United Kingdom by CPI Group (UK) Ltd, Croydon CR0 4YY

The manufacturer's authorised representative in the EU for product safety is eucomply OÜ - Pärnu mnt 139b-14, 11317 Tallinn, Estonia, hello@eucompliancepartner.com; www.eucompliancepartner.com

9 8 7 6 5 4 3 2 1

For all those who look up at the night sky to take in the ancient light of unimaginably distant stars.

PROLOGUE

"You must meet the most interesting people on the gallows," Whitlaw Goddard said to the black-hooded man readying his noose. The wooden stool creaked beneath his bare feet as he shifted, earning him a cuff that left his ear throbbing. The large audience chattered among themselves, making jokes and mocking, waiting for the day's entertainment to begin.

The silent executioner didn't dare talk with the heretic the corrupt hierarchs held responsible for conniving to land a mage on the holy moon, home of the gods. He ignored the condemned mage and pulled a length of rough rope taut, checking that it would hold the weight of his portly criminal. The man grunted in satisfaction and tied the end into a looping knot just large enough to accommodate Whitlaw's head.

The mage shuddered and swallowed back down the sudden burn of bile. He'd never been one for pointless small talk, but with his hands bound and his magic sealed, a rising panic lent desperate energy to his tongue – as if by some miracle he might charm the dour executioner into sparing his life. Behind him, chains rattled, and the prison door clanked open for a second time as his official partner in crime emerged.

Komissar Taeban Tereshkova was escorted out of the black gate by seven grim-faced Imperial guards in full mail, iron-bound clubs at the ready. She was a muscular, scar-faced career warrior with short, severe, salt-and-pepper hair and a gravelly voice, but her cold demeanour was very much at odds with what he had gleaned from their exchanges though a crack in the prison wall.

Like himself, she was barefoot and dressed only in a sweat-stained linen long-shirt, with her hands bound so tight with styxsteel chain that they were almost purple. Mages were rightly feared, especially this close to death when desperation might cause one to call up the most terrible of powers. These chains, marinated in death and despair, disrupted a mage's ability to draw aether from the well of magic inside them. Whitlaw's own hands throbbed in empathy, his skin slowly scalding from the touch of that accursed steel.

Komissar Tereshkova held her head high, climbed the steps, and walked out onto the creaking wooden platform to meet her fate beside him. She mounted the stool, ready for the noose. He wished he'd shown such composure when they dragged him out sobbing.

The prison they had spent the last two months in, being tortured and interrogated, was named The Howling, after the incessant shrieks of the inhabitants that made sleep all but impossible – a torture all of its own. As bad as the mouldering prison was, the area it had been built in was worse. The Forest of the End was silent save the noise of the gathering audience. A morning mist clung to the red grass and twisted black boughs that had seen so much death over the centuries. A river of blood had been spilled here on the Unity side of the border with the Empire: the mountain of corpses slumbering beneath its dirt had spiritually tainted the land, and now only the worst mages, traitors, and criminals were brought here in the hope that their souls would be carried off to the Nine Hells in torment. As a mage, the whole place tasted like rotten meat in Whitlaw's mouth, and the touch of the mist itched like maggots burrowing into his skin. The only magically twisted hellhole worse than this was No Man's Land, the wide strip of border between the warring nations.

Twenty armoured guards and a full squad of gold-masked Unity battlemages with rune-encrusted robes and glowing staves stood ready to ensure there would be no escape. Not that anybody would ever ride out to rescue the likes of Whitlaw Goddard.

He smiled at his counterpart from the Ranneas Empire, his lips cracking and bleeding anew. "We finally meet face to face." After the momentous events of the last three years, and despite their current sorry state, it was a pleasure.

She nodded back, dignified until the end. She was one of the Empire's old guard, from a distinguished and powerful noble family, a warrior mage cut from very different cloth than podgy, balding, middle-aged manager Whitlaw Goddard, who had happened to become Chief of the Unity's Research and Design Workshop – no, he would definitely be pissing himself right now had there been any piss left in him.

"Head back," the hooded executioner demanded. Whitlaw winced as his head was yanked back and the rough rope pulled tight around his throat. His mouth was a desert. The rope wouldn't allow him to swallow. He started to squirm. The rope tightened, squeezed harder. Panic welled up.

Komissar Tereshkova shot him a look that simply said, *Endure*. Her glance was a bucket of cool water that quenched his rising panic.

Whitlaw's gaze slid past a few familiar faces in the crowd, amidst the guards there to make sure they stayed to watch his execution. The surviving staff from the workshop, those hardworking subordinates who had dared to dream of a better world and were willing to risk their lives to do it. Of course they would be forced to watch his demise as an object lesson in obedience! Then he spotted his darling daughter Katherine, her dark hair limp and unbrushed, eyes red and face drawn. Half of the right sleeve of her coat was missing, unneeded now, the hole sewn up just like the flesh beneath. He nearly lost all composure, almost dissolved into a flood of tears and snot. She had already lost her mother and her arm, and now she would lose her father too.

But she will live, he reassured himself. *You saw to that.*

The image of his own father appeared unbidden in his mind, half-blind, grey and bent over his writing desk, painstakingly writing Whitlaw's letter of recommendation to the second-best magic guild in Orialis. *If you reach for the moon,* he had said, *be assured that many people will try and keep you shackled in the mud beside them.* He hadn't meant it literally, but his father had been more correct than he'd known. A sudden wave of grief arrived. The old man would have approved of his son's actions, despite the cost.

So, the hierarchy wanted him to break and beg for his life for all to see? No, he refused to let Katherine's last memory of him be so pathetic. Instead, he lifted his head and straightened his back, denying the bastards the chance to record for the history books that Whitlaw Goddard died wailing. One day, many years hence, he mused, Katherine might even live to see her father considered a hero: that was the only comfort he had left, and a feeble one at that. He looked out at his wet-eyed staff, and his beautiful and loving daughter, and did not regret putting his neck in the noose to save their skins… but he knew the hierarchy would have just hung all the rest, too, had he not publicly claimed total responsibility for their great deeds.

As Whitlaw regained his composure, Tereshkova's lips curved upwards in a brief sign of approval. He swallowed, tried to ignore the rope around his throat, and looked out at the crowd gathered before the gallows. Nobody who was anybody would miss this execution. It was likely this was the first time most of them had even heard his name.

At the front of the throng, velvet-cushioned seats were occupied by hierarchs of the Unity and the wealthy merchants that backed them, the senior battlemages, and generals. A delegation of Empire officials sat off to the side, clad in thick black bear furs and hats with their red griffin emblem pinned to the front. He thought it ironic that this was what it took for both sides to agree on anything.

Behind them, enraged priests had gathered from all over the world to glare death at the heathens who had dared to set mortal foot upon the holy moon. The head priests of Gildanas, god of abundance and patron deity of the Unity; and Perunuk, The Thunderer, chief god in the official religion of the Ranneas Empire, stood frothing at the mouth and spitting abjurations at him.

Their religions might have started the war, despite the doctrines of both sides holding only minor differences, but money and power and the pride of the rich and powerful had turned a skirmish or three into genocide, exploring new depths of the Nine Hells right here. Behind the seething ecclesiastics stood a semicircle of bureaucrats, mages from far-flung lands, tradesfolk, scribes, and news carriers eager to record the death of the most notorious criminals of the age – or maverick heroes, depending on who you talked to. At the back were a horde of unwashed workers from the local towns and villages whose sweat greased the Unity's march of industry, all dressed in drab brown and grey coats and flat felted caps. Many of them looked at the sky, peering up at the waning crescent of the moon and pondering the feat of magic and engineering that mankind had achieved.

The way people had once looked at the world had shattered. It was a unique moment in history, and they all felt that the pieces would never quite fit back the way they had before.

Mere mortals had touched the moon and had explored the Garden of the Gods. The high and mighty battlemages with all their power and potent arcane artefacts had not been the ones to achieve such a feat; oh, no, that belonged to the low-born and weakling mages of the Research and Design Workshop, with naught but their ingenuity and hard work. Whitlaw grinned down at the battlemages from the gallows. Most of them shifted uncomfortably and looked away.

A greying man in a black formal tunic and silver brocade coat approached the gallows, a sealed scroll clutched in gloved hands. He wore a pure white cloak stitched with the Unity's emblem, the gilded eagle. This man was the voice of the hierarchs. The executioner yanked the nooses tighter until Whitlaw and Tereshkova were on the very tips of their toes, struggling to breathe.

The man mounted the steps, stood in front of Whitlaw and turned to address his audience, breaking the wax seal of the scroll with a thumbnail. He cleared his throat and unfurled the parchment with a dramatic flourish.

"To all you gods-fearing ladies and gentlemen here today in the Forest of the End," he intoned, "I ask you to bear witness to the sanctioned execution of these two criminals: Whitlaw Goddard and Taeban Tereshkova. These wayward souls have been declared anathema by the most holy Churches of the Unity and the Ranneas Empire, and have been sentenced to death. I tell you this, it is quite the feat to bring the Unity and the Empire together in agreement on anything!"

His attempt at humour fell on deaf ears, managing only a few nervous titters and a lot of shuffling of feet.

He cleared his throat and continued. "Let their crimes be listed... Grand thievery! Fraud! Destruction of government property! The death of mages and men enmeshed in their treachery!" He paused for dramatic effect, the crowd still and listening, rapt.

"And finally, heresy against the gods!"

Whitlaw snorted at that last charge. Could they get any more ludicrous?

"The condemned will now be allowed to say a few last words before divine Akerbis reaps their souls for final judgement." He motioned the executioner to ease up and let Tereshkova speak.

"I am Taeban Tereshkova, Komissar in the Imperial Army," she said, voice hoarse and guttural with a strong Imperial accent. "And I am not afraid of a good death. Magic was a gift of the gods meant to lift mankind out of the dirt and enable us to understand the world. It was never meant for war. That is all I have to say."

The delegation from the Empire showed little emotion, but the grim-faced old man who seemed to be in charge gave a slight nod of approval, for her bravery if not for her words.

Whitlaw ground his teeth. She'd said what he so yearned to say, and now his last words would be outright lies glorifying the hierarch who had condemned him to death. His gaze was drawn to Grubman-Lordrach IV, who'd had a golden throne brought out especially for the occasion. The man sat there gloating, and with his daughter's life held hostage, there was nothing Whitlaw could do about it.

"I am Whitlaw Goddard, Chief of the Unity's Research and Design Workshop, and I confess to all charges. By order of the great and farsighted Hierarch Grubman-Lordrach IV, I strove to enable mortal hands to reach up into the void between worlds and show the entire world the marvels of the Unity's arcane engineering. Instead, in my hubris and heresy, I ordered my brave and loyal mages to collaborate with a rogue Imperial mage to trespass upon the home of the gods itself. His grace offered the world a gift of knowledge, and I instead betrayed it for my personal glory." The lies burned like acid on his tongue.

The speaker shot him a scowl. "Enough grovelling. Your fate is sealed, traitor. Let these criminals hang."

The executioner kicked the stools out from beneath them. The rope pulled tight, cutting off most of his air. His feet flailed for purchase as his own weight began choking him to death. Blood pounded in his skull. Lungs strained for breath that wouldn't come. He dangled here, slowing dying, legs jerking as panic filled him. Hanging was not a quick death without a drop to break the neck. His vision narrowed, the darkness of death eroding the edges of his world.

Katherine did not look away, and their eyes met one last time across the jeering crowd. Tears rolled down her cheeks, but the set of her jaw was firm. She was no longer his naïve young child, but a strong woman in her own right. She would survive and she would thrive.

The pain and panic peaked, beyond enduring. Then all terror fled, replaced with a soft and unexpected peace that suffused every fibre of his being. A glorious silver light appeared directly ahead, a beacon summoning him to the afterlife. Whitlaw Goddard left his slowly swaying corpse behind and accepted the warm embrace of death.

CHAPTER 1

Three years before…

Ella Pickering woke at dawn with the rest of the workers and commoner mages, groaning and burying her head beneath her blanket as the mistress of the flophouse marched down the hallway, beating on her copper pot with a wooden spoon.

"Up and out to work, you layabouts," Mrs Beaton yelled. "Porridge is two copper bits. Three with bread and butter."

Ella stirred and stared up at the black mould creeping across her ceiling, trying to decide if she could make out the pattern of a demonic face or not. Once, in another, more grandiose life, this old building had been an inn's stable, thus its doorways were wide enough to accommodate her wheeled chair. As wretched as the dingy, damp, and lopsided old building was, it still offered more freedom and colour than the soulless barracks at the fort, locked up at sundown with the conscripts, debtors, and indentured criminals treated every bit like the slaves of old.

Another joyous day, she thought, wiping gritty sleep from her eyes. The cracked and blistered skin of her hands was a gift of the caustic alchemical substances used in her work, and she weighed up using the last dregs of her hand cream to soothe the sting. She grudgingly decided to save it for a truly bad day. The wheel-callouses on her palms throbbed at the thought of another day's travel and work.

Ella sighed and peeled back her bedding to expose herself to the chilly spring air. After the accident, it had taken a while to learn how to manage even the simplest day to day tasks, but she decided early on she'd be damned if she let that stop her. Through trial and error, she'd found her own solutions. She wiped herself down with wet rags, brushed her unruly straw-blonde hair back and double-pinned it into a bun well out of the reach of machinery or fire. After pulling on her patched, drab brown work robes, the belt and pouches went on next, followed by a thick leather apron. She swung her legs out of bed, using wooden crutches to shift herself into the battered, third-hand wheeled chair.

The two front wheels were old, yet still sturdy enough, but the stabilising central wheel at the back squeaked with every revolution. The chair's wooden frame and tarnished brass spokes creaked in complaince as she settled herself into the wickerwork seat and hooked her crutches over the upright handles. Her tailbone felt raw from the cobbled streets and the sores that resulted from spending all day seated, but there was nothing she could do about that. She slung her bag over the back and forewent the stale bread and questionable butter, instead wheeling herself out of the mouldering flophouse she called home.

A fat drop of cold rain promptly plopped onto her scalp. The rivulet wound down her forehead to hang at the end of her nose.

Ella wiped it away and cursed the black and swollen sky. Rain was no friend of hers – iron-rimmed wheels fared terribly on cobblestones and muddy tracks, and once she got going the only way to slow down or stop was to use her palms on the wheels. She prayed the spring storms would be light this year, and that those black clouds would hold their rains until they hit the hills further east.

Another worker stepped out into the doorway beside her, the older man's skin sallow and his cheeks and bulbous nose red from another night on the alehouse's special sauce. Jim smiled, revealing missing teeth. "Tough day ahead, my little chicken?" His rough accent was from the far north of Unity lands, somewhere cold and dark and dreary where hard men and women lived tough lives, ate pickled herring, drank buckets of eye-watering booze, and dared to fight bears for fun. Or so they claimed.

"You know it," she replied. "Same as always, Jim."

"Don't let the bastards get you down, hen. You have a good one, now," he said, completing their daily ritual. He pulled up the stiff collar of his work coat and weaved his way past the temples of the gods and down the road towards the fort, joining a stream of horse and cart and gloomy workers disgorged from their housing. More than a few limped or walked with canes and crutches, lacking an eye or an arm: the gifts of a long war that sucked in the young and healthy, chewed them up, and spat out people broken in mind and body.

Watching Jim's broad back shudder as he hacked up phlegm before he went wherever it was he went every day, Ella pondered if someday she would care enough to learn anything about the man other than his name and his local drinking den, The Muddy Mare.

She steeled herself against the day, took a deep breath, and wheeled herself down the cobbled street, avoiding a dozen potholes deep enough to lose a child in. The mounds of horse droppings were the worst – if it was on her wheels then it was on her hands. The road between the fort and the ramshackle village of Newsark had been built on the cheap and in a hurry to accommodate the servants and staff assigned to work there. Ella's teeth and tailbone rattled as she juddered over the cobblestones – they didn't call wheeled contraptions like hers boneshakers for nothing. Without any ability to stop beyond grabbing the wheels, slopes were a nightmare. The road ran through the village and round the edge of the lake: Ella reckoned it might have once been a picturesque location before the alchemical run-off from the fort killed everything that had once lived there. The oily brown scum on the surface rippled as the wind picked up.

Beggars, orphans, crafters, alewives, and hedge witches were out in force along the roadside, offering repaired goods richer folk had thrown into the midden, handicrafts, ointments, potions, and foodstuffs long past their prime – anything that could net them a quick coin or two. As the stream of workers heading to the fort began to thin, most of them moved off to richer pastures, biding their time until the bulk of traffic reversed at the end of the day.

Half a bell spent lurching over the cobblestones led her to the ramparts of the fort. Aether stirred all around her, the tang of magic fizzing on Ella's tongue – the huge, grey stone walls boasted hundreds of magical protections that sucked in the ambient aether of the world and stored it against the day somebody tried to breach the defences. The passive protection those ambient defensive runes offered didn't require the use of expensive gems of concentrated aether to operate, but they could be swiftly drained by a sustained, concerted offensive. Which is when a second line of ruinously expensive protections would be activated.

She joined the line of workers and carts queuing at the fortified gatehouse. Four huge, stone war golems in the form of muscular men in old-fashioned armour flanked the entranceway, their glowing ruby eyes and rune-encrusted spear points offering a warning to any and all that might dare cause trouble. Guards with red-painted iron breastplates and wickedly hooked halberds yawned and looked on in boredom from beneath wide-brimmed helmets. They rested their weapons on their shoulders while a grizzled sergeant ran a wand over the back of people's right hands, studying the red glow of the permit tattoos that appeared before ushering them through.

A sandy-haired young musician with a patchy thicket pretending to be a beard tried to slip past the guards by hiding behind a bulky labourer. He ducked his head and clutched his lyre tight, trying to stay in the bigger man's shadow. A guard spotted the hapless intruder and tripped him up with the butt of his halberd. The man went down face-first to the muck. His lyre shattered beneath him, strings snapping with loud twangs. Guards clapped hands on him and yanked him upright.

"What do we have here?" the sergeant said. "Some young dolt trying to sneak in. What are you, son? A spy?"

The young man struggled in their steely grip and his face flushed red. "I jusht wanna see her."

A guard's nose wrinkled. He sniffed at the fumes escaping the man's mouth. "This one's still drunk as a tavern rat from the night before."

The sergeant's eyebrow arched. "Who are you here to see?"

"Katherine," he growled.

"Oho," The sergeant said. "Katherine Goddard?"

The intruder nodded, his eyes bright and furious. "Let go of me, you dolt, I needsh my inshpiration."

Ella rolled her eyes. Of course it was that shy little alchemist. She wasn't the prettiest woman on the fort by a bow shot, but oh, what a stunning singing voice! A prodigy in mathematics and academia, too. Ella might have been envious if Katherine didn't also seem like a genuine and warm-hearted woman, one she wished she knew better than in passing – a shame they moved in very different social circles.

The sergeant whistled. "So, you are the scabby musician who's been sniffing around the Chief of Research and Design's daughter. That, you odious little sack of shit, was a mistake." He looked to the nearest war golem. "Toss this wretch into the lake. As far as you can without killing him."

The golem's eyes burned bright. Stone ground as it reached out and plucked the fool from the guards' grip, imprisoning him inside a fist that could squish him like a grape. The man gasped for breath, his ribs straining against implacable stone.

"Try not to drown," a guard shouted as the golem took off at speed, its pounding feet causing miniature earthquakes.

As terrifying as the war golem was, Ella thought it lucky the man hadn't just been slain on the spot. When it was her turn, she offered up her hand and felt the tingle of magic playing over her skin. The blood-red tattoo swam to the surface of her skin, a swirling circle of runes and glyphs that set his wand buzzing.

The sergeant grunted and waved her onwards.

She wheeled herself through the gatehouse, past massive brass-bound oak doors that throbbed with defensive arcane runes and under the portcullis made of cast iron, a metal that served to thwart hexes and curses and disrupt many a spell. Spearmen in clinking iron mail and wide-brimmed helmets trooped after mounted knights whose elaborate and disastrously expensive dragon-forged steel plate armour reeked of potent enchantments that made them nigh on invulnerable killing machines on the field of battle, so long as they had enough aether gems to keep it powered. Labourers worked to unload supply carts, gossiping about last night's drunken indiscretions. Mages tinkered with bladed war machines and directed hulking stone golems, most of them crude and clumsily formed, only suitable for lugging heavy equipment about. The Unity's fort was vast, comprising of parade ground, barracks, arcane artillery ranges, workshops, and dozens of enormous warehouses.

She rolled past a row of forges, hammer and anvils ringing in thunderous tempo making swords and spears, nails and horseshoes, and whatever else the army was short of. They were always short of something. Some few craftsfolk of a more sorcerous bent cast bronze and brass implements and fittings for the exclusive use of mages, for whom crude iron, and even normal steel, proved an impediment to their spells. Chimneys bellowed smoke and steam into the air, gifting every breath the tang of metal.

Ella was stationed at the very back of the fort, where the downtrodden and less-skilled mages laboured away in the production booths day in and day out. Behind the corner of the Research and Design workshop she was lucky enough to be stationed in, there was only an empty area of craters and broken statues used for testing new weapons.

At the raised lip of the main doorway, she summoned aether up from inside her along with a levitation cantrip to help her chair up and over the threshold. The crude, rusty iron rims of her wheels tried to twist the spell askew, but her will held firm and the chair bumped up and in.

The cavernous warehouse workshop was hot and sticky, with several forge fires already belching out heat as mages possessing the lore of steel resisted its malign influence to bend metal to their will, hammering it out on anvils. They used the raw power of their aether to keep their work hot and pliable for far longer than otherwise possible, eschewing the use of tongs for the push and pull of their minds when it came to the more delicate work. They were making weapons and armour for the ranking warriors, whereas others worked on intricate gold, bronze, silver, and brass, inserting crystals bearing elemental power to the tips of staves to form the deadly weapons wielded by the combat mages of the Unity.

The fort's temple bell rang out the start of the workday, and Ella rolled to her section in the corner. Every booth was isolated by thumb-thick oak walls, as much to stop meaningless chatter as it was to try and contain shrapnel from explosions. She washed her hands in the bowl on the workbench, sat up painfully straight so she could reach, and got to work on the new line of blasting crystals. The day went past in a haze of monotony, exactly the same as every other: Cut the crystal. Polish the crystal. Insert her aether into the graver to inscribe a miniscule circle of arcane runes into the face of the crystal. Wash it all with caustic binding solutions. Concentrate and move aether from the well inside her to empower and activate the runes. Carefully set it down in a wool-lined crate beside a dozen other weapons of its kind, and then begin the next, on and on until a bell rang, summoning workers to the dining hall for luncheon.

A small army of grease-spattered cooks stirred cauldrons and ferried food to and from the ovens while pot-washers frantically laboured away in troughs behind them. Workers marched past, bowls in their hands ready to accept the mysterious bounty of the ladles. Every worker was allowed one big ladle of stew and one spongey dumpling before sitting at a table to chow down. Mages got two.

At least the fort provided me with decent food, Ella thought, tucking into a hefty bowl of beef stewed in red wine, carrot, and herb dumplings. It was all free, too, helping to make up for all that internal energy the war effort demanded of mages like her. Utilising aether took as much energy as physical labour, though the mental muscles involved were very different. For poor folk like her, this was their only real meal of the day. She spooned down the last shreds of beef and carrot at the bottom of her bowl, wiped her lips, and wheeled back to work. Her quota wouldn't change, and any dawdling now would mean a later finish. She stretched, repositioned her magnifying glass and got back to cutting the crystal, polishing the crystal…

Being locked away inside a sweaty, stinking workshop was not at all what Ella Pickering had signed up for when the local lord's recruiters came to call on her sleepy little village in the countryside, searching for those with the talent. Of course, that was before her accident.

The dishevelled mage yawed and blinked tired eyes, trying to shake off the mind-numbing repetition of her job. She stirred and sat up straighter in her wheeled chair, finding that she had missed the nightfall bell. Most of the other workers had long since extinguished their oil lamps and gone off to their beds. What light there was did not touch the edges of the cavernous workshop, a glorified stone barn crammed with all manner of magical apparatus, most of which she had yet to determine the use of. Rain drummed on the tin roof, driven by fierce wind.

Just two more to finish off her extra quota, she told herself, and her debts would be another day closer to being paid off. She swept an errant lock of hair back from her eyes and squinted through the magnifying glass at the octagonal thumbnail-sized piece of quartz clamped to the workbench in front of her. Ever so carefully, she forced an edge of magic onto the fine edge of her jeweller's graver. She cut the rune of blasting into the polished face and poured aether into it: the rune caught light, a stuttering inhale suckling on her magic. She withdrew her power from the newborn weapon and placed it into the wool-padded crate to slowly absorb the ambient aether. In ten days, it would be fully charged and ready to blow some unfortunate patrol of Empire warriors to smithereens.

All the painstaking effort crafting these weapons, only for some arrogant battlemage with more magical might than brain power to toss them about like bent pennies, shattering them to make big bangs and bloodshed.

A shadow fell over her. She started, looking up.

"You are wilting, hen," Jackan Grissom said, setting a mug of steaming tea down in front of her. "Double shifts are brutal, and you do more than your fair share. Take a break before you make a mistake, is what I always say."

The grey-haired northlands engineer had a bushy moustache, which hid his lips entirely, and bore a deeply lined face that might charitably be described as having "seen some serious shit go down". The hems and cuffs of his work robes were singed and stained. That raggedy old leather apron he wore over his robes had many stories to tell. They had met a few times before, but she was a production mage – the lowest of the low when it came to their ilk – and he was a senior engineer in the Research and Design team, offering them little chance to mix.

She curled her fingers around the hot mug. A tentative sip revealed perfection – the tiny dash of milk she preferred. Ella sighed. He had obviously done his research, and she imagined him measuring the amount added down to the droplet.

He grinned with the satisfaction of a job well done. "Is it coming up on two seasons now that we've had the pleasure of your presence?"

She glanced at her calloused hands, the irritated, cracked skin. “Yes,” she replied. “It feels like a whole year already.”

He chuckled knowingly. “I remember that all too well. I used to design bridges once, back before the old war heated up again. I had such grand plans – soaring spans of stone and glass steadied with ropes of steel cable. I had imagined a group of metal mages working beside me, forging masterpieces together. Now… well, we do what we are told and make this shit.”

She sipped her tea and said nothing.

Jackan’s dark eyes studied her like one of his faulty machines of steel and brass and sorcery. “You were a skymage, yes? Piloting one of the Unity’s rarest and most expensive aerial vessels?”

She tapped the brass spokes of her wheeled chair. “Was.”

He didn’t ask what happened. None of them had done since she arrived under a very obvious dark cloud of the Unity’s displeasure. Most of them had once been something else, and they didn’t want to pry. But it had been a while now since she had spoken to anybody about anything other than work, and his gentle query had Ella wanting to tell somebody about her woes, at least a little.

“I messed up bad,” she said. “As bad as it gets. I crash-landed my ship on a hierarch’s gilded chariot and ruined them both. My back, too.”

He winced. “Aye, that would certainly do it. Was it your fault or did they just assign you the blame?”

She blinked at his bluntness, then nodded. “They said I made an error in wind speed calculations. I was sent up on a windy day, but still…”

“Was that your first mistake?”

“The only one that ever mattered.”

He nodded sagely. “One mistake and they dump a promising young mage like you on the production benches. Sounds about right. As if anybody is perfect all the time. Never mind; I wager you won’t make that mistake again, eh.”

Ella scowled and sagged in her chair. “As if I’ll ever get the chance.”

Jackan shrugged. “What goes down can sometimes go back up again. Who knows what the future might bring.” He looked around at the deserted workshop. “Maybe this accursed war will end some day, and we’ll all go back to having real, useful jobs.”

He patted her on the shoulder and wandered off down the other end of the workshop, a restricted area screened off by heavy canvas curtains hanging from rails on the ceiling. As he drew the entry flap back, she glimpsed a half-built arcane contraption up on a wooden scaffold, its weight supported by chains. She had no idea what this secret project was, but the other worker-mages on her line speculated – from what few details they had glimpsed – that it was a new model of cannon, based on it being a long metal tube with a flaring muzzle at one end.

She was alone with her thoughts in the darkened workshop, listening to the rain and wind. She cricked her neck, cracked her knuckles and got back to work; one last blasting crystal and she was done for the day. Her head throbbed from the drain on her aether well, and her back ached from sitting up so straight to work on a bench too tall for her wheeled chair. She managed to get it finished before her concentration failed completely, a dangerous prospect when potent arcane energies were in play: if she overloaded her graving tool, it would explode in her hand, likely taking a few of her fingers with it. She packed the crate and nailed it shut, ready for transport to the front lines.

The war she slaved away for had grown stale, mere skirmishes between dozens rather than actual battles these days, but nobody knew how long that relative peace would last. Over the centuries, millions had died on bloodstained and cratered fields of conflict littered with the ruins of arcane war machines and the twisted skeletons of vat-grown warbeasts. This seemingly endless war periodically exhausted the resources of both the Unity and the Empire, but a brand-new generation of mages and warriors were coming of age, and the hierarchs were rearming their forces at a punishing pace, no matter the cost to impoverished rural villages and towns already struggling to bring in the harvests. So long as the administrative capital Orialis was flush with fresh produce and luxury items, the rulers of the Unity didn't much care what happened out in the sticks.

Ella packed away her tools and locked them in the cabinet of her workbench, then brushed the debris of a day's work into a bin and set it aside, ready for the specially trained cleaners to dispose of. She peered at the high windows in the workshop, where sheets of rain poured down the wavy glass panes, and did not relish the thought of the trip back to the flophouse, with its damp walls and leaking roof.

A squeal of steel from the other side of the workshop and the clang of something heavy hitting the stone was followed by Jackan yelling, and cursing blue enough to offend black-hearted pirates and brigands.

Ella sped down the walkway towards the curtains of the restricted section, iron-rimmed wheels clicking across stone. "Jackan? Are you hurt?"

A hiss of pain and more cursing.

Rules and regulations be damned. She pulled the flap in the curtain open and entered.

By the lights of multiple oil lamps, she could tell the scaffolding had collapsed on one side, steel poles bent and wood splintered. Chains with snapped links lay all over the floor. The machine Jackan had been working on was almost upright now, the dented muzzle on the floor. It was a thick cylinder of metal double his height. A hatch in the thing's belly dangled open, its guts of copper tubing glimmering with sequences of arcane runes.

The engineer himself was on his knees, cradling a nasty gash that split his palm. Splinters of wood jutted from the skin, and one thumbnail was already blackening.

She rolled towards him. "What happened?"

He scowled at the scaffolding. "Should have taken my own advice and called it a night. What a daftie. I'm fine, lass. Just a few scratches, is all."

"Let me see that hand."

He obliged and she plucked out the offending splinters. "Can you bend your fingers?"

Blood welled up from the gash and dripped freely as he curled them, wincing.

Ella looked around and spotted a mage's medical kit in its Unity-standard square tin stamped with the eagle emblem. "At least it's a shallow wound." She popped the lid open and retrieved healing paste, smearing the pungent green substance over his cuts. The skin flushed red, and his wounds slowly closed over until they were pale scars.

"All done," she said as wind and rain battered the windows and roof. "Uh, am I allowed to ask what you're working on?"

He glanced at the machinery. "You are definitely allowed to ask..."

After a moment's pause, she added: "And are you allowed to tell me what it is?"

He smiled, the corners of his eyes crinkling. "Now that's a better question, lass. I don't see why not: this is merely an experiment, not any kind of secret weapon. The battlemages keep on asking us for better siege weapons. More range. Bigger explosions. You know the drill. Whitlaw Goddard has given me a decent budget and free rein to try and develop a weapon delivery system more sophisticated than a mage staff or crude heavy cannon."

Ella studied the contraption, hanging on its chains. "Oh, so this won't blow up in your face if something goes wrong? Say, if somebody were to drop it?"

Jackan cleared his throat, shifting uncomfortably. "Ach, of course not. There is nothing to ignite the black powder loaded into this thing. Why–"

Lightning flashed.

The roof boomed from a direct strike, causing them to flinch and cover their heads. Glowing droplets of molten tin showered them, sizzling in the rain falling through a gaping hole in the ceiling above them.

Lightning snapped and sparked through the chains connected to the arcane machine. The copper guts of the thing began to smoke as whatever was inside coughed and spluttered to life. Protective wards flickered and failed, and the air smelled of burnt hair and hot metal. A whistle of smoke and sparks jetted from its muzzle and an ominous rumble in its belly promised something more extreme.

Jackan's eyes bulged. "Oh, damn. Oh, shitting hells."

Ella was already fleeing, hands powered by panic pushing her wheels as fast as she could move them.

After a moment's hesitation, the engineer hurried after her.

The arcane machine roared to life. Blue and orange flame exploded from the flaring muzzle, setting papers and wood burning. The blast knocked Jackan off his feet, sending him careering right into Ella. They went down in a bruising tangle of limbs and wheels. Chains and scaffold groaned as the machine heaved at its restraints. Its steel casing glowed hot and the stone floor bubbled and melted beneath relentless blasting flame. The machine roared in anger, smoke and debris billowing out across the workshop, stinging her eyes.

Chains squealed and parted. The machine howled at its sudden freedom, launching itself at the ceiling. The damaged roof exploded outwards as the machine punched through to roar into the night sky.

Ella and Jackan lay on their backs, coughing and squinting up into the rain as the flaming machine rose on a pillar of black smoke, soaring higher than any skymage had ever reached.

Ella's wheeled chair was on its side, spokes bent, one missing entirely. Terror punched her in the gut. There was no possibility of replacing something so expensive. If the chair was broken, then her independence was gone. She'd need help to get to the toilet, to wash, get food… everything, and she had nobody. Jackan rose and righted the chair, then helped her back into the seat. She found it a little more battered, but still functional. Her heartbeat slowed; fear replaced with awe as she looked up at the bright spark in the sky.

"By the gods," Ella said. "It's still going. That weird contraption of yours might even touch the moon!" She sighed. "Just imagine if we were actually able to talk to the gods face to face and ask them to stop this wretched war."

As if cosmically unimpressed gods heard her, the device listed and began to spin round and round with fearsome speed. The rear-end of the device came apart under intense heat. It began falling back to earth, jerked this way and that by steam and flame jetting from between twisted metal plates. The mass of hot metal plummeted like a shooting star somewhere over the contested No Man's Land between the Unity and the Empire.

Jackan scratched the singed bristles on his chin. His eyes sparkled as he looked up into the night sky. "The moon, you say…"

New designs and figures began rampaging through his mind.

CHAPTER 2

Guylan Bluford stifled a yawn and combed fingers through his curly black hair in a hopeless attempt to tame it. He'd been hauled out of bed first thing in the morning and sent off half-dressed to assess extensive damage to the rear of the workshop. While the Chief of Research and Design struggled to open the heavy canvas partition, the young engineer pulled a stick of charcoal from his belt pouch and tapped his notepad impatiently.

"The bloody mess is in here," Whitlaw Goddard said, ushering him through. The chief was in his fine formal robes, rather than work browns and leather apron, and the white cloth was now stained. It really wasn't like him to get his hands dirty, Guylan thought, and he had a feeling he was about to have a very bad day.

His nose wrinkled at the acrid stench of burning. The entire space was a mess: blackened canvas that was meant to be fire-resistant. Charred wood. Melted glass pooled in pitted stone. Sagging, deformed steel supports, tools, and the remnants of chains. He ran a dark finger along the ruins of a shelf and rubbed grey ash between thumb and forefinger, studying the consistency. The young arcane engineer whistled in surprise at the clouds showing through a massive hole punched through the roof: the edges were curled outwards, evidence that something had left rather than entered. A flock of inquisitive pigeons clustered around the opening and the sooty floor was already crusted white with their droppings.

Guylan dusted off his hands and looked back at the chief, who stood, red-faced, his arms crossed and his foot tapping.

"What in the blazes happened here?" he asked. "It looks like an angry battlemage struck the place."

Whitlaw Goddard's lips thinned. "That," he said, jowls shaking, "is a very good question. Jackan, would you care to comment?"

The older man lurking in the back shrugged. "Lightning strike."

"Mmm-hmm," Whitlaw replied. "Unless I am very much mistaken, lightning alone does not usually result in an explosion and a pit melted in the floor. Nor does it explain your missing eyebrows and singed beard."

Jackan shuffled his feet and cleared his throat. "Aye, well, one of my experiments might have been under construction and I was here tinkering with it last night. I swear, it wasn't my fault, old friend."

Whitlaw massaged the bridge of his nose. "I don't have an unlimited budget to play with. Where are the remnants? Can any of it be salvaged?"

Jackan refused to meet his superior's eyes. "Ah. Well. That I am not rightly sure of."

"And why is that?" Whitlaw asked.

"I've no idea where it landed," the old engineer admitted. "It blasted right through the roof and took off like a bat on fire towards No Man's Land."

The chief sighed and his shoulders sagged. "How much did that experiment of yours just cost me?"

Jackan winced. "Five thousand crowns, give or take."

Whitlaw cursed. That was enough to buy a good-sized inn on a main street of Orialis itself – and an unskilled labourer might only earn five crowns in an entire year. They were friends, but he was also Jackan's superior, and that amount of loss had to be dealt with harshly.

The chief's hands clenched, trembling. He took a series of deep and calming breaths. "You will be the death of me some day, you mad northern oaf. Guylan, have the roof repaired and this side of the workshop refitted as a priority. Rumour has it that the war is starting to heat up again, and we cannot afford any reduction in productivity."

Guylan nodded. "I'll get the apprentices on it this morning. I will need to requisition a dozen labourers as well."

The chief nodded, pulled a crumpled paper out of his belt pouch and stared at it for a moment, muttering a spell to char letters into the page. He spun his signet ring on his hand and pressed the face into the bottom of the permit, stamping it with his seal before he handed it over. "Jackan, come with me. You have a mountain of paperwork to fill out."

The old engineer's face fell. He sighed and trudged off to the chief's study, grumbling all the way. The door slammed shut and the shouting began.

Guylan shook his head and turned back to the ruined section of the workshop. A chisel and a handsaw lay on the floor, the wooden handles charcoal and the temper of the steel destroyed. He prodded an abacus with his little finger and the side promptly crumbled, sending ceramic balls rolling about the floor. He noted down those few tools and equipment that may be salvageable. The melted blobs and piles of ash he would leave to Jackan to identify and request replacements for.

Once the inventory of damage was complete, Guylan calculated the likely cost of repairs. He winced, but then a smile grew. If Jackan wasn't in the doghouse already, he certainly would be when the chief saw this report. Served the old bastard right.

There was a large fragment of tin roof under a blackened bench. He bent down and studied the melted edge. Every mage worth his staff could tell lightning bolt damage when he saw it. While Jackan hadn't lied to the chief about the events of last night, he certainly hadn't volunteered the whole truth, either. Wheel marks ran across the sooty floor, and there was a bent brass spoke that had come from an unusual wheel. He knew of exactly one person in the workshop using a wheeled chair like that: though he was loath to confront her, Ella Pickering needed to be questioned – after all, he had to ensure the fault was attributed to the right person.

He paused at the fire-resistant canvas, somehow scorched beyond repair by temperatures far beyond any mere lick of flame. He poked the worst section with a finger, and it went right through in a shower of black flakes. Guylan noted the need for a replacement down on his notepad before pushing through.

The roped-off areas beyond the curtain contained well-provisioned workbenches and tool racks belonging to senior mages. Many older members still clung to the secretive ways of the past, hiding individual workspaces behind curtains and nets, but others had clustered together to form collaborative coteries studying new weapons of the Empire under magnifying glasses, probing their encrypted glyphs and arcane circles with fine-tuned scrying spells. Other groups laboured on developing devastating new weapons for the Unity, or novel methods of penetrating enemy defences to uncover information on troop movements. Apart from the mighty battlemages, with their huge aether wells that allowed the casting of large-scale spells, these research mages were the cream of the crop. During the war's previous fifteen-year lull, some had been renowned scholars and lore keepers, or masters or journeymen in the various magic guilds, while others had run independent workshops crafting bespoke ensorcelled items and services to those with enough coin to hire them. All were highly educated and wealthy, just not obscenely rich and connected enough to avoid conscription when the hierarchs turned their minds back towards warfare.

The production mages had their own sad little area down near the entrance to the building, with old, scarred benches bearing only those tools needed for a particular task. Each bench was kept separate: not just to discourage talking and timewasting, but because of the inherent dangers of mass-producing the newest line of arcane weaponry. A slip of concentration at the wrong moment and aether overload would make that mage very dead, most likely along with the poor git next to them. The separation of workbenches meant only two would die. Probably.

The mages assigned to mass production were deemed lesser by the hierarchs in all manner of ways, and treated as such. Some were pacifists or cowards – the same thing in the eyes of their superiors – while others were disabled veterans ruled out of deployment on the front lines. Some had only possessed weaker magical abilities in the first place, and they would only ever have been admitted to the lowest rung of the mage guilds before their betters were slaughtered in battle. Or there was that most relevant of tests to the hierarchs: those who simply failed due to the shallowness of their personal treasury and thus limited the reach of their education. They were almost all commoners, and what fallen nobles and merchants there were among them must have been considered failures to their respectable families. One or two once-promising mages had been demoted and consigned here to languish in ignominy after pissing off the wrong people – much like Ella had.

Ella Pickering's booth was cramped and gloomy and isolated. Even among the dregs of magery consigned to these tedious production tasks, nobody wanted proximity to somebody who had earned the displeasure of a hierarch. She had her head down, eye to the magnifying glass, working hard. Guylan noted that she wore new work robes, despite her debts and general state of poverty. Of all people, why did it have to be her…

Guylan took a deep, steadying breath and approached, waiting for her to finish graving the last curving line of a blasting rune into her crystal before he cleared his throat to announce his presence. She carefully set down her graver and glass. Her face was drawn and her eyes dark and sunken, as if she hadn't slept at all last night. "Can I help you, Mage Bluford?"

"I certainly hope you can clarify something for me," he said, glancing down at the wheel of her chair, then circling round to the other side. The wheel was scuffed, two spokes dented and one missing entirely. He leaned in close and sniffed. "Is that smoke I smell?"

The woman didn't react as he'd expected. She didn't blanch and shrink down into her chair or start shaking and sweating with guilt. Her eyes were steady and her expression unchanged. The last year had served to harden her.

"I think you'll find I smell of soap," she replied. "And if you believe I smell at all of smoke, then it must be the scent of the forge clinging to my clothing."

Guylan raised an eyebrow. "New robes, I see. Did the last garment get damaged somehow? And what do you have to say about this?" He tossed the lost spoke of her wheel into her lap.

She swallowed, then smiled. "I wondered where that went. Must have fallen off a few days ago. Thanks, I'll get it reattached."

"Jackan is in with the chief now," he said. "That spoke was found in the restricted section next to wheel marks among the debris of last night's excitement, and your own meeting to discuss the damage to the workshop has been scheduled directly after his."

Her false smile fractured and fell apart. "Shit. What did that daft old man tell you?"

"He didn't even say you were there last night," Guylan replied. "But you just did."

She shrunk into her chair. "Great. Just great. I had nothing to do with that... whatever it was... being set off. I swear, I was just in there when the lightning struck the roof."

Guylan sighed in relief. "Well thank the gods for that, then."

Ella blinked. "Eh?"

"I thought you might have messed up his experiment," he said. "I was worried that arse-of-an-engineer was going to pin it all on you. If it was natural lightning, I can write this up as an act of the gods."

"Oh," she said. "I see. I'd thought..."

He shook his head knowingly. "That I was going to hang you from the nearest tree? Quite the reverse, I assure you. I was trying to figure out how much I might have to... ah... massage the reporting to keep your name out of the official record."

She studied his dark eyes, frowning. "We don't know each other nearly well enough for that – what exactly are you wanting from me? Blackmail? I don't have anything worth the effort, and if you expect me to suck–"

He held his hands up and took a step back. "No, no, goodness, nothing like that! I've, er, a soft spot for folks shat upon by the higher-ups."

Her eyes narrowed. "Pull the other one. What is your real reason?"

Guylan grimaced and mulled over his answer for a few moments. "I felt that you deserved a chance. Plus, you obliterated Hierarch Deva-Mokaren III's second-best golden carriage. I saw the wreckage up close, and I must say, it amused me greatly."

Ella's lips thinned. "I'm glad it amused somebody..."

He paused, struggling with a choice he should never have had to make. "It is likely a mistake to tell you this, but I was one of the team called in to investigate the treason charges against you after the accident."

She stiffened. Frozen like a small animal caught in a trap.

"They pushed hard for a death sentence," he added.

Ella shivered and wrung her hands, staring at her lap. "I know."

"What they never told you," he continued, "what they never admitted, is that the skyship you piloted was a disaster waiting to happen. If not you, it would have soon been another – though perhaps a pilot not quite so unlucky in their choice of landing site."

She looked up, puzzled. "What do you mean?"

Guylan glanced around, checking for eavesdroppers. "It was a miracle you were able to fly that thing at all. The control enchantments were old and decaying, the seams of the gasbags frayed, and the wooden structure was warped and rotten from rainwater ingress. Honestly, we were impressed with your ability to keep it aloft as long as you did."

She gaped. "But I was told… I thought…"

"A hierarch was enraged," Guylan said. "Somebody had to face the fire, and the mages in charge of maintaining expensive skyships were hardly going to blame themselves, were they? Silver changed hands, and most of the investigators found a junior skymage solely at fault."

Her hands curled into fists, shaking as she ground her teeth. "Bastards. Utter bastards. Why the hells am I still alive, then?"

Guylan cleared his throat. "Because the investigation team's decision was not unanimous. One idealistic young idiot feeling too much guilt at his involvement dissented." He paused, guilt at his failure swirling. "As it turns out, honesty does not get you terribly far in the bureaucracy of the Unity, nor does it make you friends in high places. And so here we both are, stuck in this dump, lapping up all the glory offered by our glittering new careers." He chuckled, sad and bitter. "I owe you nothing in truth, and I never wanted to bring it up again, but what they did to you was an atrocity, and I felt like you deserved some good luck in your life for a change."

Ella's chair creaked as she shifted uncomfortably, a churning mass of anger, resentment, and gratitude. "You saved my life, Guylan Bluford. I'll not forget that. I always pay my debts… uh, eventually." She closed her eyes for a moment, taking deep shuddering breaths to soothe frayed nerves.

"Yes, well," he said. "That's all done and gone, and it will do neither of us any good to bring it up again. I would be forced to deny everything if you did."

She opened her eyes and met his firm gaze. "I understand."

Guylan took a deep breath. "Now, what in the Nine Hells really happened last night?"

She relented and told him everything, lapsing into a worried silence awaiting his scathing reply.

He chewed on his bottom lip, tapping his notepad with the charcoal stick while mulling over the implications of her tale. "So, it really was just a bolt of lightning. That should not have happened. The weather enchantments on the building may have failed, or it could be a case of sabotage. Either way, it will require me to climb up onto that bloody roof to check." He shuddered at the thought.

"Are you afraid of heights?" she asked.

"Perhaps a little," he replied, a grotesque understatement. "It must sound like nonsense to you, given that you used to pilot skyships."

Ella shrugged. "We all have our flaws. I never learned to swim; it felt like I was drowning. I suppose I never will now." Her jaw muscles flexed, grinding her teeth. He reckoned her emotional wounds would lay open for years, even before considering her broken back caused by the negligence of others. And all this time, she believed she was to blame for her own accident. He had not the faintest idea of what that would do to a person.

They loitered in awkward silence for entirely too long before he managed to break it. "Well, Jackan is still on the hook for the loss of his experiment," he blurted out. "I'd, er, best be off to gather proof that it wasn't all his fault before Goddard skins him alive. Much as I'd enjoy that."

She nodded absently.

Guylan muttered a goodbye and rushed off, cheeks flaming and feeling like a complete imbecile. He could feel her eyes burning a hole in his back as he fled the workshop to gather a group of labourers, fetch ladders, and source roofing material. He had finally mustered the courage to tell Ella he had been part of the events that ruined her life. While the guilt – unwarranted or not, it was undeniably there – still gnawed at him, it felt oddly freeing to release that secret into the world, despite the risk to both of their lives if she decided to start shouting about it.

It took him an age to climb the wooden ladder, carefully taking the rungs one by one, his hands clamped to the rails hard enough to leave fingernail impressions. By the time he reached the top, he could feel sweat drenching his back. He mopped his forehead with a sleeve and hesitantly set a foot on the workshop's tin roofing, yelping as it flexed underfoot.

Steeling his nerves, he swung his other foot from the ladder and onto the roof, easing his weight down until he was sure it would hold. His heart thudded heavily as he took baby steps forward.

Then, Anemotus, god of wind, caught him with a gust and set him swaying.

His stomach dropped away, along with his courage.

"Nope nope nope, not happening," he wheezed, falling to all fours. He crawled towards the lightning rod, intent on getting this damnable excursion over with.

The iron roof rod that was meant to have channelled the crackling energy of a lightning strike away from the building and disperse it safely into the earth was missing. The stonework it had been embedded in was old and crumbling; judging by the crude and mismatched blocks, its housing had been patched multiple times rather than being properly replaced. The damage itself was far from fresh, as evidenced by an abundance of moss jutting from the cracks and the weather-wear along the edges of the breakage.

Guylan tutted loud and long, studying every aspect of the damage.

He retrieved his charcoal stick and notepad from his pouch and sketched the scene, paying particular attention to the sloppy repairs. "Happy days," he murmured, picturing the chief's face when he found out the maintenance team's dereliction of duty made them liable for the cost of repairing his building and replacing his tools. The lazy rat in charge of keeping the fort in war-worthy condition would have his stonemasons and mages flogged for making him look bad when Guylan's report was kicked up the chain of command.

The massive cost of Jackan's ruined experiment was another matter entirely. That steaming pile of shit would land squarely in the lap of the Research and Design Workshop. Five thousand crowns worth of material was not something the chief would dismiss with a wry laugh and wave of the hand. He pitied the poor gits who would be charged with retrieving it from the toxic battlefield of No Man's Land, assuming they ever found the crash site.

CHAPTER 3

Several days after the explosion, Ella was in the final stage of another long and gruelling double shift that had dragged on into the hours of darkness.

She yawned and rubbed tired eyes, trying to focus through the glass at the miniscule carved runes. Her aether-flow fluctuated, shaking the point of her graver. She carefully set the tool down and stretched her arms – at best, a mistake would mean starting all over again, but even in her short tenure in this workshop, she'd seen two tired mages lose fingers to aether-overload when it backwashed into them. The stench of their charred meat had served as a potent warning.

Ella nibbled on half a dry biscuit before cracking her knuckles and diving back in, taking it step by laborious step. Her mind wandered as she fell into the well-trod rhythm of work. Two more months of working at this punishing pace and she would be able to pay off another of her smaller debts, reducing the crippling interest she'd owed to several unsavoury characters to just one large amount owed to a single terrifying woman: the owner of the black market who'd gouge Ella's eye out with a spoon if she dared miss a payment. At least Ella was a mage and had been deemed worth the hefty investment. She'd taken on a whole heap of debt to afford medical care administered by mage-priests of the divine Mogranus, god of healing and medicine. They had saved her life, if not the use of her legs. That, too, could probably be fixed, were she a far richer woman.

Another debt paid off was a step in the right direction, something that would ease the vice of stress slowly crushing her, and maybe even allow a decent night's sleep outside Mrs

Beaton's flophouse – somewhere with clean blankets, no black mould, and no rats in the walls. Though, she mused, she would miss the big brown one she'd dubbed Top Rat due to his white crown of fur.

"Really, Ella?" she muttered. "If you are making pets out of vermin, then you must be going slightly mad." She snorted. "And now you are talking to yourself..."

Guylan's revelations had set her emotions spinning. She wasn't sure what was worse: that she'd been left to think her debts and broken body were all her fault, or that the negligence of higher-ranking mages had caused her downfall and there was absolutely nothing she could do about it. Her self-recrimination gave way to anger and a measure of paranoia. Was the hierarch done with her? Had she just been overlooked, and if so, for how long? She felt vulnerable inside and out, and she hated that with a passion. As for Guylan... she wasn't sure what to make of the engineer. Was he to be hated or admired? He had kept the truth from her, but the man had also suffered greatly for trying to do the right thing.

She shook her head and threw herself back into work. It was better than giving herself time to think about the wretched state of her life.

The other oil lamps in the workshop had been snuffed out hours ago, leaving her working alone in a small island of light amidst the gloom. Other than her own little lamp, the vast space was lit only by moonlight shining through the narrow upper windows and shards of light that escaped the brand-new heavy canvas curtain at the restricted end.

On the benches of the more senior mages, arcane instruments emitted a dull green glow. She *tch*ed, mentally chiding the lazy gits who hadn't disabled their tools properly, draining their aether storage – they would likely just hand the tools over to her to charge them back up again, draining her strength to make up for their carelessness.

The roof had been recently patched by workers, and the burnt stench was almost gone. Jackan had been back in his workspace the moment it reopened, sawing and swearing as he returned things to the way he liked them. The muffled blows of hammer on hot iron meant she was not the last to finish up. That old man had impressive stamina.

She finished graving her last crystal and packed it away with its deadly kin, yawning and daring to imagine some food in her growling belly. Halfway through packing away her tools, Jackan sidled over to her booth, appearing worrisomely eager to see her. The soot-stained man stopped behind the wheeled chair, his shadow looming over her as he blocked her only exit.

Ella became acutely aware she was alone with a bigger, older, and more senior mage that she didn't really know. She wasn't even aware if he was married, had a wife and children, or if he liked women that way at all. Or if any of that would matter a jot if this man was in a foul mood. He seemed nice enough, but then many people did, right up until the moment they didn't – as a young woman, living in the flophouse with some of the dregs of society, she had learnt not to trust. What did he want? To blackmail her by threatening to pin the failure of his experiment on her? She suppressed a shiver and shifted in her chair to keep an eye on him.

He smiled disarmingly. "Can I get a skymage's opinion on something?" His bushy moustache quivered as he spoke.

"As soon as you can find one," she replied bitterly, wrapping her magnifying glass in protective wool and leather. "There's only a lowly production mage here."

Jackan loitered, a scrap of paper clutched in his hairy, calloused hands. His eyes were wide and dark, like a chastised puppy.

She regretted her harshness and shook off the unwarranted fears. "Can't it wait for the morning? I'm dog tired. I'm hungry. And I'm not in the mood for more explosions."

He slid the paper across her workbench and stood there, waiting expectantly.

She sighed and glanced down, paused, then looked harder at the scrawl of handwriting. On the page was a circle representing their world, and another, smaller circle with a crude palace of the gods crowning it, depicting the moon. A straight dotted line ran from one circle to the other, surrounded by numbers and calculations, many scored out.

"What is this unholy mess?" she asked.

Jackan nodded at his workings. "You tell me, lass."

She studied it, determining distance and speed and… "What is this number?"

"Weight," he said.

She frowned, trying to fit it all together. "It looks like you are trying to figure out the speed you would need to achieve to get something the weight of a stone golem to the surface of the moon."

He rocked backwards and forwards on his heels. "Mmm-hmm. Thoughts?"

She looked up at him, eyes widening as she took in his sincerity and remembered an off-hand comment made the day before. "Why the moon? Is it just a thought experiment?"

He nodded. "Sure is." Then, under his breath: "For now."

Ella was far too tired to deal with such flights of fancy. "Even if you have the distance calculated correctly, this plan is too simple to ever work."

"Why is that?" he said. "Pretty sure the mathematics check out."

"I'm sure it would," she replied. "If it was a straight line between here and there, and if there was no wind to drag you off course and slow you down. And you do know the moon dances rings around her mother, right? Always moving round and round in an oval orbitus, sometimes closer to us and sometimes further away. Even if we work the mathematics out perfectly for one particular time of year, that distance figure will change."

Jackan coughed and fiddled with the tips of his moustache. "Yes, well, this research is still in an early stage. What were you saying about the air?"

"Air resists you. It tries to drag you back when you move through it at speed," she explained. "The faster you move and the larger your surface, the more it pushes against you, like running into the wind with your hands up. That's why our skyships with big, bulky gasbags move so slowly through the air. That's also the reason arrows and javelins are shaped the way they are."

Jackan stroked his moustache, nodding. "I see. I see. The spear-shape reduces the drag, and the fletching on an arrow uses the flow of air to stabilise its flight. I would need something similar to reduce the force needed for flight."

"Then there are the materials used," she continued, deep in thought. "Rock and metal and suchlike are heavy and follow their chthonic natures by being drawn towards the earthen body of the Great Mother where they belong, whereas fire and smoke, being light and more divine in nature, yearn for the sky and the moon and the domain of the gods. Does any of that help you?"

"Oh, aye," he said. "Very much so. That gives me a wagonful of food for thought." Jackan reached for his paper. "Thank you for your expertise, Mage Pickering. I will let you get home to your bed now." With that, he wandered off towards the restricted section of the workshop, his eyes glazed and his mind focused inwards.

She watched him stop, fish a monocle attached to a fine chain from a small pocket sewn into the breast of his robes and place it to his eye. He squinted at the page in surprise, walked a bit more and stopped again, his brow furrowed. He muttered and scratched at the page with his stick of charcoal. His eyes abruptly widened and the monocle fell free to dangle on its chain. "Yes! Of course," he exclaimed, speeding off into the restricted section, where a series of clanks and thuds announced furious activity.

Ella shook her head and hastily packed up all her equipment. She wheeled herself out into the darkness before the mad old engineer could come back for more enlightenment. It was a dry and starless night, but the fort was well lit by lanterns set on poles every thirty or so paces, gifting the paths a ruddy hue. A pair of guards kept desultory night watch over the rearmost buildings, patrolling with spears on their shoulders and a skin of wine hidden behind a hand. Their role was largely redundant; no enemy had ever breached these walls, and nobody sane would dare try with packs of specialised guardian golems packed full of magical detection devices guarding the exterior once darkness fell. Their standing order was to kill everything that approached the walls, and they did it tirelessly. A few wolves and bears sometimes ventured too close under the cover of darkness and ended up filleted, but, so far as she knew, no mutilated human remains had ever been found scattered like so much trash.

She slowed halfway to the gatehouse, her mind drawn back to Jackan's diagram and workings like mice to grain storage. Her belly rumbled, but she was far too curious to pay it much attention. Was the old man seriously trying to calculate how to rework his experiment to launch a weapon into the very lap of the gods? That seemed like a spectacularly bad idea. Or was it just some flight of mathematical fancy that had caught his interest? She pictured his odd contraption soaring into the sky again, born aloft on that fearsome pillar of flame. It had looked majestic, as if the hands of humans were reaching for the very stars – right before it began a death-spin, cut out, and plummeted back to earth. But, for a moment there…

What if we added fletching to it? she mused. That would help avoid that uncontrolled spin. Feathers wouldn't do the job, given the size of the thing, so it would have to be more solid – metal fins, most likely…

It was at that point Ella realised she was actually interested in something. Excited, even. She hadn't been able to claim that since her last, ill-fated flight in a skyship.

"Damn," she said. "Gods damn that mad engineer." It seemed that his scheme was infectious. She couldn't help but wonder what he was really up to. She gritted her teeth and growled, then, going against her better judgement, swung herself round and returned to the workshop.

Ella grabbed an oil lamp and focused her will upon the wick. Touching it with a finger, she forced a stream of aether to well up inside her and gush down her arm. It had been a long day, and the effort of transforming aether into heat without using a tool was a strain. The wick flared bright and shed a dim, ruddy glow across the empty workshop. She attached the lantern to a hook screwed into the arm of her chair and navigated her way down the walkway to the restricted section. Beyond the curtain, Jackan still hammered away, followed by the hiss of hot metal being cooled by water.

She itched to find out what he was up to, working so late in secret. Whatever mania consumed the engineer, she had definitely caught it.

She rolled to a stop before the slit in the curtains. "Jackan?"

Something clanged to the floor on the other side. The din of industry ceased.

"Jackan? Are you there?"

Footsteps approached and a sooty hand speared through the curtains, pulling them back to reveal a guilty face. He blinked down at her and his face softened. "Oh, it's just you, Mage Pickering. Scared the shit out of me there. What are you still doing here?"

She cleared her throat. "I couldn't stop thinking about your, ah, special project. I have more thoughts on it."

He hesitated a shade too long.

She raised an eyebrow. "Come off it. We both know you are not working on a secret weapon in there."

He frowned, then shrugged and held back the curtain for her. "In you come, then. Not like you haven't seen the prototype before up close and personal, eh. Just don't go telling tales to stuffy old Goddard."

Tools and bits and pieces of wood and metal were scattered all over the place, a hazard for his feet more than her wheels. He scowled and kicked them into neater piles.

A framework of hefty rods of oak and leather cording contained the skeleton of a new device. It was half the size of the old one, the same height as Jackan himself, and consisted of a flaring metal muzzle at the base attached to a thin steel cylinder. Above that hung a snarl of copper tubing attached to an iron box.

Jackan ambled over to the roaring forge fire and picked up something on the anvil that he had been working on. He gingerly placed a cone of paper-thin beaten iron at the tip of his device. To her eye, it looked much like the head of a spear.

"I had been told to experiment on a way to launch aether-empowered munitions much farther than ever before," he explained. "I, ah, may have got a tad overexcited about the engineering side of it. Who could have imagined lightning would ignite the alchemical powder inside and make the whole thing take off like a demon escaping the Nine Hells?"

Ella looked it over. "What are these tubes and boxes for?"

"I'm not sure yet," he admitted. "The previous experiment used a black powder developed by ancient alchemists. It burns fiercely, and if you cram it into a paper tube, it explodes in a puff of colourful smoke. It's nothing compared to magic, of course – more of a toy, really – but I reckoned it might help reduce the strain on our siege mages. With this Mark II device, I am working on better ways to control the rate of burning. The last one just went whoosh, half-melted itself and burned out all in a one-er, so this little lot is just my way of better understanding the problems."

She pursed her lips and examined his setup. "Only the mightiest of battlemages would have the aether reserves to lift something this heavy so high into the sky. You would probably need a large cabal of them all working in concert to reach the heavens, unless you used an alchemical process in conjunction with magic."

The old engineer snorted. "Well, getting a hold of a battlemage is never going to happen. Haven't seen any of them glory-hounds at the fort for months."

Ella refrained from voicing her own opinions on the cream of the mage crop. Her mind was aflame with far more important ideas. "Fins," she said. "Metal fins to guide it aloft, like a fish swimming through water."

Jackan grinned. "I had been thinking along similar lines."

She marshalled her courage and decided to chance her arm. She was in the restricted section already, his confidante, of sorts, and the worst he could do was say no – well, that was not entirely true, she corrected herself. The man could probably ruin what was left of her career if he wanted, but she didn't think he was the type, and she didn't have much worth losing anyway. "Do you," she said, hesitating, "by any chance, need an assistant?"

He squinted at her. "Eh? Who did you have in mind?"

She jabbed a thumb at her chest. "Me."

"Oh," he replied. "You? An assistant… um…"

She prepared herself for the acid sting of rejection. She was, after all, just a failed skymage working on the production benches.

"You work a lot of double shifts," he said. "Do you have any qualms about working long hours on this side of the workshop?"

"None at all."

He chewed on his lower lip, thinking. "How are you with levitation runes?"

"Excellent. Levitation and wind manipulation were the powers I used most when I was a skymage. They're a vital skill to keep you aloft." Her lips twisted for a moment, tasting a sour memory.

The senior engineer held out a hand. "Then, Chief Goddard willing, I will happily welcome you aboard my little crew, Ella."

She shook it, besieged by a heady mix of feelings she hadn't felt in ages: hope, accomplishment, and the gratification of just being useful. "Thank you. I am looking forward to working on something new." Carried away, she decided to push her luck that little bit further. "I don't suppose this role comes with a raise?"

He chuckled and backed away, eyeing her shrewdly. "You can argue that one with Goddard yourself. I expect he'll demand you serve some kind of probation period on your current pay before he stumps up more coin." He scratched at his beard. "Now, were I you, I'd counter the grumpy old bastard by stating that you will be serving as a journeyman runesmith and then follow up with queries about overtime payments for working the long hours I require. If you argue him down to the standard pay for a journeyman in return for taking the threat of overtime payments off the table, that would still net you more than you currently do from double shifts as a production mage."

She goggled at him. "They get paid that much? No wonder they head home so early."

"Oh, yes, and that pay is for the lowest-level mages among their ranks."

"Well, damn," she muttered. It was even more than she had earned as a junior skymage.

"So, back onto these levitation runes of yours. If we can reduce the weight of the Mark II, then it won't have to burn so fast and hot to send it to the heavens. By how much can you reduce it?"

"I'd need to do some calculations," she replied. "It depends on the materials we have to work with and the power level you need them to work at. The more power, the faster the structures will degrade, and then there's interference from other nearby magical workings…" she cut off her line of thought and looked over what he was currently building. "I'm assuming you'll want them powered by expensive aether gems?"

Jackan nodded.

"For something the size and weight you want, I could probably reduce the weight by half for a hundred and fifty heartbeats before the runes start to come apart under the strain. Perhaps longer, but not reliably."

The engineer rubbed his blackened and blistered hands together. "That is a very good start. I only wish we could find out what happened to the previous version. I imagine the debris would prove most enlightening."

CHAPTER 4

Tensions and tempers were running high in Whitlaw Goddard's study. The chief was still in a foul mood after being forced to approve the funding for Jackan's new assistant, her current pay having tripled after she passed a scant two-week probation period.

Goddard sat at his desk, fingers steepled and a sour twist to his lips as Guylan Bluford and Jackan Grissom snapped and barked at each other like two hunting hounds straining at the end of their leashes. His personal chamber was heaving with dusty old tomes, scrolls, and fired clay tablets from vanished civilisations. Charts and diagrams of arcane devices littered two side tables, and the tooth of an actual dragon sat pride of place in its glass case in the corner of the room, fizzing and sparking with stray magic. It was a lifetime's work curating and collecting all of these precious artefacts, and he displayed them with pride, out where every eye could see them.

Now, a map of No Man's Land had been spread out across his massive old writing desk heaving with paperwork. The outline of the area was clear enough, but the interior consisted only of vague lines of ink, more suggestion than certainty. Every detailed map of that tainted place became obsolete a season after its creation.

"You cannot be serious," Guylan spluttered. "You want me to head out into that twisted wasteland to recover *his* blasted experiment? I am a First Circle graduate of the Orialis Guild of Mages, not some porter. Get his new assistant – whoever it is – to do their master's bidding."

The older engineer polished his monocle with a cloth and set the glass to his eye. He peered at the younger mage like he'd just found dog dirt on his shoe. "Oh lah-de-dah, your big fancy mage guild accreditation means diddly squat. All I care about is if you can do the job – or not, in your case."

"Can't you find me somebody better?" Jackan asked the chief. "Some brave young buck who can climb a tree without fainting would be grand."

Guylan's fists clenched, and he opened his mouth to spit venom – quite literally, since his old-blood mage family forced magical adaptations upon their children when they came of age. It could cause agony and blind the old git for a good hour, but would leave no lasting damage. Somehow, he managed to restrain himself.

"Now, now," Whitlaw Goddard said, studying the map. "No squabbling in my study. You are both experienced mages and you should act like it. You are an old friend, Jackan, but badly mistaken if you think I will not hold you to account. I play no favourites when it comes to work."

The two engineers glowered at each other. Ever since Jackan had been awarded the bulk of their research budget, Guylan had made do with funding scraped from the bottom of the barrel. Though he tried to deny it, all present knew resentment clouded his opinion whenever it came to his senior colleague and his unorthodox ways.

"Five thousand crowns, Guylan," the chief stated. "That small fortune is what you are heading out to recover. If all is lost, then it is lost, but I will not write good materials off if any can be salvaged. A squad of the fort's warriors will go with you – oh, and our good friend Jackan Grissom here as well."

That was news to the old engineer, judging from his dropped jaw and bulging eyes. Jackan coughed and spluttered, struggling to voice an appropriately foul-mouthed objection.

"Is that wise?" Guylan said, gleefully changing tack. "Going out there with somebody younger would be preferable, since we wouldn't want the *venerable* Mage Grissom here putting his back out by bending over too fast."

Whitlaw stabbed a finger into a point on the map. "Scouts have located the crash site, here. Jackan, you know the device. You know what is worth recovering, and what might be too dangerous to meddle with. Guylan, get over yourself; jealousy is not a good look. You are both going and I will brook no whining. Two such proficient mages retrieving an item from No Man's Land is better than one." He searched his desk for a scroll stamped with his personal seal and slid it towards them. "Here are your orders. Visit the fort's armoury on the way out."

Jackan's jaw snapped shut. He snatched up the scroll, unfurled it, and scanned the contents before rolling it back up. "Very well, Chief. But I am the senior mage of this expedition, and I will be in charge."

Whitlaw's eyebrows raised. "Oh? A mighty battlemage now, are we? I must have missed your promotion from research mage into their heady ranks. Don't be a fool. You can lead the recovery effort, but an old friend of mine will be in charge of the expedition itself – and of keeping you both alive."

The arcane engineers both simmered with annoyance as Whitlaw studied them critically. "Just bring me back something good I can use to placate the hierarchs' accountants. Those ice-blooded fiends are relentless." He leaned forward and fixed a cold stare on Jackan. "Do *not* force me to submit request forms for more resources without anything to show for the previous lot. You promised me a new weapon delivery system and all you have done so far is give me a gods-damned headache. Are we clear?"

Jackan gritted his teeth and nodded, then turned on his heels and marched from the chief's study. Guylan swallowed his own ire and followed, making sure to keep a goodly distance between the two of them lest anybody think they were colleagues, or worse, friends.

They left the workshop behind and marched to the armoury in silence, seething, hands curling into fists. A harassed-looking maintenance team making their rounds inspecting buildings gave the research mages an accusing look. Guylan sniffed in derision and ignored their glares.

Two lines of mail-clad warriors marched past with spears on their shoulders and leather bags on their backs, heading out on patrol. A pack of tan and black hounds with wiry coats trotted beside them: hunting dogs trained to track down unfamiliar scents and magics. Their trailing knot of porters carrying cooking implements and supplies made way for Jackan and Guylan, heads bobbing in nods of respect; two of them were only boys, barely able to grow a moustache.

The foot patrol was heading off to secure the border and ward off whatever new horrors the Empire mages had loosed into the contested lands. Even with the dogs helping to sniff out magical dangers and monstrous creatures, it was likely that some of them would not come back. It cooled the tempers of both engineers, their own feud suddenly seeming petty. Things could always be worse.

The armoury was accessed by a thick oak door encased by solid stone walls, warded with all manner of arcane protections that would take mundane siege weapons days to break down. Jackan frowned at the two bronze guard constructs shaped like lions perched on either side of the doorway, their razor-sharp claws and maws stained brown from old blood, then he grimaced and stuck his right hand between the nearest lion's teeth. The construct's eyes glowed a baleful red as it tasted his tattoo, then the door to the armoury unlocked with a heavy thump. He snatched his hand back, checking to make sure all his fingers were still there.

The older engineer put a hand on the door, then turned to Guylan and sighed. "So, we don't like each other much. That's fine, but know I will watch your back out there. Let's get this over with and get back to proper work as soon as we can."

"Sounds good to me," Guylan answered gruffly. "Er, have you ever been in actual battle? I've been through basic training, but... well..."

"Only the once," Jackan answered, staring off into the distance. "I'm a builder, not a butcher of men." He shoved the heavy door, which opened surprisingly easily on well-oiled hinges.

The door slammed shut behind them, trapping them in the windowless fortress of the armoury. It was well lit, with evenly spaced oil lanterns burning steadily.

A heavy-set, greying woman in drab brown commoner's dress and green woollen stole sat at a massive edifice of a desk, guarding a single doorway in a wall of steel bars that led to the storeroom beyond. She glanced up at them as they entered, then returned to toting up numbers using an abacus, ignoring them utterly.

They stopped at a painted line set two paces back from the desk. The woman in charge still showed no sign of acknowledgement. Guylan cleared his throat, pointedly. She dipped quill to ink and began marking something down in a thick, leather-bound ledger.

Guylan moved to rouse her, but Jackan put a hand of warning on his shoulder and whispered: "Never piss off the folks in charge of your supplies."

The younger mage shook off his hand. "She's just a commoner. We are mages."

Jackan's brow lowered. He shook his head in disgust and said nothing more.

The younger man's temper threatened to reignite, but he heeded the man's sage advice, at least for now...

The woman took her time with her ledger. She laid down her quill and blew on the page to dry the ink before closing the book and sliding it into a drawer in her desk. Only then did she look up. "Hello m'dears, and how may I help you two fine mages today?"

"Unfortunately, we are on a foray out into No Man's Land, my good woman," Jackan said, stepping forward. "Could you please provide us with all the necessities?"

She winced.

Jackan handed over their papers from Goddard. The woman lifted horn-rimmed eyeglasses attached to a silver chain around her neck and scrutinised both letter and mage's seal, her eyes distorted through the thick lenses.

"All seems to be in order," she said. "I'll be back with your weapons in two shakes of a lamb's tail." She heaved herself off her chair and flicked through a ring of keys hanging from her belt.

"Huh," Guylan said. "There is no keyhole in that door."

"Indeed, there is not," the woman replied. She found the key she was looking for and brandished it like a wand, muttering something under her breath. The tattoo on her right hand glowed for a moment and the door swung open.

Jackan smirked as the woman revealed she too was a mage, and probably one who outranked them to boot – who better to oversee an armoury filled with all matter of arcane weaponry?

"Shut up," Guylan growled.

"Didn't say a thing," he replied.

The woman came back clutching a pair of battered war staves and a small leather knapsack. "Here you go. Standard issue weaponry for a short-duration mission."

Jackan's scorch-marked staff was marred by sanded-down nicks and cuts and boasted a blood-dark ruby at the tip. The other staff was crowned with a sapphire, the blue so deep it was almost black. Something with terrifying sharp teeth had once done its best to chew through the haft. Both weapons thrummed with hidden power, hot against their hands.

Jackan ran his fingers over the marks in the pale wood. "Ash, eh? Very nice indeed. It'll make for a good walking stick, or a stout quarterstaff in a pinch."

"Fire and ice," the armoury mage stated. "If one doesn't work, the other surely will. Once you have attuned them to your magic, these weapons will provide eight offensive charges each, with an average ambient recharge time of one spell per hour, depending on aether density, of course."

She leaned forward over the desk, fixing Guylan with a grim look. "If your staff is not returned in a timely manner, it comes out of your wages. Are we clear?"

The young mage swallowed. "Understood."

The woman pursed her lips. "The items in this bag are classed as consumable items, but we would very much appreciate that anything going unused is returned for reissue." She opened up the knapsack and withdrew two small wooden boxes, sliding the lids back to reveal two blasting crystals and one smokescreen crystal nestled inside woollen cocoons. She repacked them and thrust the bag into Guylan's hands, then slid a sheet of paper across the desk towards them.

"Do you require swords or knives?" she asked. "Bows, perhaps?"

They shook their heads and pointed to the knives sheathed at their belts. They were daily tools more than weapons, mostly used for carving wood and cutting leather and cloth, but they would serve just as well as some blade from the armoury far less familiar to them.

The woman looked doubtful for a moment. "On your own heads be it. Please check the listed items and sign your receipt," she said, offering quill and ink. Once that was done, she gave them a nod. "Good luck out there, lads. Do try to come back in one piece."

With a wave, the armoury door clanked open and they were ushered out, blinking and clutching their new weapons. They walked in silence towards the front gate, where a horse and cart, a heavy labour golem, and the main force of their expedition awaited them. Fifteen mailed warriors, all having seen less than twenty summers, stood to rigid attention at their approach, cocky smiles spread across their faces. Each boasted a stout spear, a sword and knife at their hip, and a shield on their back. The leader was an older, bald, one-eyed mage in combat robes festooned with pockets bulging with unseen items of death and devastation. His eyepatch had been crafted from a scaled leather they couldn't readily identify, and a disc of black onyx was set into the centre like a pupil, where it seemed to suck in the light.

"Greetings," the man said, flashing a smile and extending a hand.

They fumbled with their staves in order to shake it, finding the man's arm like a bar of iron. He was no soft-bellied academic.

"I'm Rojer Glenn, your expedition leader," he said. "My old friend Goddard has already briefed me on all the particulars of this mission, so get your arses on the cart and we can get going. It will take us three days to get there, so no sense in wasting the gods-given sunlight."

They circled round the hulking stone golem, a crude, four-legged construct that could only obey the most simplistic of orders: carry this, pull that. Which was more or less what it was intended for: carrying back what was left of Jackan's experiment.

"If you get too scared you can always hide behind that big brute, eh," Jackan said, nudging Guylan.

The younger mage's lips thinned. He might have been thinking the very same thing, but he disliked his courage being questioned again, especially by Jackan. "Let's just agree to stay out of each other's way as much as possible, old man."

Jackan smirked and shrugged.

They clambered aboard the back of the cart and settled down amidst the sacks and crates, coils of rope, and barrels of water.

"Best get attuned to your staff," Rojer said, climbing onto the front of the cart beside the driver. He grinned and chuckled. "I wager you will probably need it sooner rather than later." He waved a hand forward and the retrieval expedition set out for No Man's Land.

CHAPTER 5

Ella had to admit, working in the research section of the workshop was a far more pleasant role than slaving away in the production booths. Here, she only needed to use magic sparingly, avoiding the headaches and crushing weariness brought on every night by the constant draining of her aether well.

It was a scorching day, with the suffocating sort of humidity that sticks like sweat and smothers any hope of cooling down. Heatstroke threatened to claim many of the fort's workers as they toiled under the relentless sun, but, as Ella had just discovered, the mages were fine. She sat in the shade of the workshop and picked up a cold mug of juiced apples brought up from the kitchen cellar. She sipped that nectar of the gods; sharp and sweet burst across her tongue, a delightful chill sliding down her throat. Jackan had been gone for a few days, and it was only now that she discovered mages above the lowest rank could simply request food and drink whenever they liked. Chilled juices. Frozen grapes. Something deliciously decadent called iced cream… It took all her restraint not to abuse her newfound power. Well, too much.

She set her mug down on the bench and picked up a tiny pot of expensive mineral oil requisitioned earlier. She twisted round in her chair, poured a little into the axle joints, then took an experimental trip around the workspace. The squeaking rear wheel of her chair had finally been silenced. It was galling that all it had taken was a little oil to vanquish one of the more annoying aspects of her daily life.

Back at the workbench, she used a wooden mallet to tap a tiny copper pin into a triangular sheet of metal she was fashioning into the third fin for the Mark II model, ready for Jackan to inspect upon return from his expedition. Drawings were well and good, but the old man was a firm believer that a proper engineer should always translate designs to physical scale models before they broke ground at a construction site. He had dusted off the original wooden model of a stone bridge built twenty years ago and explained how he'd been forced to increase the arch and reinforce the supports to accommodate floodwaters – a problem that had only come to light when he showed the model to a local fisherman who had spent thirty years working the river it was meant to span.

She'd taken Jackan's point. It was difficult trying to explain aerial concepts to an earth-bound mage when they had come so naturally to her as a skymage floating up in the air, immersed in its currents. If models could help, then she would just have to build them. What she hadn't expected was for it to be so much fun to construct something that wasn't a horrific weapon. There was great satisfaction in crafting, even if her model wasn't very good.

Ella attached the fin to the thin steel tube that was the main body of the Mark II, then added a small clay figurine into a cut-out section she imagined as the passenger area. She wheeled back to check the scale of it, nodding in satisfaction. When she ran a hand along the steel, Ella noticed her skin was no longer cracked, paper-dry, and crying out for expensive beeswax hand lotions; it was starting to recover from the abuse of alchemical solutions used in the production-line process. The lack of pain was a revelation.

It occurred to her that the excitement of testing out new theories had replaced the mind-rotting tedium of churning out the same thing the same way every day. She was something more than a pair of hands with an aether well, and she had begun to enjoy Jackan's amiable company instead of the enforced silence of her old workbench.

And then, of course, there was the increased pay – the vastly increased pay. The crushing despair of her debt had faded, and pulling double shifts at her workbench was now a thing of the past. Stresses and burdens she hadn't even really been aware of had lightened: this week, she had enjoyed full nights of sleep devoid of nightmares. As a result, her mood soared almost as high as when she had been piloting skyships.

"Am I… happy?" Ella asked herself, wheeling around to survey her section of the workshop, newly patched roof and all. It had been a while.

A broken part of her, long downtrodden and dragging itself through the muck, rejected the idea. Ever since the accident, nothing good had come her way. What if Jackan Grissom died out there in No Man's Land? She was under no illusion that Goddard would keep her in her current role. He would kick her back down into the filth before she could blink. Her good fortune could be as fleeting as the life of a fly.

The thought of returning to that production booth caused her throat and chest to tighten. She couldn't face going back! Her hands shook and tears rolled down her cheeks.

She slapped herself. "Get a grip, Ella." The pain centred her, and the tide of blind frothing panic retreated. She wiped away the tears and stared at the model.

"You have a chance here, woman," she chided. "Work hard and work well, and they will see your worth."

Your worth? the sick and sad part of her mind mocked.

She stamped it back down. Jackan was no hot-headed young fool. He would return with the wreckage of his Mark I experiment, and when he did, he would expect to see what his new assistant could do in her new role. The model was one thing, but that alone would be nowhere near enough to impress the canny old engineer.

The Mark II device was only part of the solution to the quest he had assigned her, and perhaps the lesser part, at that. The rest was buried in a mess of arcane mathematics and mechanics of angles, arcs, forces, thrust, and drag. Ella pulled out sheets of diagrams and calculations and spread them across a long, narrow table. Jackan had modified this table for her, sawing the legs shorter so she could better reach items and equipment from her wheeled chair. He had also augmented another workbench with an attached writing desk: a slab of wood on metal rails that slid out over her lap to be used as a writing surface from the comfort of her chair.

Those accommodations to her disability had been simple tasks for him after watching her work for a day, but they meant the world to her – it helped that her back no longer ached from sitting so straight all day without sufficient support. She had resigned herself to struggling with the world as it had been presented to her, whereas Jackan looked on the world with an engineer's eyes: he noticed a problem and designed and built her a solution. He hadn't said a word. It was just there one morning, all ready for her. No wonder he couldn't resist the lure of sending a mage to the moon. He had to know not *if* it could be done, but *how* it might be done.

She worked on her calculations until an hour before sundown, then thumbed through a series of old tomes she last read during apprenticeship as a skymage to refresh knowledge she hadn't expected to need again. To her chagrin, much of the advanced mathematics were still beyond her, a weakness that once upon a time might have stopped her progressing up the ranks. Her talents and enjoyment leaned more towards the practical piloting and enchantments of the ships themselves, the courses meticulously plotted by others via laborious calculations that she'd just had a natural feel for.

Ella sank back into her chair, pondering. She had an insane-seeming plan in mind that she was sure could work in practice. If only she had the skills to prove it on paper. She shook her head, locked away the most sensitive of her research materials in a warded steel strongbox, stuffed a few sheets of calculations in progress into her bag and then left for home before it got too dark..

She didn't remember the journey. Her head was too stuffed full of equations and ideas to pay a blind bit of notice. One blink, she was at work; the next, she was outside of her decrepit home.

Mrs Beaton's flophouse was far from Newsark's finest accommodation. It was filthy and halfway to falling down, but it had been a roof over her head when she'd had nothing but the clothes on her back. Ella harboured a strange sort of affection for the dingy place and its downtrodden residents, moreso because she would not be staying much longer now that a goodly amount of coin was flowing into her purse.

Old Jim was leaning against the wall, puffs of blue smoke rising from a long-stemmed clay pipe. His generous nose seemed redder than ever as the sun sank towards its slumber. He looked up at the rattle of her wheels over cobbles and nodded in greeting.

She paused in the doorway and looked up at him. "Jim, I've never asked you before, but what do you actually do up at the fort?"

The worker flashed a gap-toothed grin. "Me? Nothin' much. I just sweep up broken glass, dust, and dirt down the alky… achemic… the place where they mix up weird potions and powders." His breath reeked of dark ale, a mix of yeasty bread and burnt barrel-scrapings.

Ella blinked as an idea came to her. "Interesting. Does a Katherine Goddard work in your section by any chance?"

Jim took another puff on his pipe, looking thoughtful. "The singer?" he replied, in a cloud of sweet smoke that most definitely had the tinge of narcotics added to the shredded tobacco leaves.

The singer, Ella mused. The girl was a genius in mathematics and the alchemic arts, and this man called her a singer… but she realised that particular talent probably had more direct value to him than the others. Perhaps, for him, her singing made each and every day that little bit more bearable.

"That's the one," she replied, all bright and breezy. "I don't suppose you could show me around your workplace tomorrow and introduce us?"

He eyed her for a long moment, thinking his way slow and steady through the mental haze. "Don't see why not. You're a sweet little chicken, so I can't see you causing any trouble."

She smiled, loving it when a plan came together. "Thank you so much. You are doing me a big favour here. Can I ask, what is it with you and chickens?"

He shrugged, staring up as the stars started to unveil themselves. "I like chickens more than cows. Leastways, I did back on my farm."

"You owned a farm?" She immediately regretted the surprise in her voice.

He didn't bother to look down at her. "Wasn't always a dirt sweeper. Nor a drunkard." He sucked on his pipe and blew out a plume of smoke. "Shit happens, you know? People and places don't last forever. Best you head off to bed now, lass, before you get me all maudlin. See you in the morn'."

"Well… you have a good night's sleep," she said. "And thanks again." She wheeled herself off to bed before she made more of a judgemental arse of herself.

Jim nodded absently, staring up into the night sky as stars spread across the expanse of the void.

For once, the dark, damp interior of the flophouse worked in Ella's favour. The decrepit old building did smell like rotting vegetables left out in the sun, but it had kept out the worst of the day's heat, allowing her to swiftly fall asleep instead of sweating atop her blankets all night long.

The next morning was a fine and sunny day, but the gods had taken pity on her and made it a tad cooler and less sticky. She washed away the night sweats, packed her bag, and by the time she emerged from the gloomy flophouse, Jim was already waiting for her, whistling a merry tune and looking none the worse from his heavy night. If anything, he'd cleaned himself up a bit and put on his best cloak and tunic with the neater patches.

"Mornin'," he said, tapping the burnt ends out of his pipe on the wall before stashing it away into a hidden pocket in his cloak.

"Good morning," she replied, navigating through the doorway and out into the street. *Ah, the cobbles. My daily enemy,* she thought as her chair juddered fortwards. "Did you sleep well?"

He shrugged, yawned, and without another word began the walk to work.

The two of them joined the stream of workers heading for the fort, immersed in the drone of their chatter. Jim didn't say much. He walked fast, and her arms had to work hard to keep pace, wheels spinning so fast she expected to see sparks fly.

The lake on a hot day spread its swampy, sewage perfume far and wide, overpowering even the odorous summer sweat of the massing crowd.

Approaching the gatehouse, the flow of workers slowed, stymied by the security checks, but of course Ella couldn't see a damned thing from her chair – just a wall of backs, shoulders, and heads, and looming above those, the muscular figures of the fort's guardian golems. Bit by bit, she moved forward, trying to avoid getting jostled in the crowd. A big man in a red tunic shoved ahead of her, almost tipping her out of the chair. He glanced down and sneered.

"Oi! C'mere, you ignorant prick," Jim yelled, grabbing the man by the back of his collar and yanking him aside. The man fell and Jim's boot went in, hard. He spat on the groaning, prone man and then turned to her. "You all right, chicken?"

Ella looked around for the brutalised man, but he had already been swallowed up by the crowd. "Uh, yes, thanks. That really wasn't necessary." She eyed Jim, newly wary of the man's temper.

Jim shrugged. "Arsehole deserved it." He stepped a pace forward, and Ella followed.

Soon enough, they were at the front of the queue. The guard had been doubled, operating under the raptor gaze of two gold-masked battlemages wielding war staves bearing the seal of the Unity on the front of their shimmering crimson robes.

Jim wandered forward and had his tattoo scanned, then he was quickly ushered through the gate.

The battlemages watched Ella intently as she wheeled herself up to the guard sergeant. They could sense the aether of another mage and would obliterate her if she made a wrong move. The sergeant nodded to her, quickly scanned her tattoo and waved her on. She could feel the eyes of the battlemages burning into her back as she passed through the gate.

"Them sorts give me the jitters," Jim admitted. His hands fiddled with the pouch on his belt, as if his nerves demanded he fill his pipe up with something stronger than tobacco but didn't dare.

Ella shivered. "You and me both. Shall we head to your alchemical laboratorium?" They passed a great number of armoured men and a line of three horseless carriages, all gaudy in gilt and drawn up as if on parade.

"Somebody of great importance must be visiting the fort," Ella said.

Jim scowled and spat. "Self-important, aye. Bloody hierarchs."

He led her towards the alchemy buildings on the other side of the base from the Research and Design area: a series of long, low-roofed barns, some with tall chimneys belching odd-coloured smoke, and others, like their destination, with glistening glass domes bulging like blisters from their sides.

"Morning, Jim," a sleepy-eyed guard in rusting mail said, opening the door. He yawned and barely gave Ella a glance as Jim waved her in before him.

"See you in the Muddy Mare tonight, Mikas?" Jim asked, clapping a hand on his armoured shoulder. "Lors's turn to get the next round of drinks in, ain't it?"

That woke Mikas up. He blinked and worked his jaw. "Righto. Wouldn't miss it, mate."

Ella gazed around the alchemical laboratorium, so tidy and clean when compared to the rough and ready Research and Design workshop, where mages were wont to leave scraps of wood and metal, half-built contraptions, and sharp tools laying all over the place like caltrops for the unwary.

She whistled in admiration. "You keep this place clean as anything, Jim."

He looked at her quizzically, as if unsure what to do with a compliment from somebody without a flagon of ale in their hand and another in their belly. "I just clean up any messes I see." He nodded towards the plant beds bathed in sunlight through the glass dome, to where a young woman was already working, her long dark hair pulled into a ponytail, tutting and pulling up shoots of stringy weeds.

"Is that Katherine?" Ella asked.

As if alerted by some sixth sense, the woman's head lifted and turned towards them. She rose, dusted her hands off on an apron, and then made a beeline towards them.

"Er, you're on your own now, chicken." Jim sidled off, grabbed a broom, and began sweeping before Ella could remind him to provide an introduction.

Katherine Goddard's eyes were pale blue, wide, and inquisitive as her gaze flicked over Ella, cataloguing everything about her. "Ella Pickering," she said. Then, after a moment's pause, she winced and added: "Uh. Hello. I'm Katherine."

Ella blinked up at her. "You… know me?"

"I do. You are quite famous."

It was Ella's turn to wince. "For demolishing the hierarch's carriage, I presume?"

Katherine grinned. "Oh, yes. What, may I ask, brings you here to my plant beds?"

Ella looked to Jim for a measure of reassurance, but the man had fled the scene, whistling nonchalantly as he swept the walkways between plant beds and workbenches. "Actually, I am here to see you. I asked Jim to bring me–"

"The janitor?" Katherine queried. "The man who cultivates sativa plants behind the compost heap?"

Ella searched the woman's eyes. "Sativa?" She had a horrible feeling that she knew the sort of thing old Jim was growing on the side.

"Narcotics," Katherine explained. "Shredded leaves people smoke in pipes to give them that special relaxed feeling."

Ella gaped at her. "Um…" She did not want to land Jim in any more trouble than he was already in.

Katherine tilted her head, frowning. "Oh, don't you worry. He's not in any trouble, at least not from me." She looked left and then right, and then lifted a hand to her mouth conspiratorially. "Between us, half the people here are growing a little something of their own on the side."

Ella stared at her, mouth opening and shutting. *This* was Whitlaw Goddard's daughter? That officious paper tyrant? The chief that quibbled the expenditure of every single gold crown?

"We are both rebels," Katherine said, eyes sparkling and fist pumping the air. "Oh! You said you were here to see me? Why? Are you up to something off the books? I bet you are."

Ella felt like she'd been leapt on by a ferociously friendly shaggy dog, experiencing the sort of joyous enthusiasm she rarely encountered and had no idea how to deal with. She reached into her bag and thrust her unfinished papers into Katherine's hands. "Mathematics!" she squeaked.

Katherine flipped through the pages, eyes flicking back and forth over the calculations. "What are you trying to hit?" she asked. "These forces are immense, and the parabolic arc these numbers describe is simply huge." She paused, her eyes glazed as she worked something through. Then she blinked and looked at Ella in surprise. "Why, if I didn't know any better, I would say you are trying to hit the moon." She chuckled. "But that is…" she spotted Ella's appalled expression. "Wait, you are? Why in the name of the gods are you trying to calculate that? I mean, this is rudimentary, and it wouldn't work in reality, but it is a fair attempt at solving the problem."

Ella snatched the papers back and rolled them up in her hands. She swallowed and offered a sickly smile. "Could we perhaps talk about this somewhere more private?"

"Katherine!" Whitlaw Goddard's voice boomed large in the confines of the building. "I have been looking for you everywhere. Did you not get my message?"

Ella craned her neck, eyes widening at the sight of the Chief of the Research and Design Workshop bearing down on them. A well-groomed mage of indeterminate age in exquisite black and red robes ambled in behind him, flanked by two gods-damned battlemages wearing impassive golden masks.

The chief spotted her. One eye twitched in annoyance.

Gods damn it, she thought, shocked into immobility like a frightened rabbit. The visiting hierarch! The very last person she wanted to encounter...

CHAPTER 6

"Your Grace, Hierarch Grubman-Lordrach IV," Whitlaw said, his chest puffing up in pride. "May I present to you my daughter Katherine, a First Circle graduate of the Orialis Guild of Mages, winner of the Svarman Award for mathematics, and a most accomplished alchemist."

Katherine fell to one knee and bowed her head in greeting. "Your Grace, I do apologise for my working attire," she said, standing again. "Had I known you would be visiting the fort so early in the morning I would have made other arrangements."

"Oh, that is quite all right, my dear girl," the hierarch said, greased lips spreading in a smile. His face was painted in the current style of the capital, shade and light artfully sculpted to accentuate high cheekbones, and he bore a thin, waxed moustache on his top lip. "The early bird catches the worm, as my beloved papa used to say. I find it most revealing to begin my inspections early. Why, often, I arrive before the slovenly workers have finished sweeping all their undesirables beneath the rugs, so to speak. I find it gives one a far more honest overview of a workforce, and unveils the measures necessary to reinvigorate their love of labour for the war effort."

Ella swallowed. In her past role as a skymage she had seen exhausted workers consigned to the stocks for days, backs torn up by floggings, and for the worst offenders, a hot-iron brand – the first on their chest, the second on their cheek so that all could see their shame.

The hierarch turned to face Ella, an eyebrow raised as he took in her wheeled chair. "And who have we here? A distinguished colleague of yours, Katherine?"

A spark of worry kindled in the eyes of Katherine and her father, reflecting Ella's own billowing panic. Her throat ran dry as if she'd been chewing five-day-old bread. "Ella Pickering, Your Grace," she said, her voice cracking as she copied the terminology of the others. "Assistant Engineer to Senior Mage Jackan Grissom in the Research and Design Workshop." She briefly bowed her head.

The distinguished hierarch of the Unity waited for her fall to one knee, as custom dictated.

Ella stared back at him.

The moment stretched on into deep awkwardness and lingered there like the reek of a rotten fish on one's pillow.

She smiled, hopefully disarmingly. Her thoughts scattered like a flock of pigeons put to flight. What to say? How to avoid calling the hierarch an idiot? All she wanted was to bury her head in the plant beds until he went away.

It took a while for the fact that she was in a wheeled chair to dawn on the hierarch. A faint flush crept through the paint on his cheeks. He cleared his throat. "Ahahaha, one of yours, eh, Whitlaw? Most excellent. With the redoubtable Jackan Grissom away on a mission of derring-do, I had despaired of seeing what progress he was making with such a sizeable budget. It is all so complicated; what luck that his assistant is here to explain his experiments to me."

The chief's eyes bulged as he begged Ella to pull off the best magic trick she had ever attempted.

Her body went rigid as her mind raced ahead like a riderless horse. All that worry about her future... here, now, she had the chance to secure the chief's gratitude, and she was not going to miss it. All her fear melted away, replaced with a bucket of distilled bullshit.

Ella cleared her throat. "I would be delighted to, Your Grace." She would sprinkle her explanation with as many technical terms as she could manage. He was a mighty and learned hierarch, and unlikely to admit to not knowing something.

"Shall we move to the restricted area of our workshop?" Ella asked, flicking the chief a look that said: *Trust me. No, seriously. Please trust me or we are both face down in boiling water.*

All doubt in Goddard's eyes was quickly masked. "Absolutely," he replied. "Let us explore the knife-edge of arcane engineering."

"Marvellous," Hierarch Grubman-Lordrach IV said. His lips pursed in thought. "Hmm, Ella Pickering... I do believe I have heard that name somewhere before..."

Everybody froze.

The hierarch shook his head. "I cannot quite recall from whom, however. I believe it likely that an officer in the higher ranks of the Unity was singing your praises."

Ella chuckled, a little strained. "Yes, that must be it." One of the battlemages, a woman with ice-blue eyes stared right at her, any expression hidden behind the golden mask. By the weight of her regard, Ella suspected the woman knew exactly who she was and what she had done. It was a blessing that she chose not to give voice to the truth.

They made their way into the cavernous Research and Design workshop. Ella was unsurprised to find it cleaner and more orderly than she had ever seen it. It must have been a sizeable job, and she reckoned an entire team of janitors must have worked on it throughout the night. The mages in the production booths were studiously hard at work, churning out more crates of blasting crystals. Two of the more senior members of the workshop had left their workbenches and their own projects to patrol the walkways, pretending they were hard taskmasters for the day.

While the hierarch was engrossed in the sights of the workshop, Whitlaw Goddard mopped the sheen from his brow with a linen kerchief. Every time he tried to snatch a word with Ella in secret, the hierarch or his battlemages would look round and his mouth would clamp shut to avoid incriminating himself.

The chief gave Grubman-Lordrach a brief tour of the facility, describing the production of the new type of spell-crystals they had developed. They stopped at the booths of several senior mages, who fell over themselves trying to impress one of the few people with the power to grant them increased funding. Their grandiose ideas and explanations of their work elicited little more than vaguely interested nods and bland smiles. None of it was earth-shattering: all modifications or additions to old spells and research.

All too soon, they entered Jackan's work area in the restricted section. Ella bitterly regretted leaving her model out on the table for all to see, but what was done was done, and she would just have to weasel her way out of it. The hierarch wandered closer, bending over to peer at the cylindrical Mark II with its new metal fins.

"This does not look like a cannon," he said. "The metal is far too thin."

His head turned this way and that, trying to figure out what the device was for. He paused and reached out to retrieve the little clay figurine from the cut-out section in the belly of the model, holding it up to his eye, peering at it and then where it had come from, trying to piece this puzzle together.

Katherine too seemed most interested in the model. She looked at Ella with dawning comprehension of what it was all about. Ella had never meant for her to be here to link the calculations to this model and Jackan's experiment, but it was too late now. That was an awkward conversation for another time, assuming she survived this one.

"I must throw myself on your mercy and ask," the hierarch said. "What does this strange device do?"

That was exactly what the chief wanted to know as well, judging from his brittle expression and flop-sweat.

The younger skymage Ella – naïve, loyal, and diligent – would have babbled some nonsense and given herself away immediately. Now? That loyalty was ashes. Their lies had reduced her to a broken, sorry, debt-ridden mess, and now she had no compunction about lying right back at them to preserve her newfound freedoms.

What had Jackan said to her about his experiment? *A weapon delivery system more sophisticated than a mage staff or crude heavy cannon.* An idea formed in her head, the only idea.

"That clay figure," Ella said, "represents a war golem."

Grubman-Lordrach turned the little clay figure over in his hands, his lips pursed.

"Imagine this scenario," she continued. "You are a young nobleman of the Ranneas Empire tasked with carting supplies to the front lines. You feel entirely safe so far from the heavy cannon and magic of the perfidious Unity. Your brave warriors and unmatched mages patrol the borders eliminating any intruders or war machines, so all your caravan must contend with are some local bandits or a smaller monstrosity birthed from No Man's Land that managed to slip through the net. No real threat to big brave men like you..."

The hierarch did not look suitably impressed, his eyes hooded and his pursed lips threating to turn into a frown. He misliked being compared to a man of the Empire, especially because however much the Unity hierarchy espoused equality, there was little real difference between the wealthy hierarchs of the Unity and the noble houses of the Empire.

Ella nodded to the clay figure. "Imagine a Unity war golem emerging from the mud to destroy that supply caravan and all with it, stone fists smashing everything to paste. This model device is many times smaller than the real thing. And as for the range, well, we could land war golems deep behind enemy lines to devastate their entire line of supply. Attack their iron mines and their farming heartlands, and they would have to divert mages and men from the front line to deal with it."

Ella kept her glee deep inside. She was damn proud of this spur-of-the-moment lie. All that military education had not gone to waste: lines of supply were one of the main things that skymages were deployed to spy upon.

The hierarch replaced the clay figurine back in the belly of the device and stepped back to study it. His hand stroked waxed whiskers. "What progress has been made in developing it?"

Whitlaw Goddard cleared his throat. "Jackan Grissom and a crack team of specialists are in No Man's Land as we speak, recovering the wreckage of the initial test launch of the weapon – one several times the size of this little model here."

Grubman-Lordrach's eyebrows lifted. "This has advanced beyond theoretical research already?" He did some quick mental calculations. "Why, that is already thrice the range of our heaviest cannon. Impressive. You are to be commended. Chief Goddard, let us retire to your study to discuss an increase in funding for this project of ours."

The chief positively salivated at the thought. "Right this way, Your Grace." He shot Ella a look that mixed gratitude and deadly warning before they entered his study.

She winced, not relishing the talk they would be having later.

The hierarch paused on the threshold. "What a quaint little collection of artefacts you have in here."

Whitlaw's lips tightened, but he nodded and ushered his guests inside, closing the door firmly behind him.

Katherine waited just long enough to ensure they wouldn't re-emerge any time soon before she rounded on Ella with such feral glee that it seemed to radiate from her. "You are in so much trouble if you don't spill your guts and tell me everything."

No Man's Land. The arse-end of nowhere. A gods-forsaken barren expanse of sucking mud, spell-craters, deathtrap ravines, dusty riverbeds, and ambulatory corpses. It was a canker upon the face of the Great Mother, a weeping sore in the world.

"Why is it so accursedly cold here?" Guylan complained, pulling his cloak tighter around his body as the cart lurched along the heavily rutted track. "I thought predictions were for a heatwave."

Jackan, too, was huddled up inside his cloak. He kept an eye on the dead, twisted trees and the shadows beneath scorched boulders, wary of *something* mad enough to attack a party of armed men and mages.

From his seat at the front of the cart, Rojer twisted round and the two mages discovered his ever-present smile had vanished. The man had cracked jokes and told amusing stories all through their tedious trek, but now he wore a sober mien like a suit of armour.

"The weather here is… different," he explained. "Unnatural and undecipherable, like the dreams of a mad god unleashed upon the land. Whatever you have heard and whatever you have read, discard it. This mutilated land is one of the Nine Hells made manifest, and only once you have walked this scorched, frozen earth will you understand." He turned back to face No Man's Land and lifted a hand. "Stop the cart. We proceed on foot from here."

The trackway vanished fifty paces ahead. It hadn't been worn away by scouring wind and rain; it just stopped. A clean line cut through the land like a giant had taken a butcher's knife to it. On the one side, patchy sunshine, a track and scrubby grass, bushes, and withered trees with the occasional surly crow; on the other, black clouds, barren earth, glassed rock, steaming hollows and bubbling puddles squatting in the craters left by the impact of siege-spells.

"Listen up," Rojer said to his men, his eyes finding the two mages in his charge to ensure they knew he also spoke to them and expected them to heed his words. "For some of you, this is your first time in No Man's Land. Touch nothing. Take nothing. For the sake of the gods and your life, watch your footing: if you break a leg on the way in, you are on your own until we return. Keep your eyes peeled and your weapons handy; war has made this land into an unholy death trap. Right, who among you has the keenest eyes?"

The grinning warriors all looked at each other until a hesitant hand lifted. "I'm a fair archer," the warrior said. "I'd say my eyes are better than most."

"Right, then," Rojer said. "Climb atop the golem. From here on out, you are our scout." The man shrugged and clambered up the craggy legs of the golem, sitting pretty while everybody else trudged through the mud and dirt.

"Why are we not sitting up there instead of him?" Guylan asked. "Seems like an easier way to travel."

The leader of their expedition offered him a flat look and leaned in to whisper. "If you want to make yourself a big ol' target for enemy mages, by all means, climb right on up there."

The younger mage looked doubtful. "You don't like me much, do you?"

Rojer snorted and ignored the question. He cracked the lid on a small barrel carried in the cart. One by one, the warriors painted the thick brown paste over every exposed surface of their boots. The air reeked like a fisherman's shack on a hot summer's day.

"It's the cursed dirt here," Jackan explained to his younger colleague. "It'll eat away at the leather and then your skin if you don't protect it. You first."

Guylan stepped forward, nose wrinkling at the alchemical mix. "What is in this?"

Rojer shook his head as he coated his own footwear. "You don't want to know."

The younger mage gagged as he applied it, much to Jackan's amusement.

The warriors transferred provisions from the cart into backpacks and readied their shields and weapons for battle. The party formed a loose semicircle, looking at Rojer expectantly as their nervousness and excitement ramped up.

"The plan is to go slow and careful," their leader said. "We go, we recover the wreckage, and we get the fuck out. If we are lucky, we won't see a damned thing out there other than ourselves." He looked to the sky. "May divine Gildanas bring us luck and safe passage."

Three men stayed behind with the horse and cart while the rest of the party pushed on, heads bowed against biting wind and scouring dust. They talked among themselves of what they might find, boasting of their prowess and the glory and gold they expected to be heaped upon them. Overhead, black clouds boiled, blocking out the sun and casting a pall of gloom over the land as far as the eye could see.

They marched onwards, eyes scanning the broken terrain. The chill gradually deepened, their breath misting the air. Hoarfrost gathered on the tips of their spears as they circled a hill and followed the path of a dried-up riverbed leading to a small lake of sulphurous, bubbling mud.

"I see something up ahead," the scout yelled. "But I can't quite make it out."

Rojer lifted a land and signalled them to lay low. They watched a thick bank of fog roll in through the ravine they had planned to travel through.

"What is it?" Jackan whispered as the fog gushed from the ravine and flooded towards them. He shivered as its icy coils wrapped around him, nipping at his nose and ears.

The scout clambered atop the golem's rocky brow and peered into the gloom. "I can see people moving in the fog."

Rojer readied his staff. "Those ain't people. Listen up, lads, looks like we have a fight on our hands. Ditch your spears and draw your swords, because you'll need to hack these things apart to put them down permanently. That is what we call an *arisen* – it's what's left of a mage killed by magic and left here to rot. The evil of this place has seeped into their bones and set a corpse to walking. Make no mistake, its brains might have rotted away, but it still thinks it's fighting the war, and it sees anything living as the enemy. There is only ever one main body, guarded by mindless corpse thralls, so if you put that dead mage back down, they'll fall too."

He urged the eleven warriors on foot into a semicircle, shields up front and swords ready. The three mages stood at the centre with their war staves ready to unleash destruction. Rojer grabbed Guylan's hand. "Don't waste your time launching wide-area ice attacks using that staff in your hand. It's largely useless on the arisen. Focus on cutting blades of ice and restricting their movement, or just use your own aether."

He turned to Jackan. "The fire from your staff will prove much more effective. Don't waste it all on the thralls, though – save it for the arisen itself."

"What about me?" their scout said from atop the golem.

"You? Hang on for dear life." Rojer looked to the construct that had been coded to obey him. "Golem: smash anything that approaches us." It was no swift war golem, but a huge lump of stone could crush skulls just as easy. If nothing else, it would serve as a mobile wall.

The thick blanket of fog rolled in, turning their world to whites and greys and the darker shadows of scared men. They shuffled closer to one another, breath rasping in the sudden silence. Leather and wood creaked. Steel rattled as armoured men shifted nervously.

An enraged voice boomed through the fog. "Destroy the enemy of the Unity!" The cultured accent originated a few days east of Orialis.

Figures raced in, silent apart from the thudding of bare feet across the ground. What was left of a woman in tattered mail and leather, with one arm missing and a face squirming with bloated maggots, slammed into a warrior's shield. His sword split her skull in two and came back up ready for the next. The boastful young warriors snarled and swung as more corpse thralls slammed into their shield wall. A man on the right screamed as black blood and brains sprayed his face: he fought all the harder from sheer disgust.

The golem swung stone fists like anvils, crushing anything that dared to come close. Its blows were slow and clumsy, and would be easily avoided by anything with a sense of self-preservation, which these cursed things evidently lacked. The scout on its broad back screamed and kicked out at skeletal hands that reached up for him.

"There's the main body," Guylan said, pointing into the fog.

Behind the crowd of its undead thralls, the septic-green glow of a mage's staff appeared at the mouth of the ravine.

"Cast!" the one-eyed mage commanded.

Jackan's staff snapped forward, pointing into the fog. He focused his will upon the weapon and unleashed the aether stored within it, conjuring a fist-sized sphere of roiling flame. It grew brighter and hotter as more aether converted into heat and flame, straining the very fabric of the spell and beginning to sear his hands. He snarled and unleashed it upon the enemy. Flame blasted ahead, burning a tunnel through the fog. It hit and detonated, the explosion showering them with smoking debris.

Guylan stared into the billowing smoke. "Did you get it?"

"Cast your ice," Rojer demanded. "Maintain the assault!"

The young engineer swung the staff like a spear, willing a blade of ice to scythe across the battlefield. Several thralls fell in pieces, falling shadows in the smoke and fog, but the attack shattered against something far more solid inside the smog.

The ragged figure of a dead mage stepped forward, once-exquisite runed crimson robes now black and scorched. Half of his jawless skull was missing, just broken teeth, white bone, and loose grey skin flapping. It screamed and launched a dart of emerald light.

Rojer snarled and spun his staff, a lattice of energy strands forming a spinning shield of blue light. The attack struck and deflected up and away to the right.

Swords rose and fell as fists and teeth shattered on the warrior's shields. Men roared. Corpses in old Unity garb wheezed and drooled vileness as they pressed forward, threatening to overwhelm the beleaguered defenders.

Jackan and Guylan struck again, their attacks on target but ineffective.

"Damned battlemage robes," Rojer yelled over the din of battle. "Of all things, it had to be a dead fucking battlemage."

Its robes were the highest grade crafted by the Unity's artisan mages. Woven throughout with thrice-blessed gold thread, fortified by slivers of dragonbone, and ensorcelled with runes to make it highly resistant to fire and ice and all imaginable manner of offensive magics launched by enemy mages – and the three of them were far from wielding the might of dedicated combat mages. Most arcane engineering drew power from the world, slowly storing it for later use, and the more potent types utilised external gems of solidified aether to produce far stronger effects, but so exceptional were the materials forming this creature's robes that they generated their own power. It would never run out unless overtaxed to complete destruction – more's the pity for the living.

"What do we do?" Guylan shouted, launching a block of ice at the thing. The force of impact knocked it back a few paces but did no lasting damage.

"I'm thinking!" Rojer snapped.

As the fog dissipated in the heat of his flames, Jackan studied the ravine with its high rocky cliffs on either side. He nudged Guylan. "We're not bloody battlemages, but we are engineers." Jackan gritted his teeth and directed several charges of magic through his staff. Fire billowed out to rage against the cliff face. The hair on his hands burnt away and blisters formed as he endured the stream of flame until the rock was hot and steaming

Guylan knew exactly what he was about: when the old engineer's staff fell, he layered the rock face with sheets of ice that immediately melted to water then turned to steam. Heating rock and cooling with water was one of the oldest ways of quarrying stone, but here they were making a weapon of it.

Fractures webbed out across the cliff face. Rock cracked and snapped. The entire wall of the ravine suddenly slid free.

The arisen looked up as the slab of stone blotted out the sky. It didn't try to defend itself: there wasn't much point in fighting a falling mountain.

The impact knocked everybody off their feet. An entire cliffside of stone crushed the enemy, filling up the mouth of the ravine with dust and debris. With the arisen permanently disposed of, the magic animating its corpse thralls faded and they collapsed into lifeless piles of meat and bone.

Warriors climbed to their feet, panting for breath and wiping sweat and gore from their hands and faces. The scout sat up from his golem, peering into the dust and whooping with joy. Their boasting began again, this time with increased enthusiasm.

Guylan offered Jackan a hand up. After a moment's wonderment, the older man took it, wincing as blisters popped and oozed clear fluid.

Rojer Glenn surveyed the devastation. He looked at his two charges with a grudging respect. "Well done. That was an effective solution."

"We're engineers," Jackan said. "We're no' just pretty faces."

"You are old and dried up," Guylan muttered. "If anybody has a pretty face here, then it's me."

Jackan cupped a hand to his ear. "Eh? What was that? Was that a 'thank you' I heard? Ach, don't mention it, youngster. You are most welcome for saving your life."

"Right, lads," Rojer shouted, steadfastly ignoring their bickering. "See to your wounds. We move on before this mess attracts something worse that our big-brained boys here can't outthink."

CHAPTER 7

"Please do avoid the death machine," Rojer Glenn said as the two other mages and their guards edged along the path closer to the spinning torso of a bisected Empire construct.

Unlike wholesome Unity golems crafted from stone infused with natural aether, this Imperial machine was a blasphemous amalgam of brass rods, steel plates, and the living flesh of a vat-grown monstrosity crafted by the twisted minds of the enemy's research mages. Its lower half lay in scattered bits, the half-melted torso fused to glassed rock by some mighty spell. The rubbery head was a shattered stump with shards of glass where eyes must once have been, but some sorcerous sense still enabled it to notice their presence. Hinged blade-limbs spun in squealing circles, cutting and stabbing in a vain attempt to reach them – the command to kill was still in force despite its ruined condition.

A slitted yellow eye opened inside a hole in the thing's armoured midsection, fixating on Guylan as he crept past. The man shuddered as mewling mouths with translucent needle-teeth burst from blisters on its neck. Its voice was high and childlike as it called out to them, the words a crooning nonsense. "That is vile," he said, spitting the acid tang of bile from his mouth.

Jackan scratched his chin. "Aye. Undeniably sturdy, though, to have survived a spell of this intensity."

Its call ignored, the thing shrieked like a demonic toddler, sending Guylan lurching away from it, his staff raised into combat position.

"It's just throwing a tantrum," Jackan scoffed. "Calm down; it can't reach us."

The younger engineer ground his teeth and shook his head, muttering obscenities about his colleague's parentage.

The party left the construct to its impotent rage and spent the next day picking their way across the remnants of an old battlefield. Broken Unity war golems littered the ground like weather-worn statues in the remains of a ruined manse, still entwined in fatal battle with the Empire's own constructs of war. Twisted skeletons of huge, vat-grown war beasts sprouted from the lifeless earth like albino tree trunks. Rusted mounds of human corpses littered the area, their armoured bodies entombed by an orange-brown mass of corrosion.

They pressed on, silent and watchful. The wind whistled though the graveyard of a battlefield and their boots crunched through dry grass and debris.

"Who do you think won?" Guylan asked.

Rojer glanced back. "Nobody won. Some were lucky enough to survive."

Guylan lowered his head, brooding.

One of their warriors paused. The young man kicked over a broken shield and peered down at the ground. He gasped and his eyes lit up with avarice. "Gildanas has granted me luck – I've found a war staff! These things are worth a damned fortune."

"Don't touch that," Rojer snapped. "We are here for the wreckage of Jackan's experiment and nothing else." He moved on, but a blood-curdling scream set him spinning with an attack spell on his lips.

The greedy warrior had ignored his order and picked up the staff. The crystal embedded in the tip was cracked, leaking its deadly aether at the touch of unwary human hands. Sparks of lightning filled the air, crackling and snapping. His leather gloves melted onto the shaft, the flesh beneath bubbling and hissing as he flailed about, trying to dislodge the damaged weapon. He took a breath to scream some more.

Then he exploded.

Jackan and Guylan ducked. The other warriors hid behind their shields as chunks of meat, metal, and shattered staff rained down on them. Where the man had stood there was now a steaming crater.

"Let that be a lesson to all of you," Rojer snarled. "I told you not to touch or take anything from this accursed place. There's always one greedy little prick that thinks he knows better than me. Do what I say, and the rest of you might live through this." He stomped ahead, muttering profanities.

The two engineers and remaining warriors followed him, eyes fervently scanning the ground for more hidden dangers and skirting anything that even looked like it had been created by human hands. The golem stomped ahead, the scout atop its stone back unconcerned.

A field of floating boulders lay ahead, massive rocks drifting like clouds at head-height, spinning and rebounding from one another but never straying beyond a certain nebulous boundary.

Jackan approached the nearest rock, hand outstretched. He incanted a detection spell, trying to determine just what manner of magic had caused such an effect. He turned back, shaking his head. "No levitation magic. No earth magic. Nothing I can decipher. Somehow, the laws of the world have been twisted beyond bearing in this place, but by what?"

Rojer just shrugged and wove through the field of spinning rocks, keeping his head down.

They passed through without incident, then clambered up a rocky hill to proceed along its narrow ridge. The sun slowly followed its arc as they marched, the Research and Design mages' feet growing sore on the rocky landscape and their complaints becoming more vociferous. The view was less than spectacular, with the barren, cratered land below mostly lumpen brown mud and grey rock, or obscured by oddly coloured mists seeping from the broken earth.

Several times during their trek, Guylan stiffened and glanced back, feeling like somebody or something was watching him. Each time, he summoned his aether and willed it to form a cone of force around his ear. He listened intently, but all he could hear was Jackan's wheezing, the wind and the occasional pebble tumbling down the hillside. He dismissed his worries and continued onwards but couldn't shake that itch between his shoulder blades.

Rojer called a halt to confer with the scout atop his golem. To the east, their ridge descended down the opposite side of the hill to an expanse of sucking swampland riddled with geysers of liquid metal, steam, and green gas. Glowing shards of rock jutted from the morass, surrounded by the skeletons of small birds and other twisted things with too many legs that none there could identify.

The air reeked of pepper and a metallic tang, irritating the back of their throats and causing their eyes to tear up in the wind. The mage clambered up to join the scout, and together they surveyed the terrain for a while before he jumped back down, looking none too happy.

"Right, lads," he said. "We are closing in on the crash site, but it looks like the route I had been intending to take has become a deathtrap. Unfortunately, we will need to take the more stable western route that some call the Shredding Slide. It's not as bad as it sounds. Unless you fall. So, don't. If one of you proves inept enough to fall, your only chance is to get your shield beneath you and ride it down the slope."

"What about us?" Guylan asked. "We don't have shields."

Their leader gave him a disparaging stare. "No... but you do have magic. You could, oh, I don't know, *use it*." He shook his head and walked away.

Rojer bid the party ease themselves down a treacherous slope of broken black glass, the remains of a firestorm beyond anything they had ever seen. They used their spears and staves to steady themselves and test the way forward for unstable footing. The golem began its descent off to the side, taking one unsure step at a time, the heavier weight of its tread threatening to cause an avalanche of razor-sharp shards.

"You first," Jackan muttered.

Guylan scowled and shoved past him. "Which one of us is the coward now, eh?"

Every step was accompanied with a crunch of shattering glass, and they winced at the din as fragments clattered and screeched their way downhill. Stealthy they were not.

They were halfway down the slope when a hulking white shape crested the ridge they had recently vacated. A great forest cat of some sort – or at least it had been before corrupting magic got into its flesh and warped its growth. This creature was easily ten times the size it should have been, with bulbous tumours all along the spine and an oily spiked tail. Overgrown incisors and claws like swords jutted from swollen, bloodied lips and paws. Glowing pink eyes surveyed prey from under two vicious spikes of bone jutting from its forehead.

"Don't move a muscle!" Rojer hissed as the party balanced precariously on the shifting slope, entirely exposed and vulnerable.

"What is that thing?" Guylan gasped.

Rojer glared. "Nobody move. Nobody panic. Keep your voices down. Calmly look back at the abomination and show it that you are unafraid. It is a hunter, and the worst thing you can do is flee like prey."

The monstrosity stared down at them and the Unity expedition stared right back. Time ground past, every moment excruciating. Slowly, ever so slowly, Rojer raised his staff.

Whatever the creature was, it knew a mage's war staff when it saw one. Its chewed-up ears pricked, then it turned away, leaving to find easier prey elsewhere.

A plate of black glass broke beneath Jackan's foot. He cursed and lurched sideways, the fragments clattering down the slope.

The white beast's head snapped around at the skitter of glass shards.

More glass shattered underfoot. Jackan's arms windmilled, trying to regain his balance. "Shit, shit, shit," he yelled, keeping a death grip on his staff.

The old engineer began muttering a levitation spell, but his concentration was broken by a shard of glass stabbing through the side of his boot. He began to slide downhill upon a shifting sheet of broken glass.

The abomination snarled and leapt, massive muscles launching it down the slope, paws wide and sword-claws splayed.

Guylan's hand snapped out and barely grabbed hold of Jackan's staff as the sheet of sliding glass picked up speed. The old engineer swung out sideways, legs kicking, holding on to the staff for dear life. The ground cricked and cracked under Guylan's boots, but his footing held.

The white beast sailed overhead, an avatar of hissing frustration as it missed decapitating Jackan by half a claw-length. It hit the slope and slid, spinning round ready to launch itself back towards its prey. Heavy paws scrabbled at the razor-sharp shards of glass. The monstrosity yowled in pain as its blood spattered the surroundings.

It slipped.

It fell.

An avalanche of broken glass flowed over it. The creature was flayed alive by shifting, slicing shards of glass, shredded and spread across the expanse of the hillside. The human party watched wide-eyed as the glass-slide hit the valley floor and what was left of the beast's deformed skeleton tumbled free of the bloody tide, red and gory and glistening.

Rojer looked on impassively. "And that's exactly why I said not to fall." He shrugged and resumed where he had left off, carefully picking his way downwards, leaving the rest of them staring at his back and shivering.

Jackan found sure footing again and shot a grateful look at Guylan. "Thank you," he said, trying and failing to keep a hint of surprise from his voice. "If not for you..."

Guylan simply shrugged, staring down the treacherous slope at the bloody remains.

The rest of them turned envious eyes upon the scout atop the golem, but the man flashed a grin and urged the construct onward, off to one side of the rest of them, its stone feet dislodging more broken glass with every heavy step.

It took a while, but they achieved the descent with only a collection of nicks and scrapes and a few deeper cuts needing to be bound, one of which was on Jackan's ankle – painful but not debilitating. He bit his lip and limped on without complaint.

They came to a forest of charred, dead trees. A fire had swept through the entire area and the stink of smoke and ash was still strong upon the air. Overhead, clouds gathered like a thick, grey blanket, turning the day overcast and gloomy. The silent forest all around was shades of black and grey and nothing else.

"This is the place," Rojer stated. "The wreckage the skymages spotted is somewhere ahead."

"And what do they call this gods-forsaken hellhole?" Guylan asked. "The Dead Forest? No, wait, the Forest of Living Death? Will these trees come alive at night and try to suck our blood?"

Rojer shrugged. "It wasn't here last season, so it probably doesn't have a name yet." He eyed the trees, if true trees they had been. "If they were ever going to try and eat you, I reckon the wildfire caused by your colleague's crashed weapon put an end to that."

"Silver linings," Jackan muttered.

They took a brief rest, gnawing on jerky and drinking from water skins, then readied their weapons and pushed on into the dead forest. Twigs disintegrated at their touch, and the breeze caused ash to fall like a soft snow, turning heads and faces as grey as the land around them.

Up on the golem's back, the scout stiffened and craned his neck. He pointed ahead and to the right. "I see a campfire. Tents and people moving in front of the light – don't know how many. They seem to be encamped at the edge of a crater."

Rojer gave his warriors a nod and they formed a battle line, shields out in front and spears and swords ready. He turned to Guylan and Jackan. "I don't suppose either of you are well-practised with invisibility spells?"

"Actually," Guylan said, chest puffing out, "I was in the top three of my class at the Orialis Guild of Mages. I specialised in advanced spellform design."

Rojer gave him a flat look. "And have you ever used it in a combat situation?"

The young engineer deflated somewhat. "Well, no, but I can perform the spell without flaw."

"Right, then, on your head be it," the man replied. "I want you to mask yourself with magic and scout ahead. See what sort of force we are facing and then return without getting caught. Think you can manage that?"

Guylan's lips thinned. He nodded.

"Off you go, then," Rojer said. "Be careful."

One incantation later and Guylan's aether wrapped light around him like a cloak. If one looked close enough, or if Guylan moved too quickly, an onlooker might see distortions and eddies in the air as the spellform bent light around the mage inside. If you looked even closer, you might spot the dark dots where Guylan's eyes were – there wasn't much point in a cloak if the caster couldn't see through it.

Footprints appeared in the forest floor as Guylan ranged ahead.

"Didn't think the lad had that sort of magic in him," Jackan admitted grudgingly.

The leader of the expedition chuckled. "No love lost between the two of you, eh. What happened?"

The old engineer scowled. "Orialis Guild this, Orialis Guild that. The arrogant twit won't shut up about it, and somehow he reckons that makes him better than the rest of us. As if we had the money and connections to enrol in such a vaunted guild with bottomless resources. Nah, we had to make do with what we had and forge our own path."

Rojer raised an eyebrow. "So what did you do?"

He shifted uncomfortably. "Aye, well, I may have sabotaged his funding application somewhat. The lad was boasting about it for weeks to any that would listen, so I knew exactly what resources he was going to ask for and I got there first. Us old dogs know how to work the system, and I can write a proposal in my sleep. Thought I'd take him down a peg or two."

"And that would be this expensive experiment that has old Goddard in such an uproar? No wonder Guylan is in such a sour mood if he's been roped into helping you on it. It's like rubbing his face in the dirt. Even so, he did save your life."

Jackan's lips pursed. "That he did. The bastard."

They waited, warily watching the treeline.

At the sound of cracking branches rushing towards them, the Unity expedition came to alert. Guylan appeared, his cloak of invisibility torn away by his panicked rush, arms waving to catch their attention.

"Ambush!" he yelled. "An Imperial patrol. Ten men and two mages that I could see."

The scout stood atop the golem, helmet tilted upwards as his keen eyes peered into the trees. "I see–"

The young warrior's head exploded. Spears of ice thudded into his body, piercing his armour and launching his mangled corpse into the air. More shattered on the golem's stony hide.

"Shields up," Rojer yelled as arrows whooshed through the trees. "Warriors forward! Mages, cover them. I'll hunt that blasted ice mage."

He nodded to Guylan. "Told you it wasn't a great idea to ride the golem."

A shudder rippled up the younger mage's spine and he gripped his war staff tighter.

The expedition advanced towards the Empire encampment as more enemy magic bloomed in the distance.

CHAPTER 8

Katherine Goddard freed her long dark hair from its ponytail, ruffled it out, and then sat, tearing through their notes in a joyous academic frenzy. Little noises of interest and appreciation escaped her lips as she flipped through Jackan's initial sketches and Ella's notes on why it wasn't as simple as flying in a straight line to the moon.

Ella sat beside her, fidgeting and chewing on her bottom lip as the woman devoured their notes. The embarrassment of their flight of fancy being exposed to outside scrutiny was immense, like being stripped naked – and by the chief's own daughter at that. She fully expected the woman to laugh at their mad thoughts and speculations about landing a mage on the moon. The model she'd been so proud of now seemed like a cheap children's toy.

"This really started as an accident?" Katherine asked, peering at her over a handful of pages. She tapped one of Jackan's early diagrams, rich black soil ingrained beneath her fingernail.

Ella took a measure of solace that she faced a hardworking woman not afraid to get her own hands dirty. "A lightning strike set off Jackan's device," she admitted. "It was supposed to be a new sort of heavy cannon he was tinkering with, but, well, instead it took off into the sky atop a pillar of flame."

Katherine set the pages down and leaned back, chair creaking. One hand absently drummed a rhythm on the table. She glanced down at the papers again, then looked over to Ella and ceased the drumming. "I love it."

Ella blinked. "Excuse me?"

"I love it. It is quite mad, of course, but a world away from the research we have been stuck doing here for years. I am thoroughly sick of brewing up poisonous concoctions that maim and kill." Katherine scowled and spun to face Ella. "You have no idea how many promising lines of research have been tossed into the bottom of a scrapheap in favour of this endless bloody war of theirs."

Ella straightened in her chair. "Oh? Like what?"

"Alchemical powers and potions made from rare minerals that could possibly revolutionise several domestic industries. Medicines and cures of all sorts: I have grown exotic plants that could have enormous health benefits for the populace at large, but oh, no, the hierarchs have no interest in us exploring that sort of thing – they all have cadres of personal healing mages, after all! Imagine if all these resources were spent doing something good for the world."

"I made blasting crystals for months," Ella replied, looking at her still-recovering hands. "I know what it's like spending my days helping to kill people."

The two women locked gazes. A bond of shared professional commiseration and understanding formed.

Katherine cleared her throat. "Um. So. This is the bit where I blackmail you."

Ella's jaw dropped. "Excuse me?"

"You will make a request to my father that I join your team," she added. "You desperately need my mathematical abilities, and I assure you, my alchemical prowess will prove most useful."

"Wait, what?" Ella blurted. "You want to attach yourself to this debacle?" She waved at her model. "You did realise I was lying to the hierarch, right? We are nowhere near making this into a weapon even if we wanted to, which I don't. This is highly likely to blow up in our faces. I don't exactly have much to lose, but you do."

Katherine grabbed Ella's hand. "I am so bored! Every day is mind-numbing tedium. This is a magnificently mad endeavour, and for the first time since I can remember, I am actually excited about something. I feel alive even contemplating the challenge ahead. Please! I don't care if there are risks."

Ella stared at her. "I'm not sure you understand what blackmail is..."

"Oh. Yes." Katherine's nose scrunched up, deep in thought. "I could… tell my father?"

"I suppose that works," Ella muttered. "Well, guess I have no choice but to put in the request. Anything more than that is up to the chief, though."

Katherine's eyes lit up with the fire of determination. "You leave Father to me, my new colleague." As if a lever had been pulled, her attention snapped to Ella's model of the Mark II. "So, can you please explain why the device looks the way it does?"

Faintly stunned by the speed of events, Ella launched into the trimmed-down version of skymage basics that she had related to Jackan, all about the forces involved in aether-powered flight.

Katherine studied the smooth pointed nose of the Mark II and the metal fins Ella had recently added to the base. "And these modifications will help to steady the flight?"

Ella nodded. "They will. The gods shaped birds and fish the way they are for a reason. I can steady the flight of an object, but getting something so large and heavy up into the air and flying it fast enough and far enough are very different matters."

"They are, indeed," Katherine replied. "Did Mage Grissom detail what alchemical powder he was using in his device that took fire so readily?"

She shook her head. "He did not, and many of his notes didn't survive the accident. I do know that it was black, if that helps?"

Katherine's shoulders slumped. "You have much to learn about alchemy. Most mixtures are grey, black, or brown. I find it interesting he thought of empowering his device with the transition of a chthonic state of matter into flame, which, as we all know, is drawn towards the heavens. Do you suppose he has read Empedocles's treatise?"

That sort of nitty-gritty detail of magical theory was lost on a practical mage like Ella. She could only shrug.

"No matter," Katherine said, waving a hand. "I also have much to learn about the intricacies of being a skymage." She paused. "Given the way that arcane device launched itself through the roof and into the sky, you are both lucky it did not just explode. They would have had to scrape you off the walls with a knife." She chuckled awkwardly.

Ella felt distinctly green around the gills. "Thanks for that lovely image."

A faint flush crept onto Katherine's cheeks. She hung her head, hiding behind a veil of hair. "Sorry, I... um... I am a bit nervous. I'm not good at talking about things outside of work matters."

"Nervous?" Ella asked, incredulous. "Of what? Me?"

She nodded. "You were a skymage. You destroyed a hierarch's carriage, survived the crash, and now you are building a device to land a mage on the moon; you are a marvellous rebel. All I have ever done is what was expected of me: first in my class at the guild examinations, a solid no-nonsense practical job that keeps me out of danger..." She chewed on her lower lip, then swept her hair back over her ear to look Ella in the eye. "I want to be like you."

Ella couldn't help it. She laughed, great heaving guffaws that set Katherine's face burning with embarrassment.

"Sorry," she said to Ella, voice trembling. "I'll... I'll go... Forget I said anything."

Ella fought for breath, wiping the tears from her eyes. "No, no. I'm sorry for laughing, but nobody wants to be like me. My life is a steaming pile of cow dung. I've only started to feel alive again since I became Jackan's assistant."

She told her would-be blackmailer everything, the woman's eyes growing wider with every revelation. The accident that, as it turned out, was not her fault. The massive debts taken on to pay for her recovery. The poverty and the flophouse, where she survived on one good meal a day. The tedium of the production benches, and the joy of constantly cracked and stinging skin.

"I had no idea," Katherine said, visibly disturbed.

"Safety and security are not such a bad thing," Ella added. "Your father's just trying to look out for you."

"That may be," the woman replied, her expression hardening. "But I am not some precious piece of glassware that needs to be wrapped in wool and consigned to a chest locked away in a darkened cellar where nobody can ever find it."

"So I see," Ella said. "Well... it's up to you. I can't speak for Jackan Grissom, but I have no objections. We could certainly use your expertise in mathematics and alchemy.

Just… please don't tell anybody else what we are really doing here? If word gets out that we're diverting resources to this project and aren't working on a horrific new weapon, then we'll be–"

She hurriedly cut off her treasonous words at the sound of approaching feet.

One of the hierarch's guardians entered first, hard eyes behind the golden mask scanning the workshop. A tingle of magic swept through them as she employed a divination spell searching for concealed and magical threats. Apparently satisfied, the woman stepped aside to allow Hierarch Grubman-Lordrach IV to stroll in. The man's gloved hands were folded behind his back, and he wore a broad smile upon his handsome face.

Katherine leapt to her feet, smoothing out soiled work clothing.

Whitlaw Goddard came in behind him, flushed and somewhat shocked by whatever they had talked about. He flashed a worried smile at his daughter.

"What a marvellous weapon this will be," the hierarch stated. "I shall take a personal interest in its development." His expression hardened. "And, of course, in any problems, should there be any." He pivoted to face the chief. "Other than yourself, who among the staff and servants of your workshop know the details of this particular project?"

"Ah, well, Jackan Grissom, of course," Goddard said. "Ella Pickering here is his assistant. Guylan Bluford and Rojer Glenn are aware of some but not all of it. I believe that is all."

The hierarch arched a perfectly plucked eyebrow. "Consider them assigned to this project." Then he looked at Katherine, standing as she was before a table of mathematical diagrams and sketches relating to the usage of their experimental device.

Katherine swallowed and stepped forward. "It is my honour to consult on mathematical and alchemical issues for this project, Your Grace."

Her father paled, hands trembling. "Ahaha, my daughter overstates the matter. Her work lies in the seedbeds, nurturing plants."

Grubman-Lordrach IV scoffed at that. "Now now, my good man. There is no need for such humility. Your daughter is a First Circle graduate of the most prestigious guild in the Unity, and you said yourself that she was the winner of the Svarman Award for mathematics – which, I do believe, would prove a vital resource for such an ambitious endeavour."

Goddard looked ready to throw up his breakfast, but he nodded in submission.

The hierarch looked to Ella. "Now, are there any others you have omitted to mention?"

The battlemage shifted ever-so-slightly, her impassive gold mask facing them directly. Somehow, her cold eyes managed to exude an overt air of menace that had the young women quaking.

They hastily shook their heads and the hierarch smiled. "Excellent," he said. "A small but skilled team will mean no loose lips carrying secrets to enemy ears. Do you require any more personnel? Any unique skillsets?"

Ella cleared her throat. "I, ah, no, not at this early stage... Your Grace. Most of it will be working out the theory and building more test devices."

"I see," he replied, deep in thought. "More labour will be required later, of course." He blinked and looked around the workshop, nose wrinkling as he took in old cloth, rusty chains, patched roof, and a security system consisting of heavy canvas curtains and a painted sign. "This will not do. No, this will not do at all."

He snapped his fingers in the air. "Battlemage, is there a more secure location nearby that could be requisitioned?"

Behind that golden mask, her eyes remained unfazed and unoffended. The icy eyes of a hardened killer. "There is an old motte and bailey castle several hours ride west from here," she replied in a voice like gravel. "It is, I believe, currently used as a training camp for conscripts gathered from The Howling prison, but the walls have recently been rebuilt in stone and a new moat dug. There should be enough space inside the bailey to allow for the construction of workshops and all manner of arcane devices."

"There you have it, Goddard, my old fellow," the hierarch said, clapping him on the shoulder. "A secure new home for this project. Once my people have renovated the place, it is all yours."

"Thank you, Your Grace," Goddard mumbled, looking forlornly at his daughter, now irreversibly entangled in Jackan's foolishness. "You are most kind and wise."

CHAPTER 9

An arrow thudded into the trunk of a tree near Jackan's head. He yelped and ducked as another followed, hitting only air. Yet more thunked into the warriors' shields as they advanced upon the Empire encampment set up at the lip of where Jackan's falling device cratered the earth.

Over to the left, a flash of light as Rojer deflected an incoming enemy spell. A nearby tree exploded into frozen shards that pattered off an invisible shield surrounding the one-eyed mage. In response, he roared and unleashed a crackling bolt of lightning from his staff. The spell seared a line of white across the old engineer's eyes. Ahead, one of the enemy screamed and burst into flame, greasy black smoke billowing from his flailing form.

Rojer lifted his staff. "Divine Gildanas is with us! Charge!"

The research engineers kept their heads down as the Unity battle line raced ahead of them, shielding the mages with their armoured bodies and their very lives. Grim men wearing the Imperial red griffin on grey tabards over their mail swapped bows for sword and spear and advanced to meet them with a dirge dedicating their souls to Perunuk the Thunderer upon their lips.

Steel clashed. Men roared and screamed. Blood splattered the ground.

Jackan and Guylan stood frozen with indecision as the battle swirled around them, too afraid of mistakenly hurting their own men to take any offensive action.

A construct of brass and steel clambered from the crater, resembling a massive metal spider. Crystal lenses in its head whirred as it focused on the battle. The open end of a long, thin metal tube riveted to its side began to glow a baleful red – some manner of weapon, though Jackan had no idea what.

The two engineers glanced at each other in an instant of understanding: an enemy war machine was something they were better equipped to take apart.

"Ice and fire again," Jackan snarled.

Guylan struck first, draining aether from his staff to direct a blast of icy wind at the construct. Frost spiderwebbed across its surfaces while blocks of ice coalesced around its metal limbs and joints. It stumbled, mechanisms grumbling as it tried and failed to walk. A beam of ruby-red death lanced from its weapon to cut a furrow deep into dirt and stone like a spear thrust through human flesh.

Then it was Jackan's turn: a jet of flame that roared through the dead forest, turning charred trees to candles. His spell struck the frozen construct and the ice flashed to steam. Metal cracked under the strain of going from frozen to superheated in a single instant. Its weapon split, broken parts dangling on strands of copper wire. Eye-lenses shattered. Legs snapped. The construct fell apart, its torso split open to reveal turning cogs and glowing crystal spheres. Stumps of legs jerked and flailed to no effect. It was out of the fight.

Overwhelmed by his victory, Jackan stood grinning. "Take that, you–"

Guylan slammed into the old engineer, carrying them both to the ground. Blades of ice scythed across the area, cutting through trees and one of their own warriors with equal ease. That man flopped to the ground in two parts, blinking and gasping in shock as he stared at his own legs sitting three paces away from his torso. Jackan stared at the dying man, fighting the urge to vomit.

"Saved your life twice now," Guylan snarled, rising to his knees and muttering a shielding spell. He rocked back and lost the spell as something heavy slammed off it to explode against a nearby tree.

Jackan looked to his younger colleague with equal parts gratitude and annoyance, then his eyes widened as the tree next to them split in two and fell towards him.

"Rise!" Jackan shouted, forgoing the intricacies of a proper levitation spell for raw will and power. His aether obeyed, staying the trunk from crushing Guylan beneath its bulk. "Call it only one debt owed," he said through gritted teeth as the younger mage rolled out from under it. Jackan let go of his will-working and the heavy trunk crashed down. He staggered back, exhausted.

Bolts of fire streaked through the dead forest, setting shields and branches alight and filling the area with smoke.

The older engineer lost sight of his young colleague within the smoke. The sounds of fighting drifted towards him, closing in. He staggered to his feet and tried to back away, quickly getting lost with no idea which way led back to his own lines.

A young man with a war staff came through the smoke, head down and coughing.

Jackan sighed with relief. "Guylan! Where have…"

It wasn't Guylan. This man wore the red and grey of the Ranneas Empire.

The Imperial mage seemed just as shocked at the encounter, both of them staring at one another open-mouthed. As one, their weapons snapped up into spell-launching position, arcane crystals crackling angrily. The moment one loosed his spell, so would the other, and then both would die.

Jackan's gaze met the enemy's fearful eyes. This mage was exhausted and even younger than Guylan. He was no battlemage, judging from the terror-sweat glistening on his brow and the bulging toolbelt much like Jackan's own hanging around his waist. Shaking hands held the staff in a death grip.

Jackan cleared his throat. "Are you an arcane engineer?"

The man stared back, confused.

"I, too, build things," Jackan said. When the man didn't reply, he added: "Do you understand me?"

The enemy mage hesitated, conflicted, and then offered a swift nod.

Jackan took a deep shuddering breath. "I don't want to hurt you, lad. I prefer to make things. So howsabout you and me just back away slowly and head back to our own lines?"

The man licked his lips. "We must trust each other, yes?" he said, his voice deep and guttural. "How do I know you will not, ah, how you say, knife me in the back?"

The old engineer shrugged. "Aye, well, looking at your tools, you also prefer to build things than kill people. Maybe we are not so different, eh?" He chewed on his lower lip, sweating as the man's hands tightened around the staff. "We are not here for you," he said. "We are here to fetch my device."

A flicker of understanding in the man's eyes. "You are here to retrieve your weapon?"

Jackan couldn't help it. The stress bubbled up into strained laughter. "It's not even a weapon, lad; it's a bloody accident – I'm sick to death of this endless war."

The mage didn't look convinced, and he didn't lower his staff. "Then what was this device used for?"

"We tried to touch the moon," he replied with a chuckle. "Mad as it sounds, it's true." In his thoughts, he added: *More true than calling it a misfired weapon, anyway.*

The enemy mage blinked, some of the fear fading into curiosity. "The moon? Hah. Impossible."

Jackan shrugged. "Is that so? Have you ever tried?" He'd heard somewhere that giving an aggressor your name made you less of a faceless, nameless enemy to them. It humanised you, made it less likely they would kill you out of hand. "My name is Jackan Grissom – and you are…?"

The mage searched his eyes, then chose to answer. "Andriyan Korolev, adjunct to Komissar Taeban Tereshkova."

"I know that name," Jackan replied. "That would make you my counterpart in the Empire."

The man nodded. "You destroyed assigned construct. We cannot now take all of salvaged device back to the Empire. We could… how might you say… go halfsies?"

Jackan chewed his lip bloody, thinking furiously. Goddard would be enraged if he returned with only half of the wreckage, but what were a few chunks of twisted metal and crystal when weighed against the lives of himself and all those young men only here because of him?

"That sounds… wise," he said. "Call off your men and I will call off mine."

He took a chance on the lad. He lowered his staff a little. The other mage didn't, but he did slowly back away without attacking, gradually fading away into the smoke. The mage's voice yelled out something in the Imperial tongue: the shriek of steel and roars of rage dwindled as Imperial forces pulled back to their camp under the spell-cover of their mages. Silence fell, save for the screams of the wounded and the dying.

He sagged, holding onto his staff for support. Soon the smoke began to clear, and the scattered Unity force gathered around him. Four young and arrogant warriors were dead; only seven shaken survivors remained, and one of those clutched a dangling, broken arm with the shattered remnants of his shield still attached. Rojer and Guylan's robes were scorched and torn and bore the melting remnants of ice-spells sparkling on the cloth.

Guylan reached him first, the mage's eyes wide and staring, his hands shaking. "Are you well?"

"I'm alive," he replied. "Not sure about well."

Rojer crept towards him, keeping low and keeping trees between him and the enemy position whenever possible. His robes were shredded across one shoulder and the flesh beneath was bloody and black from frostbite. Given the extent of his injuries, it was a miracle he was even standing. "Good bit of work there, lads," he hissed through his pain. "Didn't expect we'd be tangling with the Empire today. Looks like they are pulling back."

"How are you faring?" Guylan asked.

Rojer gritted his teeth and grimaced. "I'll survive."

"I made a deal," Jackan muttered, staring at his feet. "Came face to face with one of the enemy mages in the fracas there. An engineer like us, by the look of him. They take half my device and leave, and then we recover the rest. Nobody else needs to die here." He looked up to meet the gaze of the other mages and found no condemnation in their eyes, not even Guylan.

Rojer just nodded.

"I wanted to get in and get out without killing anybody," Jackan added.

"Depends on them now," the one-eyed mage replied. "I doubt they know how few we really are. Were it me, I'd want to retreat as soon as possible." He turned to the warriors. "I'll keep watch – you see to the wounded."

Wounds were swiftly cleaned and bandaged, as best as could be managed on a battlefield. There was no trace left of their previous boasting behaviour, no grins or talk of gold and glory.

Soon, they advanced on the Empire encampment only to find the enemy in full retreat. Several of the warriors carried sacks with shards of metal piercing the cloth, but true to the mage's word, much of the twisted wreckage remained untouched in the crater. Andriyan Korolev acted as the rearguard for the enemy force, setting up shimmering shielding spells to cover their flight. He looked across the ruined landscape of No Man's Land and nodded to Jackan, then turned and fled.

"Go about your business," Rojer ordered. "I need to see to the men and rig our golem ready for transport – sort out what we are taking back. Don't dawdle. We don't have days to linger here picking over every tiny fragment." In their haste to depart, the Imperial forces had left behind sacks, tools, and other goods in their tents. The experienced mage began requisitioning whatever they might need for the journey home. He handed the two engineers a shovel each and shooed them off.

Jackan and Guylan walked the floor of the crater, examining what was left of the experimental device. Plates of metal warped by heat and bent by impact. Flattened copper tubing. Shards of crystal. Much of it was unidentifiable.

"What did they take?" Guylan ventured.

"Hard to say what survived the impact," Jackan replied. "At a guess, they took the wind-element aether crystal I was using to power some of the spell arrays, and a good chunk of the interior structure that survived around it."

"That's the most expensive part," Guylan said, groaning. "Goddard will not be happy they got away with that."

The old engineer glanced at him. "Lucky for us, I'd say."

"How do you mean?"

"Those are the parts I had least interest in recovering – well, beyond the obvious monetary value."

Guylan frowned and scanned the scattered wreckage. "You were more interested in... this?" He turned over a metal plate with the toe of his boot, noting that rivets had been sheared off from the remnants of frame beneath.

Jackan nodded. "Oh, yes. I am keener on finding out what set it off, what failed in flight, and the structural damage the device suffered before it landed. That is worth much more than what powered it."

"I... see," the younger man replied. "Very well. I would not like to linger too long in case they come back with reinforcements."

Jackan shuddered. “Most sensible thing you’ve said in months.”

A sigh emerged from Guylan’s lips. He made no reply, simply frowned and shook his head.

“That was unwarranted,” the old engineer admitted. “My apologies. Old habits die hard, it seems.”

“It’s fine,” Guylan said. “I accept your apology. Now can we please get a move on? I really need to get back home and have a long, hot bath.”

They began a systematic survey of the crater, scouring it for any materials that might grant them insight into the flight of the device, and the perils of trying to duplicate it. Every piece of importance that they dug from the muck and ash was retrieved and loaded up onto the back of the golem ready for transportation back to the workshop.

By the next dawn, they had gathered a hefty haul of material and began their journey back to the borders of the Unity, and to safety. Their prayers were answered with an uneventful journey.

CHAPTER 10

Ella scowled at her slate of lopsided calculations. "Add up, damn you!" She attacked the problem from multiple angles for hours before finally admitting defeat, wiping away the offending lines of chalk with a rag. She threw it aside in a huff, beyond frustrated.

She still had much to learn about the mathematics that presumed to illuminate the workings of the world. Katherine could only teach her so much; the rest she had to learn by doing, or she would forever be forced to rely on somebody else. Over the last few days, she had taken to using slate and chalk instead of expensive paper or parchment – it was only while cleaning up the piles of wastage that she'd considered how much her errors had cost the project. It was a shock, and she lived in fear of the chief's wrath. So, reusable materials it was until she had something worth recording for posterity.

She growled at her empty slate and got back to work, trying to build upon mathematics and barely understood theories they'd cribbed from dusty tomes in the workshop's library. Knowledge not directly applicable to warfare had languished unread and unloved for many years. She and Katherine had taken to raiding the stacks for the most obscure texts, finding some nuggets of gold buried inside their crackling pages.

At the sound of raised voices, she looked up. The mages sounded excited. Happy, even – a rarity in this dour place.

Guylan and Jackan sauntered into the restricted area, wearing tired grins. Her eyes grew wide as she took in their dishevelled state. The mages' robes were caked in mud and their faces dusty masks around tired, red eyes. Jackan's leg bore a bloodstained bandage. The two men carried the weight of combat on them – a weariness of the soul that she had often seen but was glad to have never experienced herself. They were home safe and sound – and likely looking forward to a bath and a cold ale or three.

Jackan drew back a section of the canvas curtain to admit a stone golem loaded up with bulging sacks. The construct settled itself on the floor and waited to be unloaded.

The old engineer thumped down into a chair, dried mud flaking off him. "Hello, lass."

"Welcome home," Ella said, wheeling herself over. She looked them up and down, noting the scrapes and bruises, torn clothing, and scorch marks. "Was it so very awful out there?"

Both men shuddered.

Guylan frowned. He stared at her with narrowed eyes. "What in the blazes are you doing in the restricted area?"

She arched an eyebrow, unimpressed. "I'm Jackan's assistant," she replied. "Where else would I be?"

The young mage scowled. "Jackan has you fooled as well, then? The man is a hawk and not to be trusted. He will steal your funding and your glory at the first opportunity."

Ella looked over to her superior, who simply shrugged and rolled his eyes. "I don't need your protection, Guylan. This is the only good thing to happen to me since my accident."

The man's lips thinned. "Well, you might be able to stomach the old bastard, but after this venture, I don't have to."

She winced. "Ah. About that. You might want to have a chat with Whitlaw Goddard sometime soon."

"Why?" he asked, suspicious.

She swallowed. "Umm… just, maybe you should."

"Spit it out," he demanded, a sudden dread stealing over his expression.

"Oh!" Katherine cried as she peeled back the curtain and entered. "My new colleagues have returned from their adventures. I look forward to hearing all about it once you have had a chance to wash and eat a hot meal, and I do hope we can create marvellous things together."

Guylan looked to the newcomer, then back at Ella. "New… colleagues?" he said in a strangled voice.

Katherine offered him an awkward smile. "Um. Yes. The four of us, and that Rojer fellow, too."

"No. I will not have it," Guylan growled.

"Ach, get over yourself," Jackan muttered. "Like it or not, we made a good team out there. You even saved my life."

Guylan ground his teeth, having no scathing response to that.

"I fear I have put my foot in it," Katherine said, stiffening up and wringing her hands. "I apologise, if so."

"Not at all," Ella said. "Guylan here is just sour about it, but even he won't go against the direct order of a hierarch."

"What?" Jackan and Guylan blurted.

Ella explained the situation. "And, er, so that's what I told Hierarch Grubman-Lordrach IV we were building in here."

"This will not stand," Guylan raged. "We will see about this." He stormed off towards the chief's study without another word.

In appalled silence, they watched him go. The pounding of a fist on old wood was followed moments later by the squeak of a door opening and closing.

Jackan groaned as he forced himself to his feet. "Let me wash off the blood and sweat and we'll speak about this again. Ella, perhaps you should have a word with that man in private, and maybe give him the kick up the arse he needs."

Ella looked at her feet, motionless in the wheeled chair. "Unlikely."

Colour bloomed on the old engineer's cheeks. "Ach, you know fine well what I mean, lass. Punch him in the bollocks, then!"

She grinned. "Just kidding. Now go and get that leg of yours properly seen to by a priest of Mogranus before the rot takes a hold of it. Unless you really want my advice on wheeled chairs?"

"Aye, aye, and I'll let Rojer know he's been conscripted while I'm there – the poor man's shoulder was black with frostbite from one of those Empire bastards' spells. It'll take him months to recover from that. I'm sure he'll be delighted with this spot of news."

Ella's eyes grew wide. "You fought Imperial troops?"

"More like a bunch of scavengers, same as us lot." He shook his head and limped out of the workshop leaving Katherine and Ella and the motionless stone golem behind.

"Um. Should I unload it then?" Katherine asked.

"If you wouldn't mind," Ella said, eyeing the shards of metal piercing the sacking. "Best wear some thick work gloves or you'll do yourself an injury."

Katherine untied the sacks and emptied them onto the table for Ella to catalogue the wreckage. They sorted out structural items of buckled iron plates and half-melted bronze hoops, separating them from what was left of the bent copper pipes and more arcane fragments that made up the device's internal construction. There was even a tiny pair of scuffed red aether crystals that had somehow survived the crash and could be reused. Ella had only briefly seen the device before the accident set it screaming off into the night, so much of the material before her was a mystery.

Darkness was drawing in by the time they finished sorting it. "I believe that is all we can do for now," Katherine said, surveying the piles of scrap. She picked up one of the small crystals and held it up to her eye, studying the ruddy colour. "Fire-aspected aether, low quality. I cannot fathom why they went to such great effort to retrieve all of this. These crystals are common as dirt."

Ella twitched, thinking that if she sold one of those crystals, she could feed herself for an entire month. It was another reminder that they inhabited very different social strata. "I haven't the faintest idea what manner of arcane secrets Jackan might be able to glean from this mess," she admitted. "But he wouldn't have bothered to fetch it back if there was nothing to be gained. I expect we will find out in the morning."

Ella was up and out of the flophouse early, waiting for Guylan by the gatehouse. He caught sight of her and she had the distinct impression that his day had just gotten worse.

"Good morning, Mage Pickering," he said. "How may I assist you today?"

"I'm sorry," she said. "I know you don't like Jackan, and I wager some – maybe even most of it – is warranted, but I really don't need protecting from him."

Guylan's lips thinned. "Don't say you were not warned."

She sighed and looked up at him, her gaze hardening. "I know our own history is... complicated. It seems like you still feel a need to protect me, but you're no longer a member of the investigation team that condemned me to the production benches. You saved my damn life, and in doing so suffered their wrath as much as I did. After all of that, I think you can just call me Ella."

He clenched his jaw. "I–"

"I'm not finished," she said. "Now it's my turn to protect you."

He remained silent, weighing up her words.

She looked left and right, ensuring nobody was close enough to overhear. "Like it or not, we are stuck together until we're finished with this project, and you deserve to know the truth of things. Which is to say that we're not really building a weapon for the hierarchs."

He blinked in shock. "Continue."

"We misled Chief Goddard, and I lied to Hierarch Grubman-Lordrach IV's face."

"Fuck," he muttered. "Are you mad, woman? Was one charge of treason not enough for you?"

"It is not a device for dropping war golems behind enemy lines," she admitted, then had to clear her throat before continuing. "In truth, we're designing a device to carry mages to the moon."

He couldn't stifle the laugh. It cut off when he realised she was deadly serious. "You are quite, quite mad, Ella. Why would you ever attempt that?"

"People need to be reminded that magic is for something more than war," she replied. "This pointless conflict grinds up thousands of lives every year. How can the gods possibly allow it? What if you could build a vessel to go up there, knock on their door and ask: 'Why? Why will you not intercede and stop the slaughter?'"

He had no immediate answer for that.

She swallowed, chewing on her lower lip. "Look, all I ask is that you look over our workings before doing anything rash. If you want to help, fine. If not, I'll help you find a way out of this, or you can rat us out and you won't hear a word of complaint from me.

"Come, let me show you what I have been up to while you and Jackan were off sightseeing…"

* * *

Guylan sat down at Ella's workbench and tidied the strewn papers into a neat pile. He silently and solemnly worked his way through them. Ella waited nervously for any hint of what he was thinking, but his face was every bit as stony as the golem still squatting in the corner of the space. Every whisper of paper and creak of his chair echoed loud in her ears. Her fate once more rested in this man's hands. Several times, she opened her mouth to query him, then slowly shut it again – he'd be done when he was done.

An age passed before the engineer set down the last of her papers, sat back and sighed, closing his eyes and massaging his temples. "Using war funds and material like this will not go well for you," he said.

"I already know that," Ella replied.

"Do you?" He opened his eyes and swung round to face her. "You promised the hierarch a weapon. What do you think will happen when you fail to provide one? Do you believe that the production benches are the worst they can do to you? You will dance at the end of a rope for this. If you are lucky."

Ella crossed her arms and set her jaw. "Do you mean to rat us out to Goddard?"

"If I did," he snarled. "It would be well-deserved! And it might save your lives – all our lives, apparently."

"If?" she asked, hope hanging by a gossamer thread.

He groaned. "This… it is a lot to process."

"I understand," she said, moving in close. "Look, you said that you felt guilty over your involvement in my… in what was done to me."

Pain and regret flickered in his eyes.

She calmly met his gaze. "That's bullshit, of course. You did nothing wrong. Nothing. But if it makes you feel any better, all I ask in exchange for that debt is that you hold off on a decision for now and witness what we are doing here. I know Jackan can be an arse to you at times, but please try to tolerate him."

Guylan twitched and frowned at the very idea of working with Jackan, but eventually he sighed. "I will hold off. For now." He blinked and his lips twisted into a vindictive smile.

"It suddenly occurs to me that I can always blame everything on the senior engineer of this fake project. But what of Chief Goddard's daughter? How did you rope her into this insane scheme? I do not believe her the type of woman to willingly engage in deceit and law-breaking."

"Ah, yes, about that," Ella said, scrubbing at her hair and looking at the floor in embarrassment. "I'd asked her for some help with the mathematics, but she blackmailed me into joining the team instead."

He gaped at her. "She did what?"

"Blackmailed me."

"Katherine?"

"Yes, her."

"But she is…"

"Sweet and naïve? Possibly, but she was like a war dog with a bone."

"Katherine? Really?"

She could only nod.

Guylan sat back and shook his head in disbelief. "Well, well, what a dark horse she turned out to be. The chief cannot have liked that one bit."

Ella winced. "Yes, well, she was helping me with some of my work when the hierarch strolled in, and he decided that anybody that knew anything at all about this project was on the team and had to be sworn to secrecy. That was a done deal there and then."

"Ahhh, that explains it," he replied, waving one of her sheets of workings at her. "The reason you asked her for aid, I mean. These calculations are abysmal."

She scowled at him and rolled past, ensuring the iron rims of her wheels passed right over the tip of his toes.

He yelped and yanked his foot out of the way. "I suppose I deserved that."

She huffed. "And more. In all honesty, I prefer seeing you this way instead of sulking over past misdeeds."

"I don't sulk!" he objected, mortally offended.

"You like to complain a lot."

"Ah. That, I cannot deny," he admitted. "In all fairness, there is a lot to complain about."

She nodded in genial agreement.

Katherine chose that moment to pull back the curtain and enter. She looked from Ella to Guylan and back again. "Am I interrupting something… private?"

"Not in the slightest," Guylan growled. "Mage Pickering was just bringing me up to speed on the status of this project. And of its true purpose."

Katherine turned wide eyes upon Ella, who nodded. "I see," she said, relaxing. "Well, I look forward to working with you. Mage Grissom will arrive momentarily. He was delayed at the infirmary: I gather that the leader of your expedition will be spending some more time in recovery before he is able to join us."

They waited in awkward silence.

"So," Guylan said to the newcomer. "While we wait, what is this I hear about you being a blackmailer?"

Katherine flushed hot enough to cook an egg. "Ella!"

CHAPTER 11

Jackan entered his workplace and paused, taken aback by the heated argument he encountered. All three of the young mages were too consumed with bickering and barking expletives at one another to note his arrival.

The old engineer stood in the doorway, eyebrows raised and stroking his bushy moustache. He coughed to announce his presence. "And what exactly happened here?"

All three spoke at once, fingers pointing, accusations flying.

Jackan drew on his aether. He muttered a spell of silence and snapped his fingers three times, his concentration focused on each of them in turn. His magic hung in the air like a thick cloak, and while the mouths of the others opened and closed, no sounds emerged.

"Much better," he said. "This is a place of work, not an alehouse filled with gossip and bickering. There is sharp metal and wood, tools, and bloody expensive and fragile arcane apparatus lying about – a moment of inattention could bring the chief's wrath down upon you like a golem's fist."

Guylan looked at him, and then pointedly looked at the patched roof.

He scowled. "That was an act of the gods, and you know it. Now I don't know what this fracas was about, and I don't rightly want to know." He glanced at the younger engineer. "I, for one, intend to leave my own grievances outside. Now, have you all calmed down enough to get back to work?" They nodded and he dropped the spell.

"That was unpleasant," Ella said. "I didn't know you were so proficient in that branch of magic."

Jackan strode over to the sorted piles of wreckage. "I am an accredited mage, and all of us who live long enough keep a few tricks up our sleeves. Now, let's look at what we were able to salvage of my original experiment."

"What, the remains of your moonshot device?" Guylan asked.

Jackan paused and turned to look at Ella, who steadfastly refused to meet his gaze. "I suppose it was inevitable." He straightened up and faced his junior. "This," he explained, "was originally envisioned as an alchemy-assisted spell launcher – until the lightning strike turned it into something quite different."

He related the events of that night down to the most precise detail, including Ella and his discussions in the aftermath. "That was when we chose to explore this new idea further. It's been a damned long time since I worked on something that generated any kind of joy or excitement. What I need to know from our new colleagues is if you choose to join us in this research. If not, the best I can do is order you to work on something on the very periphery of the project so you may rightly claim to be unaware of its true purpose if – no – *when* the truth is uncovered."

Ella shifted, uncomfortable in her chair.

"It will come out sooner or later," Jackan added. "That's a gods-damned certainty. I don't know if it will be to a clamour of applause from a world dazzled by our advancement of humanity's knowledge or if we'll end up dangling at the end of a noose for misuse of war material." He slumped into a chair. "I'm old and I want to leave behind something beyond a legacy of developing deadly weapons. Something worthy. It's not like I have so many more years to risk. Make no mistake, this is bloody dangerous and blatantly treasonous business we are engaged in, and I can't make these decisions for you."

Katherine wasted no time. "I am in as far as we can go. Even the thought that we might be able to touch the moon has set my mind on fire."

Guylan scratched his chin, mulling it over. He looked over the wreckage, shaking his head. "Am I correct in thinking that this research really could be used for transporting war golems?"

"Aye, I suppose it could at that," Jackan admitted. "Much easier than people, too, given how fragile we are."

The young engineer took a deep breath and let it out low and slow. "As the basic research will serve both purposes equally... I am in, for the moment."

"Yes!" Katherine's fist pumped the air, causing everybody to look at her. Then her face flushed and she hid away behind her long hair.

Jackan surveyed his team and smiled. "I very much appreciate your discretion, and also your enthusiasm, Katherine. Now, let's stop nattering like fishwives on a becalmed day and see what knowledge can be gleaned from the debris."

They combed through the piles of parts, with Jackan picking out whatever he could still recognise. "Aha," he cried, pulling out a length of twisted copper tubing. "This channelled fresh air into the combustion chamber, so that the black powder could burn faster and hotter." He turned it over in his hands, noting the internal heat damage and soot in the piping. He set it down on the floor, just above part of a curved metal plate that had been the mouth of the cannon – before extreme and unexpected heat and heavy impact left it deformed.

Katherine turned over an iron box in her hand, noting that the hole matched up with the tubing, and the broken wind rune that had been inscribed into it. "And this was powered with a wind-element crystal to suck in the fresh air?"

Jackan nodded. "I figured that if you blow on hot embers, they glow hotter and burst into flame, so this would provide the same. I tried various mixes of powder alone a few times and the darned things failed to burn well, so I thought to myself, maybe it was the lack of air. Have to admit, I'm not exactly well-read on modern alchemical matters – as I said, the whole thing was an experiment."

"You were trying to cause a small explosion?" Guylan queried. "A contained – nay, directed – one?" At Jackan's nod he continued, picking up a shard of the device's barrel with force runes inscribed into it. "The usual array of force runes that power our heavy cannon, supplemented with an additional alchemical source of power to overcome the magical interference limit?"

"Aye," the old engineer said. "Most guild-taught mages think that every little problem can be solved by using the right magic, but there's only so many arcane runes and enchantments you can add to something before they snarl each other up and explode in your face. I was a stonemason and an engineer before I was an accredited mage, so I thought to myself 'alchemy, now that's a different matter entirely'. If we use our brains as well as our aether, we are bound to improve the efficiency of both."

Guylan grunted a vague approval. "I've seen a shocking amount of shoddily crafted buildings here at the fort only held together by regular magical maintenance. They were built in a hurry: if they were not magically hardened against mundane and magical attacks, and the ambient enchantments redrawn on a regular basis, I wager they would crumble in a year or two at most."

"I have noticed that," Jackan said, glancing up at the roof above their heads.

Guylan set down the metal shard he'd been holding. "Looks like some of that iron you used failed to hold its shape and strength due to extreme heat: that'll be a problem for sure."

"I agree, looking at this lot," Jackan said. "We will need good dragon-forged steel instead."

They continued to arrange pieces on the floor in an approximation of where they had originally come from. Eventually, they managed to reconstruct a partial skeleton of Jackan's device. A much larger pile of blackened, bent, and twisted scrap gave no hint as to what it once had been: those Jackan set aside to go to the blacksmiths to melt down and make whatever new tools they could from it.

Ella, Katherine, and Guylan studied the construction of his device:

– A heavy, tubular shape, open at one end. The muzzle of his cannon, which had instead become the maw of a fire-gushing monster propelling it upwards into the night sky. The remnants were a molten ruin, having utterly failed to contain the raging inferno.
– The barrel of the weapon had been heavily inscribed with force runes designed to propel spell-crystals and other shot as far as it could fling them.
– A boxy iron container built into the base of the barrel containing alchemical powder, and the jury-rigged airflow device and tubing that Jackan had subsequently grafted onto it.

"Deceptively simple in design," Guylan muttered. "But how you would precisely time the activation of the runes with the ignition of the powder escapes me."

"Aye, that was a problem," Jackan admitted. "Fortunately, one that no longer matters. This great big lump of metal flew into the air without the use of any levitation spell. If something so heavy can do that by accident, imagine what we could achieve if we actually tried?"

Katherine ran a finger across what was left of the powder box and studied the sooty residue, rubbing it between thumb and forefinger. She sniffed it and her nose wrinkled. "What alchemical mix did you use?"

The old engineer shuffled his feet. "Er, the black powder used for those little fireworks they sell in Newsark village, for celebrations and the like."

Katherine tutted and shook her head. "What you mean is, you used some cheap black powder brewed up by a failed alchemist or shoddy illusionist. Probably made with pot ash and hearth soot." She scowled at him, and even the old engineer quailed before her scorn. "With poor materials like that, is it any wonder most mages consider alchemy outdated mumbo-jumbo only used by charlatans and hedge witches."

"I would have tried better powders, had that lot worked," he protested.

"Well, that's being added onto my own work list," she said, eyes glazing over as she looked inwards and began thinking up plans. "Developing a proper black powder mix first, and then perhaps something better."

"Hold your horses there, girl," Jackan said, hands raised. "We don't even know if that line of research is worth pursuing at this early stage. Let's get a nice pot of tea brewing and we can all talk this through."

Once they all had a steaming mug of tea in their hands, they sat around the table with diagrams and calculations spread out before them.

Jackan took a scalding sip and began. "The way I see it, we have a number of things to discover before we dare use the chief's funding to build anything substantial. The first thing we need to study are the limitations of levitation – Ella, I want you to work on that. The lighter we can make our... carriage?

Ship? What the blazes do we even call this long metal tube ferrying mages to the moon anyway?"

They sipped at their tea, mulling names over.

Guylan smirked. "Hah. With that tubular shape and rounded head, it looks a bit like a giant c–"

Ella interrupted: "A fire dragon," she said firmly, her cheeks colouring. "It flies, and breathes fire, and carries people in its belly."

"Oh, that is a good suggestion," Katherine said. "Guylan, what were you about to suggest?" She leaned forward, looking directly into his eyes. "Do go on."

Jackan fought to keep a straight face, savouring Guylan's sudden discomfort.

The younger engineer endured Ella's glare as he stared into the younger woman's earnest, open eyes. "Ah, er, a... commoner's drop spindle? Yes, you know, for spinning wool into yarn?" He wiped a bead of sweat from his brow whilst Ella nodded in satisfaction.

"Oh, I suppose it does look a little like that," Katherine said. "A rocchetto, I think they call it. I like fire dragon more."

"Then Fire Dragon it is," Jackan said. "Now that's settled... where was I?"

Guylan relaxed and perused the arcing diagrams of sending a device to the moon.

"You wanted me to work on levitation?" Ella prompted.

Jackan snapped his fingers. "Yes! When we build a full-scale device, the lighter the better, so we need to know how many levitation runes we could use before they start interfering with one another – we most certainly cannot exhaust the passengers' aether trying to maintain active spells to do the job. However we intend on powering this Fire Dragon, we'll need to overcome the pull of the Great Mother wanting to gather it back to her bosom. Katherine, alchemy aside, work with Ella on the mathematics of launching something and hitting the moon – work out how high and how fast this Fire Dragon must travel to achieve our goal."

Guylan cleared his throat and tapped a finger on one of Ella's sketches. "I hate to bring up such an obvious question, but these figures represent launching something fast enough to touch the moon, yes?"

Ella looked on her calculations with a measure of pride. "I know they are not complete, and more work needs done to factor in various forces at play, but they are along the right lines."

He glanced at the diagram. "I am assuming that you might want to slow down near the end, as well? You know, to avoid hitting the moon like an egg thrown at a stone wall?"

The others stared at Guylan for a long, horrified moment as they imagined that impact.

Jackan slammed a palm to his forehead, muttering expletives.

Ella swallowed, then leaned over and carefully took the page from him. "That's a very valid point," she said while scrawling that on the paper. "More work for Katherine and myself, I think."

"Good catch," Jackan said. "I hadn't considered that bit yet."

Guylan groaned and rose to his feet to look at the Mark II model under construction. He rapped a knuckle on its steel shell. "Not only do we need to slow down, we must ask the question: will the moon love the material of her Great Mother and wish to gather us to her bosom, or will she push us away? That affects the mathematics involved. I also note that nobody has yet discussed how the first mage on the moon might affect a return home."

The team appeared shaken, not having any answer to that, either.

"We are trying to run before we can walk," Guylan said. "This project is a shambles."

"If you do it first, you do it worst," Jackan rebutted. "That's just the way it is."

"A fair point," the young engineer admitted. "I pray any mistakes we make won't prove fatal. We must work on the basic ideas first to give us something solid to work towards. How high has a mage ever flown before?"

"The highest a skyship reached was half a league," Ella said. "Three thousand steps doesn't sound a lot; there are taller mountains in the world, like the Godspire, but not many."

"Battlemage Breo the Brilliant managed four leagues into the sky before his aether well ran dry and his spells failed," Katherine said. "And he had to scale a mountain first to reach that height. We covered his life and writings in one of our classes at the guild."

"I took that class as well," Guylan added. "If memory serves, he half-froze, couldn't breathe, and passed out, waking just in time to avoid hitting the ground headfirst." He clapped his hands together to illustrate it. "And we are nowhere near the lofty rank of battlemage. How high would we even need to propel this proposed device of yours? How far away is the moon? Anybody?"

Jackan grinned. "Eighty thousand leagues, give or take, according to modern theory. I propose this: Katherine, Ella, you two work on the theory and mathematics of getting something so heavy aloft and then getting it to the moon and back. Guylan and I will work on the Mark II device with an aim of generating enough power to overcome the heavy, chthonic nature of its metal and materials – oh, and Katherine, if you could supply me with some better black powders for testing, that'd be most welcome."

"That will be a simple task," she replied. "I can have a sample ready in a few days. Perfecting it for our needs, well, that will take far longer."

"Excellent," Jackan said. "Now get to it, you two. There'll be no layabouts tolerated on my workforce." He watched Ella and Katherine settle down and begin their discussion before he turned to Guylan.

Jackan extended a hand. "I could really use your help on this. There is only so much one engineer can do on his own."

Guylan stared at it for a moment, then reluctantly shook the hand. "I suppose it is more interesting than clambering onto the roof to spot the Maintenance Team's mistakes."

"No doubt about that," Jackan said. He eyed the Mark II. "It does look like I've built a massive metal cock, now that you mention it."

"Must be compensating for something," Guylan muttered.

"Nah, no need for that," Jackan said. "Anyway, can you help me fit the black powder box and air tubing into this thing. My strength is not what it was back when I was a young lad like you."

They got to work rigging the device for their team's second launch, and the first intentional one, but given their current state of unreadiness, such a costly event was going to be many months down the road.

CHAPTER 12

After six months of hardcore theorising, red-eyed research through stacks of dusty tomes, and nineteen inadequate and un-launched iterations of the Mark II, Jackan was taking no chances with this latest darling device, the fruit of their many failures that showed such promise. The Fire Dragon was chained up and secured to a metal scaffold, bolted to steel beams sunk deep into the floor of the workshop using earth magic. The entire structure was warded with potent enchantments to prevent any kind of escape – and more roofing repairs that would leave the chief weeping. Its gaping mouth was pointed at a stone wall treated to resist heat and flame; runes of air had been configured to suck any smoke and fumes out of the high windows.

Learning from his previous close call with incineration, Jackan had built a stone bunker. His team huddled inside, peering out of a pane of impressively ensorcelled glass.

Katherine carefully poured a cupful of black grains into the new and improved powder box and set one end of a fuse cord into it.

She retreated to the bunker, unwinding the cord, and laying it down at Jackan's feet.

He called on his aether and it sparked into life. The powder-impregnated cord hissed and burned swiftly, the team tensing behind their fortifications as the flame raced towards the powder box. "Here it comes!"

There was a puff of blue smoke and… that was it. The first test firing was over.

"A little underwhelming," Ella complained.

"Best start small and work our way up," Jackan chided. "Three cups next, I think."

The next test produced a bigger puff of smoke and a brief flame. Four cups produced a bang, a lick of flame, and an even larger puff of smoke from the end of it.

Jackan sucked on his teeth. "This is exactly what I was talking about with my original experiment. I tried powder and it did so little that I fashioned an extra air source. This time, we try six cups and I trigger the increased airflow." The result was a larger flame and a louder bang, but the device barely shuddered in its metal prison.

"What I don't understand," Ella said, "is why that lightning strike didn't set off all the powder at once in an explosion. Instead, it seemed to run out somewhere in the sky."

"I pondered that myself," Jackan said. "I think it may have been my wind runes. Judging from the damage to the copper piping, I suspect the lightning might have caused some of the runes to reverse and suck up powder instead of blowing air in, resulting in a more gradual burn from a series of smaller explosions."

They slowly scaled up the amount of powder until the device bucked and heaved against its restraints with each detonation.

"It is obviously an unsuitable method for human transport," Guylan said. "An explosion powerful enough to fling our Fire Dragon into the air with sufficient force to reach the moon would break every bone in a passenger's body."

"We could use padded chairs and protection spells to guard against such an impact," Katherine suggested.

Jackan hummed and hawed over it. "Any device we could fashion would take too much damage from an explosion that large. What we require is something slower burning but more sustained – is there such a thing, Katherine?"

She thought on it. "I could mix black powder with a paste of pitch and dried lacquer and let it dry. That might serve to control the burn. I will research alternatives."

At ten cups of powder, the combustion box blew apart. Shards of metal tinkled off the bunker.

"Well, I think that concludes today's experiments," Jackan said as he inspected the damage.

"There was very little force pushing the device forward," Guylan said. "After the first one took off like a bird with its tail feathers aflame, I had expected the chains and ropes to take more punishment." He took a deep breath and let it out through pursed lips, scratching his head.

Jackan stared at his lips. He grabbed his shoulder. "Do that again."

"Do what?" Guylan asked.

"Your lips, man, your lips!"

Guylan did as he was asked, utterly confused.

The old engineer copied him, his hand in front of his face, expelling air through pursed lips, and then he repeated it with his mouth wide open. "Could it really be so simple?"

"What are you talking about?" Guylan said, watching his antics. "I would claim you have gone mad, but I thought you were to begin with."

"It needs more... more... thrust! Yes, a force thrusting it forward. The problem is that the muzzle I crafted for the Mark II is much too wide for its size. It doesn't need to launch any kind physical weapon, so it should be narrower, like blowing air through pursed lips."

The younger man held his hand up in front of his face, blowing as hard as he could both ways. The light of realisation dawned in his eyes. "Like sand trickling through an hourglass. If we shaped the combustion box and muzzle with a narrowed waist, just like an hourglass, that might serve to compress the hot gases given off by the exhausted powder."

"Yes!" Jackan cried. "Since this is not a cannon, henceforth what we have been calling the muzzle should be called the exhaust – either that, or we call it the arse?"

"Exhaust it is," Guylan replied firmly.

On the other side of the workspace, Ella and Katherine looked on with increasing puzzlement.

"Are they blowing kisses at each other?" Katherine asked. "Why are they so excited?"

The two men extracted the remnants of the combustion box and rushed over to the forge, wide-eyed and chattering like over-stimulated children.

Ella shook her head and rolled her eyes. "I think it's best not to enquire further. At least they seem to be getting on better."

They turned their attention back to the mathematics and theory underpinning all they were trying to achieve.

"There is a treatise on the use of cannon shot we might find useful," Katherine continued. "I think there was a copy in the workshop's library. The writer worked out the mathematics behind the arc of cannonfire, and the force runes necessary to propel stones certain distances. Those workings might allow us to adapt our calculations to something far larger."

"It's certainly worth a read," Ella replied. "But the more of this mad plan I try and figure out, the more I come up against the unknown. We know that physical materials yearn to return to the womb of the Great Mother where they were born, and we know the higher one climbs towards the heavens the colder and thinner air gets, but how we might overcome these problems ourselves..." she shrugged. "Theory can only get us so far, and too much of our knowledge was written down piecemeal or in cypher by various mages intent on hoarding their secret knowledge."

They began throwing theories and questions at each other, discussing the use of skyship gas bags, flapping wings like a giant bird, and even the terrifying prospect of flinging a carriage of people skywards using giant catapults.

Eventually they ran out of half-baked ideas, and Katherine peered up through small windows at the rising moon. "The moon arcs across the sky, looming larger or smaller depending on the month and season – the mathematics are complex. Do you know what would happen if we missed landing on the moon?"

"I..." Ella frowned. "I actually have no idea. I assume that at some point we would just fall back down."

"We assume," Katherine reiterated. "In truth, we know very little about what awaits beyond this world the gods made for us. I very much fear we are like fish that have chosen to investigate the land."

They fell silent, minds churning.

Ella looked over at the Mark II. "It might be wise to run a series of small tests to discover some of those things we don't know. I wonder how high we can propel something of this size, and how we might return it safely to land instead of making a pile of scrap and a burning crater."

The two women began writing down a list of the things they were sure they did not have a clue about. It was worryingly long.

A month and a half later, the team rose at an ungodly time in the morning and braved sleeting rain to trudge along the cart track near the fort, heading down towards a fallow field surrounded by trees that offered a semi-secluded spot for the first test launch. A four-legged stone golem, borrowed from the quartermaster, followed after them towing a wooden cart bearing the Mark II and sacks of supplies protected from the rain by a tarred canvas.

Ella's wheeled chair splashed through muddy puddles. Her hands were soon grimy, cold, and wet as she laboured along the half-gravelled rutted track, tossed from side to side by the uneven surface. She was panting and aching by the time they reached the field and was forced to pause atop a slope. Her heart sank.

"What's up, lass?" Jackan asked as the others squelched their way down.

"I'll need to use magic to get down there," she said. "There's no way to stop this wheeled chair once it gets going. When the wheels are wet, they are too slippery to get a proper grip."

The old engineer's eyes flicked to and fro, cataloguing the construction of her chair. His lip curled in displeasure. "Can't say I've really taken it in before. Shoddy – that's all I'll say about that wheeled deathtrap of yours. This'll not do at all. No, not at all. Let's get that sorted for you as soon as we get back to the workshop."

She swallowed her pride and dared to ask. "Could you help me down? Just this once?"

"Of course," he replied. "Always good to conserve the old magic in case it's needed, eh."

His aid was happily given without a hint of her being a burden. To her surprise, Ella found she didn't mind his help as much as she'd thought she might. It wasn't a threat to her sense of independence to rely on the old engineer once in a while.

Guylan cleared a space for the launch, scythes of air cutting through the tall grasses that had taken over the fallow field and blowing away flammable debris. The golem set the Mark II down in the centre and the mages gathered around it, their burning excitement rising above the cold and wet conditions.

Katherine opened a small chest from the cart and transferred the solidified black block inside into a slot in the Mark II's body. "The fuel is in the reservoir," she stated, backing off. She wasn't yet satisfied with her fragile formulation but felt it should work well enough.

Guylan double-checked the rune array inscribed into the cone-shaped nose of the Fire Dragon. He held a bronze plate in his hand, its markings their twin. "The recovery slowfall spell is paired and ready to be remotely triggered."

Then it was Ella's turn. Her wheels spun in the mud, making it a chore to circle and check the runes she'd etched in a spiralling pattern along the shaft of the device. Their adaptation had proved no small task when skymage arrays were normally sprawling affairs meant for much larger ships. "Levitation runes are ready to be activated, configured to negate half the weight of this device."

"Good work, team," Jackan said. "Now, all of you back off and take cover behind the golem. I'll take it from here."

His team beat a hasty retreat, fortifying themselves behind its solid stone bulk and their own shielding spells.

Jackan peered suspiciously at the grey clouds overhead, checking for any hint of lightning. He donned thick leather work gloves and the latest in military helmet design: a visored metal pot with extra padded lining and a cushioned chin strap that wouldn't choke him. His robes were also enchanted for flame resistance. Lessons had been learned, and he'd be damned if a silly mistake killed him.

He double-checked all their work. Satisfied, he inserted the fuse cord to the fuel reservoir and lit the end with a spark of magic.

He retreated as the cord fizzed to life, incandescent white flame burning its way towards the heart of the device.

"Levitation runes active," Ella said, her voice trembling with anticipation.

The flame travelled inside the metal body of the Mark II.

For a moment, utter silence, their breaths held.

Then…

WHOOSH.

The Mark II screamed into the heavens on a pillar of fire and sulphurous smoke. Suddenly, Fire Dragon seemed an apt name.

"She's holding steady," Ella yelled over the roar.

They craned their heads, following its ascent, eyes squinted against the rain. Their hearts pounded with the excitement of seeing a small piece of their hard work coming to fruition.

"Those fins are doing a fine job of stabilising the ascent," Guylan added. "What a majestic sight."

Sodden strands of dark hair blew across Katherine's face. "The wind is picking up."

"Damnation," Jackan snarled. "She's listing."

The Fire Dragon's climb began to curve as it scraped the clouds, gradually listing groundward instead of heading straight up.

"We don't have any way to correct that," Ella said. "Yet."

The nose of the Fire Dragon dipped earthwards. It began to spin and wobble.

"Ah, shit," Jackan snarled.

The exhaust flame flickered and spurted.

Katherine paled. "It's going to–"

A flash turned the grey clouds white.

The volume of the explosion surprised everybody: they instinctively lifted their hands and triggered shielding spells. Flaming debris rained down. Reflexively, Guylan triggered the slowfall spell worked into the bronze plate clutched in his fist, for all the good it would do now.

Shards of hot metal hit the ground with angry hisses while the shattered remnants of the Mark II's nosecone drifted down like a leaf on the wind. They stood in stunned silence, watching its descent with macabre fascination.

"If you do it first, you do it worst," Jackan reiterated. "Ach, this won't be our last failure, not by a long shot. We just need to figure out what we did wrong this time, and find better ways moving forward." He sighed heavily. "Come on, then, let's go gather up what's left of her ready for inspection tomorrow."

CHAPTER 13

Jackan waved as Rojer Glenn exited the temple of Mogranus after one of his regular visits to the priests for healing. The one-eyed mage's arm, neck, and shoulder were still shrouded in bandages, with puckered pink edges of extensive scarring showed through white gauze. "Are you on the mend, then?"

"Getting there," Rojer replied with a wry smile. "Hardly the first time I've been struck by a combat spell that pierced my shield, but this was a particularly nasty one bearing a secondary curse. Lucky the army are crying out for experienced combat mages like me, eh. I'll be seeing healing mages monthly until the new skin grows back smooth as a baby's bottom. How goes the project?"

The old engineer pulled a face. "A true voyage of discovery."

"Getting lost a fair bit, are you?" Rojer replied.

Jackan chuckled and nodded. "How about yourself? Are they keeping you busy?"

Rojer stopped and sighed, circling his shoulder and wincing from the pain. "Soon as this thing is fixed and the priests deem me combat-capable, they'll be sending me back out on another bloody mission to No Man's Land. Having a particular set of skills is damned inconvenient." He turned to the engineer. "That said, your boss is currently occupying a lot of my time. He's got me going here, there, and everywhere ferreting out rare materials for… well, you, I assume."

"I wonder, does that make you my underling?" Jackan mused.

The one-eyed mage frowned dramatically. "Shoulder or not, I'm fully capable of knocking you to the dirt, old man."

"I've no doubt," he replied. "Good to see you in such fine fettle. Well, I'd better be off – I have an appointment to inspect a truly woeful piece of construction. I'll let Guylan know you're healing up well – the lad's been asking after you."

A smile creased Rojer's lips. "Tell him I prefer good wishes to arrive in pints of ale."

"I'll do just that," Jackan said. "Take care out there!"

"What manner of imbecile designed this vehicle?" Jackan cried, incredulous. "Is there no way to stop these wheels from moving?"

Ella shook her head. "Even this old chair was ruinously expensive – that was a good chunk of my debt, right there, and I've only just paid it off. Were I not a mage, I'd have starved to death by now. Most peasants probably just lie in their bed until they die, unable to earn a living. I wager most people who can easily afford one of these would have servants to wheel them about."

He reached out to casually lay a hand on the chair and she flinched. He paused, puzzled by her reaction.

"Sorry, this chair feels like an extension of my own body," she explained. "It's as vital to me as your legs are to you. I'm a little… touchy about people handling it without permission."

Jackan nodded. "Understood. Don't think I'd like folk feeling so free about handling me, either." He circled her, his brow furrowed in thought. "They really just stuck a pair of wheels and an axle off a cart onto a wicker chair, added a little wheel at the back so it doesn't topple over, and then thought, 'That'll do.'"

Ella licked her lips, looking down at the rickety old chair that had nevertheless proved a godsend for her, allowing her to regain her independence. It had warded off the dark thoughts of suicide that almost consumed her after her accident and as the accusations were heaped upon her.

"Could you design something better?" she ventured, voice quivering with a spark of hope.

He snorted. "Who do you think you are talking to? That was never in question. What I need to know is, what problems do you actually have when using this chair, beyond the inability to stop?"

She blinked, thinking.

"You are not a skymage now, Ella," he chided. "You have shifted onto the path of the arcane engineer. It's not all lightning bolts, runes, and dusty old tomes of secret knowledge. You need to adjust your thinking. Identify a problem and come up with ways to solve it. In your case, none of those in positions of power have ever given a blind bit of thought to people that require the use of this kind of chair. And they never will unless they are forced."

"I…" She looked at her calloused hands coated in street-dust and ingrained mud. "I'm bloody well fed up of having filthy hands."

He grinned. "That's it! That's a problem. So, you propel this chair with your hands directly on the wheels. As it is, this is unavoidable. So, what would you change without resorting to the use of magic?"

"Ummm…"

"Gloves?" he suggested.

"I can't afford…" she began, then realised that, actually, she could now – as many pairs of thick work gloves as she needed. She swore, glaring at her grimy hands.

Jackan cackled. "You'd be surprised at how often we can overlook something blindingly obvious to others. Our ingrained habits and assumptions get in the way. Tacit acceptance that things are the way they are, and that they can't be changed, is too damned common." He patted her on the shoulder. "Gloves would work, but what would be even better?"

She looked down at the wheels, thinking. "Handles?" she ventured. "Maybe attached to the spokes so I don't actually have to touch these dirty iron rims."

Jackan quirked an eyebrow, tapping a finger to his lips. "Huh. I'd been thinking of some manner of crankshaft, cogs, and handles up front to spin a mechanism that turned the wheels. Handles on the wheels themselves would be far simpler. What else plagues you?"

"Cobbles," Ella replied with vehemence. "You have no idea how sore I get juddering down the streets of Newsark."

Jackan bent down, examining the wicker seat that sat directly on the wooden frame. "I see. Like riding a bony horse without a saddle." He stepped back, awaiting her response.

"Cushions?" she said. "Perhaps a layer of cork?"

"Cushions and cork might work, but would wear out quickly," he replied. "What might be more permanent?"

She wracked her brains for ideas of what was flexible or soft, but hard-wearing. She remembered the guards who had been stationed in the skyship hangers and recalled an afternoon of sparring with them on a windy day. "Swords," she said firmly.

"Eh?" He stared at her, confused. "Did you say swords?"

Ella nodded. "I did. The best swords are flexible and spring back to their proper shape. Too hard and they break, too soft and they bend out of shape and stay that way."

"Well, well," he muttered. "Now you really are thinking like an engineer. Good steel might serve well. I'd been thinking of rope and cord and some sort of suspension of the chair above the solid frame. I'd not thought of steel." He stroked his moustache. "Aye, I could make you something that will consign this heap of crap to the fire."

"I'd rather donate it to somebody else in need," Ella said. "With a way to stop it rolling, if that's not too much bother?" She cleared her throat and looked around the workshop. "I'm not sure how much I can pay for it. Even if your labour is a gift, the materials will be more than I can afford."

Jackan waved her off. "Enough of that. If this gets you working with increased capacity then it's well worth the investment."

Ella smiled up at him. "Don't worry, I won't tell a soul you're not the grumpy old bastard you pretend to be. Especially Guylan."

"Ugh," Jackan looked like he'd bitten into a lemon. "What do you even see in that self-important twit? Your favourable attitude hasn't escaped my notice."

So Ella told him about her accident, and what the younger engineer had done to save her hide from Hierarch Deva-Mokaren III's wrath in the aftermath of destroying his gaudy carriage, all at the expense of him enjoying a cushy life in the capital.

"Guylan Bluford?" Jackan queried. "Are you sure we are talking about the same man?"

She nodded.

The old engineer had to sit down. "Well, I'll be. There is something good inside that sack of shit. Buried deep, deep inside."

She glowered at him and he looked away, defeated. "Fine! I'll try to be nicer to the man."

"Nicer?" Guylan asked as he pulled back the canvas curtain and entered the workspace, Katherine at his back. "You? Pull the other one. Who are you talking about anyway, old man?"

Ella and Jackan exchanged a startled glance. She shook her head.

Jackan stood. "Well done for volunteering," he said.

The younger mage's brow furrowed. "For what?"

"Why, our first crewed launch!" Jackan said. "As you continually claim, I am an old man, and we can't very well ask these young ladies to do an engineer's job. I'm almost positive the Mark III won't blow up."

"Hang on a minute," Guylan said, hands up and backing away. "When did this get decided? I didn't agree to get strapped to a Fire Dragon. I… hang on a minute, you're taking the piss, aren't you?"

Jackan patted him on the shoulder, turned his back to hide his grin, and made his way over to inspect the wreckage of the Mark II.

"He was kidding, right?" Guylan asked Ella.

"It only makes sense," she replied, hurrying to join Jackan. She couldn't quite manage to keep the laughter in.

"Oh, very droll," Guylan said. "There is no way I'm going to let you strap me to a bomb and light the fuse."

Katherine ambled past him. "But imagine being the first person to travel beyond the confines of our world," she mused. "Even Breo the Brilliant could not claim that glory."

Guylan's jaw snapped shut. That set him thinking, hard.

"Gods damn it, now you've gone and done it," Jackan said. "He really will want to be the first one up there. I was joking."

Guylan shrugged. "An offer was made, and it is accepted. I volunteer." He looked over the mangled remnants of the last Fire Dragon. "Er, once we have all the problems smoothed out."

The other three mages stared at him. Jackan looked to the two women beside him. "Ach, so be it, unless one of you two want to contest the honours?"

"I've had more than enough of flying high," Ella said. "The landings are a bitch."

Katherine shuddered. "No, thank you."

"It's settled, then," Guylan stated, smug at his victory. He grinned and skipped over, thrumming with hopes and dreams of future glory. His smile faltered a little as he looked at the wreckage. "Do you have any idea what caused it to explode?"

Jackan browsed the blackened parts and pulled out a scorched section of the fuel reservoir. "I reckon when it listed, the fire in the combustion chamber made its way back into the reservoir."

"The fuel brick was too crumbly," Guylan said. "It may have broken up from all the vibration. Katherine, could you make us something more solid?"

"Soon," she advised. "I just need to work on the proportions of pitch so it burns a little swifter. It will be something we can press into moulds, and once it dries it will turn solid and hold its shape."

There was little else they could glean from the remnants of the Mark II, so Jackan began sweeping it into sacks ready for smelting down.

The door to the chief's study squeaked open. A little oil might have sorted that particular annoyance, save for the fact Jackan felt he might need a little warning from time to time. He'd carefully tuned it to be as loud as it was. "Look busy," he ordered.

A few moments later, Whitlaw Goddard arrived, a scroll case bearing the wax seal of the hierarchy clutched in his hands. "Ahem, may I please have your attention."

They all looked up from their papers and parts they had been pretending to work on. Katherine met her father's worried gaze and her lips thinned with stubborn determination.

The chief drew the scroll from its case and unfurled it. "Hierarch Grubman-Lordrach IV, having deemed your project as Vital to the War Effort, has ordered the refurbishment of nearby Abelin Castle for your exclusive use. As such, you are commanded to provide details of what tools and materials you require to ensure your research comes to fruition."

Jackan took the scroll and scanned the text. "There is no mention of budget."

"No," Whitlaw said, his eyes wide. He licked his lips. "There is no set budget."

The team's eyes lit up with the burning fervour of academics the world over when given unlimited funding instead of scrimping and scraping to gather even half of what they needed.

"I could have a fully stocked alchemy lab to myself," Katherine said with wonder.

Guylan's hands trembled. "An arcane engineering workshop with the very latest machining tools from Orialis."

"I could have ramps installed," Ella added. "Wait, no, I could have crystal-powered levitation runes built into a new chair!"

"Think bigger, people," Jackan snapped, smacking a fist into his palm. "Bigger. Better. I want you to… Bleed. Them. Dry!"

The old engineer dragged himself away from the frenzy over who got to write the massive shopping list. He retreated into the corner of the room to speak in private with his superior. "Is everything well, Chief?"

Whitlaw watched his daughter for a moment. A small smile grew as he took in her friendly squabbling with Ella and Guylan. "It is a wonderful thing to see her making friends. She has always been a little… awkward. Promise me you will look after her, and keep her out of trouble?"

Jackan scrubbed a hand through his hair, wracked with guilt and trying not to show it. "Ach, you need have no worries there. She's a good lass and a fine mage."

Whitlaw nodded his thanks, his eyes unerringly finding the sacks of scrap. "Did your latest experiment also end in failure?"

He stiffened. "Not in the slightest. Every time we fail, we learn something new. Nobody has ever tried to do what we are attempting – they've all been sucked into the cult of aether being the answer to everything."

The chief held up his hands. "Oh, I meant no criticism. I fully understand you need to break a few eggs to make a good breakfast. That said, the hierarchs may not see things that way." He set his jaw and looked Jackan in the eye, filled with one of his rare moments of iron resolve. "Here, I can shield you all somewhat. When you are in Abelin Castle, you will be watched. A word to the wise, my old friend: give their spies something good to report back to their masters in Orialis."

Jackan cleared his throat. "Is it going to be that bad?"

"You have been given a nigh-unlimited budget," Whitlaw said. "Do you believe their eyes will not be upon you? The more resources you use, the greater the attention you gather, and the greater your results must also be. I have seen it play out elsewhere. Failures are taken personally by the hierarchs involved. Your successes become their glory and bragging rights, but for those who fail them…" He shuddered.

"I…" Jackan felt all at sea.

"The military and the secretive leaders of the old mage guilds never had much faith in this Research and Design Workshop," the chief said. "It swims against the tide of history, and their very beings, to freely share knowledge. I have done my best to toe the line and manage the resources we have been given – and exceed their expectations, might I add – but now you have caught Hierarch Grubman-Lordrach IV's attention. He has high expectations, and he absolutely does not understand a single thing about the ups and downs of research and testing."

"What am I to do?" Jackan asked. "Conjure miracles out of thin air like the gods themselves? All things take time."

Whitlaw clapped a hand on his shoulder. "What you do is hoard your successes: delay reporting them to me if you must. Dole them out at regular intervals as evidence of the project's development. He wants big, showy wins suitable for display and bragging rights. Think of the hierarch like a…" he checked who was in earshot, "a spoilt brat who always gets his own way."

"An apt description," Jackan replied.

Whitlaw chuckled, but there was a weary, strained edge to it. "Distract him with shiny things and fancy new toys while you get on with the rest of the work."

"Aye, Chief. I'll do my best. You have my oath that Katherine will come to no harm under my watch."

Whitlaw Goddard's eyes again sought out his daughter. "You had better make sure of it. Otherwise, you'll find yourself on the front lines even before you feel my boot up your arse."

The old engineer watched the chief head back to his study and contemplated the mess they had all landed in. Jackan had never had the faintest interest in fame and glory. Some riches might have been nice, but that had not been the will of the gods. What he had received was a profound sense of accomplishment at seeing his designs emerge from imagination and paper and ink to something real. He was a maker – that was who he was in blood and bone. And now there was this accidental project born from an act of the gods, a spark of genius that had gained a life all its own. It consumed his thoughts, desperately struggling to be born to world.

Ella, Katherine, and Guylan were still gleefully squabbling over their list of treasures to request from the hierarch, unaware of the growing peril that had them in its grip. Sooner or later, he'd have to sit them down and determine just how far they truly wanted to take this mad dream, and what they would be willing to risk in order to achieve it.

"By the gods," he whispered. "I'll complete it myself if it comes to that."

His course was set. At least one mage would go to the moon – and back.

CHAPTER 14

Komissar Taeban Tereshkova's desk was a temple to order, devoid of the clutter of paperwork and miscellanea that plagued the lives of lesser mages wallowing in their own disorganisation. Her quill, silver inkpot, and a neat stack of paper sat ready for her many missives. On her walls, tapestries depicting glorious heroes of the Ranneas Empire were draped in midnight black and vibrant red, and in the corner, a full suit of archaic bronze armour inlaid with golden wards stood proud on a wooden mannequin: Aleksandr Tereshkova's battle plate, a man whose stern face adorned the walls of Imperial outposts all across the empire, and the doting grandfather who had raised her. His portrait took pride of place on the wall facing her desk.

It was late, and she was tired, but the Empire's work was never done. She uncorked the small flask hanging at her hip. The aroma of potent alcohol filled her nose as she saluted her beloved ancestor and took a deep draught. The vodka burned warm inside her.

A knock at the door had her hastily replacing the cork and wiping her lips. There was no hiding the smell, but what was an Imperial officer without their drink?

"Come!" she barked.

Andriyan Korolev entered carrying a sheaf of papers. His face still bore some scabbing wounds from his foray into No Man's Land, a place so profaned by the corrupt power of Unity mages that even the gods averted their gaze from it.

"You have the report?" she asked.

The young mage came to attention before her. "Yes, Komissar." He handed over the papers.

She set them aside for later review, ensuring all the edges were lined up neatly. "Your conclusions?"

"Confusing," he admitted. "The device itself resembles a heavy cannon designed to propel solid shot. The fragments of Unity-standard force runes salvaged from the wreckage would seem to back that conclusion. However, those runes were not activated as I would expect. Instead of launching a deadly payload, our spies at Fort Newsark reported that this 'cannon' itself flew through the air. We also found traces of a heat source from inside the casing and a sooty residue that indicates non-magical burning."

"Alchemy?" she queried.

"It seems likely."

Tereshkova pursed her lips. Alchemy was a far greater drain on materials, manpower, and supply lines than simply using magic, an inexhaustible and ubiquitous source of divine power utilised by imperfect, limited human beings. Powders and potions were also unreliable and less efficient methods of doing anything. She pondered why the Unity would dabble with such outdated methodology.

"What of the enemy mage? This Jackan Grissom's claims that it was an accident and not a new weapon at all?"

Korolev hummed and hawed. "I believe that may have some truth to it. Why go to the effort of inscribing and empowering force runes if they were never to be used as intended? The aether gems alone must have cost their corrupt and decadent hierarchy several thousand Unity crowns."

Tereshkova drummed her fingers on the table.

"The mage is listed as a senior engineer stationed in the Research and Design Workshop at Fort Newsark," Korolev reported.

"The man is a designer of death, then," she said.

He nodded. "However, before the war grew heated again, he was listed as a civic engineer with a number of bridges built in the north, according to his plans."

Korolev cleared his throat. "And then I must verbally report something the mage said to me upon our meeting. Due to its ludicrous nature, I have not recorded it on the official report, but..."

She eyed her subordinate. "Spit it out, soldier."

"He claimed this device was meant to touch the moon."

She snorted. Her eyebrows climbed as her subordinate stood before her, stony faced. She leaned back in her chair, fingers steepled. "The moon? You are certain of his words?"

"Yes, Komissar."

"A lie," she stated. "No mage will ever be mighty enough to reach the lofty heights of Konstantin the Great, much less the moon."

Soldier Korolev said nothing, but she detected some dissent in his expression. "You disagree, mage?"

"What if," he said haltingly, "you did not rely upon magic alone to bear you into the heavens. I too once made studies into such a thing. A boyhood fantasy before I found magic, no more than that. And yet..."

She regarded him with interest. "You truly think this to be an experiment meant to achieve an impossible task?"

"I did not think this man to be a fanatic warmonger, nor an obvious liar," he replied. "I have been trained to detect falsehoods during interrogation, and this mage was certainly more scholar than hardened battlemage."

"The corrupt hierarchs of the Unity would never waste their beloved coin on such a fantasy," she said, then paused as a thought struck her. "Unless they do not know."

"A rogue mage?" Korolev asked.

"It is a possibility," she replied. "Pacifists and traitors sprout like weeds if the garden is not well tended. I shall have our spies keep track of this Jackan Grissom. It may be that he could be of use to us. You are dismissed."

He saluted, turned on his heels and marched out of her study.

Taeban Tereshkova rose from her desk, vodka in hand, and moved to the window. She pulled back the curtain and looked up at the silvery disc of the moon rising above the darkling trees.

She thought back to the many times she was bounced on her grandfather's knee before bedtime, looking up at the moon and listening to Aleksandr's tales of the gods that dwelled there, in a magnificent silver city ruled by divine Perunuk. Her grandfather had been as famous for his recording of folk tales from across the many lands of the Empire as for his magery. She vividly recalled her favourite story from his books, about an orphan taken away to dwell on the moon beside the gods, returning years later when his homeland was in desperate need of a hero. To visit the moon was a thing beyond all realistic imagining, and yet, as a child she had tried so hard – many were the drawings she had made for her grandfather before his end, and many were the wishes she had made with all the pure heart and stubborn will of a child to make it come true.

"I had once thought to skip through its silver halls," she said ruefully, her thoughts filled with honoured ancestors and girlish dreams she had almost forgotten. "To touch the moon…" She sighed, savouring the moonlight in her eyes. "That would be a most marvellous undertaking, do you not agree, Grandfather?"

She lifted her flask in salute to the moon and drained it. Moments later, she filed away all thoughts of fantasy and nostalgia and got back to work. More scrolls and paper arrived shortly, all marked as urgent and needing to be processed yesterday. She dipped her quill into the inkwell and began, immersing herself in the minutiae of running an entire section of the border.

Tereshkova tried to focus on weaponry and warfare, supplies and soldiers, but she found her mind continually drifting back towards the mage who wanted to touch the moon. That cork of interest had been popped, and she found it exceedingly difficult to stuff it back into its flask. She shook her head, setting the letters and ledgers aside in favour of a single leaf of thick, creamy paper meant for people of far more importance.

Komissar Taeban Tereshkova was a woman of personal and political power, but the Empire's spymasters could vanish her as quickly as any other. Accidents happened every day…

She inked a missive to her superior, detailing a curated list of the strange events in the Unity's weapon development programme, and enclosed a report from an informant embedded within Abelin Castle saying they had received orders to refit and prepare the fortress to host an undisclosed secret project. Perhaps there was something here that could be exploited.

In Orialis, Hierarch Deva-Mokaren III's twentieth Ascension Day ball was winding down. All twelve courses of the sumptuous meal had been devoured, along with their matched wines of the utmost rarity – only a sip of each, but every swallow expensive enough to purchase a countryside village. Any leftover scraps would be fed to the servants and the paupers on the streets of the capital as a display of the magnanimity of their rulers.

As was traditional, the women retreated to the drawing room while their menfolk moved to a parlour, well stocked with the best brandy and whisky the Unity could provide, and more than a few liquors smuggled in from the Ranneas Empire. Pipes were filled with leaf imported from the furthest lands known to merchants, and the men relaxed into the serious business of running a nation from their comfy chairs.

"Drink, my fine fellows!" Hierarch Deva-Mokaren III cried, already quite inebriated. "To your wealth, and the health of the Unity!"

Their host, an older man, resplendent in a lofty curled wig, purple silk robes, and a pink cravat dripping with diamond studs, sat at the table closest to the fireplace laughing with the scions of the old families – those whose ancestors had been kings and queens, dukes, and members of grand dynasties before the survival of their nations demanded they join together in the Unity to stand against the advancing Empire. Most of them had been related in some way to begin with.

Hierarch Grubman-Lordrach IV sat fuming and nursing his brandy at one of the tables on the periphery. Even among fellow hierarchs, a social pecking order was upheld: the old guard closest to the centre, and those younger upstarts uplifted by mercantile wealth radiating outwards depending on whatever diluted noble blood flowed through their veins.

The young man boasted none of that so-called noble blood, and they reminded him of that deficiency at any given opportunity. Sixty years ago, the common-born owners of the Grubman iron mines and the Lordrach farming investment company had joined their bloodlines to produce a titan of industry that benefited mightily from the ongoing war: iron to outfit the Unity's warriors and food for its armies. His grandparents' obscene wealth had bought their way into the ruling council of the Unity, and granted their offspring this lofty position. His eyes burned as he watched the host make a fool of himself with his inbred cronies, all protruding chins and underbites.

Jerae, a newly minted hierarch of the Eastward-Fuzals family, leaned across their table, drink slopping over his lace cuff. "You were saying that you have a secret project?"

Grubman-Lordrach IV fought to contain his smile. The young man was an entitled dolt with less sense than a donkey, but not without his uses.

He looked around, very obviously checking who was listening. "I do, indeed, my friend," he whispered. "I know you can be trusted to keep this under your wig, but I have funded the developments of a most potent new weapon. When those under my patronage achieve great success, as they most certainly shall, I will shower them with unmatched glory."

Oh, how he yearned to raise that broken-backed chit of a girl high and watch Deva-Mokaren III's face turn purple with rage when he realised this was the very same mage who had transformed his prize golden carriage into a pile of scrap – and on his Ascension Day, to boot! At the Research and Design Workshop, his acting had been top-notch – as if he would not know the name of the girl who had amused him so greatly. Still, deniability was a grand thing. He could not be expected to know the name of every minor mage.

Jerae tittered into his drink. "You can trust me, my good sir. What manner of weapon is it?"

"You will need to wait and see," he replied, grinning. "When it is further along in its development, you will be the first hierarch I invite to witness its testing."

The boy was suitably flattered, as he should be. He began wittering on about something involving his estates, but Grubman-Lordrach IV's mind was elsewhere. He made the appropriate sounds and nods of interest, of course, but in reality, he was dwelling on the many slights tonight's host had heaped upon him over the years.

Normally, he had little to do with the development of weaponry or magic, only showing face and providing the minimum war funding expected of a hierarch of his grandeur. None of the richest hierarchs actually wanted to win the war, not when maintaining their positions of privilege depended upon its continuation. With the threat of the Empire looming large in their minds, the populace of the Unity were kept in a permanent state of fear. Without that, the unwashed masses might start contemplating their lowly position in life and begin demanding 'rights' – or worse, wanting a say in the governing of the Unity itself.

That idea was downright distasteful.

He would happily spend a fortune to spite the pompous prick by the fireplace. Tens of thousands of crowns was nothing to a man that dealt in millions on a weekly basis, and he'd happily spend hundreds of thousands on a worthy jape. If all worked out even half as well as he'd been promised, he felt it coin well spent.

CHAPTER 15

"What do you think?" Guylan asked, smug as anything.

The others clustered around his crude but functional device, studying the system of string, weights, and pulleys as he tilted it. The metal plate suspended in the centre always returned to horizontal, weights shifting to compensate for the tilt.

"If a version of this was attached to movable metal fins on the outer body of the Fire Dragon," he explained, "perhaps we could ensure it flies straight."

Jackan gave it a prod with his finger, watching the play of string and pulley. "Now that is using your head." His rough hand slapped the younger engineer on the back. "Well done."

Guylan preened, but only for a moment before he realised who it was commending him.

Jackan turned to the next member of his team. "Katherine, you are up next. What do you have for us today?"

She moved across to the second table, this one a heavy beast made of solid iron with the goal of diminishing the chance of interference – or ignition – by magic. A horizontal steel tube, an arm's length, was securely riveted in place, one end sealed and the other with an hourglass shaped piece of pottery attached as an exhaust. She swept back a wing of dark hair and cleared her throat, glancing at Ella, who nodded reassuringly. "I have improved the alchemic powder recipe that was being used for propulsion."

Katherine retrieved a wooden box from beneath the table and opened it up to reveal a hollow-centred tube of solidified black powder. "With this, there will be no unforeseen shifting of material, and no requirements for complicated air systems or external combustion chambers."

"Oho, this looks like the stuff we needed," Jackan said. "But why is it hollow?"

She smiled. "It burns from the inside out, and the centre there is your combustion chamber. Other substances are mixed in to feed and steady the burn." The pottery exhaust was removed, the tube of fuel carefully inserted, and then it was refitted, ready to go. She fed a fuse cord up through the narrowed hole in the pottery and into the fuel.

"Please step back," she advised. "I expect this test firing will prove rather exciting."

They retreated to a safe distance behind potent shielding runes, and then set light to the fuse. The fizzing, sparking flame raced towards the device.

A weak flame puffed out of the exhaust, all very underwhelming. The others shifted their feet and looked at one another. Katherine smiled – she knew what was coming. The flame gradually grew fiercer until fire and fumes shrieked through the exhaust at the rear, compressed by fireproof pottery.

Ella winced. "That's awfully loud!"

"What?" Jackan yelled.

She waved him off as the shriek grew to deafening volume.

The iron table rattled and groaned as the force roaring through the metal tube fought to fling it through the wall.

Katherine laughed gleefully, her skill in alchemy vindicated.

Nobody heard Whitlaw Goddard shouting, nor noticed his approach until the thick curtain was yanked aside. "What fresh hell is this?" he shouted.

One of the rivets securing the experiment to the table snapped. The protective runes around the mages flared as a fragment of metal bounced off it. The chief ducked behind them as the tube began to spin, spewing a wheel of flame around the workspace. Fortunately, due to past events, they had ensured nothing flammable was within its reach.

The fuel soon burnt itself out. Flames flickered and faded, and the spinning slowed, then stopped. The pottery exhaust was scorched and soot-blackened, but it had withstood the fierce heat.

"Yes!" Katherine cried, fist in the air. "It worked!"

"Did it, now?" her father snarled.

She spun, startled. "Ah... I... uh... did not see you there."

"I thought you'd summoned a bloody howler demon!" he yelled. "What were you all thinking? The other mages thought it was an enemy attack!"

"I had no idea it would be so loud," she protested.

"A minor hiccup," Jackan added. "It's a learning process. Next time, we'll be sure to inform everybody that an experiment is taking place."

Whitlaw Goddard mumbled expletives as he ducked his head out of the curtain for a moment. "It's just Jackan's lot. Thank the gods he didn't blow up the roof this time."

The other mages voiced their complaints, but nobody sounded terribly shocked. It was that sort of place.

The chief rounded on them again. "Ensure you do inform me next time. We'll have no more of you going rogue and disturbing the rest of us! Maybe it's a good thing you will all be shipped off elsewhere soon." He looked to his daughter and his fury drained. "What *was* this experiment?"

She explained every detail, and the more she did, the more interested he became.

"I see. And this new fuel was your idea, Katherine?" At her nod, he straightened his back and lifted his chin. "That's my daughter. Keep up the good work and the hierarchs will surely take notice."

"That's what I'm afraid of," Jackan muttered under his breath.

Whitlaw Goddard's gaze found him. "What was that?"

"Nothing, Chief. Just an old man talking to himself."

Their superior frowned at them. "Remember, a warning is not too much to ask."

They all gave their word, and he retreated to his study to wage war against his eternal enemy: paperwork.

Jackan took a deep, calming breath. "Well, Ella, I think it must be your turn now. You said you had an interesting idea for the next test launch?"

"That I do," she said, wheeling herself over to a cupboard to pull out a large, dusty, leather-bound box. It thunked down onto the metal table beside the steaming experiment.

She flipped the lid up and grunted with the effort of pulling a crystal ball from the velvet-cushioned interior. "I found this in one of the storerooms. I thought we might want to see what's up there beyond the clouds. If we secure it to the outside, we'll be able to see everything."

"And who do you expect will go up there to operate it?" Guylan asked. "I know that I volunteered, but there is not a chance I am strapping myself to a lit Fire Dragon just yet."

Ella grinned. "I thought, perhaps, we could book some time with the Fort's summoner – an imp should do the job nicely. With slowfall runes to ensure its safe return, we could learn a whole lot more. We don't even know if mortals can survive up there without magical protections, and I'd much rather send a demon than an innocent animal."

"I am not keen on fraternising with infernal beings," Guylan stated.

Jackan nodded in agreement. "Aye, it's a dicey thing, that. Give me a good honest elemental any time, but those things are thick as my ma's mincemeat pies."

"Pies?" Katherine queried.

"Lovely woman," he replied. "Salt of the earth, but a piss-poor cook. You could crack a bear's skull at fifty paces with a fling of one of her pies."

"That's what specialised summoners are for," Ella said. "Unless you can think of another way to get a crystal ball to work from so far away?"

They could not.

The crystal ball was squirreled away back into its protective box. "It's settled, then," Ella said. "We go and see the summoner."

Jackan slumped down into a chair, his face twisted like he was chewing a wasp. "You lot can piss off on your own. I'll not be spending a second more than I have to with that grumpy old bastard – I'll be here working on your wheeled chair."

"Are you sure?" Katherine asked. "You are the senior mage overseeing this project."

He pulled a face. "I'd rather lick the latrine clean. Off with you! Give me peace and quiet to work." He shooed them out.

* * *

Ella's wheels clicked and clacked over the floorboards of the workshop as they made their way towards the exit, past other mages toiling away at their benches. "What was that all about?" she asked, avoiding looking at her old booth and its dour-faced new occupant. "Guylan, you've known him the longest."

"I have not the faintest idea," he replied. They stepped out into morning sunshine. "Perhaps he is secretly intensely religious."

They exchanged a glance. Ella raised an eyebrow.

"Well, maybe not," he admitted. "He's far too foul-mouthed for that."

"I imagine we are about to find out," Katherine said. "Assuming the fort's summoner has time to see us today. Have any of you met him before?"

Nobody had. Summoners had a somewhat ominous reputation as being ever-so-slightly mad.

"I heard he was originally a shaman of some savage tribe dwelling far to the north," Katherine said. "They still practise the old ways and sacrifice animals to the gods. Even people, some of them."

Guylan scratched his cheek. "Oh? I heard he was from one of the more prestigious guilds but was thrown out for exploring a little too deep into the infernal. It was said he had a pact with an eldritch entity that corrupted the minds of all who beheld it. Were it not for the war, they would have hung him. Or so they say."

"So... nobody actually knows anything about him for sure," Ella clarified. "This will be interesting. Oh, did you hear that the Empire's raiders have been probing outposts all along the border, using some new kind of winged war beasts?" They had not, and they discussed the worsening political situation as they made their way to the summoner's home.

The only specialised summoner attached to Fort Newsark resided in a decrepit tomb directly across the path to the temple. It was an ancient structure of megalithic stones, a grave barrow built in ancient times by a people long vanished into the mists of time. The temple to the gods occupied a site of similar antiquity, but that ancient circle of standing stones had been enveloped by marble columns and mage-grown jade walls for a far more modern, glorifying aesthetic.

Standing in the sunshine, they looked down the narrow, footworn steps leading into the darkened depths of the tomb. There was barely room for a single person to pass through.

Ella sighed and settled back into her chair. "I guess I'm waiting here, then."

Katherine looked at her quizzically for a moment before it dawned on her. "Ah, right. Sorry."

She had become inured to such things. Much of the world was not built to accommodate her needs. "You can tell me everything when you come back up. At least it's sunny today."

Guylan led the way, a sphere of light forming in the palm of his hand. He brushed away cobwebs and descended into darkness. Katherine followed more reluctantly, taking each step carefully.

The stairs opened out to a circular chamber with an arched, irregular ceiling supported by massive, unworked pillars of stone. The floor was gravel, every footstep an echoing crunch. The entire place oozed untouched antiquity. At the far side of the chamber was a crude open doorway lit by a single green corpse flame hanging in the air, burning without candle, lantern, or aether source. It was the sort of flickering flame travellers reported seeing in marshes and bogs, and it smelt like it too.

Katherine glanced at Guylan.

"You first," she said.

He rolled his eyes and walked confidently towards the passageway. His steps faltered when he noticed the corpse flame had tiny hollow eyes and was looking directly at him. He stepped sideways to pass it by, but the flame moved to block his path.

Guylan cleared his throat. "We are here to see the summoner."

The little green flame closed its eyes for a moment, then bobbed in the air as if nodding. It drifted up the passageway.

"I guess we follow it," he said faintly.

"Why would anybody choose to live in a creepy tomb?" Katherine asked, sticking to Guylan like glue.

He chuckled nervously. "There are always some apprentices that like to wear black and hang around in graveyards. I didn't like to ask them too many questions."

The sound of their footsteps gradually changed from a solid, hard-edged crunch of stone to something altogether more brittle.

"Don't look down," Guylan said through gritted teeth.

Katherine immediately did. She squeaked at the sight of shattered human bones and countless rat skeletons, grabbing at him as if she intended to climb to safety.

He winced and fended her off. "Calm yourself, woman! You are a First Circle graduate of the Orialis Guild. What is there to fear in this place?"

Her eyes grew wide at the sight of something behind him. Guylan turned, yelped, and jumped back as something with far too many glistening eyes and legs squeezed through a crack in the wall. They ran for it, dashing for a door at the end of the tunnel.

Guylan slammed into the door. It was solid oak and didn't even shudder. He pushed and pulled at the iron ring set into it to no avail, then set his shoulder to it, trying to force it open. "It's locked!" he snarled.

Katherine turned, ready to raise a shield and blast the passageway with fire.

The little corpse flame accompanying them slipped into a keyhole; a second later, the locking mechanism clicked open. The door yawned wide. Guylan tumbled through, his flailing hands grabbing onto Katherine. Both mages fell into the domain of the summoner, sprawling on something blood-red and hairy.

CHAPTER 16

Guylan lay face down on a plush red rug with Katherine's elbow jabbing painfully into his spine. The floor was clean, smelling faintly of pipe smoke and cedar wood.

"Oh!" she said, rolling off him. "I was not expecting... all of this."

He lifted his head to discover that the summoner's abode was not at all what he'd imagined in an ancient tomb. The walls had been whitewashed and decorated with tapestries and murals. Vases crammed with bright and bold flowers occupied niches where he could only imagine yellowed grinning skulls once sat. A crackling fireplace gifted the room a homely, welcoming light and warmth, with two worn but cosy leather armchairs set at either side. Bookcases lined one wall, the shelves heaving with tomes, scrolls, and a riot of strange curios – some glowing, and others only visible by the lack of light reflected from their abyssal blackness. A doorway led to a bedchamber, silken sheets and the carved posts of a large bed visible.

"Are you well?" a deep male voice asked.

A hefty old table sat in the middle of the room, right in the centre of a summoning circle painted the colour of blood upon the floor. On one side sat Fort Newsark's summoner, a bald, bearded old man in sagging undergarments and a greying vest. Spilling over his wood-framed spectacles were two bushy eyebrows, now raised in surprise at finding two mages sprawled on his floor. On the opposite side of the table, perched atop a high stool, was a creature of the infernal: a yellow-eyed imp, with mottled crimson skin rough as stone, stubby black horns, grey wings, and a forked tail and tongue. Both of them were smoking pipes, held a hand of painted cards, and had a pile of coin in front of them. They stared at the two intruders with a mix of curiosity and annoyance.

Guylan rose to his feet and dusted himself off. "Please forgive our rude entry. There was... something horrible out there... Lots of eyes..."

The imp removed his pipe from between razor-sharp teeth. "S'quite alright, my good fellow," it said in the deep voice that had just enquired as to his health. "This old fool's outside décor leaves a lot to be desired. He seems to enjoy discomfiting others."

The summoner glared at the imp. "Don't make me dunk you in holy water again, you little red rat. The temple is right across the path..."

The imp hissed, forked tail flicking.

Guylan and Katherine stood closer together, watching the two bicker.

"Oh, for hells' sake," the imp cried. "Put your robes on, you dotard. Can't you see we have company."

The old man looked at his undergarments, then to the young woman in his presence. His cheeks reddened. "Ah. Yes. I shall be back in a moment." He set his cards face down on the table and scuttled off to his bed chamber.

The two mages stood there awkwardly, the imp's slitted yellow eyes watching them unblinking.

Eventually, the summoner returned, dressed in fine black and white robes with a black silken hood pulled up over his shiny pate. It was all very impressive. "What brings you to seek the wisdom of the mighty Wilfred Berkhoff this late in the evening?"

"It's morning, dimwit," the imp interjected.

The summoner shot the creature a glare that might have boiled blood, but the creature seemed to revel in his ire. "Mouth. Shut. Or else! We're underground, and it's hard to keep track of the time."

The imp looked at the visitors, then glanced meaningfully at the empty jugs of ale on a side table and grinned a shark's jagged smile.

Guylan cleared his throat, then introduced them both. "We have a research project that we could use your assistance with."

"What did you have in mind?" he asked them. "Do you wish to converse with a powerful demon from one of the Nine Hells? An unfathomable being from beyond the stars? No, I sense it is not either of those... Aha! I have it! You require an elemental prince to do your bidding."

Guylan shook his head. "We thought that perhaps, we could enlist the services of one of your lesser summons for a time. An–"

Wilfred's eyes lit up with joy. "An evil chicken?" His slow, sinister cackle sounded much like a laugh. "Ooh, or a flying squid – those are tremendous fun at children's parties."

Katherine spoke up before the summoner could continue. "An imp would be perfect. We require something that can talk and describe what it sees."

Wilfred turned a gleeful grin on the little creature at the table.

It looked worried. "Hang on one minute–"

"Excellent. Most excellent," Wilfred said, rubbing his hands gleefully. "Let this layabout earn his keep, eh. What foul task do you require of him? Is it dangerous?"

"I hope not," Guylan said. "We just wanted something – er, somebody – to operate a crystal ball for us at a distance."

Wilfred tutted. "Ach, you had my hopes up and everything. Yes, this little pest can easily do that."

"Well, he would be strapped into a flying device," Katherine advised. Guylan frowned at her, but she shrugged it off, not willing to subject anybody to dangers they had not knowingly signed up for.

Wilfred's eyes looked hopeful. "Oh? Please elaborate."

She tried to explain as best she could what it would involve without giving away their secrets, but emphasised the experimental nature of their endeavours.

"A previous device exploded in the sky, you say?" the summoner asked. "That does sound fun, does it not, my dreadful little demon?"

"Does it, hells," it replied. "Let me get this straight: you want to strap me to some sort of explosive and fire me up into the heavens?"

"Well, yes," Katherine said. "If that is acceptable, sir."

The imp smiled in surprise, not a pleasant sight. "Sir? Oh, I like this one. Have you ever thought about entering into an infernal pact, my dear? My terms are most reasonable."

"No recruiting for your cult on my time," Wilfred chided. "This sounds exactly like the sort of dangerous task these foul little demons are good for."

"You vile slavemaster," the imp hissed. "One day there will be a reckoning! Your soul will burn in my fiery pit."

"Yes, yes, you are very scary," Wilfred replied to his summoned creature, distracted as he looked around the chamber. "Let me go fetch a request form to fill out and we can make this official. I was just about to win this game of cards anyway – I find it far too easy playing with the likes of a lesser demon." He moved to the bedroom and began rummaging through a massive chest of paperwork.

The imp set down his hand of cards – a full noble house. "Don't tell him I was just about to win." It swapped out the king for a two-pip nothing card from the deck.

"Why are you cheating to lose?" Katherine asked.

It tapped a claw to its nose. "He likes to think himself so very wise. It's a ruse to lower his guard. One day, his overconfidence will lead to a terrible mistake, and then I will claim his soul."

"Aha!" Wilfred cried. He returned with an old scroll, blew the dust off and unrolled it. "One of you please state your division, official position, and sign the form here and here." He waved a hand. An inkpot and quill appeared on the table.

Guylan completed, signed, and handed back the form.

"The Research and Design Workshop, is it?" Wilfred said. "Well, well. And how is my cute little cousin doing these days?" He waved a hand and the implements and form disappeared in a puff of aether.

Guylan and Katherine exchanged a puzzled look. "Your cousin?"

"Jackan Grissom," he said. "Grumpy bastard? Likes buildings more than people?"

They stared at him, for the first time noticing a vague resemblance.

The summoner chuckled. "He didn't mention me, then. And here I changed that little shit's swaddling when he soiled himself as a babe. Tsk, ungrateful prick. When you get back, you tell him he still owes me money. Families, eh? Bah. Ach, well, let's get this imp's summoning stone prepared for you."

Wilfred bid them back away from the elaborate magic circle painted on the floor. He shoved the card table off to one side, grunting with the effort.

The imp stood by, looking mightily suspicious.

Its summoner's eyes narrowed. "Trying to hide a break in the lines, eh? I am on to you, vile little creature. Any more of your shenanigans and there will be no fried chicken wings for you next time."

The imp looked aghast at the threat to its food. It kept out of the way as its master took pot and brush and filled in a break in the line just behind the imp. "One day…" it muttered, showing far too many viciously sharp teeth as it squatted in the centre of the circle.

The summoner paced the outside of his working. "Perfect. Now, we begin." He lifted his hands, fore and small fingers pointed heavenwards like horns, and struck a pose of power, legs spread and hips thrust forward. "By my will and by my name – Wilfred Berkhoff – I command thee, infamous imp of the nine hells, Jeff be thy name, to come at the command of Guylan and Katherine of the Research and Design Workshop, and do their bidding for a single task to the best of your ability."

Dark power pulsed forth from the summoner. Candle flames flickered madly, casting shadows around the chamber.

The imp exploded into a cloud of boiling red mist. Sulphurous fumes wafted through the chamber, making the two research mages gag and pinch their noses. The disembodied demon swirled around the circle, seeking a break in the lines or a malformed rune. Finding none, it condensed into a small gem the colour of dark blood in the centre of the circle.

The flames in the room steadied, and the stench of sulphur faded.

Wilfred picked up the tiny gem and popped it into Katherine's hand. "There you go. This gem should contain him for a year or so. When you need to use him, just hold it and concentrate on calling Jeff back to this mortal plane."

"Jeff?" she queried. "Just… call Jeff? I was expecting something a bit more elaborate. I don't have to cut my palm and bleed on it or anything?"

"Holy moon, no," the summoner replied. "No need for any of that old-fashioned claptrap. He has a hundred names. I just call him Jeff around these parts, but he seems to like it."

"Thank you for your time and your skill," Guylan said. "This will prove most useful. We had best head back."

"You are most welcome," the summoner replied. He sat down and peeked at the imp's cards. His eyes crinkled in amusement. "Hah. Loser."

Katherine paused in the doorway and turned back. "If something goes wrong, it won't kill him, will it?"

Wilfred laughed. "Oh, don't worry about that. This is not his real body. When demons intrude upon the mortal plane, they manifest one formed from aether."

"That's a relief," she replied, smiling. "I didn't like to think we might hurt him. This undertaking will be scary enough as it is."

The summoner smirked. "I shall let you into a secret, girl, as you clearly know nothing of these infernal creatures. That wicked little beast is no doubt tremendously excited to be strapped to a fiery flying device and launched into the heavens on an insane mission no human would dare to contemplate. Demons crave the rush of danger." He paused, thinking. "And good food. If you want to be nice to him, make him an omelette before you send him up on your contraption."

"I will do just that," she replied. "You must like him a lot to treat him like a friend more than a summoned slave."

"Get out," Wilfred replied, a sour look on his face. "Right now. The very thought of it... go! Shoo, before I set an evil chicken on you."

She bobbed her head and fled his wrath, racing after Guylan.

When they were at the entrance and about to climb back up to Ella, Katherine asked: "Are we really going to remind Jackan about the money he owes? I don't think he will be pleased."

The engineer smiled, smug at the thought. "Leave that task to me. I can't wait to see his face."

The sunlight was blinding, forcing them to shade their eyes from its glare. Ella was there waiting on them.

"Did you get us an imp?" she asked.

"Oh, yes," Guylan replied. "And some red-hot gossip. The summoner is Jackan's older cousin."

She gaped at him. "No way! He's never once mentioned him."

"Wilfred used to change our beloved senior mage's dirty diapers, back when Jackan was a mewling babe."

"That, I cannot imagine," Ella said. "It's not a pleasant thought. I keep picturing a wizened old baby crying."

"Not much different to now," Guylan quipped.

"Come on, you said you would try to be nice to him," she said, folding her arms. "He's your project leader."

"I did say 'try'. But come on, Ella, this is a gold mine. A true gift! Think of all the embarrassing stories we can glean from his cousin."

Katherine let them get on with it and began walking back without them. She turned the imp's summoning stone over and over in her hand. It was smooth and warm, and felt somehow alive, tingling against her skin. All her training with the guild had warned her off even dabbling with anything even vaguely infernal, but this Jeff creature had not seemed so bad, assuming suitable precautions were taken.

She began to wonder what else she had blindly steered herself away from on the advice of others: her masters at the guild, her father, the senior alchemy mages at the fort… it was all food for thought.

CHAPTER 17

After long months of mind-numbing work, the three parts of the Mark III Fire Dragon were finally ready and being carried out onto the launch field for assembly. It was a cold but dry day, with no breeze and sparse clouds, affording a good view of the ascent.

"Hurry up, slowpoke," Jackan yelled, setting the crystal ball down on a portable scrying table set up for the viewing. It consisted of an aether gem-socket for power, a wooden frame with a sheet copper base that vibrated to reproduce sound, and a brass mouthpiece to speak into. A chest of tools and supplies had been carried down earlier and set a small distance away from a crackling campfire.

Serving as the team's packhorse, Guylan staggered over carrying a crate of well-packed crystals and metal plates inscribed with levitation runes. The aether from active levitation spells might interfere with those delicate runes, justifying Jackan's order of manual labour. It was certainly not out of revenge for the many "humorous" comments involving his cousin…

"Serves you right," Ella said, wheeling past the over-laden engineer with a crate of Fire Dragon fuel nestled in her lap. With the ground dry, her wheels were a boon.

Katherine hummed the tune to a bawdy alehouse song while transferring the blocks of fuel into the base of the device and preparing it for ignition. Ella raised an eyebrow, wondering if the chief's daughter knew the rather explicit words that went with the tune.

Guylan groaned as he set down his load, then wiped sweat from his brow. "Please tell me that is all we need."

Their leader glowered at him. "For now."

Katherine finished her work and gave a thumbs-up. They came together to lift the second stage of the device into place, then carefully affixed the metal plates bearing structural support runes, already fully charged with ambient aether, and the more power-intensive levitation runes that would require gems to function. The guidance system of weights and pulleys was fastened to the fins with steel wire, tightened and tested to ensure it would keep the device on course for the heavens.

Stages one and two were packed full of fuel and designed to be ejected once they were exhausted. There was no point dragging dead weight about.

The third and final stage was an entirely new creation: a hollow section of padded metal and safety straps, outfitted with small panes of thick, enchanted glass. It was just large enough for a single imp and the crystal ball it was to use. The cone-shaped nose bore slowfall runes of Ella's crafting, after they discovered that – to the surprise of no-one except Guylan – the ex-skymage's work was indisputably superior to the rest of them. They set it up and marvelled at the fully assembled device, standing six times the height of a tall man. It was ready for the passenger to climb a wooden ladder and board through a small hatch.

"We are ready for the summoning," Jackan said.

Katherine nodded. "I'll just get the frying pan and eggs ready."

The old engineer scratched his head. "Eh? Is it time for lunch already?"

"It's for the imp," she replied. "Wilfred said to cook him an omelette before he goes up."

Jackan stared at her. "Are you honestly going to waste your time cooking for a bloody demon?"

She shrugged, uncomfortable and hiding behind her dark veil of hair.

He shook his head. "Waste of good eggs, but fine, do as you will. Summon my ugly cousin's stupid imp and feed the damned thing."

While Katherine prepared to cook, Guylan and Ella checked that the runes on the Mark III were all correct.

"What do you have on your wrist?" she asked, peering at the bulky item attached to his arm.

"An engineer's book bracelet," he said, flipping through the hundreds of miniature pages bound into a circular bracelet. "Every page bears the diagram of an arcane rune and its variations. When you have your hands full, you don't want to be running back and forth to consult your grimoires." He found the diagram of a slowfall rune and showed her. "I don't know every line of every rune by heart, and this way I don't have to."

Ella licked her lips. "Ye gods, I want that."

"Then I'll make you one," he said breezily, busy working his way through the runes on the device. "At least the beginnings of one. You can fill in whatever other runes you might think you need."

"That's... very kind of you," she replied.

"You have the makings of a half-decent engineer in you," he stated. "That sort of thing should be encouraged."

"Does Jackan have a book bracelet as well?" she asked.

He paused. "Possibly? I've never seen him use one, but he is quite... traditional in some ways. It pains me to admit it, but he's also damnably good at remembering details."

"I could definitely use one," she replied. "I hate not having a reference to follow. I'm always paranoid I'll inscribe it backwards or something."

He laughed. "Why do you think I use this?" Then he winced at a bad memory. "All I will say is that mistakes were made. Here, let me show you my rune collection..."

While they pored over runes and inscriptions, Katherine finished her preparations. The frying pan and utensils were ready, along with eggs and a jug with a little water set out beside paper twists of salt and pepper, a knob of butter, and scraps of ham. All she had to do now was summon the imp that would crew the Fire Dragon.

Jackan watched with disdain as she cradled the strangely warm gem in her hands. "Jeff," she called. "I, Katherine Goddard, summon you to carry out the agreed task."

The gem shattered, and a red mist boiled from between her fingers, accompanied by the infernal stench of sulphur.

She yelped and flinched.

Jackan jerked upright, about to come to her aid, but she waved him back as the imp coalesced. "Blasted cousin of mine," he snarled. "Rotten black sheep of the family for a good reason."

She could feel him drawing on his aether, readying to blast the imp back to the Nine Hells if she needed him to. Katherine didn't think it necessary, but it was still a comfort.

"Hello, my dear girl," Jeff said, yawning, razor teeth on terrifying display. He bowed theatrically. "Are you ready to strap me down and have your wicked way with me?"

She flushed and hid behind her hair. "Omelette," she blurted, pointing to the frying pan.

The imp's eyes bulged grotesquely. "For me?" it asked in amazement. A forked tail flicked side to side. Bubbling black drool oozed down its chin.

She set the frying pan on the campfire, grabbed the eggs and cracked them on the edge of the jar, emptying them into the water. She added the salt and pepper, and beat it all together. Once it was ready, she added the butter and ham to the hot frying pan before pouring the eggy mixture on top.

The foul little creature seemed to vibrate with excitement; his drool dripped freely to the ground in hissing droplets that withered the grass.

With a shy smile, she handed Jeff a plate bearing a fragrant crescent of fluffy omelette.

The imp stared at it for a long moment, turning it this way and that, as if admiring the sight. Then it tore into the meal like a shark and finished it in two seconds. It carelessly dropped the plate, which shattered, and patted its scaly, bulging belly. "That's the good stuff, right there. Just for that, I'll do an extra-good job for you today."

Jackan sat shaking his head. "Get that creature strapped in and ready the crystal ball for transmission."

Katherine led Jeff over to the Mark III, explaining his role in the experiment.

The imp whistled though its teeth, a sound like a gale howling through twisted trees. "That's quite some contraption you have here. I've lived a long time, girl, and never seen its like. You say the last two versions exploded?"

She paused, then nodded. "We think we have that fixed."

The imp looked saddened for a moment, then perked up. "An imp that hopes humans will fuck up is rarely disappointed! Let's hope it blows me to bits and what's left of me rains down on the fields." It hissed with mirth and scampered up the ladder like a deformed squirrel, climbing inside the top section to study the padding and straps they had provided. It tutted and ripped them out, tossing shreds of leather and wool out.

"What are you doing?" Guylan shrieked.

"Lightening the load," Jeff replied. "Don't need no stinking safety straps. Or padding! The very thought of any demon putting up with cosy *padding...*"

The engineer looked to Jackan, who flung his hands up in despair. He watched sullenly as every safety precaution they had taken was tossed out like trash, leaving only sharp metal edges and hard plates, and Ella's slowfall runes in place for the descent.

"Much better," the imp said, pressing a finger to a sharp metal edge. It pierced his hide and black blood oozed out, resulting in a purr of pleasure. It curled up inside the metal shell and placed its claws on the crystal ball embedded in the wall. A flicker of its aether established the connection to the next nearest scrying device – so long as it kept that connection powered, the link would remain for the next hour before the transmission of sound and images began to degrade.

Ella peered into the ground team's ball, seeing a big yellow demonic eye looking back at her. "It's working fine. Seal him in now."

"With pleasure," Guylan said. He climbed up, closed the door, locking the imp inside the Mark III, then removed the ladder.

Jackan brought over the tiny wind-crystals that would power the levitation and slowfall runes and installed them as the final preparations for launch. He stepped back and gave it one last inspection. "Ready."

They retreated to the scrying platform. The ball was glowing, showing the imp and the interior compartment. The view of the outside world through the device's thick windows proved to be restricted, but better than nothing. Jackan bent over the brass mouthpiece. "Can you hear me, imp?"

"Set fire to it!" the demon cried, a tinny voice emerging from the vibrating sheet of copper on the scrying table. "Fire! Fire! Fire!"

"I'll take that as a 'yes'," Jackan replied. He spotted Whitlaw Goddard observing from the edge of the field. He was guarded by a pair of warriors and accompanied by a man in nondescript clothing and hooded cloak. Jackan could only imagine he was a minion of the hierarch that funded them.

Whitlaw offered Jackan a grim nod.

The old engineer returned it and hoped they would not disappoint the hierarch with another catastrophic failure. He cast a proud eye over their construction. "Over a year of our labour has gone into this moment – Ella, would you please do the honours."

She wheeled herself over to the Fire Dragon and powered up the spell-array controlling the levitation runes. A thread of her aether set them flaring to life and she swiftly withdrew her touch before it could suckle at her own lifeforce. The runes drank in the gem's stored aether and the device grew lighter. Ella picked up a smouldering stick from the campfire, set light to the end of the long fuse cord, then beat a hasty retreat from the blast area. Their expectations, fear, and excitement built to fever pitch as the fire burned its way towards its destination.

The initial whoosh of sparks swiftly escalated into a deafening roar. The Mark III shuddered, slowly rising from the earth on a pillar of fire and smoke. Its ascent swiftly accelerated. Displayed in the crystal ball, the imp was slammed to the floor by incredible force.

As it rose into the sky, wind hit the device, snatching at its smoke trail and threatening to push it astray. Wires pulled, fins twisted, but the course stayed true.

"Angle of ascent looks stable," Guylan said proudly. "The guidance system is working as intended."

Katherine leaned over the mouthpiece, yelling over the din. "How are you faring, Jeff?"

Inside the crystal ball, the structure rattled and shook with the strain. The imp's reply was unintelligible, pinned as it was to the floor. One yellow eye winked at them and a mad giggle emerged from the scrying apparatus, sounding somewhat strained.

The Fire Dragon lanced into the sky, diminishing to a black dot, then vanished into the heavens.

All eyes focused on the crystal ball. Jackan set both hands on it, and a thread of his aether changed the viewing angle until they could partially see out one of the thick glass viewing panes. The view lurched as the exhausted first stage detached and fell away.

The second stage roared into life. Inside the Mark III, black vomit spewed across the wall as the imp howled with laughter.

"Weird little masochist," Jackan muttered. "Right unnatural so it is. That bloody cousin of mine..."

Katherine swallowed and averted her eyes from the spinning scenery. "I feel nauseous just looking at that."

Guylan nodded in emphatic agreement. "Definitely not something we would ever want to experience ourselves. I am sure that is a problem we can fix."

The Fire Dragon roared onwards, mountains, forests and distant sea growing ever smaller. The imp managed to pry itself off the floor, looking a little battered and bruised. Its mouth moved, but no voice emerged from their scrying apparatus. They could hear the dull rattle of metal and bolts but no speech. It clutched at its throat, eyes bulging, then looked directly into the crystal. The horned head shook, and it lifted a claw to its fanged maw. The roaring ceased, leaving an eerie silence.

"Fuel is exhausted," Ella stated.

The second stage fell away, leaving only the passenger capsule rising heavenwards, its ascent slowing. The blue haze of the horizon gave way to darkness, a void of nothingness that existed between worlds.

"Oh, no," Katherine cried, wringing her hands. "We sealed Jeff into a tiny metal tin and forgot about air holes!"

"I don't think there is much air up there in the first place," Ella said. "Uh, do imps even need to breathe?"

Jackan could only shrug.

The imp himself didn't seem too bothered. The Fire Dragon had stopped rising and was now hanging suspended in nothingness. Jeff seemed to lose purchase on the floor, and began floating freely around the small chamber, bouncing off the walls like an overactive child.

Guylan gasped in amazement. "Our device has broken free from the chthonic attraction of this world. The Great Mother has no hold over him."

The imp caught sight of something interesting. It dug its claws into the wall and pressed its face up against a window. The moon came into view, huge and clear and brilliant silver.

The mages' breath caught in their throats at the sight of such magnificence. It was still too far to see the Silver Palace with the naked eye, but this was the closest anybody had ever come to the home of the gods.

The blue haze crept up the window to envelop the Mark III again, and the imp was soon flattened to the top of its chamber.

"Not quite beyond the yearning to rejoin its earthen home, it seems," Jackan said.

They watched it plummet towards the ground, still spinning. Tiny mountain ranges grew to shadowed hills, swooping past with nauseating speed.

The imp found a voice again, and its mad laughter returned as it rattled off the walls.

Guylan palmed the activation plate for his slowfall rune, eyes fixed on the horrifying descent.

"Press it," Katherine demanded, agitated.

He flexed his fingers around the plate. "Not yet."

She tried to grab it, but he lifted it out of her reach. "It only has limited power," he explained. "If we activate it too early, it will do no good at all."

She grimaced and forced her hands to keep to themselves.

"It's just a bloody imp," Jackan spat.

Katherine glowered at him.

"Not like it's the thing's real body," he said, scowling back.

Ella rolled over and held her friend's hand. "It'll all be fine. Just wait and see."

Rivers and plains came into view, a god's-eye view of the sprawling lands of the Unity. The ground was approaching at a sickening rate.

"It's going to land aways to the west of here," Guylan said. "We'll need to get a golem, and a horse and cart to retrieve it."

The Mark III began to tumble end over end, slamming the imp into the walls. Black blood spattered the inside. Metal and wood groaned under the strain of descent. A window shattered, shards ripped out into howling winds.

The imp was sucked half out of the window, its flesh shredded by broken glass and metal.

"Press it!" Katherine screamed.

Guylan's thumb stabbed down to activate his runes.

Through the crystal ball, they watched the Fire Dragon's descent slow to a more sedate, survivable pace. A clawed hand came into view, followed by a yellow eye peering in from the outside of the Mark III.

Ella sighed and gave her friend's hand a squeeze. "See, told you it would be fine."

Grey wings spread out past the windows, an astonishing wingspan for such a tiny creature. "I'll bring this heap of scrap right back to you," it yelled. "No heavier than a snack horse now."

Guylan looked back to their team leader, mouthing *snack horse*?

"Don't ask," Jackan said.

The team watched as the black dot in the sky grew larger, their device borne home from the heavens on infernal wings.

CHAPTER 18

"Told you I'd do a hellish good job," Jeff said, crawling over broken glass and scorched metal. He'd dropped the nosecone at their feet, then flown off to retrieve the ejected first and second stages.

The demon's right arm was a floppy mess of broken bone, and the muscles of one leg showed grey through gaping lacerations as he preened atop the ruins of their device.

The mages stared at the broken and bloodied mess it had become.

Katherine rushed over and enveloped the little demon in a hug.

The imp stiffened, shocked to its very core. Its claws trembled, a frozen moment of struggle against instinctive murder.

She stepped back a moment later, flushed and fidgeting.

The infernal creature shook off its surprise, spat black blood and grinned. "That trip was bloody brilliant! When can we go again?"

Jackan threw his hands up. "Told you they were vicious little masochists."

Its horned head bobbed. "'Tis very true. Oh, I cannot wait to tell this tale to my brood! The excitement of wondering if I would be blown to tiny bits at any moment, the brutal pressure and being slammed off metal walls. Being choked of air, too! What a delight."

Guylan leaned in. "Air? Tell us about that."

"Two problems there, pal: first, all the air got sucked out when we went up high – need to seal that bastard up tight next time. Problem number two: what air there was went bad real fast before that. You're going to need some way of purifying it, or you animals will keel over when it's your turn to get locked in. Wanna test that yourself? Stick some weights in the bottom of a barrel, climb in and get dropped into a pond. You'll catch on real quick. Or maybe not. I don't much care."

The young engineer pursed his lips. "Bad air, like in the mines when they breathe toxic gas? Huh. That was actually very helpful." He paused, feeling awkward about saying this to a demon. "Thank you."

The imp spat on his shoes. "Did it for the omelette. Jeffrozon the Black Wind of Pain and Suffering pays his debts. Now piss off, the lot of you – 'cept for you, my girl; you can call on me anytime." He winked at Katherine. "With eggs, o'course, just to make sure I don't swallow your soul by mistake." The demon dissolved into a cloud of stinking smoke.

Jackan wrinkled his nose in disgust. "Right then, team. Let's get this back to the workshop." He noted the chief leading the emissary of the hierarchs away, deep in conversation as they headed back to the fort. Jackan could only hope the man had been suitably impressed with their progress.

A golem carried the remnants of the Mark III back to the workshop. The mages gathered round, disassembling the hull to poke and prod the device's guts. It was in remarkably better condition than previous efforts, in that it didn't have to be shovelled up into sacks.

Ella patted the cold metal. "How far up did it go?" She examined the metal plates bearing her levitation runes, which seemed undamaged and reusable – though the small aether gems powering them had been drained until they cracked.

"Further than that boaster, Breo the Brilliant, ever did; that's for sure," Jackan said. "I don't believe any human has ever seen our world laid out like that. For all our cities and our wars, from that high up we couldn't see a damn thing our race has ever made."

They began taking notes of what parts were damaged or destroyed, and any other defects in their construction that would need to be corrected in the next iteration. Guylan cracked open the nosecone: the stench of imp blood and vomit caused him to retch – he hastily closed it all back up and plugged the broken window with a spare rag while Ella worked a spell to eliminate the reek.

"The fuel worked well," Katherine said, running a finger down the interior of the ejected first stage. She examined the residue and pulled a face. "I need to put more work into the consistency – there are still too many impurities in this mix for my liking."

"I think that's the least of our worries," Jackan said. "Look at the window frames and the structure here and here. The metal is twisted from that spinning force."

"We can reduce that," Guylan added, studying the construction. "I wonder if our work was lopsided, causing the spin. If we divide it like a pie and ensure all segments are the same weight, that should do the trick."

"What about the air problem?" Ella asked. "I know it sounds insane, but Jeff's idea was not bad. Sealing one of us up in a big barrel would be a good test – better that than getting all the way to the moon and running out of air. Who knows if the moon even has air?" She looked at each of them in turn. "Do gods even breathe?"

Maybe priests had an answer to that – some apocrypha buried in a footnote of a dusty religious text, perhaps – but mages certainly didn't.

"I volunteer," Katherine said. "It was a good idea."

Guylan snorted. "Be my guest. I can't be the only one daft enough to volunteer for this madness."

Jackan winced. "Not sure your da will thank me for that, lass."

Her lips thinned and her nostrils flared. "I am not helpless. As a mage, I am every bit as good as the rest of you, and I can most certainly escape a poxy barrel if I have to."

He waved a hand in defeat. "Fine, fine, it's your call. Just save me the headache and don't go tellin' your da all about it, eh."

"Not a problem," she replied. "What he does not know will not hurt him."

Their leader sighed and scratched his head. "Many a youngster has said the same, but aye, lass, it's your life. You and Guylan can work on the air problem while Ella and I make a start on plans for scaling the Mark IV up to full size, though it will only carry a single sacrificial mage on the first launch."

Guylan's eyes narrowed theatrically. He glanced at Ella and rolled his eyes, fighting the urge to snap back.

In response, Jackan leaned in close to her. "I'm a bit worried – do you think our colleague is unwell? He seems to be developing a sense of humour."

"Let's go before you rub each other up the wrong way again," she replied.

"Follow me," the old engineer said, leading her to the back corner of the workspace. "I have something for you to test."

He pulled canvas off a cunningly built wheeled chair of brass rods and woven wicker, still somewhat unfinished. "I apologise for this taking so long – there were issues with... well, no point spouting excuses. What do you think?" He stood there awkwardly, like a child submitting its first artistic creation to a parent for approval. "No doubt it will need more modifications, but best to consult the expert first."

Ella stared at the gleaming metal and wiped a tear from the corner of her eye. She took a deep breath and studied his work carefully. The large front wheels bore circular handles just offset from the rims, so she could spin them without getting filthy hands. It had some manner of braking mechanism using a lever that operated clever mechanical wood and leather clamps, and the wicker seat seemed to balance on a flexible arch of dragon-forged steel.

"May I?" she asked.

"Of course! Do you need a hand?"

"If you could hold this chair in place while I transfer across, that would be wonderful."

He did as he was asked, steadying the battered old chair as she used crutches to move herself to the new.

She bounced several times, feeling the steel flex beneath her. "Just like a sword blade," she said.

"Fine bit of dragon-forging, that," he said. "It'll bear enchantment well, if needs be. That's the part I had to outsource, of course, what with me not being a fire-breathing dragon. Give her a spin."

Ella cracked her knuckles and laid hands on her wheels. She used the handles to propel herself forward with alarming speed. She squeaked in surprise as she careered towards the wall, and Jackan had to step in to save her.

"Maybes should have showed you the brake first, eh," he admitted. He showed her how to use the lever that worked the clamps squeezing on the wheel to slow and stop it, and the steel bolts used to lock the wheels in place and stop them turning at all.

She tried again, zipping across the floor. "So fast and light," she said with wonder.

"Hollow tubes," he replied. "That old thing was built like a bloody battle wagon. No need for solid brass and cast iron to support a little thing like you."

"Soft seating, too," she said. "I bet this would stop my teeth rattling when I roll over those damned cobblestones. Only problem with the seat is that it's a little big."

He slapped his forehead. "O'course it is! I used my own fat arse when I was measuring it. That's an easy fix. Anything else?"

She looked up at him, eyes brimming with gratitude. "Not that I can think of. I–"

The gruff old engineer cleared his throat, cheeks reddening with awkward embarrassment. "Right, well, enough of this lazing about, eh, lass. Back into your old chair for now and get on with your work. I'll have this adjusted for tomorrow."

Jackan spread papers out and they began to sketch out initial ideas for the Mark IV Fire Dragon. It would need to be larger, mightier, and far more complex than anything they had attempted before. Stage one was dedicated to launching them off the ground, and stage two powered the transition to orbitus. Each was designed to be ejected when it became exhausted. The third stage hosted the pilot, allowing re-entry and safe landing.

Ella sketched the necessary structural support and protection runes, then an array of levitation runes that spiralled along its entire length. "I'm worried about the massive number of runes necessary to lighten something of this size. The interference will be problematic if we continue the way we are going. Even if we use more stable ambient runes for the structural support, levitation runes require the extra power that only aether gems offer. Some of them might fail, or even explode if we are unlucky. And then there are the sheer number of them we'd need to power all this." She winced at the eye-watering expense of it all.

He shrugged. "That's what we need to figure out. Where there's a problem, there's a way to solve it."

Ella sighed. If he was breaking out his tired old engineer's idioms, then she was in for another long day. They got to work, sketching and planning, scoring out and starting again…

None of them noticed the cloud of smoke loitering in the eaves of the workshop, nor felt the demonic eyes watching their every movement. It flowed out through a gap in the roof and seeped back into the tomb-chamber of its master, Wilfred Berkhoff, reforming as a whole and healthy imp inside the crackling fireplace.

Jeff stepped from the flames, brushing off specks of ash. "Shame nobody told them how to properly dismiss a summoned creature. Bit of an omission on our part, eh."

The summoner set down his steaming mug of tea next to a second that had been freshly made. "So, what is my little cousin up to?"

"Mad as prophets, the lot of you," the imp said, crawling up his lap. "He's only building a device to send mages to the moon – launched me right up into the void between worlds as a test." It told its master everything.

Wilfred stared into the lying little creature's yellow eyes and found no iota of falsehood there, nor even a bad joke. "I… I am gods-smacked speechless."

"If only that were true," Jeff grumbled, picking at a tooth with a dirty claw.

"By all the guardians of the backdoor to the Nine Hells," the summoner said. "I wasn't expecting that answer. Little Jackan never was into all that blood and guts and glory like the rest of his side of the family. You think I should cut my cousin some slack after all these years of shunning me?"

Jeff snorted. "Nah. He's a grumpy old sod. Going to get themselves killed if they go up there, though. Ain't no air to breathe nor water to drink. Ain't nothing at all between here and there."

Wilfred plucked a white feather sticking out of the imp's leathery wing, he frowned at it and tossed it into the fire where it crisped and curled up. "Is that a note of concern I hear in your voice? Not turning good on me, are you?"

It glared at him, exposing wicked, rending fangs. "Shut up."

He laughed at the little demon. "Maybe you could see your way to offering them a little advice, then? Perhaps a friendly summoner who might be willing to provide a few minor air elementals to refresh their air supply…"

"For a price, sure," Jeff said.

Wilfred nodded. "But of course! And only if my wayward little cousin comes down here and asks for it himself."

"Now who is being good?" Jeff replied, picking up his cup and sipping scalding tea. "You stink of concern."

Wilfred huffed and didn't reply. He drank his tea and stared into the crackling fireplace.

Ella stared at the two mages arguing over some tiny piece of engineering minutiae, brandishing tiny pieces of bent wire at each other.

Something something five degrees…

Centrifugal force… structural integrity…

It was just like being back in the guild classrooms of yesteryear: every bit as bewildering and full of the same windbag bores stuffed full of their own certainty.

She fished a small jar of mead from her bag and winked at Katherine. "Shall we get out of here?"

The dark-haired woman hesitated. "Should we not stay and work on? Won't they notice if we leave?"

Ella chuckled. "You are too good for this place, Katherine. They'll be at loggerheads until the break of dawn. Let's roll!"

Nobody noticed them leave. Most of the workshop had already gone home, save a few glum souls on the production benches with too much debt to pay off.

It was early evening, and the heat of the sun still lingered. The moon was rising as they settled themselves in a leafy copse just outside of Newsark, looking up at the darkening sky as the twinkling stars began unveiling themselves. Ella sipped the mead, and honeyed alcohol slid down her throat, its warmth settling in her belly. She passed the drink over.

"I've always wondered what the moon and stars really are," Katherine said. "I mean, of course we have the stories recorded in the temple scriptures, but nobody really knows for certain."

"Sailors and scholars both discovered our world is a sphere long ago," Ella replied. "It's hardly difficult when you have a stick and measure the angle of its shadows cast at the same time of day in various locales. It's basic arithmetic. When I was little, I always believed the stories that said we were on a globe inside a greater, heavenly globe with little holes poked through to let the rains in. Later, when I became a skymage, I began to doubt that when it became obvious that we *believed* in much but actually *knew* close to nothing."

She pointed at one particularly bright star. "There's the evening wanderer beginning his travels. Unlike other stars, the wanderers travel across the sky, and I always imagined they had more of a story beyond the temples' tales of celestial charioteers and silver-winged messengers."

"Sometimes, I wonder…" Katherine began. "Do you ever feel like, instead of looking up into the shifting sky, that we are really sitting here on a spinning ball staring out into the vastness of the void, with nothing more than the love of our Great Mother stopping us from flying off into endless nothingness?"

"Damn, that's deep," Ella mused. "And you are very drunk. Pass me that mead back – I'm not yet drunk enough to ponder that sort of thing." She took a big swallow.

"Perhaps we will find out someday," Katherine said. "We are going to go up into the void beyond this world, and for the first time in history, we will see exactly what is up there."

Ella sighed, wickerwork creaking as she shifted in her wheeled chair. "You might go, but I fear my flying days are behind me. I'm content helping from down here in the mud."

Katherine had no idea how to reply to that, so she fell quiet. They sipped mead and stared up at the sky. It was a soft, companionable silence. Eventually, she turned to her friend and marshalled her courage. "You occasionally talk about your accident and the difficulties, but you *never* talk about any family."

"Dead and gone," Ella replied. "Well, my mother is. The man that sired me pissed off years before that. Hopefully he died in a ditch."

Katherine winced. "I'm so sorry. I didn't mean to open old wounds."

"No need for that," Ella said. "It was a long time ago, and he's not worth thinking about." She turned to her friend, a wicked smile on her lips. "So, tell me about that sandy-haired young musician that was so besotted with you he tried to sneak into the fort." Even in the darkness, she could feel the sudden heat coming off the woman's face. Ella chuckled and took another drink.

Katherine fidgeted awkwardly. "I only shagged him the once."

Mead spurted out of Ella's nose. She coughed and choked, staring at her friend. "You did what?"

Her friend flashed a coy smile. "I'm not all sweet and innocent. I like an ale or three, and pretty men."

Ella grabbed her hand and stared into dark eyes, shining bright in the moonlight. "You must tell me *everything*!"

CHAPTER 19

The Research and Design Workshop team, nominally under Whitlaw Goddard's oversight, had spent the past few months building and testing different variations of the Mark III. They fine-tuned different parts of their design and construction methods before deciding it was time to embark on the next new and improved version. It was not an unusual development cycle for an arcane engineering project, just an incredibly expensive one.

The chief watched some of the launches from a distance, not wanting his daughter to feel like he was sticking his nose into her affairs. It was an interesting project, and he took heart that there was little personal risk to Katherine. It was not a traditional weapon, after all – more of a transportation method – but there was a concerning number of mid-air explosions. Jackan had assured him these were not failures and that it was all part of the learning process, but he could not help but worry, especially with the war growing increasingly volatile, with frequent cross-border raids exchanged by both sides leaving bodies on the ground.

When the leaves turned red and yellow, and began to carpet the earth with their golden glory, the day that Whitlaw Goddard had been dreading finally arrived: Abelin Castle was ready to welcome Jackan's team. A guarded caravan would arrive at Fort Newsark that very day to transfer everything and everyone involved. Due to the spreading conflict, messengers had been disrupted of late, and he now had only hours to say his farewells to Katherine. He was not remotely ready for their parting.

Whitlaw dropped the orders to the desk and hunched over, his face in his hands. "Oh, my darling daughter," he moaned, fear warring with pride. She was coming out of her shell and blossoming, largely thanks to that young Ella Pickering he had initially been so doubtful of. He was in mixed minds about their association: on the one hand, everybody deserved a second chance, but on the other, the woman had once earned the wrath of a hierarch, and their sort were not known to let go of grudges.

It was far too late for him to try and do anything about it. Grubman-Lordrach IV had been explicit in his orders. The only saving grace was that their project seemed to be coming along very well indeed. Still... there was something niggling at him he couldn't quite place, as if his people were keeping something from him. Conversations had cut off mid-flow when he showed his face, and Katherine... why, as utterly absurd as it sounded, she had almost looked *guilty* on occasion.

He shook it off. It was her first secret project, after all. He was hardly objective about his daughter's participation, but she would only be a few hours' hard ride away in an emergency.

He fished the brass locket from beneath his robes and flipped it open. As always, he took strength from seeing the face of Lillian, his late beloved wife. The painting was true to life, crafted by one of the finest artists of Orialis. She almost looked alive, save for the stillness. That woman had never remained still a moment in her life, always busy doing something with her hands: working, knitting, painting, or gardening.

"Your daughter is strong," he said, stroking the case with a sad smile. "Would that you could see her now. What a mind she has, my darling – she most definitely takes after you."

He stared at Lillian's portrait, lost in thought, until a knock at his door snapped him out of it. He closed the locket and slipped it beneath his robes, then took a few deep breaths to centre himself in the here and now.

"Come!"

Whitlaw leapt to his feet as a golden-masked battlemage strolled into his study, her crimson robes glimmering with arcane runes, active and glowing with ravenous power. She hadn't needed to wait for his permission to enter – that had been mere courtesy.

"Sit," she said, her voice hoarse.

He sat, sweating while she walked around his study, examining the collection of arcane relics gathered over the course of his life.

"Impressive," she said, "given your personal resources. And entirely appropriate, when some in your position might skim some cream off the top of their budget for personal excess."

He swallowed. "Thank you. Are there any items you wish to examine closer?"

Behind the mask her ice-blue eyes were cold and uncaring. "No."

She sat in the chair facing him, composed and in control. "You have received the communication about Abelin Castle?"

"I have," he replied. "A few moments ago."

Her eyes hardened at that response, radiating displeasure. "You should have received that missive two days ago. Such delays are unacceptable."

Whitlaw could only nod in agreement. Some poor messenger would be getting posted to the front lines for a little laziness, assuming she didn't incinerate them on the spot.

"May I enquire as to what brings you to Fort Newsark in person?" he asked, resisting the nervous urge to bite or pick at his fingernails.

She stared at him, her mask displaying his own distorted reflection. "I am here to ask if there are any more of your staff who have become aware of the true nature of Mage Jackan Grissom's project. If so, inform me now."

He relaxed slightly, which did not go unnoticed. "No additions to your list," he assured her. "We have been most careful to keep the details restricted. It has been impossible to hide the tests, of course, but all assume it is just one of many new weapons currently under development."

"Excellent," she said. Her gaze softened slightly. "I am aware of your familial connection, and I do sympathise, but I will have it understood that there will be no casual visitors allowed to Abelin Castle. Any necessary consultations with specialists will be conducted via the usual remote scrying methods, and all requests for materials will go through me first, before you."

Whitlaw Goddard sat straighter, and leaned towards her. "I will require regular reports via crystal ball that my people are safe and happy."

She calmly met his gaze, saying nothing. He held it, unwilling to back down.

The corners of her eyes crinkled – in a smile or a scowl behind the mask, he could not tell.

"You tread an exceedingly thin and very dangerous line, Chief Goddard."

"A necessary one," he countered. "The wellbeing of those under my command is my grave responsibility."

She held up a gloved hand and flexed it, knuckles cracking. "And if I do not agree to this… request?"

He smiled coldly. "I am in no position to demand anything of you, or the hierarchs."

There was another moment of fraught silence between them. She was waiting for the 'but'.

He cleared his throat. "The paperwork involved in a Research and Design project is considerable. Sourcing the varied and rare materials required by my teams is more of a dark art than simple organisational ability, and there are so many teams vying for my time. Without my knowledge and skill of Unity bureaucracy, the delays to any project would be… unfortunate."

The battlemage's eyes narrowed. "Is that a threat, Chief Whitlaw Goddard?"

The air felt so charged with aether a single spark might obliterate him. He carefully folded his hands on the desk in front of him to stop them trembling. "I have been perfectly clear it is not, and I would never dream of threatening an esteemed agent of the hierarchy. I would certainly never try and threaten you with matters of lowly, tedious, and time-consuming bureaucracy, not when the sponsoring hierarch is so keen to see this project succeed."

She appeared to mull that over for a while before she sighed and sat back. "Very well. You will have their wellbeing reported via crystal ball." Power, battlemages understood. Arcane might, such as her own, was one thing, the political and monetary influence of the hierarchs another, but Unity bureaucracy held a dread power all of its own, and her sort did not relish the drudgery of navigating that labyrinthine mess. Nobody did, which is why mages with low ambition but an eye for detail, like Whitlaw Goddard, rose up through the middling ranks.

He fought to keep the relief from his face. "I will sleep better at night knowing my people are being correctly cared for."

"Is there anything else that you *require* of His Grace's battlemage?" she asked.

He was acutely aware of the cold sweat slicking his armpits and dampening his back. "Nothing at all. If there is anything that you require from the Research and Design Workshop, I shall see it done."

The battlemage turned her head, staring off into the distance. "The escort caravan is about to arrive. I will see to its preparation, and you will hurry your people along. We leave for Abelin Castle in four hours." She rose and strode from his study. There was no further debate to be had – it would be leaving with all aboard, whether he liked it or not.

He sat there locked in place until he was sure she was not returning to claim a forgotten glove or some such. Then he flopped into his seat, shaking and wiping away the sweat. All his strength had drained away and his body ached from the tension.

Whitlaw Goddard had just faced down one of the hierarch's own battlemages with only the threat of bureaucracy. "What in the blazes were you thinking?" he hissed, "you utter fool of a man!" Whitlaw knew he was not brave, but until now had never considered himself foolish. His Lillian had been the brave one, gods bless her soul.

He was surprised to discover that he would do it all again if his daughter were at risk. But he had no time to explore that feeling; the sands were running out of his glass, and he had to get his people as ready as they could be.

The chief rose on shaky feet and hurried into Jackan's workspace. Apart from Rojer Glenn, the rest were gathered together, saving him the trouble of sending people to hunt them down.

Katherine looked up and saw something in his expression. She put down her quill and hurried over. "Father? What's wrong?"

He enveloped her in a hug. "A caravan has arrived to take you all to Abelin Castle. You have four hours to gather your belongings and vital work materials."

Jackan's nostrils flared. "Preposterous! What bloody idiot thinks we can get everything done in that time?"

Whitlaw winced, hoping the heavy curtain helped to muffle the engineer's words "Keep your voice down. The hierarch has sent a battlemage to take charge of your relocation. Apparently, we should have had a couple of days to pack up, but… well, I fear some of the fort's messengers are soon to have a very bad time."

They all had the good sense to look worried.

"Gods, what a mess," Jackan said, scrubbing a filthy hand through his hair. "Guylan, help me with our papers. We absolutely need every one of them." The two engineers tore through the place, collecting armloads of papers and scrolls and stuffing them into an old chest hastily emptied of tools.

"I need to go," Ella said, her hands shaking around the handles of her wheeled chair. "All my things are back in town, and I've tools and aids necessary to manage my condition."

"Hurry," Whitlaw replied. "That battlemage will brook no delays. It will not go well if she must go and fetch you."

Ella shuddered and wheeled herself off in a hurry, her new chair proving much speedier and more manoeuvrable than the clunky old thing she had been using previously.

That left father and daughter to say their goodbyes.

"No need to worry," Katherine said, sniffing as she escaped from another hug. "I'm a grown woman, and I won't be on my own."

"You have never been so far from me," he replied, lower lip trembling.

She squeezed his hand. "I did live in the dorms at the Guild, if you recall."

"I remember," he said. "But I was only a short walk away through well-patrolled streets if you had need of me."

"I was perfectly fine then, and I will be fine now." She drew back and took a deep breath. "I had best gather my things before we run out of time."

"I'll help," he said.

She held up a hand. "Please stay and help the others to pack up our tools. I will be back soon as I can."

His daughter marched off before he could object, leaving him with a cartload of nervous energy to work off, so he rolled up his sleeves and got to work.

* * *

°Despite her show of confidence, it didn't take long for Katherine's nerves to get the better of her. She strode from the workshop full of fire and determination, and then she caught sight of the caravan forming up at the front of the fort, and warriors loading supplies onto six armoured wagons.

Halfway to the quarters she shared with her father, she stopped and leaned against a wall, taking several deep breaths to calm her racing heart and rising nausea.

Her guts felt all twisted up. She didn't cope well with sudden changes, and loathed having to deceive her father. If he knew what she was really working on, he would have been in torment, and she would not choose to inflict that upon him. She had made her choice and she had to live with it.

"Oh, hello there." Wilfred Berkhoff stood before her, his brow furrowed in concern. "Are you feeling ill?"

She stood straight and cleared her throat, forcing a smile onto her face. "I'm fine, thank you."

"No need to fake it on my account," the summoner said. "Me, I'm more than happy to tell folks when I'm upset. If that ruffles their feathers, they weren't worth caring about in the first place."

Her false smile crumbled. "We are being transferred to a new, more secure location."

The old man glanced back to the hive of activity surrounding the caravan. "That little lot for you folks, is it? That is unfortunate." He looked around, ensuring that nobody was close enough to overhear, and then flicked his fingers to and fro, working a spell to detect magical scrying attempts.

"Good," he said. "Nobody is eavesdropping. Let's make this quick. Here, take this." He handed over a summoning stone with a demonic sigil on it.

Katherine looked at him quizzically.

"In case you need assistance," the summoner said. "Jeff can carry secret messages for you, even under the noses of battlemages." He snorted. "All that personal power and they show an atrocious neglect for the subtler infernal arts. You need to talk to me or your father in confidence, you send me a message."

She fought back a tide of emotion. "I cannot imagine we will have cause to need it but... thank you, sir."

Wilfred frowned at her, about to say something more and then thinking better of it. Instead, he said: "Even the most thought-through projects can go awry or find themselves going in intriguing new directions. I'd bloody love to see you folks succeed – more than you might imagine. Don't be afraid of summoning up old Jeffrozon if you need aid."

He winked at her. "Don't be a stranger now! Say hello to that arse of a cousin for me – and remind him that he still owes me money." He patted her on the shoulder as he passed by on his way to the fort's kitchen.

Katherine shook her head and hurried to her room, quickly packing her favourite clothing and other necessities into her bedside chest. She opened her jewellery case and paused, fingers tracing over chains and earrings of silver and gold, ruby and emerald. The non-magical but beautiful gems were small and modest by the standards of those she had apprenticed with in Orialis, but costly all the same, especially on her father's modest budget.

After a moment's thought, she took only the most important item, a plain silver locket engraved with her mother's and father's names above her own. Inside was a tiny painting made one glorious summer day twenty years ago. Katherine herself was a small, pudgy, and grumpy blob perched on her father's lap. She smiled and fastened it around her neck. She could do without gold and jewels, but she could not do without her family.

Katherine made one last sweep for whatever might be needed in the coming weeks. She could easily fill three or more large chests with her belongings, but she restrained herself by limiting it to the largest of her travel chests. She made a snap decision to leave all but one of her formal gowns behind, along with most of her gloves and fancier footwear. She winnowed it down to the necessities. That nagging feeling of forgetting something important was already rearing its ugly head as she forced the lip closed.

She shook it off and waved her father's manservant over, an aging man with matching salt and pepper moustache. "Charles, please see that this chest is carried to the caravan preparing for departure to Abelin Castle."

The man bobbed his head and made to carry out his task immediately, but Katherine stopped him. "I will be gone for some time. Can you please look after Father for me?"

Charles's eyes creased as he smiled. "No worries on that score, Mistress. Looked after this family since before you were born, so I have, and I don't intend to stop now."

A sigh escaped her lips. It was less than a day's ride to the west, but the distance loomed like a mountain. "Thank you," she said. "Whatever would we do without you?"

"Have to eat your father's cooking, probably," he replied.

They both pulled sour expressions, sharing the same unpleasant memories of charcoaled vegetables, chicken still pink in the middle, and handfuls of spices randomly tossed into a pot of stew, with her father thinking that expense equalled good cooking. He'd never been good at alchemy either, for similar reasons.

"May fine weather and fortune follow you on your travels, Mistress," Charles said.

She let him be about his work and ventured outside to watch the caravan's preparations for a moment before she returned to the workshop. The latest version of the Fire Dragon had been covered in canvas for secrecy: its parts were being loaded onto the back of wagons by two battered old stone golems, supervised by an experienced team. Groaning chests and half-finished pieces of metalwork were being loaded into others.

Ella came speeding through the gatehouse, hands working her wheels hard. She drew up, sweating and panting. "I'm not late, am I?"

Katherine shook her head, looking at the small sack on Ella's lap, precariously balanced on some sort of wooden frame with handles that she couldn't determine the usage of. Crutches and various oddly handled wooden tools were tied to the back of the chair. "Is that all of your belongings?"

Her friend nodded. "Some tools and necessities. Spare robes and undergarments. Don't own much at all, really."

Suddenly, Katherine's single large travel chest seemed entirely adequate. Her cheeks coloured as she thought of Ella's face if she had arrived with more.

CHAPTER 20

With the judicious use of a levitation spell and some helping hands, Ella's wheeled chair was loaded onto the back of a wagon and securely lashed in place at the rear. She sat on the bare wooden bench beside Katherine and Rojer Glenn, devoid of bandages, his scars now thin silvery lines on his weathered skin.

"All healed up and pretty again?" Jackan asked, thumping his rear down opposite Rojer. Guylan climbed aboard the wagon and reluctantly sat beside his team leader, keeping as much of a gap between them as he could.

"Never felt better," Rojer replied with a wry smile. "Fixed my shoulder up good as new, and they got rid of that twinge in my back as well."

The older mage nodded to Ella. "Katherine I've met before; you must be Ella Pickering. I've heard good things."

"Nice to meet you," she replied. "Sorry we got you caught up in all of this."

He waved a hand dismissively. "Better back here with you lot than freezing my cock off patrolling the borders of No Man's Land."

Guylan and Jackan shuddered.

Katherine flushed, uncomfortable with his coarseness, but Ella just laughed. "Always looking on the bright side, eh? I get that."

He eyed her, nodding. "I bet you do. Gets us though the day when the world turns to shit."

A few familiar faces had been compelled to join the caravan's escort: that same band of the Fort's warriors who had ventured into No Man's Land to recover Jackan's original device – or the survivors, anyway. They shouldered marching packs and seemed to be in good spirits, likely keen for a good dose of boring guard duty away from monsters and magical mayhem.

Voices yelled out. The caravan began to move out and their wagon lurched into motion beneath them. After two year's hard graft in the bosom of Fort Newsark, they were spreading their wings and heading off to an uncertain future.

The mages looked out the back, waving to family, friends, and the few colleagues that cared enough to wave them off. Whitlaw Goddard was there of course, standing beside Wilfred Berkhoff. And old Jim, in dusty overalls, a broom in one hand and a smoking pipe in the other, which he lifted in salute.

Off to one side, mounted on a fine black warhorse that any armoured knight would covet, was the hierarch's battlemage in her crimson robes and sinister golden mask. The woman's cold eyes scoured them, and one by one they fell silent under the weight of her regard, cowed until Fort Newsark was visible only by its many plumes of smoke.

It was seven hours journey to Abelin Castle on foot at a reasonable pace, or what felt like ten on a wagon thumping up and down and side to side along rutted tracks.

The first part of the journey was unremarkable, passing through the narrow lanes of Newsark, where decrepit wooden buildings leaned precariously over the street at alarming angles, like slowly toppling drunkards. Warriors marched ahead of them to secure the route, kicking sullen riffraff and squawking traders and their blankets strewn with oddments off the cobbled streets.

"This is intolerable," Guylan griped as they juddered over the cobbles. He shifted his seating, unable to find comfort.

Ella couldn't help but laugh. "Now you know how I felt every day."

"Really?" he asked, appalled. "I had no idea it was this bad."

"Better with this chair than the old one," she admitted, stretching to pat her shiny new wheels.

Guylan and Jackan began a spirited discussion about how to improve the wagons, the basic design of which had barely changed in centuries. The two engineers were still going strong, the construction costs climbing ever higher, as the caravan left the town behind and passed though outlying hamlets and fields of crops. Tanned and weathered farmers were hard at work in muddy fields bringing in the autumn harvest of cabbage, turnip, carrot, and onions, loading them onto baskets borne off by their children. As soon as a child could walk, they had to work, and even the littlest carried their fair share of the produce.

Farm folk lifted sweaty hands to shade their eyes from the sun as they turned curious eyes towards the caravan and its escort. Escaping their labours for a moment, children raced barefoot through the fields alongside the lurching wagons, waving and squealing.

"Shall we give them a little show?" Ella said to Katherine.

They drew on their aether and sent balls of coloured light and birds of blue smoke out from the back of the wagon to whizz around the fields, delighting in the joy of the children as they tried in vain to catch the sparkling spells.

The happy sounds cut off as the masked rider turned back from the front of the caravan. The older children knew what crimson robes and a golden mask meant, and their sudden fear confused and stilled their younger siblings.

"Return to your work," the battlemage boomed, her voice cold and dead, like the heart inside her fancy robes.

The terrified children scattered.

Those disapproving eyes turned on Ella and Katherine, who swallowed and sank back into their seats, eyes downcast.

"No more magic unless we are under attack," the battlemage stated, then rode on ahead.

Ella waited until she was sure the battlemage was back at the front of the caravan before speaking up. "Do you think she was born from an egg, or do they undergo some arcane process that sucks all the joy out of normal humans?"

The battlemage's voice emerged from behind Ella's left ear: "I can still hear you, Ella Pickering. We shall discuss your questions and your lack of decorum once we arrive at our destination."

Ella yelped and looked around wildly, then her face grew red as she realised the woman had left a scrying spellform behind.

The others stared at her horrified expression for a long moment, then their lips trembled, trying to restrain their laughter. Guylan broke the tableau, unable to control himself. "You are in deep shit," he said, then broke into uproarious guffaws, infecting the others with his mirth.

Ella sat there red-faced and fuming, arms crossed and eyes like thunder.

"Let that be a lesson to us all," said Jackan as their laughter subsided. "Watch what you say and where you say it; you never know when the enemy might be spying on you." His words had a sobering effect – they knew he didn't just mean the Empire. The attention of the hierarchs was upon them all.

The rest of the journey was a quiet affair. What had been a joyous, exuberant exploration of the arcane arts suddenly seemed a deathly dangerous endeavour with the iron fist of the hierarchs tightening around them.

The caravan rattled over a timeworn fortified bridge spanning a rocky gorge. Chilly black waters churned to foam and mist far, far below. A dozen guards and guardian golems waited on the far side, weapons ready, while the flustered young mage in charge checked the caravan's credentials.

Jackan craned his head out of their carriage. He watched the poor sod, faced with the golden mask of a battlemage, fumble the orders scroll. His hands were shaking so violently he almost dropped it to the dirt. A snatch and a save, and he managed to avoid complete humiliation. He couldn't give it back to the battlemage fast enough, hastily waving the caravan onwards.

The Research and Design team waved to the bemused guards as they passed through the gate, busy rolling their eyes at their young leader leaning on a wall mopping his brow.

"At least I wasn't quite that flustered," Ella said, eying their surroundings as if she could detect sorcerous eavesdroppers by sight alone.

Guylan's eyebrows climbed and he smirked. "Entirely correct. You were indeed far more composed… when you insulted her directly."

Ella's lips thinned. She glared at her colleague until his smile fell away.

They took greater care over their words and made small talk as the caravan climbed and descended a series of small hillocks, then wound its way along a sinuous old trackway dotted with quarry sites gouged into the stone.

"Is that our castle?" Katherine said, hanging out to peer at a dark shape cresting the hill they were ascending.

The terrain flattened out to a wide hilltop that seemed suitable for launching the Fire Dragon. A dark stone keep atop its high grassy motte became more distinct, followed by the crenellated battlements of the bailey below the mound, its walls encompassing fifteen good-sized buildings. The motte and bailey style of castle was an old and obsolete fortification, one that in the past had been mostly built using logs and wood, but somebody had clearly been told to enhance it, rather than bother building a new fortification from scratch. The walls were unmarked grey stone, thrown up – or grown up – by a team of mages with extensive earth-moving experience, and a substantial moat had been dug into the bedrock around the fortress.

The battlemage rode ahead to talk to the archers stationed on the wall at either side of the lowered drawbridge. After a very brief exchange of credentials, the gate swung open to admit their caravan.

The wagons crossed the moat and drew up in the centre of the bailey, an open staging area circled by newly constructed dwellings and workshops.

"Welcome to Abelin Castle," Jackan said sourly. "Looks like a right fun place." He surveyed the dozen or so people present: ten grizzled and disgruntled guards, a wide-shouldered blacksmith, and a young apprentice – the blacksmith's son, by the look of the boy. "Doesn't look like many folk here. Guess the hierarch wants this kept real quiet."

As the team disembarked and gathered their personal belongings, the battlemage walked down the line, barking orders and directing the newcomers to their assigned stations. When the golden-masked mage came to the Research and Design team, she pointed to various sturdy stone-walled and slate-roofed buildings one by one. "Forge. Four workshops. Construction barn. Barracks. Kitchen. Bakery. Stable. Storeroom. Two smaller buildings to be used however you see fit. One house for the blacksmith and baker. One house for the overseer who will be your liaison with His Grace, Hierarch Grubman-Lordrach IV. There is a small temple located on the second floor of the keep along the north wall, where you may offer your prayers."

Ella looked up at the keep, perched high on its steep, grassy motte with a hundred steps leading up. "Um. Where, exactly, are our living quarters?"

The battlemage looked down on her. There was a notable pause as the cogs in her mind turned, and then she looked at the steep hill leading to the keep. Ella had the distinct impression the woman was scowling behind her mask. "Requisition one of the smaller buildings and have beds brought down while you modify your chair with crystal-powered levitation runes. Unless you would rather use crutches? No? Very well, follow me."

The team followed her to the building she had pointed out as the storeroom. There was no keyhole in the heavy wooden door, just a black glass plate.

"The doors have been set to admit only those bearing the correct tattoos," the battlemage explained. "Mage Jackan Grissom, please present your right hand."

The old engineer pressed his hand to the cold glass plate. The tattoo on the back of his hand glowed blood-red for a moment, and then the door clicked open to reveal a wealth of metal bars, cases of arcane crystals, and all manner of hideously expensive equipment.

They stared. They stared hard. It was more than enough to outfit several workshops with the very latest magical and mundane tools from Orialis. Fitting Ella's chair with powered levitation runes would not even make a dent in their inventory.

The masked mage studied them. "Is this suitable for your needs?"

After a moment's lingering shock, they nodded mutely.

The representative of the hierarch closed the door. "Follow me to the forge."

Hammering died off as the burly, balding blacksmith outside downed tools and stood straight and proud as they approached. The shaggy-haired boy by his side was still to come into his full growth, but it was evidence he would be every bit as bullish as his father in a year or two. Smoke was already rising from the chimney of the forge. He'd wasted no time in getting to work, doing what needed to be done in the castle without needing to be asked.

To everybody's surprise, the battlemage nodded in respect. "This is Master Smith Borman."

The man wiped sooty fingers on his apron and stuck out a hand.

Jackan stepped forward to take it, his hand enveloped by the big man's calloused, fire-scarred paw. "Good to meet you, Master Smith."

Borman's eyes crinkled in amiable amusement. "Good ta meet ya. Now here is a man used to working with his hands, Anders." The boy nodded nervously.

"I'm an engineer," Jackan explained. "I used to build bridges and the like before the war. Now, I suppose, we mostly build weapons."

The blacksmith nodded. Then turned his attention on the others, enthusiastically shaking their hands – and their entire bodies, if he wasn't careful.

He whistled at Ella's chair. "That's a fine bit of work you have there."

Jackan's eyes lit up. Ella and Katherine exchanged knowing glances, and made their excuses to leave before the old engineer launched into a full-fledged discussion with the like-minded soul.

Together, the two women claimed one of the smaller houses, finding the doorway just wide enough for Ella's chair. The furnishings seemed basic but well-made, and the walls were bare stone, freshly whitewashed.

"It's not ideal," Ella said, "but with a little help, it won't take me long to make the adjustments I need."

Katherine wrinkled her nose at it. "Are you sure? This is all a bit grim."

"I'm used to far worse," Ella assured her, studying the ceiling and the walls and finding not a speck of rot or mould. In truth, this was luxury to her. Her own bed on a raised wooden frame, sturdy and unbroken. A fireplace and the fuel for it meant an end to nights huddled under old blankets. Plenty of storage, and all of it without layer upon layer of soot, grime and various bodily fluids accumulated over years of grubby occupants.

"I had best stay here with you until we modify your chair," Katherine added, testing the shutters on the windows and examining the locking mechanism on the door. Just in case. You know… because of all the scary, scarred men."

Ella shook her head, a wry smile on her lips. Her friend would not have survived a single night in her old flophouse without sturdy doors or guards around every corner, having to keep a crutch ready to crack some skulls. Her chair clacked over smooth flagstone, and she took a series of deep breaths.

Katherine sniffed the air. "What's wrong? Do you smell something bad?"

"Quite the reverse," Ella said, sighing. She closed her eyes and inhaled the subtle aroma of wood and whitewash. This would do just fine.

CHAPTER 21

The battlemage departed the very next morning, riding out into the wilderness alone to carry out her master's will, leaving them safely guarded by stout stone walls, guardian golems, and heavily armoured men. The team watched her leave, pitying any poor fools that might dare to get in her way.

"I'm glad to see the back of her," Ella muttered once she was out of sight. "Sour old witch."

Jackan chuckled, nudging Rojer in the ribs. "The lass got on the battlemage's bad side right enough."

"From the very beginning, too," Guylan added. "A most magnificent achievement even for you, Ella. You truly have a knack for pissing off people in power."

She scowled at him, vowing to pay his flippancy back threefold. "Katherine, come help me sort out our documents. You three big burly men can lug all the heavy stuff into the workshops."

The team busied themselves with sorting out the supplies and materials brought over from Fort Newsark, inventorying the bounty inside the storeroom, and planning the layout and functions of their new workspaces while touring the area within the walls.

"Look at this little lot," Ella gasped, eyes wide as she took in the crates and baskets of goods. "They really did provide every piece of the rare and expensive equipment we requested."

Guylan salivated over having an entire arcane engineering workshop of their very own, just waiting to be assembled and configured. "Oh, how nice it is to have a wealthy patron."

"Aye, until they have no more use for us," Jackan grumbled. "Ach, let's check out the forge." He chuckled. "Maybe they really got us a dragon so we can make steel that'll hold enchantments."

One-eyed Rojer stepped aside. "I'll leave all that scholarly squealing to you lot of scrollworms; I'm going to stretch my legs awhile." He wandered off, leaving the others to explore the site.

Inside the smithy, massive banks of metal bellows used magically compressed air to keep the coals burning hot and bright. "Holy moon," Ella gasped, staring at an actual, real-life pony-sized dragon shackled to the forge beside a massive black anvil. "A dragon-forge! For gods' sake, they really did get us a dragon." The red-scaled beast with stubby horns and vestigial wings was a sad shadow of its mighty ancestors. Its kind had been originally hatched from the small, rejected eggs kicked out of their mother's mountain nests, and further bred by mages over generations to become dull and docile beasts of industry. These lazy dragons were more than happy to exchange food for the use of their aether-infused flame. The steel they helped forge carried a sorcerous strength unmatched by the mundane skill of mortals – the why or how of it, nobody had yet discovered; all they knew was that it worked.

"This here is Red Bess," Master Smith Borman said, scratching the squat dragon behind the horns. It closed its golden eyes and rumbled in pleasure. "She'll help me make whatever you need."

"Can I touch her?" Ella asked.

The big smith's shoulders rose and fell. "Just don't get your fingers near her mouth or she'll have them off."

Ella wheeled closer, hand outstretched.

A golden eye opened to regard her with indifference.

Hesitant fingers stroked her scales. "They are so smooth," she murmured. "And hot." The beast rumbled approval and leaned into Ella's hand as she stroked with greater force. One eye started to twitch, and the smith quickly drew her hand back. "Gets right snappy when she's overexcited."

"Let us move on before Ella gets too attached," Katherine said, rolling her eyes at her friend.

In addition to the dragon-forge, elsewhere in the castle grounds they discovered a summoning chamber, a scrying room, an alchemy lab, and a surprisingly extensive library. They were well stocked – almost overwhelmingly so. There would be a few weeks of sorting, arranging, sawing, and lugging pieces of equipment about before they could even think about resuming work on their project.

Ella's experience with magical eavesdropping in the wagon had given them all a healthy dose of paranoia, and – apart from Rojer Glenn, who was still unaware of certain illicit goals – they had made a pact never to mention the true purpose of the project until the room had been thoroughly swept for scrying spellforms.

Two days after the departure of the battlemage, the castle's overseer finally arrived on the back of a wagon loaded down with grain, flour, and, best of all – according to Jackan, Rojer and every one of the guards – beer barrels. The overseer, also appointed by the hierarch, was a fine-featured, middle-aged woman with shoulder-length greying hair, a jovial grin, and deep hazel eyes that peered at them through thick spectacle lenses. The woman was wearing, of all things, an eye-wateringly bright yellow and purple dress crowded with lace floral embellishments. There was not a whiff of aether about her, but she clearly came from a wealthy background if she could afford dyes and dress designs so exquisitely awful.

"Hello, my good fellows!" she cried, leaping off the vehicle. She strode over to meet Jackan, clasping his hand in a firm grip. "Mage Jackan Grissom, I presume. Marvellous to meet you. I have been told you are inventing amazing new things for the Unity, and I will do my utmost to see that the day-to-day running of this place proceeds smoothly."

The old engineer cleared his throat, quite bowled over by her enthusiasm for a remote post way out here in the back of beyond. "Ach, well, I'm sure we are lucky to have you here, Ms..."

"Lucid," she stated. "Overseer Lucid."

Jackan's gaze dipped to her left hand, which bore no ring, nor the finger tattoos they used instead in the far north.

She noted his investigation, and a smile quirked her lips. Dark eyes peered over the rim of her glasses at him. "That is forward indeed, my good fellow."

His cheeks flushed as he foisted her off on somebody else. "This is Guylan."

The woman's eyes lingered on their leader a little too long for his ease before fixing on the younger engineer. "Ah, yes, a distinguished First Circle graduate of the Orialis Guild of Mages," she said, shaking his hand. "A fine achievement, indeed, one I believe you share with your colleague here." She nodded to Katherine, who shyly offered only a little wave of greeting.

"We do share a healthy love of knowledge," Guylan admitted, his chest puffed out ever-so-slightly.

Rojer Glenn stepped forward and their hands slapped together, holding firm. "Rojer."

"Quite the service record you have," she replied. "An accomplished skymage wounded in battle, now a combat mage. I had not expected to see your like on a project run by the Research and Design Workshop."

The one-eyed man shrugged and withdrew. "Strange winds blow in all sorts, eh."

Lucid turned to Ella. "And this must be Mage Pickering. I must admit I was surprised when I read through your service record. Interesting. Most interesting."

Ella gritted her teeth, steady as a rock as she met the woman's gaze. Her days of cowering and cringing were gone. "I'm good at what I do."

Lucid chuckled. "Of that I have no doubt. Not many can boast of destroying a hierarch's personal property and surviving the experience." She made a show of glancing around to ensure none of the guards were within earshot, then she winked. "Between us, Hierarch Deva-Mokaren III is a dreadful bore, and that carriage was a crime against art."

Ella stared. "Coming from a hierarch's appointed overseer, this is… unexpected, to say the least."

Lucid smiled. "It costs nothing to be both competent and agreeable. I am satisfied with my own abilities, so I feel no need to demean those in my charge to make myself feel superior." She tapped the wheel of Ella's chair with a fingernail. "May I say what a marvellous wheeled chair you have? I have never seen its like." She looked to Jackan. "Perchance, is this one of your constructions?"

The old engineer smiled and nodded, taking pride in a job well done.

Overseer Lucid looked from Ella's chair to the stone keep perched on its high mound, and the many steps leading up. She frowned and tutted. "I see the battlemage and her attendants have prepared this with their usual thoughtlessness." She coughed into her hand. "Pardon me. The dust of travel must be in my throat. I meant to say thoroughness." She exchanged a knowing smile with Ella. "It seems I have more work on my plate than I thought."

The overseer waved to the guards offloading the wagon she arrived on. "That chest is mine! Please carry it to…" She turned back to Ella. "Which of the buildings is for my use?"

"Um. That one has been set aside for you," the young mage replied, pointing her towards the twin of the one she and Katherine had claimed.

"Thank you kindly," Lucid replied. "Well, I shall excuse myself and head off to unpack and settle into this cosy new home of ours. I hope to get to know you all a little better in the coming weeks and I am very much looking forward to helping you to create the very best project possible."

She headed off, leaving the team somewhat spell-shocked by her whirlwind appearance.

"That woman is not what I imagined of an overseer," Guylan said.

"I like her," Ella stated. "She has spirit."

Rojer's eyes trailed after the woman. He scratched his chin thoughtfully.

"What is it?" Jackan asked him.

The ex-skymage shook his head. "Too good to be true, maybe."

"On the other hand," Jackan countered, "perhaps we just got lucky. Nobody is perfect. Who knows, the woman could be downing a jar of wine every night. She might seem nice enough now, but I wager that one has a fierce temper if you cross her."

Rojer shook it off. "You are likely right. Ah, well, it's not like we can change anything. She has a hierarch's ear, and probably for a reason."

Jackan found that a sobering thought.

"Just as well we're a legitimate project, eh, team," Rojer said, slapping him on the shoulder. "Probably here to keep an eye on us as much as help – why, I've worked with some terrible frauds in my time, and…" his words faded as he caught an undercurrent of tension in the air as the rest of his team froze, looking guilty as a murderer caught red-handed. "Something I should know?"

Jackan looked back at his team. Ella and Guylan nodded while Katherine remained silent, chewing on her lower lip.

"Er, about that," The old engineer replied. "We need to have a serious talk. Somewhere private…"

Rojer's face was an expressionless mask as they led him into the stone building they had chosen as their main workshop. He stood in stony silence staring at Jackan while Guylan checked the place for eavesdropping spells.

"Clear," the young engineer said, his tone uneasy.

The one-eyed mage noted the discomfort in the rest of his team and scowled. "Now, can you tell me what in the blazes this is all about? What have you done?"

"You might want to take a seat," Jackan advised.

He remained standing and crossed his arms. "I'm fine as I am."

Jackan cleared his throat and then told the man everything. The initial accident. The research and their wildly ambitious new goal…

Rojer Glenn thumped down into the nearest chair behind a worktop, scrutinising each of them in turn: Katherine nervously hidden behind her veil of hair, Ella's unashamed stubbornness as she met his gaze, Guylan's weary acceptance, and then, finally, Jackan's mix of excitement and knowledge of just how damned they would be even if they succeeded.

"The moon?" Rojer said. "You really want to spend our resources on setting foot in the Garden of the Gods themselves? This is truly not a bad joke?"

"It's not," Ella supplied. "This is very real." She retrieved some of her papers from their chests and handed it over. "We are far from finished, but we believe we can go where nobody has gone before."

Rojer smoothed the papers out on the worktop and studied the diagrams and calculations of trajectories and speeds taking them from muddy earth to holy silver moon. Many of the workings were familiar to him, being a former skymage, but some had been invented by Katherine, Guylan, and Ella working on mathematics cobbled together from overlooked occult knowledge, gleaned from the writings of wise sages and the ramblings of mad mages alike.

"There's still a lot we don't know," Ella added. "And a lot we don't even know that we don't know. But we aim to find out, and then we'll build a Fire Dragon to take us to the moon." She glanced down at her wheels and winced. "Some of us, at least."

A sigh escaped Rojer's lips. He set the papers down and rubbed a hand over his bald scalp. "Chief Goddard knows nothing of this, does he?" His eyes fastened on Katherine and he shook his head. "His own daughter, too."

Katherine found her voice. Quivering though it was, she was determined to be heard. She swept back her hair and met his gaze. "This is important work, and he would have stopped us."

His fist pounded the tabletop. "Gods-damned right he would have!"

Rojer stabbed a grimy finger in Jackan's direction. "Why are you dragging these youngsters into such an unholy mess? This heresy will have them dangling from a rope around their necks."

Jackan blanched. "I told them all that myself."

"I blackmailed my way onto the team," Katherine blurted.

Rojer stared at the younger mage, lips working but finding no appropriate words for a reply. He turned to Ella. "And your excuse?"

She shrugged. "I spent two seasons in a flophouse bed recovering from my accident, and then two more rotting on the production line, drowning in debt. Anything is better than that. Like Jackan, I'm heartsick of this accursed war, and I want to help make something good."

The one-eyed mage pursed his lips, thinking. After a moment, he nodded to Guylan. "And you? Didn't think you were the type to hitch your wagon to this sort of nonsense."

The younger mage considered that. "I am not. Two things have me standing here. First: much of this project is perfectly applicable to military use – the last stage of reaching the moon is simply a step or three further than that would require, and I could technically feign illness and drop out before that point. Second: how often do you get a chance to make history?" He looked around at his colleagues. "If we manage to pull this off, we will be remembered and venerated as long as people exist."

"A glory hound?" Rojer scoffed. "They will execute you before you ever see a shred of reward."

To his surprise, Guylan shrugged. "What of it? My name will still go down in history. I will have made a difference."

The older mage scratched his head, scowling. "Jackan. A crusty old bastard like you should have more sense. Why are you allowing this?"

The old engineer slumped into a nearby chair. "I am sick of making weapons," he said simply. He sounded heartfelt and bone-tired of it all. "I derived infinitely more satisfaction from constructing the most humble of bridges than all the weapons that have ever come out of the Research and Design Workshop. I want to leave something grand to the world before I go. Everybody is so wrapped up in this never-ending, grinding conflict that our dreams of anything better are smothered under the fearmongering domination of the hierarchs." He looked Rojer in the eye, his determination building. "I want to shock the world out of its stupor and make them all watch as we stride across the moon to confront the gods themselves and ask why they allow this butchering war to continue. Some may call it heresy to confront the gods, but to be frank, I'm tired of all the shit spouting from the lips of priests and hierarchs alike."

Everybody stared at Jackan, eyes wide.

"Well, fuck me," Rojer said in wonder. "You are all mad bastards." The veteran mage paused, thinking hard. "I suppose… so long as you all know you are risking your necks… Ah, gods damn it; it's not like I have any family left – I do believe I'm in too." He stretched out a hand and a surprised Jackan shook it.

"So," Rojer said, grinning wickedly. "How can I help?"

CHAPTER 22

It took a full two months just to unpack all their materials and set up workshops from scratch, requiring more manual labour, sawing, and hammering than the sweaty team of scholars were comfortable with. But some things could not be left to the burly warriors stationed in the castle – many of their delicate pieces of arcane apparatus cost more than one of them would earn in years. Another month galloped past as they assembled and arranged, constructed, and inscribed the appropriate safety and scrying wards that would protect them from accidental explosions, smoke inhalation, and eavesdropping spies. It was an exacting, and laborious business that absolutely could not be rushed.

During a rare day off, Guylan finished making a new book bracelet and presented it to Ella, showing her how to add tiny pages of runes to create a portable rune reference library of her very own, beginning with variations of levitation runes and their component parts. She swiftly discovered how much time she'd been losing going to and from the reference tomes and vowed to repay the favour someday. Jackan didn't seem impressed, which pleased Guylan all the more.

Finally, just as winter's frigid winds arrived to howl past the fortress walls, they were ready to resume full project development, with Rojer Glenn providing much-needed practical experience to supplement Ella's more limited skymage training.

The Mark IV Fire Dragon was constructed using preternaturally light and strong sheets of dragon-forged steel around a wooden frame. When fully assembled, the vessel would stand at an impressive height: twenty times that of a tall man. Ella and Katherine talked the older mage through every aspect of the device's construction and piloting, and the results of the recent launch of an imp into the void between worlds.

The ex-skymage sat for a while, sorting all this new knowledge in his head. "Guylan?" he asked. "Are you really going to strap yourself into this deathtrap?"

The younger mage scrubbed fingers through his short, dark hair. "I volunteered, actually." He looked over the Fire Dragon. "Er, well, not this exact version, to be clear. Something a little further down the line."

Rojer rubbed his eye and looked on dubiously as they explained the changes they wanted to make for the final version of the Mark IV: some for safety reasons, and some to accommodate human passengers – or a war golem, if the overseer were to ask.

"And this stinking little imp claimed there was no breathable air up there at all?" he asked the team. "I wouldn't trust a bloody demon as far as I could throw a horse, but even if you assume it's true, what exactly are you intending to do about that thorny little issue?"

Jackan grinned. "I have a plan…"

The team, aided by a few of the friendlier warriors they'd went into No Man's Land with, spent two weeks outside in harsh winter weather rigging up scaffolding, netting, and ropes across the moat to facilitate the lowering of a life-sized mock-up of the capsule that Guylan would be riding into the airless void beyond the borders of this world. In truth, it was little more than a huge, sealed metal barrel with a couple of small porthole windows and a chair inside, but it was enough for a practical test: submerging it under water.

Several days after completion, a storm blew past, driving rain scouring the castle, and howling winds keeping the huddled occupants awake. In the morning, the winds dwindled, and the rain softened to a damp but constant low hiss, allowing the team of mages to assemble outside at the moat.

Katherine wiped the cold drip from her nose and studied the construction as she nervously waited to board. The metal cylinder was suspended by a net above the moat, the brown and muddy water currently occupied by two opportunistic ducks – or, as the guards called them, the emergency food supply. A system of weights and pulleys had been set up to lower the capsule into the water, with Jackan and Ella ready to levitate rocks into the attached nets to submerge it.

"Up you get, then," Jackan said, his head bowed under a wide-brimmed straw hat that kept off the worst of the rain.

Katherine steeled her nerves and lurched across the netting to Guylan, who stood beside the capsule with the hatch door open in his hand. She offered him a worried smile as she peeled off her sodden cloak and climbed down into the uncomfortably tiny space, settling into the heavily padded chair designed to host Guylan on his ascent to the stars.

She took a glow-crystal from her belt pouch, whispered the activation words and locked it into a tiny cage set into the wall in front of her. She would have preferred a lantern, but naked flames inside a sealed metal can packed full of explosive fuel seemed like a terrible idea. As it would be on the launch day, so would it be during this test.

"Are you ready?" Guylan asked. "It is not too late for me to take your place."

She shook her head. "You have the more dangerous task by far. This is nothing, in comparison, and it's only for an hour. Proceed."

With the hatch still open, Jackan and Ella began levitating rocks into the netting on the sides until half the capsule was under water.

"Any leaks?" Guylan queried, peering down at her. One last check before he sealed her in.

Katherine surveyed the points where metal had been joined by artifice and magic, then the edges of the thick glass plates that would eventually allow Guylan to view their home from the void between worlds. For now, they showed only murky brown water. "All good so far." She swallowed the lump in her throat. "Seal me in."

He nodded and manoeuvred the hatch door into place. It thumped shut, edges of gummed leather squishing into what they hoped would be an airtight seal. Outside, a wooden mallet hammered the door in tighter. She felt a tingle of aether as

Guylan secured it further – Jackan had judged it shouldn't be necessary, but they were taking no chances.

On the inside, Katherine turned the locking beam to secure the hatch and knocked thrice on the hull to signal her readiness. She was locked in, entirely unable to escape early without resorting to the use of magic, and could now only sit there, waiting, thinking. Her fears deepened as the capsule lurched back into swaying motion, slowly sinking beneath the water as rocks dragged it down. She had felt calm before the door was sealed, but now that an easy exit proved impossible, her heart pounded and some primal panic raised its ugly head. She took deep breaths and focused on the task.

The windows turned entirely dark, accompanied by a blubbing sound as trapped air rose to the surface in a flurry of silvery bubbles. It was a relief when her prison finally settled in the mud at the bottom of the moat. Then all was silent.

Katherine lifted her glow-crystal and studied the seals on the door and windows, heartened at the absence of glistening water, or indeed a torrent. She listened, but there was no dripping or bubbling of escaping air. The engineers had done their work well.

This capsule was a tight, cramped affair, just large enough to accommodate one adult human, a few tools, and a small waterskin. She didn't have anything to do once her checks were finished, so she sat back into the chair and gazed out of the tiny windows of thick glass, trying to imagine how it would feel to see the moon and stars through them instead of moat muck. After a while, that lost its novelty, and she regretted not bringing any texts to fill the dead time.

Her introspection was interrupted by a sudden urge to urinate.

"Ah. We have forgotten something vital," she said, her voice sounding tinny in the confined space. There had been no provision made at all for those particular human needs, and Guylan would be in one of these capsules for far longer than the duration of this little test. He would need a bucket for his business. She would just have to hold it until the experiment had run its course and then chide the engineers for neglecting something so fundamental. Their heads were too far up in the clouds.

She became aware of a stuffiness in the capsule – it was growing noticeably harder to breathe, akin to very slow suffocation. Jeff had told them the air had gone bad even before it was sucked out into the void, and now she had evidence that the imp had spoken the truth.

But why? She asked herself as she breathed in and out. There was enough air. It hadn't gone anywhere. She pondered the problem and recalled the tales of miners dying, choked to death in the depths of the earth by bad air, or burnt in mysterious explosions. Mages had never got to the bottom of why some bad air burned when exposed to naked flames, and this peril had once been thought a curse. Lately, it had been linked to entirely natural but deadly gases seeping through minerals in the earth, though that particular cause did not apply here. It was known to the sages that the lungs digested air and turned it into life, but in here, it was as if all the good air in the small space was being used up.

Her chest rose and fell and rose, faster and faster with a swelling fear as the sensation of being suffocated settled around her throat and brought a fogginess to her thoughts.

She summoned all her willpower and her aether and shouted a charm to clean the air. It had served her well in eradicating smoke and bad smells from her alchemy rooms, but here it did nothing at all. Her chest still heaved for every inadequate breath.

She couldn't catch her breath. Found it hard to think…

"Experiment. Over," she wheezed.

The initial panic of being trapped surged back to the fore, and she snapped. She clawed at the hatch, yanking at the locking bar, trying to shove it open. It refused to give.

She summoned her magic and screamed a simple spell at the hatch, transforming aether into brutal crushing force.

Metal screeched and wood shattered. The side of the capsule exploded outwards in a torrent of muddy water. For a moment, she glimpsed grey sky and castle wall. Then the icy water flooded back in, shocking her and slamming her to the floor with irresistible power.

She managed to gasp a blessed breath and held it as the frigid water buffeted her.

The sudden inflow calmed, and she reached, blind and battered, to pull herself out.

She never got the chance.

Bands of force wrapped around her and yanked her out, coughing and spluttering, into glorious fresh air. Nothing had ever tasted sweeter.

"Katherine!" somebody shouted.

"Are you hurt?" another cried.

"Can you hear us?" a woman asked. Ella…

Katherine groaned a vague response, her feet kicking the air.

Rojer Glenn's hand was outstretched towards her. With a gesture, his magic deposited her onto solid ground where her friends rushed to the shivering woman's aid.

She doubled over, hacking up filthy water and gulping in air as a warm blanket wrapped around her shoulders.

"Let's… not do that again… anytime soon…" she coughed, her heart rate slowing.

Ella patted her back, trying to help. "What happened?"

"Bad air," Katherine replied. "Felt like I used it all up."

"That damned imp was right," Jackan admitted. "This will be a huge problem. You weren't even in there for a half an hour."

She glanced up at him, peeling away curtains of sopping dark hair. "And we want to send Guylan up there for much longer."

The young engineer shuddered. "We can work out that problem later. Let's get you dry and sitting by the fire with a nice mug of hot tea."

Ella and Guylan led Katherine off to rest and recover while Jackan and Rojer retrieved the mock-up capsule from the moat.

They turned the cranks, hauling up the nets and its damaged cargo.

Rojer whistled at the rent metal and shattered wood. "For a softly spoken girl, she sure does pack a hefty punch."

"Ach, she has more iron in her than she gives herself credit for," Jackan replied. "She takes after her father there. Why, he could've… well, that's not my tale to tell. I'm just glad the girl had sense enough to escape before it was too late." He worked his magic, grunting with the effort of shifting the capsule onto the dirt and rolling it until it was hatch-down.

Dirty water gushed out as the engineer bent down to examine the inside of the capsule. "When I was just a wee thing, it was a right cold winter and the neighbouring cottage decided to pack up their chimney against the cold. My da warned them it was a bad idea – he said it would keep the bad spirits from escaping – but they didn't listen." He prodded a curl of good steel, blasted open by Katherine's magic. "We found them the next week dead in their beds with not a wound on them."

"You are claiming this was due to bad spirits?" Rojer asked, eyebrow raised.

Jackan chuckled. "Nah, nothing that understandable. I've heard stories since, of cooking fires in small rooms and caves killing folk when there's not enough air... like it eats up the good air to help make heat."

They stared at the capsule in silence for a moment.

Rojer hummed in annoyance. "If we use up the goodness in the air, just like a fire, then what replenishes it? What turns bad air back to good?"

Jackan shrugged. "The gods, maybe? As good a guess as any. Anyways, best we get this back and get a new door fitted. Going to be another test once we hash the theory of this problem out."

Master Smith Borman watched from the wall as they dragged the broken contraption back inside the castle grounds for repair.

The warrior beside him scratched his arse and sniffed. "That lot are a bunch of nutters, if you ask me. You know what they are up to down there?"

Borman snorted. "Haven't the faintest idea. They aren't likely to tell the likes of us now, are they."

Unseen by any from below, he slipped a tiny scroll into the warrior's belt pouch.

The man offered no reaction. His job was not to ask too many questions, just to drop messages in specific places whenever he went out hunting for rabbits and deer.

"A list of materials used," the blacksmith said. "And what we know about that thing."

The warrior nodded. "Some extra coin coming our way, then."

"I bloody well hope so."

"Me and you," the warrior said. "We have to look after our families back home as best we can."

Borman clapped a hand on his mailed shoulder, and then returned to his forge, where his son was waiting for him, disapproval writ large across his face.

His son was no idiot. He knew what was going on.

"Father," the boy asked, "why do you pass information to the E–"

Borman shot a deathly glare. "Hsst! Fool of a boy! Keep your mouth shut if you can't speak sense. You never know who might be listening." He checked the area and sat his son down, speaking low and quiet.

"We're borderlanders, boy. Root and stem, blood and bone. In this damn war, poor farmers and crofters are the first to suffer and the first to die by the swords and magic of either side. If we offer them gits a little sugar now and again to keep them sweet, they will look right on past our villages and our kin and aim their accursed weapons elsewhere."

They boy looked unconvinced. "That's treason."

"Only a little bit," his father replied. "Just titbits of information on new weapons and strange events. Not anything they wouldn't discover for themselves in a few months. 'Sides, folks on the other side of the border are doing the exact same thing with our lot, so it evens out, in my eyes."

"What about these research mages?"

Borman grimaced. "Not hurting them now, are we. They'll finish whatever they are making and then piss off home to their big fancy houses. No harm done, if you ask me."

Three days later, a message scroll containing details of the team's work and a list of materials used was winging its way over No Man's Land to the spymasters of the Empire, and hence to Komissar Taeban Tereshkova.

CHAPTER 23

Jackan's face was stone as he gazed into the depths of the crystal ball. "Cousin," he said in a gravelly voice.

Wilfred Berkhoff's face smiled back at him. "Well, well, if it isn't my long-lost kinsman. To what do I owe the pleasure?"

The engineer's right cheek ticced. "Katherine advised me to contact you regarding our team's summoning requirements."

One eyebrow raised, pointedly. "Oh?"

Jackan took a deep, shuddering breath and launched into a tale of their experiment carried out a week earlier.

Some of the gloating drained from Wilfred's face. "The girl is well?"

"More perturbed by the puzzle of what bad air is than anything else," he replied. "If we understood the root of the problem, then it would be something we could resolve using our spellcraft, but as it is, she thought to consult you on elemental matters."

Wilfred sat back and stroked his beard. "I doubt an air elemental could shed any light on such matters. Those things have wind for brains. That said, I wager one could indeed purify whatever goes wrong with the air in such a confined space. Assuming you could make your requirements understood."

"That would be an enormous help to Katherine," Jackan said. "She will be most grateful for whatever help you can provide."

Wilfred stared at him through the crystal. "Not good enough, cousin. This is *your* team and *your* responsibility. Don't hide behind a youngling." He fell quiet, and the moment stretched, an uncomfortable silence building.

Jackan ground his teeth and forced himself to smile. "*I* would be most grateful for your aid."

"You still owe me money," Wilfred stated.

The smile remained nailed to the old engineer's face. "I do not. You said I could have that cake."

"Not all of it!"

They bickered for a time, flinging old, entrenched accusations in each other's faces. All over the cost of a single honey cake taken over fifty years ago, a minor issue that had gradually grown wings, horns, and venomous fangs.

"Enough!" Jackan snarled. "I'll give you your damned coin and be done with it."

"I will help you under one more condition," Wilfred added, wagging a finger. "You must promise to stay in touch with your extended family. Do we have an agreement?"

His shoulder's slumped, and Jackan loosed a long sigh. "Fine. If that's what it takes."

The summoner nodded. "I will provide you with several single-use summoning crystals – you should be able to test your methods using those. I'll send over my familiar tomorrow."

"That vile imp?" Jackan spat. "Must you?"

"Do you want to wait a week or three for a supply cart to pass through the fort and then trundle over in your direction?" Wilfred asked. "Or would you prefer my winged messenger?"

"Fine, fine," Jackan knew when he was defeated. "Thank you."

The old engineer abruptly cut off the scrying spell before his older cousin drove him past the point of politeness. As he made to leave, a sudden light-headedness stole over him. He slumped into the nearest chair. It took a while to compose himself. He put it down to mental and physical exhaustion after burning the candle at both ends of late. His chest felt tight. He absently rubbed his left arm. The stupid thing had been aching on and off over the last few weeks.

"You're an old man now, Jackan, my lad," he muttered to himself. "Ease up and let the young ones do more of the labour."

He shook off his aches and pains and rose with a groan, then put on a smile before returning to the others to tell them the good news that the experiment was ready to be repeated.

* * *

"Are you sure you want to go into that capsule again?" Ella asked her friend, fussing over the safety gear and the short-range scrying apparatus that was about to be carried into the mock-up with her.

This time, they were leaving nothing to chance, and the moment Katherine indicated something was wrong – or if they lost contact – the whole thing would be hauled back up and the hatch wrenched wide open. In case something was to delay that rescue, she also wore a thick leather diving suit sealed with tar and bearing rudimentary enchantments, ready to become airtight by donning a bulbous brass helmet with a thick glass face plate. Inside a brutally heavy pack on her back was a smaller, heavily modified version of the compressed air bellows used for dragon-forged steel: Jackan and Guylan had fashioned a device that stored air, supported by cleansing arrays and cunning engineering that should – so they hoped – feed enough good air into her helmet and expel the bad to last her until they could get her out. Unfortunately, it was so heavy that it would be impractical to install a larger version for the Mark IV capsule to serve as an emergency backup system.

The dark-haired woman cradled her helmet under one arm. She nodded grimly. "This is my task. I'll play my part in this quest for the moon as best I can."

Ella finished triple-checking the portable scrying tools and the small slice of crystal with silver backing in place of a proper crystal ball. "You're clear to proceed." She handed over a velvet-lined pouch containing a fragile summoning crystal.

Katherine held the pale blue gem to her eye and examined the smoke drifting through a seemingly solid interior: an air elemental bound by Wilfred's magic.

Dangling upside down from the capsule's netting and grinning like a happy little shark, Jeff the imp gave her a cheerful wave. "Have fun, my dear girl," it cried. "Try not to die horribly." The creature hissed with laughter, forked tongue running over razor sharp fangs. Jackan and Guylan watched it warily from the earthen bank. Rojer didn't take his eye off the demon. The creature was one poor choice away from the war staff in his hand unleashing its full and deadly power.

Oblivious to the distrust of her fellows, Katherine smiled at the foul little creature and patted its horned head. "I'm not sure we have the same idea of fun. But if this works, it will prove very interesting indeed. I will do my best not to die, but thank you for your concern."

The imp stared at her, inhuman feelings flickering across its mottled red face. It picked at a stubbly black horn with a claw, then popped the squirming pink worm it found there into its maw. "Remember, elementals read feelings and intentions, not words." Jeff stuck his tongue out at Rojer Glenn and then lazily flapped his wings, lifting effortlessly into the air to circle the site.

Katherine climbed into the capsule, set up her glow-crystal, secured the scrying apparatus and adjusted its mouthpiece and copper sheet, then strapped herself into the padded seat. Her helmet hung at her hip, ready to be donned at a moment's notice. This time, there would be no need to lock the door from the inside – the replacement had no such mechanism, since it had only proved an impediment when she'd panicked. The hatch was swiftly secured from the outside and the capsule lowered into the moat once again.

The windows darkened with muddy water, casting the capsule into gloom. She methodically checked that the seals were still airtight. No leaks and no drowning today, praise the gods. She waited for the vessel to reach the bottom, trying to get comfy in the horrible, heavy suit. It smelled like a deceased otter left out in the sun to ripen.

As soon as the capsule settled in the silt and ceased groaning, she laid the pale blue summoning gem on the floor, lifted her foot and shattered it beneath her heel. Warm wind swirled up around her, hair and dust flying as a half-transparent elemental the size of her fist appeared before her.

The smoke inside the crystal formed itself into a miniature whirlwind that would have been fearsome had it been able to lift anything heavier than hair and dust and dry leaves. A spark of lightning throbbed inside its core and the air felt charged, smelling like a crisp autumn evening with a thunderstorm rolling overhead.

"Hello there, little one," she said, smiling down at it. "It is so lovely to meet you. My, what powerful winds you have!"

The elemental's blowing intensified ever-so-slightly.

"Could I ask a tiny boon from you before you return to the elemental plane? Just for a short time."

The winds dipped and rose again, which she hoped meant agreement.

She inhaled and exhaled. "I need this air to live," she explained slowly. "After a while, in this enclosed place, the air goes bad, and I can't live on it. Do you understand me?"

Wind swirled. The elemental gave no indication of understanding.

"This is good air." She inhaled and smiled, thinking nothing but good thoughts. Then she exhaled and frowned, dwelling on the feeling of suffocation from her last adventure. "This is bad air." She repeated it three times until the little summoned creature seemed to gain an inkling of her meaning. It swirled around her face, delicate puffs of air patting her cheeks as she breathed in and out, then it retreated to the front of the capsule and seemed to condense in on itself, becoming a tight ball of swirling dust and vapour.

A metallic screech made her jump. The scrying apparatus flickered into life and the metal plate vibrated, carrying Ella's voice through the aether: "How are things going down there?" A blurry nostril and Ella's staring eye appeared in the silver-backed crystal as she yelled into the mouthpiece.

"Ella… could you please back up a little? And speak a little quieter?"

Ella sat back, still squinting into their counterpart device. "I can barely see you."

"Not much light in here," Katherine replied. "We definitely need more glow-crystals in the real thing."

Peering over Ella's shoulder, Guylan scratched notes onto a slate. "More time-critical, how is the air situation? Have you made any progress with the elemental?"

She glanced down at the puffing, swirling mass of aether-infused air by her feet. "I am not certain it fully understood me, but it is doing… something. I suppose we will find out shortly."

There was little more to do but wait and make regular reports to her team through the scrying device. Eventually, Guylan leaned over Ella to peer into the crystal. "At this stage of the previous experiment you claimed you were experiencing shortness of breath. How do you feel today?"

Katherine took several deep breaths. In response, the little elemental seemed to puff up and swirl harder for a few moments before settling down again.

"I think it's working," she said. "My little friend here is somehow turning the bad air breathable."

The elemental chirped and swirled faster, flashing and roaring like a happy little storm with grand dreams of one day becoming a hurricane.

Guylan's shoulders slumped, and he sighed in relief, the flicker of a very uncertain smile playing about his lips. "That paves the way for me, then. An emergency up in the sky would not have had so easy an escape."

With that realization, being at the bottom of a muddy moat did not seem quite so bad. The thought of floating up there with no air sent a shiver up her spine, but the mission would not be all horror. Katherine sat in the chair, imagining such an incredible sight, aloft beyond the clouds with the stars and moon shining through the windows. After a time, the summoned elemental began to flag, its winds slowing and her breath becoming ever-so-slightly harder the more it slowed. She drew up a little of her aether and offered a thread of her magic to the entity – which sucked it up and chirped in glee, its tiny terrible winds whooshing around her, stirring her hair.

She made a mental note to conduct further experiments, using a sandglass to see how often this class of air elemental would require aether infusions to keep it functioning at peak efficiency. Another thought struck her: she thought it almost certain that the more people there were in a small space, the quicker they would absorb all life from the good air. They would likely require a larger elemental and more aether on the final mission to set foot on the moon.

One problem had found its answer, but from that arose more questions – which could only be called an overall success in the mind of a true scholar.

The work continued at an uneven pace: the drudgery of weeks of mundane research, scroll after scroll of mathematical workings, and the drafting of construction plans that inevitably had to be re-done as they proceeded with their project. This contrasted with the occasional flash of brilliance or sudden revelation that led them down twisting rabbit holes of promising new research, rendering much of what had come before obsolete.

Katherine discovered a dusty old text that recorded dates, times, and heights of tides and waves, matching them to the cycle of the moon. The tome answered some of their speculation on whether the love of the moon would pull them in or reject them. Waves were higher when the moon loomed large in the sky, at a closer stage of its oval orbitus around their world. This wealth of records proved the moon bore love for the body of its much larger mother, exerting a force of attraction the scholar calculated as being roughly in line with the moon's size when compared to the Great Mother: a sixth. Both hard mathematics and the somewhat fuzzier theological and thaumaturgical research agreed on the moon's power being lesser than her mother, and the team adjusted their own calculations accordingly. It would require far less power to return home than they had thought – this meant the third stage of the final Fire Dragon could be made smaller and lighter.

The twice-weekly dinner meetings with Overseer Lucid were somewhat relaxed affairs, with fresh bread, roast meats, fruits, ale, and wine in abundance. She used these events to enquire about their progress and ask what more she could do to aid them. Ella, Katherine, and Guylan were more than happy to chatter away, but after taking Rojer's words of caution to heart, Jackan joined him in holding much of his own thoughts within. It was at their latest meeting when she began asking more barbed questions…

Lucid tipped the green glass bottle upright, pouring the last of her sweet honey wine into Katherine's cup. "May I ask what your water experiments were for?" She set the bottle down and smiled disarmingly. "I thought your project involved golems, not people."

Ella and Katherine stiffened, but Jackan leapt to fill the gap in their defences. "Ach, it does," he said. "That had nowt to do with its human passenger, the kid here was just inside to check if our construction had sprung any leaks."

The castle overseer frowned and casually sipped at her wine. "Leaks?"

"Oh, aye," Jackan said, lounging back into his chair, thinking furiously and trying to hide it. "If one of our capsules were to land in a swamp or a pond, we don't want the whole blasted thing sinking right into the mud before the golems even activate."

"That makes sense," she replied. "It seems there is far more to this project than I had imagined." She flashed a smile. "Lucky I'm not the one having to dream it all up from thin air." She chuckled and reached for another bottle. "More wine?"

The candles burned down as Lucid wined and dined them, asking many more seemingly innocuous questions. Jackan sensed a harder edge creeping in behind her soft words and encouragement. It was all he could do to steer her away from the truth with long-winded tales of researching every angle of their proposed war golem delivery system. As night began to fall, the meeting wound down and they made their excuses to leave. Jackan gathered his team outside and cast a subtle ward against eavesdropping.

"I think the lot o' us should watch how much we drink around that woman," he said, glancing back at the overseer's home.

Rojer nodded. "I trust her about as much as the bastard she serves. She's the hierarch's minion and not our friend; you lot had best remember that."

"Well, that's a sobering thought," Guylan replied. "I dislike all this subterfuge. Necessary evils, I suppose."

Katherine hiccupped loudly, causing them to look at her. It was almost dark, but they had light enough to see the fire of embarrassment blooming across her cheeks.

"Uh, yes, we'll be sure to drink less and watch what we say," Ella added. "Orders acknowledged, Mage Grissom." She offered a sloppy salute, like he was the captain of a grand ship and she a drunken sailor. "Er. I think we'd best be off to bed now." Ella and Katherine headed off, but not to bed.

"I'm sooo bored," Katherine complained as they reached the door. "We've spent every night up late reading dusty old tomes and scrolls by candlelight. I am heartsick of mathematics and the motions of the moon and stars. I want to sing, and dance!"

Ella nudged her and looked up. The air was still and the stars sparkling; the moon was bright and full, a glorious and gleaming disc illuminating the realm of mortals. "Not sure I could ever get sick of that sight. Tell you what: how about you go in, bring out a chair, and we share this bottle I swiped from the overseer's table?" She slipped a bottle of honey wine out from between her back and the chair, and grinned.

Katherine's eyes gleamed as she raced to fetch a seat. They sat outside of their quarters looking at a clear night's sky, passing the bottle back and forth, feeling distinctly fuzzy around the edges from all the drink. It was too nice an evening to cut it short – a few hours away from work and study was just what they needed.

Ella sipped honey wine, savouring the floral sweetness clinging to her tongue. "Somewhere up there in the centre of the Garden of the Gods is the Silver Palace," she said. "Do you think our gods will greet us warmly after travelling so far, or do you think they will be outraged at the trespass?"

Katherine sniffed, already rosy-cheeked. "I must confess I have not given that a single thought. Our family were never terribly pious." She pondered it, staring at the heavens. "What one thing would you ask if you met divine beings?"

Ella ran a numbed tongue around her teeth. "I'd ask why they allow war. So many people dead, and for what? To prove which god is above the others? Look at what a few people can achieve with only a tiny portion of the Unity's resources. Imagine if both the Unity and the Empire instead spent all of that on medical research, engineering, and advancing the arts of magic." She looked to her friend. "There must be some reason behind it, a grand design. Right?"

Katherine could only shrug. "If there is, then it's one far beyond the likes of me. I would probably ask them what else is out there in the void. What are the stars and why do some of them wander? Where do demons and elementals originate? Things that we currently have no good answers for."

"How about the gods themselves?" Ella ventured. "Do you think it'd be blasphemous to ask where they came from? Depending on if you ask a priest inside the Unity or over in the Empire, you'll get different answers – but no mortal can really know the truth of their birth beyond what some crusty old scribe wrote down centuries ago."

They fell into companionable silence, drinking and thinking. The fact they could ask these questions and might actually get answers was… world-changing.

The river of stars wheeled above them, a spray of sparkling diamonds in the dark. Katherine sighed and slumped back into her seat. "I still find it hard to wrap my head around the fact that mathematics of the heavens seems to work in circles and not straight lines."

"It's very different," Ella admitted. "Sometimes I think my experience as a skymage helps, as I tended to think in arcs anyway – throwing something… landing… jumping… falling…"

Katherine turned, a twinkle in her eye. "Did the hierarch's golden carriage provide a soft landing?" She dodged the lazy slap in response to her black humour and laughed, peppering her friend with more humorous questions.

"What would your father think of your terrible bullying?" Ella cried. She fake-snarled: "Just for that, I'm finishing off the wine!"

"Nooo!"

Ella found it oddly cathartic to be able to laugh about the worst moment of her life. But then, as with most things, it very much depended on who it was shared with. They laughed, and they giggled, and shared tales of joy and woe until the wine was done and their stamina flagging. As night's chill began to bite, and alcohol's haze deepened, they retreated indoors towards bed and blankets.

Katherine closed one eye and carefully manoeuvred a couple of logs onto the embers of their fireplace, just enough to keep them warm until morning. She wiped sawdust and splinters off her hands and turned to see Ella sat staring at the locked chest where she stored her personal belongings. "What's wrong?"

Ella chewed on her lower lip. "Something's not right."

"Your wards, are they broken?"

She scrutinised the chest. "No, not that…" She tugged at the lid, but the lock was still in place.

Katherine hurried over to her own chests and ensured her belonging were still secure. "It all seems fine on my end."

Ella chewed on a hangnail, thinking. The feeling of wrongness persisted. Then it struck her. "When we left, there were crumbs of bread and flour on top. I'd rested a crusty end of loaf on it and couldn't be bothered sweeping it up just then."

They stared at the lid. Not even a speck of flour. Katherine looked behind it, spotting the missing crumbs fallen to the floor – this lid had been opened.

Somebody was spying on them.

"It might have been the wind," Katherine whispered.

Ella's throat clenched. "It's been calm all day and this door has been shut."

They looked at each other and shuddered.

"I miss the old workshop," Katherine whispered, glancing at all the entrances to their quarters. "I think tonight we bar the door and reinforce our wardings."

They did just that, then huddled together under the same blanket, alert and flinching at every creak and crack of settling wood instead of sleeping. Abelin Castle was far from the safe and secure place they had believed it to be. Instead of a fortress, it was more like an open prison – with unfriendly eyes and ears everywhere.

CHAPTER 24

Security was redoubled, but the team grew increasingly paranoid about spies and guarded every work-related conversation behind locked doors and a dual layer of anti-scrying wards. The staff and the warriors guarding the castle were all suspect, and the others needed no persuading to fall into line with Rojer and Jackan when it came to trusting Overseer Lucid.

With additional precautions in place, they spent months on research and building, testing and failing and trying again without further incident until, finally, it was time for the big one all of this had been building up to: the launch of the massive Mark IV Fire Dragon. They had to order a special aether gem to power something of this colossal size: one of the largest aether gems in existence. It arrived on a guarded wagon, escorted by a full squad of combat mages who carried it into the workshop inside an iron-bound enchanted chest that took a full ten minutes to unlock.

The mages couldn't tear their eyes away. The air crackled with latent potential and seductive power. A dragon heart, the condensed aether of one of the most powerful of creatures to ever live. These days, more were obtained by excavation from millennia-old gravesites than from the nigh-suicidal task of hunting such rare creatures in the mountainous areas of the world.

"Hop to it!" Jackan barked. They shook off their awe and avariceand installed it in the guts of their void-going vessel.

Hulking stone golems pulled the three constituent parts of the Fire Dragon out on great sleds. They assembled it on a flat area downslope from the castle, surrounded by wooden supports and scaffolding built atop log rollers so it could be moved back before launch. The spear-like ship reared taller than the local pine trees, seemingly eager to be launched into the heart of the heavens.

Guylan, dressed in his own thick, clumsy diving suit, stood at the bottom of the scaffolding, staring up. His forehead beaded with sweat. He swallowed and glanced at Jackan. "I… I hadn't entirely appreciated just how high up it would be," he croaked.

The old engineer clapped a hand on his colleague's shoulder. "Ach, you'd have to be dead not to feel nervous. It's not too late to back out if you want."

The younger man shuddered and shook his head. "He who does not possess the courage to take a risk will achieve no glory." He took a deep breath, steeled his nerves, and began the ascent, climbing at a snail's pace and steadfastly avoiding looking down. Jackan waited for a while before following, scampering about the scaffolding beams like he was part squirrel, and not a wrinkly old foul-mouthed git in his twilight years.

By the time Guylan reached the capsule, his hands were sweaty and his legs shaking. He caught his breath at the top, daring to look out at the view offered by such a high vantage. It was breathtaking, but terrifying. Overseer Lucid, flanked by several warriors, was watching from a castle wall. She offered him a brief wave, but he was too intent on keeping a firm grip on the scaffolding to return the gesture.

He clambered aboard and used the sleeve of his suit to wipe the sweat from his brow. The emergency air pack was donned, and with it came a new and highly experimental addition at his insistence: a metal plate sewn in, bearing a levitation rune powered by a single medium-sized crystal worth a good-sized farm in the countryside. It would last nowhere near long enough to arrest a fall from such a great height, and could only gradually slow a descent, so it would have to be triggered at *precisely* the right moment. He really, really hoped he would never have to test that. It was only a shred of comfort.

A series of deep breaths served to calm his racing heart. The dread waned, allowing him to recognise the thin sliver of excitement inside himself: this would be a true achievement for all magekind, though he was somewhat aggrieved that the secrecy around their project meant he would not have the opportunity to crow about it to every guild and scholar in the land.

"Breo the Brilliant's claim to the highest flight of a mage is about to be shattered and ground to dust by me, Guylan Bluford," he said shakily, trying to muster his courage. That only got him thinking again about heights, and how unutterably terrible he was with them.

"What was that?" Jackan called from outside, busy checking the door seals.

"Nothing," Guylan spluttered. "Just talking to myself." He busied himself with the rudimentary control panel they had fitted, checking that all was in order. Levers to manually adjust the metal fins, steering his flight through the air. More levers to control the aether fed to the force-rune thrusters on the capsule that would, in theory, propel them through the void to the moon in subsequent flights. A palm-panel allowed him to extend his magical senses through the entire structure of the vessel when it was in flight, much like a mage manually controlling a crude worker golem.

Jackan slapped a hand on the metal shell of the capsule. "I think we are good to go. Are you ready for launch?"

He swallowed the sudden searing taste of rising bile and forced an awkward smile. "As I will ever be." They secured him into the cushioned seat, slid a padded linen coif onto his head, and then his bulky helmet and breathing tubes. The glass plate was up, but could be quickly sealed if the capsule sprung a leak and all its air started to escape.

"One last check," Jackan stated.

Two pairs of eyes and magic-enhanced senses rechecked the straps, levers, and arcane protections, the summoning gem for the air elemental, and its backup in case something went wrong with that one. His backpack was ready to be activated. All was as it should be.

Guylan sat back and saluted. "See you on my return."

"The gods' own luck to you, lad." Jackan said.

Then came the thudding of the hatch being hammered in tight. The scaffolding rattled as it was withdrawn. Then... silence, save for the heavy beat of his own heart.

With a belly full of churning dread, he waited for the drumbeat that meant Katherine had set light to the fuse. She'd been right about the damned diving suit they had crafted: it reeked of sweat, leather, and something far more unsavoury. It was a sweaty, itchy, and altogether abominable thing, but it had to be endured to safeguard his life. He'd had more than enough experiments go wrong throughout his career to risk something so precious over a little discomfort.

"What in the blazes is taking so long?" he hissed, straining to hear the signal that the launch had begun. Despite the fact that this capsule was larger than the one Katherine had tested, good air was still limited – and they didn't dare risk a panicked elemental running amok during the launch itself.

Boom, boom, boom: the drum bellowed its ominous song.

He gritted his teeth, clenched his fists and waited for the roar of ignition, going over the plan in his mind for the hundredth time to soothe his nerves. The launch, the ejection of stage one's dead weight, stage two carrying him into a circular orbitus around their world, gathering just enough speed to forever fall and always miss the ground, but never fast enough to escape the Great Mother's pull entirely. Eject the exhausted stage two. Once around the world, and then a turn of the capsule and descent back to where they began.

That ignition… it was taking an oddly long time.

The hatch tore open.

Rojer dived in with a knife in his hand, the man's eye wild.

Before Guylan could react, the knife plunged down. The blade sliced through the leather straps securing him for launch.

"Move!" Rojer yelled. He hauled the young engineer out of the padded chair and shoved him towards the hatch, where he teetered on the edge, staring down. With the scaffold withdrawn, it was a nauseatingly long way down. Rojer tackled him from behind, launching them both out of the capsule and into the air.

Guylan screamed and clutched onto the older mage as they fell. Despite being terrified and confused, the young engineer could not fail to notice jets of angry flame eating holes through the steel hull of the lowest section – the part containing the most alchemical powder. If that exploded, they were all dead. Something had gone catastrophically wrong.

Veteran skymage that he was, Rojer's magic softened a bone-breaking crash to a mere jarring landing – like they had leapt off a low wall. Guylan sprawled across the earth, muscles and mind seized solid with fright. He was picked up and tossed over a shoulder like a sack of grain, carried to safety while the Fire Dragon hissed and spat and shuddered. A sheet of hot metal began peeling back, searing gases forcing the hole wider.

"Get behind the golems!" Jackan shouted. A shimmering shield of magical energies appeared in front of him and Ella as they slowly retreated behind the hulking stone bulwark of the golems that had carried their vessel to the launch field. Rojer needed no further encouragement, diving behind stone and shield. His job done, he unceremoniously dropped Guylan to the dirt.

"What caused this?" Rojer asked as the young engineer scrambled to his feet, panting and peeking back the way he had come.

They looked to Jackan and Katherine, one for the engineering of the hull, and the other for its contents. Before they could even speculate, the Fire Dragon groaned and began listing towards them like a half-felled tree, flames gushing out of cracks spreading through metal.

"We are still too close," Jackan yelled. "If that dragon heart explodes…"

An urgent need to escape gripped them. Katherine got behind Ella's chair and accelerated her into a juddering, bouncing sprint, the others running ahead under the cover of further defensive shields that sprung up behind them as they tried to outpace the inevitable explosion.

Metal shrieked as the Mark IV toppled. A flash painted the castle walls red and orange, forcing the watchers to duck and cover. A wave of smoke, grit, and searing heat hit their shimmering shields, blasting the mages off their feet. Their magical defences deflected the brunt of the blast, saving their hides but sending them tumbling through choking smoke and raining dirt. Shrapnel sprayed the castle walls, embedding itself into stone and hastily raised wooden shields.

They lay sprawled in the dirt, a tangle of legs and arms and bent wheels, moaning and coughing from smoke inhalation.

Right where they had been standing, a section of their doomed vessel had landed on the stone golems, reducing them to flaming gravel. The launch field was a pit of fire and glowing, twisted debris. Black smoke billowed towards the heavens, shot through with ribbons of lightning as aether-filled gems cracked and released their charges. A fortune up in smoke.

"Thank you," Guylan said, between coughs. "I would have been done for; I owe you my life."

Rojer spat blood from a burst lip. He waved it off like it was no big deal to risk his life by climbing into a burning ship to carry its pilot to safety.

Led by the overseer, guards boiled out of the castle gate armed with buckets of water, sticks, and brushes to beat out spreading flames, and bandages to treat any urgent wounds.

"Anybody hurt?" Jackan wheezed, helping Ella up and into her chair. It was dented and banged up, but nothing a hammer and a good polish couldn't sort. The rest of them were much the same, a mass of bruises but no broken bones or gaping wounds. The old engineer sagged against her chair, clutching his chest as he tried to catch his breath.

"Just our pride," Katherine said, surveying the disaster. "I don't think we can salvage much of this."

"That's bloody obvious," Overseer Lucid stated, her expression one of barely contained fury. "What in the Nine Hells happened here?"

"Some defect in the construction material or the fuel," Jackan said. "There's no way to know now."

Her dark eyes narrowed. "Do you know how much money just went up in smoke? You wasted a dragon heart, man. A dragon heart!"

That elicited a wince. "There was no way to predict this. We checked and double-checked everything we could beforehand."

"Then you should have checked it three times, then a gods-damned fourth!" Her hands trembled, as if eager to throttle him. It took her a moment of closing her eyes and breathing deeply before her fury subsided. "You have no idea of the grovelling letters I will have to write, nor the mountain of paperwork."

The overseer looked them over. "At least you're alive," she said, somewhat sourly. "Get yourselves cleaned up, and prepare a full and detailed report for the hierarchs. You are operating on borrowed time, using up funds and material that many say would be better spent on conventional weapons and magics." She glared at them, then stalked off to direct the firefighting.

They gathered their fried nerves and battered bodies and limped into the castle. Ella's wheels squeaked and wobbled, making for a shaky ride, but at least they didn't fall off. "Her mask of friendliness slipped there," Rojer observed as they entered the courtyard and made way for men ferrying buckets to and from the moat and well.

A groan from Jackan as he paused to catch his breath. "I cannot imagine how much that cost. What a bloody disaster."

Katherine wrapped her arms around herself and retreated behind her long hair. "Was it me? Maybe I made a mistake."

"Rubbish!" Jackan said to Ella. "Every bit of this is new and untested, and any one of two dozen things could have gone wrong. Why, my own accident was what landed us all in this mad scheme in the first place!"

"You are not to blame," Ella said, squeezing her friend's hand. "It could have been a flaw in the metalwork, a burst pipe, or blockage somewhere – it could even have been one of my own runes that burned out and sparked a fire. There is no way to know." Katherine nodded and squeezed back.

Guylan shuddered. "We are alive. It was just a hunk of metal and wood. That can be replaced." He sighed, thinking of the glory that had almost been his, and then found he didn't have one iota of regret at missing the experience of a lifetime: being launched up into the sky.

"What now?" Rojer asked.

"We regroup and rebuild," Jackan said. "The Research and Design Workshop never gives up at the first setback. Nor the fifth. I very much doubt it will be our last."

CHAPTER 25

Reconstruction was gruelling but proceeded at a swift pace, partly from a desire to prove themselves after such abject failure, and partly out of pure fear. The Unity and the Empire were only one step away from waging full-blown war again, with bodies dropping every day to magic, monsters, and old-fashioned steel – which meant the team's supply requisitions, work, and activities all came under intense external scrutiny.

A new landing capsule had been devised with the plan of reaching orbitus, then utilising the Great Mother's love and a series of transition thrusters to slingshot them around their world on a trajectory to land on the moon. Lower-powered landing thrusters should allow the capsule to land, and then to escape the weaker pull of the moon to return home to widespread acclaim and glory… or so they hoped.

The lower sections of the new Mark V had been constructed, hanging on chains and wooden scaffolds ready to be inscribed with runes and fitted with aether gems to power them. The black powders and alchemic ingredients had been carefully ground and combined, ready to fuel the next launch. They had just enough material for one more attempt, and now just lacked the magical power to go with it. An eye-watering supply order had been filled out and sent off to Fort Newsark, requesting another dragon heart crystal to act as the mighty beating heart of the Fire Dragon, and a cartload of smaller aether gems to power protective wardings, rotation thrusters, and levitation runes.

Their work on the main thruster arrays of force runes had just been completed when a flurry of messengers rode in from

Fort Newsark. The dusty riders handed unsealed missives to Overseer Lucid, then swapped mounts and tore off back down the hill without stopping to wash, eat, or drink.

Jackan wiped his hands on an oily rag and tossed it aside, emerging from his workshop to join the others. "What's occurring?"

The overseer's face grew grim as she read. She tucked the papers under her arm and then approached the mages.

"The Ranneas Empire has invaded," she stated.

A thrill of fear rippled through them.

"Are they coming this way?" Katherine asked. Her gaze flicked to the warriors on the walls, then to the stout keep with its thicker defences.

Overseer Lucid snorted. "The enemy broke through our lines to the north, raided supply depots, and razed several marching forts along the border before we forced them back. We are due to receive a share of the casualties and prisoners."

"How many are we expecting?" Rojer asked.

"A hundred or so," Lucid replied. She marched away, flinging out orders to the castle's guards and staff.

Jackan peered into the tool-strewn workshops. "Let's clear space for the wounded." They got to work, stashing away papers and tools, half-built parts and the more delicate arcane apparatus.

Half a day later, the first caravan of war wounded arrived on a motley collection of carts and wagons towed by ponies and repurposed war golems, pockmarked and blackened from battle. The gate to the castle swung wide to admit bloodied and moaning warriors and a few spell-shocked mages. Some were dying, others already covered over with stained blankets. Mail had been torn by weapon and spell; many bore weeping burns from magical fire and ice. A mutilated few had suffered the hateful touch of acids that ate through flesh, melting skin and muscle and bone.

The walking wounded were helped into the largest of the workshop buildings, where Katherine and Ella had laid out blankets and barrels of fresh well water.

The rest were carried on litters into another building, where the castle healer had laid out his knives and baskets of bandages. He got to work cutting out arrowheads and broken blades, sewing up wounds, spreading on salves, and applying poultices.

There was little for the research mages to do but carry bandages and boil sodden red rags, staying out of the way until called. The healer and those warriors who knew a little battlefield care tried to save those who could still be saved. One of the castle guards was a lapsed lay-priest of Akerbis, and he helped guide the dying in their last prayers to the god of the dead.

Katherine and Guylan were summoned into the makeshift hospital to hold patients down as shattered and septic limbs were sawn off.

The stench of spilt blood and rotting wounds filled the air, along with the screams of agony and loss. More wounded arrived at the gates in dribs and drabs, and the bodies soon piled up ready for the pyre.

Jackan slumped against a wall, exhausted and out of breath. He rubbed his sore chest with a gore-streaked hand, watching the arrival of another covered prison wagon guarded by mages and six grim, armoured men. Judging by their tattered robes, the chained passengers were mages of the Empire that the Unity valued enough to capture rather than kill.

He recognised one hollow-eyed young man staring out of the bars, his face filled with terror and despair. "Andriyan Korolev, adjunct to Komissar Taeban Tereshkova," the old engineer muttered. "We meet again, eh. Gods damn this war of ours."

The prisoners were hauled out of the wagon and thrown to the dirt. Two were dressed in bloodstained Empire uniforms with bright red trim of ranking combat mages on the lapels. Andriyan wore rough working clothes patched with thick leather, and still wore a belt with empty straps where tools had once hung – he'd likely been sent with the enemy units to keep their constructs and tools in good repair, but he'd been swept up with all the hardened killers.

The boots and weapon-butts of the Unity guards were enthusiastically applied to the prisoners' bodies. Their blood spatted the ground, and the guards showed little sign of stopping.

Overseer Lucid marched over before the captives could be beaten to death right there in the courtyard. She snarled and shouted, cowing them by threats to hang each and every one of them for disobedience. "Drag them to the keep and toss them in the dungeon."

It was more of a single cramped cell, Jackan knew, but it was still better than summary execution.

His attention was drawn away by the sputtering drone of a damaged scout skyship approaching from the battlefield to the north. Ella came to a stop beside him, hand lifted to shade her eyes against the sun. The ship told a tale of woe with its sagging gasbag and black smoke billowing from one of the two floating constructs that pulled the wicker and wood hull through the air.

She tutted. "That feckless idiot should reduce the aether-flow to the damaged pig-engine."

"Pig?" Jackan queried.

"Something about flying pigs," she replied. "I was told it started as a joke, but those things drive like a stubborn sow, so the name seems to have stuck."

The skyship lurched and leaned sideways.

"The rune arrays are overloading," Ella hissed. "It's going to–"

The arcane engine on the starboard side exploded: a flash, the distant crump coming seconds later.

Glittering metal rained down as the remaining device pulled to port, sending the skyship into an uncontrolled spin.

Ella shuddered with remembered horror of her own. "Oh no, no, no."

The remaining engine wrapped its lines around the hull, spiralling and squeezing until wood shattered. Debris rained down, and its flailing pilot, too.

With sick horror, they watched the mage fall, but – praise the gods – they were too far away to witness the brutal impact. The gasbag tore, and the falling ship crashed into the hillside. A plume of black smoke rose into the sky, marking the gravesite.

"We did this," she rasped, sniffing and fighting back tears as she looked at her own two hands, fingernails stained brown with dried blood. "And others just like us. I crafted so many blasting crystals… I hold myself responsible for killing and maiming so many people."

Jackan swallowed and put a comforting hand on Ella's shoulder. "We are all guilty of that here, lass. It's the nature of war. At least you are goodhearted enough to loathe it; so many mages don't give a blind bit of notice to the corpses they leave in their wake." He gave her shoulder a gentle squeeze and then returned to the hospital, leaving her there to stare into the past, trying to sort out her feelings and dark memories.

Screams of agony drew her back to the here and now, where the wounded needed whatever help she could provide. She was no healer, but they could load her up with linens, bandages, and pots of water for her to take where needed. It was a more worthy role than making weapons.

For two nights, Castle Abelin hosted the casualties, its guards and staff doing the best they could with severely limited resources. Spare blankets and clothing were torn up to make bandages, and cauldrons were constantly bubbling to cleanse bloodstained bedding and dressings. The water level of the well began to dip, so much was being drawn up.

Messengers came and went, reporting that aid would be slow in arriving: smaller raids had been beaten back across this whole section of the border. The number of casualties on both sides sounded horrendous to the ears of the mages, but hundreds and even thousands were a mere pen-stroke footnote to the Unity's generals and hierarchs.

On the morning of the third day, after a long night of messy, slow, and painful deaths, Katherine sat on the outer wall, hollow-eyed and staring out at the scrubby hillside. She didn't react as Rojer Glenn came to stand beside her. They sat in sombre silence for a while.

"It's hard the first few times," the older man said, easing up his eyepatch to scratch at the pink scar tissue beneath. "But you get somewhat accustomed to it after a while. You never stop feeling sick and scared, though."

She shivered. "I don't think I want to grow 'accustomed' to that kind of nightmare. It shouldn't be happening."

He nodded knowingly. "If wishes were wives, I'd have an army of disappointed women after me. You get used to it or you don't survive it. I think you would be surprised what horrors you can take in your stride. Eventually. If you don't go mad, or desert and live deep in the woods somewhere. But sometimes, the memories wake me up. The panic and the pain. It burrows into your soul and stains it red and black. An' the thing is, our lion-hearted warriors are marching off intent on protecting their loved ones – just the same as most of the poor bastards on the other side. Five years back, it was us invading their side of the border, and what a fiasco that was. Those that give the orders sit in their lofty towers feasting, scheming, and moving the rest of us about like game pieces on a board."

Jackan, Guylan, and – with the use of a levitation spell and helping hands – Ella, joined them atop the wall. They all looked haggard and grimy and shared the same morose mood.

"We have a final decision to make," Katherine said, aiming it more at Guylan than anybody else. "Do we provide the hierarchs with the weapon we promised and walk away from this unscathed? Or do we truly commit to building a ship to sail the sea of stars, and damn the consequences? You know where I stand."

The young engineer leaned on the battlements staring out at nothing. "We will be lucky if they let us live once they discover what we have been doing. It would be safer to give them what they want."

Ella had to resist the urge to rest her hands on her wheels and nervously rock back and forth – the battlements were narrow and uneven, and her position was precarious in the first place. "Is 'safe' all you want, though?"

He turned, chewing on his lower lip. His eyes were drawn to the makeshift hospital and the blanket-covered bodies piled up beside it. "No, it is not."

Jackan cleared his throat. "I'm in, lass, but this must be unanimous. I'll not have one of us condemned against their will. Rojer?"

The one-eyed mage ran a finger around the edge of his eyepatch. "As I said, the lot of you are barking mad. But then, I'm a bit mad too, so let's see this thing through."

"I've been committed since the very beginning," Ella said. "We are on the cusp of reminding the world what magic is for, and we have come too far to back out now."

All eyes turned to Guylan. He groaned and scrubbed a hand through his hair. "After this latest failure, they'd probably march me off to fight on the front lines anyway. I guess I'll take my chances up there."

Ella grabbed his hand and squeezed tight, her eyes burning with more life that they'd seen in days. "Are you sure?"

"No turning back," he confirmed.

Their course was set, the sails unfurled.

Guylan went to say more, but paused, peering out at a dark line creeping up the hillside. "Is that… yes, supply wagons and reinforcements. About time they showed up."

Wagons of medicine and supplies came in from Fort Newsark, bearing a dozen experienced healers and their helpers, including their balding leader – an overworked, accredited mage who specialised in bodily restoration. As the mages descended to help them unload, a podgy, balding, sweaty man they recognised immediately clambered down from the back of a wagon.

"Chief?" Jackan blurted out. "What are you doing here?"

"It is good to see you all well," Whitlaw Goddard said. He enveloped his daughter in a fierce hug, grinning and nodding his regards to the others. "We need to talk," he whispered to her, the smile slipping into deathly seriousness. "Alone." He turned back to Jackan. "I will have words with the rest of you shortly."

She led him off to a secluded spot behind the forge, where the clang and pounding of hot metal and the draconic snoring of Red Bess would drown out any eavesdropping. "You look exhausted," he chided, studying the bags beneath her eyes. "Is that old man overworking you?"

She shook her head, lip trembling. "Jackan has been nothing but a gentleman. I am just exhausted from tending to all the wounded."

"Oh, my sweet. I'm so sorry." He hugged her again, holding her until her breathing calmed and the threat of tears retreated.

She sniffed and stepped back. "I am not a little girl anymore, Father. I was bound to get my hands dirty in this bloody war at some point. It's just… a lot. But I don't think you came here to check up on my health, did you?"

His sorrow slowly transformed into worry-fuelled anger. "No. I am here to find out what in the Nine Hells you think you are up to. Do you think I am a fucking idiot?"

She swallowed and stepped back. Her father only cursed when he was truly upset. "I have never once thought that."

He took a deep, huffing breath. "The hierarchs' people have been looking into your team's requisition ledgers. They have spoken to the other engineers and staff in my workshop, and they are *very* interested in every little detail of what your team did under my watch."

The hairs rose on the back of her arms. First, somebody had snooped through their belongings and papers, and now this. Her throat seized up, heart hammering. The authorities were onto them.

"I have been looking into all the records as well," her father stated. "That led me to recall and review snippets of previous conversations, half-glimpsed diagrams and little clay figures. You are not working on a way to deliver war golems, are you?"

Kathrine swallowed and shook her head.

The lines of his brow deepened, and his face grew thunderous. "Explain yourself."

In the face of her father's wrath, she spilled her guts.

He stood there listening patiently, fury and fear and admiration warring across his expression. As she reached the days leading up to the arrival of the wounded, he held up his palm. "Enough."

The chief closed his eyes and pinched the bridge of his nose, groaning as a stress-induced headache bloomed. "I feared it was something like this, but I thought to myself, 'surely not my Katherine; she is far too sensible for such foolishness'. What were you thinking, girl?"

Nothing can make one feel so small like criticism from their parents. She stared at her feet and shrugged like a sulky youth.

He heaved a sigh and set his jaw. "You will be on the first cart back to Fort Newsark. When the hierarch's dogs come sniffing around, we claim you knew nothing and were just following that old fool's orders."

A moment of silence before she stood straight and lifted her chin. "No."

His cheek twitched. "What do you mean, no?"

She looked her father right in the eyes. "I won't do that. I've had this conversation with the others. They could not change my mind, and neither will you. This dream we are building will happen, with or without your blessing."

"You think so, do you?" He scoffed at the very idea. "Give me one good reason why I shouldn't tie you up on a sack and carry you home myself."

"I'll give you two," she replied holding up a bloodstained hand. "I helped build weapons, and I am partly responsible for who knows how many deaths. Somewhere across the border, because of my work, people lie broken and maimed or in shallow graves."

Whitlaw's lips were a thin line of fury. "And the second reason?"

She swallowed and clasped her hands so that he would not witness them trembling. "You are already far too late to extract me from this. You said it yourself: the authorities are actively investigating us. Somebody has been snooping through our work, and my handiwork is all over that. Like or not, our team's fates are inextricably linked. If they go to the gallows, so do I. All you can do is stand back and watch as we do something great in sending mages to the moon."

He barked a hollow, bitter laugh. "You missed your chance to send anybody anywhere. With the war heating up, and your illicit activities actively under investigation, your more expensive and rare supplies have been denied. You won't be getting any aether gems powerful enough to launch anything of note."

Katherine reeled, aghast.

The chief took a deep and steadying breath. "Your wings, my dear, have been clipped."

CHAPTER 26

With their workspace turned into a hospital and the stone keep a bustling hive of activity, the storeroom near the outer wall was the most secure place in Abelin Castle to hold illicit conversations.

Squeezed in among crates of straw-packed jars and bottles, chests of arcane apparatus, sacks of supplies, and Ella's wheeled chair, Whitlaw Goddard stood with his hands clasped behind his back. Maps of celestial movements and engineering diagrams were strewn about, having been studied at speed. The other mages nominally under his command perched on barrels, drained and eyes downcast, not daring to say another word as he absorbed all the information. As he decided their fate.

The Chief of the Research and Design Workshop had chastised the fools good and proper, and he was now deep in thought, fighting to stave off his rising panic. He could envision no future where the hierarchy and the army didn't hang his people for their crimes – they would try to execute his daughter, but he would burn the entirety of the Unity to ashes before he allowed that to happen. Whitlaw desperately attempted to think up plans of action: anything, however far-fetched, that might keep her from the gallows. He discarded his plans one by one until all he had left were half-baked ideas. Even those he tossed aside after calculating their slim odds of success.

After a good while of hard thinking, he stopped, sighed, and looked into the eyes of his people. "I can only think of three options to keep the rope from your necks. Listen well, and choose wisely." He held up a finger. "First, you build the weapon you promised."

Katherine started to object. Her father's glare snapped her mouth shut before the words could emerge.

Two fingers. "We flee, try to evade pursuit, and defect to the Empire, or anywhere else that will have us." None of them appeared comfortable with that option.

Three fingers. "Somehow, you build this accursed Fire Dragon device and go to the blessed moon to meet our gods in person. Make this project so visible and colossal in its impact that the hierarchs cannot kill you out of hand without riots erupting in every town and city of the Unity."

That last option startled them – they had not thought the reverse of secrecy would be an option.

"The safest way forward would be the first," Whitlaw added, looking into Guylan's eyes. The man was wavering, a possible ally. "Just build the damned thing and hand it over to the battlemages and all this stops. You can, with some luck, go back to how things were before this project began."

He left them to discuss it among themselves, trying to think up other ways to escape this mess. The usually fertile farmland of his mind was barren of good ideas. Whispers rose to squabbles and snarls of objection. "For gods' sake, keep your voices down."

"I already told you that I won't build a weapon," Katherine stated, folding her arms. She looked at her father and held his gaze, her chin set and her eyes full of steely determination.

"Nor will I," Ella added, patting her friend's knee.

Whitlaw's gaze fixed on Guylan. "And you? Surely you will not sacrifice your life for this madness?"

The young engineer swallowed and ran a hand through his dark hair, his expression conflicted. "I too have had my fill of it," he grudgingly admitted. "My foray into No Man's Land opened my eyes to the brutal reality of war."

"Jackan? Rojer? Can you please talk some sense into these three feckless youngsters."

The two older men glanced at each other and then shifted uncomfortably. Jackan rose, dusted himself off and faced his old friend and superior. "All here believe this thing we have created together is worth the risk. At first, it was a mere flight of fancy, a diversion of the mind away from the terrible truth of our lives. Now? It has become something more, a dream that offers hope for more than a war slaughtering generations of our young."

Whitlaw Goddard licked dry lips. "We could flee?"

Their heads shook. "Option three is the only path forward," Jackan said. "For better or for worse, we are agreed on this course."

Ella snorted. "As if I could outrun anybody in this wheeled chair of mine." She nudged Jackan. "And this old fart would be out of breath after a league, at most." She tried and failed to smile, the forced mirth falling flat.

Whitlaw searched their expressions. He found no give in them, and slumped against a stack of crates. "Then, I have no choice but to help you."

"You can't do that," Katherine blurted, appalled. "This is our choice, and we will take the blame."

The chief shook his head. "You are my daughter. Your problems are my problems. You also do not understand the politics of the Unity if you believe the hierarchs will stop at you if they are hunting for necks to stretch on the gallows."

"I..." No, she had not considered that for one second. "I'm so sorry."

He waved it off. "What's done is done. All we can do is move forward and try to make the best of it." He marshalled all his resolve and stood straight, turning his mind towards his own particular set of skills. "What do you need from me to build a fully functioning Fire Dragon?"

The swift shift caught them by surprise. "Father?" Katherine said, with furrowed brow. "Uh... what?"

"What. Do you. Need?" he demanded.

They told him.

He closed his eyes, thinking. "Most of the supplies I can get without issue, but something as grand as a dragon heart to serve as the main source of power..." He shook his head. "Given the current level of scrutiny we are under, that is likely a feat beyond me."

Jackan cleared his throat. "If you don't mind a spot of treason, I do have one idea..."

Andriyan Korolev's remaining cellmate Dmitri died slow and hard, coughing and choking and drowning in his own blood. A crushed chest and punctured lung was no way to go, but at least it wasn't a gut wound. When the decorated combat mage of the Ranneas Empire took his last gurgling breath, the silence was a blessed relief. Andriyan closed his eyes and wondered if the god of sleep might now bless him with a dreamless rest, and perhaps even carry him off to the Garden of the Gods, never to return to this forsaken place.

Sleep refused to come. He curled up on the piss-soaked straw in the corner of the narrow cell, shackled with cold iron that restricted movement and magic. It was a squat, narrow cell, big enough so you thought you might just be able to stretch out, and falling just a shade short of that. Andriyan wondered when he too would sail down the river of death.

He didn't look up as the door rattled and squealed open, and his comrade was dragged off for disposal. It clanged shut, and the locks slammed back into place. He was dimly aware than somebody had stayed behind, uncomfortably stooped in the small space.

"Never thought I'd see your sorry face again," a gruff voice said. One he recalled from his last foray beyond the borders of the Empire.

He cracked an eyelid. "Jackan Grissom?"

"None other," the old engineer said, sniffing sourly. "Least they could do is rinse this place out once in a while."

"What do you want?"

"To let you know that I'll see your friend gets a proper burial. Are there any words your lot say at funerals?"

Andriyan shook his head. "Funerals exist to assuage the grief of the living. The dead are already with the gods and care little what we say or do."

"What were you doing with a bloody invasion force?" Jackan asked. "Thought you were a decent arcane engineering mage, like us lot?"

"I am. The maintenance mages were delayed by flooding, and urgent repairs had to be made to constructs and equipment. Due to, ah, political events, I was assigned this temporary task by Komissar Taeban Tereshkova."

The old engineer nodded. "And a spot of spying, too, yes?"

After a pause, the Imperial mage nodded. He had nothing more to lose. "I would term it scouting."

His visitor sighed and leaned back against the door. "I'm sure you would. Anyway, let's get down to business: my boss wants to contact your boss directly. Is that information you can provide?"

That... was not what Andriyan had expected. "Your boss being...?"

"Whitlaw Goddard, Chief of the Research and Design Workshop. I am led to believe that Komissar Taeban Tereshkova serves the same sort of function, when it comes to the development of new weapons."

"She will not bargain for my life," Andriyan advised. "If that is your intention, it is a pointless endeavour."

Jackan chuckled. "Hah, nothing so mundane, pal. Being honest, here, we want her to supply us with some rare items."

"Oh? Like what?"

"A dragon heart, if possible,"

Andriyan choked on that. "Are you mad? Whatever could possess her to part with an aether gem of that potency?"

The old engineer smiled. "I wasn't joking back in No Man's Land when I said we were going to the moon." He explained the exact nature of the device that Andriyan and the Imperial forces had recovered, and then detailed the feverish pace of development since then.

Andriyan stared. "This is truly not an obscure joke?"

"It is not."

"So, this is what you have been working on..."

"And now we are offering you and your people a chance to be part of history."

It made a queer form of sense in Andriyan's mind. The initial accident that launched their device married up with his own deductions after examining their portion of the wreckage, and their actions since marched in lockstep with what the old man claimed to be their goal. "And now you need a dragon heart? Why would the glorious Empire ever help the corrupt hierarchs of the Unity?"

Jackan scratched his chin, bristles rasping. "Aye, well, about that... we *may* have gone a wee bit rogue."

Andriyan blinked.

"The hierarchs think we are building them a weapon," Jackan continued. "We've been using all the supplies on this, instead." He shrugged, like treason was an irrelevance. "I reckon we are on borrowed time. Hierarchy agents are investigating us and restricting our supplies."

The sodden straw stuck to Andriyan as he sat up. "And you wish me to do what about this? Even if I would be of assistance, I am a prisoner here."

"Komissar Taeban Tereshkova: put our chief in touch with her. You must have encrypted scrying spells you use."

"Your direct superior is a part of this thing too?"

The old engineer winced. "His daughter is in too deep to escape. Now he has no choice but to help."

Andriyan stood up from the straw, groaning as his joints ached. He limped closer and gazed deep into the older man's eyes. "You swear to the gods that this is no lie?"

Jackan nodded.

"You are mad." Rasping laughter followed. Taeban was no deranged visionary, but she was also not immune to taking risks on the near impossible. Such roads of research were how many past discoveries came to light. "But I will give you my encryption to contact the Komissar. Anything more is up to her."

"That's all I ask," Jackan replied. "Thank you. In the meantime…" He opened up one of his belt pouches and retrieved a handful of beef jerky. "I know it's not much, but–"

Andriyan snatched the meat from the old man's hand and gnawed it, heedless of the filth caking his hands. His care for manners and cleanliness had rotted away during his capture, beating, and confinement.

Jackan emerged from the stone keep, glad to be back out in the fresh air. He adjusted his belt and rested a bit before carefully descending the many steep steps down the hill into the bailey. At his age, and current state of exhaustion, it was a most unwelcome trial. He knew he had been burning his candle at both ends, but what choice did he have but to keep on working, even though he risked burning out.

Whitlaw was waiting for him there, studying the people moving to and fro, his eyes distrustful. Overseer Lucid offered them a nod as she passed by, two guards and a gaggle of servants trailing after her. The chief waited for her to be out of earshot before he said a word. "Well?"

Jackan nodded and passed on the cypher used to connect to the komissar's scrying device. The chief's lips thinned. "A slim chance is better than none."

The old engineer cricked his neck and rubbed his chest. "This feels all kinds of wrong."

His old friend cast a tired glance at him. "Because it is. Thanks to all of you, this is the last card we have to play, with perhaps some additional material available from the black market. Between the two, we may yet procure enough to complete the project before this rickety house of sticks and string comes crashing down around our ears. You build your void-vessel, and I will search for the needful supplies to power it."

"How long d'you reckon we have?" Jackan asked, staring at the overseer's back.

Whitlaw sucked air in through his teeth. "Not as long as you would like, but with luck, it may prove just enough for what we need. The turmoil caused by these Imperial attacks has bought us some time. Have no doubt that the harsh eyes of the hierarchs will eventually turn back towards us. Were their spies not so distracted, I expect you would be in prison already."

The chief scowled and made to set off. "I will return to the more secure confines of Fort Newsark, talk to our new friend, and see what bargain can be struck."

CHAPTER 27

To say that Komissar Taeban Tereshkova was surprised when her personal scrying device lit up displaying Soldier Andriyan Korolev's private code would have been an understatement. She had only moments ago finished signing her name at the bottom of the letter informing his family of the man's demise at the hands of the Unity, and had added it to the grim and growing pile of death notices. She had been staring out the window, mourning that there was no end in sight to this accursed conflict, when the incoming call startled her.

Her hand paused over the activation button: a robed mage matching Andriyan's description had been seen burning to death. A report, she hoped, that had been in error.

She straightened her shoulders and powered up the device, synchronising its aether currents to the incoming encrypted scrycast. Her face stilled as the image of a sweaty, middle-aged, and balding man appeared in the crystal: one she felt she recognised.

"Are you alone, Komissar?" he asked.

"Who are you?" she replied in a clipped tone.

Her caller seemed to relax. "My name is Whitlaw Goddard, Chief of the Unity's Research and Design Workshop."

A frisson of interest welled up inside her. This man boasted an entire dossier dedicated to his background and personal activities. "How did you get this code?"

"Your aide Andriyan gave it to us," he said. "Willingly, I hasten to add. I cannot claim he is happy, but he is alive."

"I see. May I assume this communication is not a social call?"

He chuckled nervously. "I am contacting you to plead for your aid."

She cleared her throat. "A senior servant of the Unity's hierarchs wishes to enlist the aid of a Komissar of the Imperial army. Do I understand you correctly?"

"You do."

"I am no traitor," she hissed.

"But we are," Chief Whitlaw replied. "Technically." He licked his lips. "I have a rather strange tale to tell you, Komissar. Please hear me out before judging as you see fit."

She sat and listened to his outlandish story of the past years, her eyes growing ever wider as she found herself believing every word of it. The reports of her spies and scholars all clicked into place, serving to verify a good portion of his claims.

Ever since Andriyan had brought back the first report of their doings, her mind had been filled with daydreams and thought experiments of seeing a mage on the moon. Her grandfather's tall tales had shed the dust of time and marched through her memory, burning bright as they had in her happy childhood. Aleksandr's visage looked down on her now from the tapestry on the wall.

"Our project is under severe scrutiny," Chief Goddard advised. "We would require certain rare items from you to complete it."

She coughed, shaking her head. "What makes you imagine I would provide such a thing to you, the enemy?"

"Your man Andriyan speaks well of you and suggests that you might at least consider it." He held up a green leather-bound tome that made her stiffen. It was one of Grandfather Aleksander's personal collection, lost or stolen long ago. "And then there is this folktale of an orphan boy living on the moon."

She fought to control her expression. "How did you come by that book?"

He shrugged. "A rare book dealer in Orialis. I collect such things. You are more than welcome to have it returned – it is dedicated to you, after all, little star-child."

Hearing her grandfather's pet name for her shook Taeban to the core. "I... I must think on this," she replied gruffly. "You will supply me with your secure scrying cypher."

With that done, she powered off her scrying apparatus and sat staring out the window, lost in thought, ignoring knocks on her door and all requests for an audience. As the hours slid past, darkness began to creep in across the horizon. With it came the rising of the moon, a glorious silver orb that seemed to stare deep into her soul.

This quest that Chief Whitlaw Goddard was on... If it were in some way possible, then the Unity would be first to realise her childhood dream of setting foot upon the moon. That was an atrocity that could not be allowed. What she should do was to immediately report all of this to her superiors and organise a full military strike to obliterate Abelin Castle, where her spies reported that this project operated from.

Or...

That she would contemplate any other course of action was treason enough. And yet, she was not done with such ideas.

She could aid them and see this thing come to fruition, with Andriyan Korolev making the journey in her place. That grand achievement and glory of exploration could be shared with her people at minimal risk to the reputation of the Empire, but only if she accepted enormous personal risk.

Surely, though, she should find out more about their plans and extort arcane engineering diagrams and details before coming to any rash conclusion. Then she would have more to report to her superiors. There could be no harm in that...

“Contact has been made, but I do not know which way this thing will fall,” the image of Whitlaw Goddard admitted.

On the other side of the crystal, Jackan Grissom nodded. “I'd expect nothing less. We're no' that lucky. Do you really think there's a chance this komissar will cooperate?”

Whitlaw paused, pondering. “I have no idea. She is a cold and cagey woman. It is a good sign that she is open to further discussions, but she is wanting copies of your plans and workings before committing herself one way or another. She may simply take all your research for the Empire.”

Jackan chewed on his lower lip. “It's a risk we have to take. It could be used to build weapons... but I suppose that would just even both sides out. If we can never make use of our hard work, I would much rather somebody else used it for good than it die with us. Maybe someday, mages would take our research forward in the way it was meant to be used.”

"Less of that sort of talk," Whitlaw chided. "If you are sure that is what you want?"

He nodded. "We'll prepare copies of all the vital details. How do we get them smuggled over the border?"

Whitlaw's cheek twitched. "Ah, about that... She says to leave them in a scroll case inside a sack buried in your smithy's spoil heap." He smiled faintly. "It seems it is not only the hierarchs' servants who have been keeping a close eye on your team."

Jackan rocked back in his seat. "We had no idea... And here we thought we'd been so secretive and secure all this time. Both sides spying on us, eh. So, what do you want us to do while these discussions are under way?"

"I have acquired a few items on the black market, but I'm afraid there are currently no available aether gems of such extreme potency as to meet the full needs of your project. I will utilise all my contacts, but I am afraid to admit that the komissar's aid may prove vital to getting it finished in time. For now, all you can do is continue construction as if the missing parts will be provided at a later date."

"We will build it as fast as we can," Jackan replied. "I pray you get us those gems before the hammer falls."

Plans were meticulously copied and surreptitiously buried in the slag heap behind the smithy, ready to be leaked to the Imperial spies. The remaining casualties of the worsening conflict were carted off by a relief convoy from the fort, freeing up the workspace in the castle grounds once more. Only a pitiful few of those passengers would recover enough to fight again.

The sound of hammer and saw and the sparking of aether filled the workshops of Castle Abelin once more as the mages got back to work. Skilled hands and minds were made swift by the fear of the hierarchs' wrath descending on them.

"Nothing motivates like a deadline," Jackan grumbled as he sat on a stool, taking a breather and wiping the sweat from his brow. His back hurt. His chest throbbed, and his indigestion was worse than ever.

He waved to a couple of the young warriors he'd ventured into No Man's Land with, hoping for a chat and a bit of a laugh, but Overseer Lucid spotted his wave and made a beeline for him instead. For once, the woman was without her gaggle of servants and scribes, but her mood appeared foul. He hurriedly masked his disquiet and forced on a smile. "Ella, Katherine: best you go and provide Master Borman with the next list of parts we need him to forge. Guylan, Rojer, keep working on the hull."

He grunted, rose to his feet and put on a cheery grin. "Lucid! How goes things? Been a while since we saw you on your own."

Ella and Katherine scurried off to the smithy as the overseer scanned the detritus of half-finished construction littering the workshop: a mix of wooden supports, brass structural components, and exhaust cones for alchemical emissions. Some parts had been recycled from wreckage salvaged from the failed launch, but even those remnants required extensive repair and refurbishment.

"What is all this hustle?" the overseer asked.

"Making up for lost time," he explained. "Running a bit behind because of all those poor bastards brought in banged up and bleeding. About that, how goes our latest requisition list?"

She tore her eyes away from their workings. "I have submitted the requests, but given recent events, materials are in very short supply. It might take several weeks before we get official word back."

Jackan grimaced. "Aye, I thought that might be the case. Ah, well, we'll get as much done as we can in the meantime. When the goods arrive, we'll be ready for the final test."

Eyebrows climbed. "Final?" she asked. "Is this the fully functioning war golem transportation device you had promised? I had understood you were still several expensive iterations away from production." She moved to examine an assemblage of metal rods, tilting her head as she tried to figure out its usage.

He cleared his throat, thinking it was probably best not to tell her those were intended to attach seats for three human crewmembers to the floor of the capsule, as opposed to housing for a single golem passenger. "We were over-complicating matters. For those initial tests, it was necessary to be aboard and manually monitor the situation. Golems don't need air, or cushioning, or much of anything, really. With the war escalating, time is now of the essence. We know enough to get the weapon working, and after this launch we should be able to make them quicker and cheaper."

The overseer smiled, a rarity these last few weeks. "Very good. You are to be commended on your diligence. I will do my best to get you those parts as soon as possible."

"Is there anything I can help you with?" he asked.

"For now, no." The overseer turned to survey her domain. "There is a vermin problem that I need to take care of. Afterwards... well, I will let you know." She nodded to him and strode off, clearly vexed by whatever this latest problem was.

Jackan watched her go, disliking the woman's less than jovial tone these days. The smile had looked good on her, and the dim recollection of his attraction raised its ugly head. He shook his head. "Glad I'm just an engineer and not in charge of running a whole place like this."

His chest and back had eased off enough for him to pick up his tools and get back to work. He swung his hammer until he felt the burn in his muscles, and then kept going. At his age, it was too much manual labour; he could feel the exhaustion settling deep into his bones. The youngsters were enthusiastic and highly motivated, but they lacked his skills and experience. If they wanted this finished in time, it was up to him. He sucked in the pain, wiped the sweat from his eyes and increased the pace.

The smithy was hot and musty, filled with a unique aroma of hot steel tang and sulphurous dragon excretions, but Ella loved it. Her fingers found the sweet spot behind Red Bess's ears, and the fiery beast closed its golden eyes and growled in pleasure, one clawed leg kicking in time with her scratching.

Master Borman stood with Katherine at his workbench, studying the diagrams scattered across scarred wood. His son shovelled fresh coal into the forge pit, then began stacking up wide but thin plates of metal against the wall. A blackened finger tapped on the thruster housings that would contain rune arrays converting aether into enormous force, propelling their vessel through the void.

"That's some real delicate work you want. It's not so easy even with dragon-forged steel, and if I'm reading this right, it'll have to cope with a lot of structural stress." He hummed and hawed, then finally nodded. "Yeah, I can do the work, but take my advice and support the joints with protective runes to ensure it doesn't fail."

"Excellent," Katherine said. "That's one more issue dealt with, then." She ambled over to the wall of the smithy and inspected the thin sheets of dragon-forged steel intended to be affixed to the framework they were building in the workshop – the hard outer scales of the Fire Dragon, riveted on and properly sealed airtight with magic.

"I have no idea how you can make it so light but strong," she marvelled. "It is plain to see this is a master's work."

The boy next to her flushed bright red.

His father chuckled. "Thank you for your kind words, but that's my boy's work right there, not mine."

"Oh," Katherine said, feeling the heat blooming in her own cheeks. "I'm so sorry, Anders." She stared at her feet, hiding behind her veil of dark hair.

"S'all good words," the boy mumbled, shifting from foot to foot. "A compliment, so it is. Red Bess does most of the work, anyways..."

Ella snickered and patted the squat dragon to signal she was done scratching behind its ears – before it got too bitey. It sighed heavily, blue flame flickering between its teeth. "Do you think you can get these done quickly?" she asked.

The burly smith nodded. "I will work on these while my boy finishes off the sheet work. Tomorrow, mayhap."

"We had better get back to the workshop before those old men get carried away and put their backs out," Ella said. "Come on, Katherine." Her friend slunk out after her, her cheeks still red.

Once the mages left the smithy, Anders turned to his father, wearing a worried frown.

"Da, are you right sure we won't get those girls hurt?"

Berman hefted his hammer, the worn wooden haft a perfect marriage to his palm. He hung it on its wall peg and slid back a slate behind his bellows to reveal a hidden space. "Nah, they'll all be fine." He retrieved the scroll case the mages had hidden in his spoil heap, turning it over in his hands. "This is likely just bits and pieces of designs and whatnot. How important can that be? It's not like they are actually building a weapon."

His son vigorously rubbed at a smear of soot that had been tickling his nose, one he'd been too self-conscious to wipe away in front of the mages. "What'ya mean by that? So what are that lot making then?"

The smith's big shoulders rolled, he waved at the diagrams of the pieces they wanted him to forge. "No idea. But all of this? Not needed for a weapon. I know that much. Let's get this passed over to our friend tonight and then we can forget all about it."

Anders looked on dubiously, but his da was a wiser man than he was. And they had more than enough work to be getting on with. His worries were pounded flat between the relentless rhythm of hammer blows on hot steel.

CHAPTER 28

Calloused fingers of a master engineer trailed across the dragon-forged steel hull of the Fire Dragon's capsule, searching for mistakes or material defects. Upon finding none, they lingered on the housings for the smaller, third-stage rune arrays that would allow their vessel to land on the surface of the moon and then return.

"Will you look at that," Jackan marvelled, peering through his monocle. "As fine a piece of work as any I've ever seen. Wish I'd had some of this steel back in the day to help build my bridges. The things I could have made..."

"Just need to fit the porthole windows in now," Rojer added, his voice muted. "Course, we'll do that closer to the launch date so nobody gets suspicious as to why we're fitting glass windows in something meant to contain a war golem."

They moved on to inspect the second stage of the Fire Dragon, housing the mighty rune-array engines that would carry their vessel into a circular orbitus around their world, and then help them to escape the pull of the Great Mother to reach the holy moon. It remained incomplete, awaiting the potent aether gems necessary to power its thrusters and protections. This stage was more complicated than the first launching stage, which was all fuel and fire and included thrusters to change its altitude and rotation up in the dark of the void.

The protective magic and sheer strength of dragon-forged materials should serve to keep the crew safe despite the structural strain of the launch and the incredible forces in play. But none of this had ever been properly tested. It was out of their hands, but what could be done was being done, and Ella and Guylan were hard at work inscribing more protection runes into key sections of the hull.

Guylan flipped through the engineer's book bracelet around his wrist, double-checking the runes he had just finished. He nodded in satisfaction, then turned to the two older men. "We are making good progress with the ambient protection runes. They should hold well enough through the strain of the launch, then fully recharge during a single revolution before we transition from orbitus to the moon and the domain of the gods."

"Are you sure that's enough time?" Rojer queried. "Mayhap twice around the world would be a safer choice?"

The young engineer's eye narrowed. "Ambient runes always gather aether at a fixed rate and store a finite amount. These calculations are fixed, the rates known."

Hands held high, Rojer admitted defeat. "Always best to clarify when your life is on the line. I'll be piloting this thing, after all."

Guylan paused and glanced back at Ella.

"Don't get disgruntled on my account," she said, not looking up from her work. "We've already talked it over, skymage to skymage. I need a bulky wheeled chair, and he has far more experience. It makes sense."

"There are three seats in the capsule," Jackan said. "A pilot, an engineer, and one more to assist. Me, I'm far too old for such adventuring, so I'll leave that job to Katherine, if you want it?"

Shoulder-deep in the alchemical guts of the first and largest stage of the Fire Dragon, the dark-haired and powder-caked mage looked up, her face a mask of dust. "Eh? Did you call for me?"

"Just saying that you're going to the moon," Ella shouted.

"Oh, righto," she said, bending back to her work. She abruptly straightened. "Wait, what? Me?"

"Yes, you," Ella replied, thumb pointing to the heavens. "Up there."

Katherine's squeal of excitement and their resulting laughter was cut short by a vibration and glow from the scrying apparatus set up in the corner of the workshop. Somebody was trying to contact them. They exchanged worried glances. Doors and windows were hastily shut, and the area scoured for evidence of eavesdroppers in person or via spellcraft.

Jackan settled himself on a stool and activated the device.

Whitlaw Goddard's face swam into focus. He seemed older, thinner, and thoroughly worn out. The backdrop was of his personal study, but the walls were now nearly bare, his prized collection of esoteric texts and arcane artefacts all gone.

"Are we secure?" Whitlaw asked.

Jackan turned. The others gave him the nod. "For now."

"To business, then. I have sent a shipment of supplies. Mid-sized aether gems to power your arcane engines, top-tier inscribing potions and powders, and a few other rare and pricey necessities sourced from the black market. You will find them hidden inside the crates of Katherine's more pungent alchemical supplies. It cost a fortune, an amount of coin the scrutiny of the hierarch's investigators rendered impossible through normal funding routes. We were lucky enough to get a good deal on many items – for some reason, the mistress of the black market held Ella Pickering in high regard."

All eyes turned to Ella. Her chair creaked as she shrugged. It seemed paying your debts in a timely fashion gained you a favourable reputation.

"Thank you, Father," Katherine said, sniffing.

The chief nodded. "Our acquaintance in the Ranneas Empire has also agreed to supply us with a dragon heart."

They crowded the crystal ball. "Really?" Ella gasped. "Just like that? Why?"

Whitlaw simply shook his head. "I think the madness of your quest is catching. She did not elaborate beyond muttering something about family history, and I did not ask. There is one proviso, however: Soldier Andriyan Korolev must be part of the crew setting foot on the moon. If mages are to make history, the Unity will not do so alone."

A groan emerged from the chief's daughter. "Andriyan, Rojer, and Guylan it is, then. My chance was brief but glorious."

"There was no way you were going up there," Whitlaw growled. "I forbid it."

She sagged. "It's a moot point now."

That did not seem to placate her fuming father.

For his part, Guylan looked from father to daughter, not exactly pleased, but neither was he willing to step away from his chance at glory.

Whitlaw regained his composure. "Along with your supplies, I have included a rather special scrying apparatus – one far more powerful than any you have at your disposal. This you must set up to show your deeds and your journey among the stars to every mage and arcane receiver on the face of the planet."

They did not like that idea much. Every one of them scowled and shifted, uncomfortable at laying themselves so open after years of secrecy. "What's your reasoning?" Jackan asked.

The chief steeped his fingers. "Even should your quest to the moon and back be successful, who would ever believe such a far-fetched tale?"

Silence, and dawning comprehension.

"To ensure your safety, you must all be renowned beyond a hierarch's ability to call you frauds and make you vanish without a trace. They control the scribes and the scholars that craft the accepted history of the Unity. They fund many of the travelling bards that spread tales from village to village and influence the thinking of the common people. If the hierarchs control the narrative, you are lost, so the world must see and hear all that happens for themselves. Knowledge of your deeds must spread through all lands like a forest fire. Only then will people believe this voyage truly occurred, and that it was not some convoluted illusionary artifice."

Guylan's smile was wide and warm enough to fry an egg. "The world as our witness… That sounds very wise."

Whitlaw leaned closer. "You must activate the device immediately before launch and take pains to show each and every one of your team preparing the Fire Dragon for flight." His gaze anchored on his daughter. "Let none be left out or they will be left vulnerable."

Jackan licked dry lips and swallowed. "Understood."

The chief nodded, sitting back and slumping into his chair. "I have deluged the Unity's investigators with a mountain of paperwork, reports and diagrams, but I cannot hold them off for much longer."

Rojer leaned to the front. "How long do we have?"

After a moment of hesitation, the chief answered, his voice cracking under the strain. "Half a month. Less, perhaps. You will have the dragon heart in eight days. How long will it take to finalise the construction?"

Jackan turned to his team. "If by some miracle we have everything else ready before delivery, how long do you reckon it will take until we can launch?"

After a brief discussion, he faced the chief once more. "Five days after we get the dragon heart."

A hiss of annoyance came through the scrying device. "Can you not launch sooner?"

"Not if we want to ensure it doesn't explode on the ground again," came the rebuttal. "We have a long list of safety checks, then we double-check everything. That alone will take two days."

Whitlaw closed his eyes. "So be it. I will let our acquaintance know to expect your scrycast being sent out to the world on that date. I pray that the gods grant us enough time."

"What about Andriyan?" Jackan asked. "How do we break a prisoner out of the dungeon beneath the keep?"

The chief sat straighter in his chair. "Leave that to me. Now, all of you had better get back to building your vessel. Good luck." His image blinked out.

Two days later, a supply caravan arrived from Fort Newsark, and hidden among its sacks and crates lay a veritable fortune in aether gems and arcane supplies, enough to facilitate the completion of their lower-powered rune arrays and protections.

Under cover of darkness, when they hoped spies would be slumbering, they stealthily fitted the aether gems into their housings, ready for the day of the launch. Once all the delicate internal connections were made, they slid the dragon-forged hull plates into their beds on the interior framework, and used focused and fierce heat magic to seal it all up into a nigh-impervious shell.

Eight days of torturous work and scraping by on the bare minimum of sleep saw the structure near completion.

Overseer Lucid strolled past at least once a day to watch them work, scrutinising everything. Her expression was impassive, but the feigned friendliness she had once displayed was long gone.

The dragon heart arrived in their workshop late at night, without any of them even noticing. Ella wheeled back from her final checks on the ceramic exhaust nozzles of the first stage and stretched sore muscles. "What's this?" she asked, picking up a heavy, tied-up sack from the workbench – one that she was sure had not been there before. She untied the yarn and reached into the straw, then yelped as sparks of purple lightning seared her fingertips.

They crowded round as she eased an aether gem the size of her head from its bedding. Katherine and Guylan reached for it, but Ella flinched and drew it back. She licked her lips and turned wary eyes to Jackan, reluctant to let go of her prize.

The old man's eyes, too, were wide and avaricious. He tutted and shook off the lingering hint of draconic power. "Bah, don't let the taint of the hoard overcome you – these blasted things always retain some sense of what they were in life. This one must have been as greedy as a bloody hierarch. Now hand it over."

He had to prise it from Ella's fingers. "Stop gawping, you lot. We need to get this plumbed in before somebody senses its presence."

The team opened up the guts of the Fire Dragon and began installing the heart of its power in the base of the capsule. This gem would supply the bulk of the aether necessary to activate all the runes of levitation and force that would carry them beyond their world – to the moon and back!

"Five days until launch," Jackan muttered. "That's not a lot of time."

He wiped gritty eyes and trudged off to sit down in front of the scrying apparatus to contact Whitlaw Goddard and let him know the last part had arrived as promised. He entered the chief's cypher and initiated the scrycast.

No answer.

"Ach, I'll contact him in the morning."

They finished off the connections to the dragon heart and then turned in. After a few hours of unsettled, snatched sleep, Jackan sat down and tried to contact the chief again. Again, no response. Whitlaw was a frustrating man and usually a stickler for the rules and due process of bureaucracy: this was not like him. Given all that was happening, it was hard not to think the worst. Which meant they might have even less time than they had imagined.

"Pick up the damn pace," he snapped at his team, keeping his worries to himself. They looked startled, but redoubled their efforts.

Jackan was not as successful at hiding his worries as he had thought. Rojer set down the enchanted staff he had been using to fuse steel together and caught him alone in the corner of the workshop. "Something is wrong." It wasn't a question.

The old engineer glanced at the rest of his team, rushing to finalise the last few components before they began to run through the extensive list of pre-launch tests and safety checks.

"I can't get in touch with the chief," he admitted, chewing on his lower lip. "I'm worried Whitlaw might have been arrested."

Rojer bit back a curse. "Contact your cousin, Wilfred. If that is so, we need to launch, and we need to do it soon."

A sour look stole over Jackan's face. "We can't go now, not without the safety checks. But, aye, I'd rather not be blindsided by anything untoward." He tried to call the summoner, but there was no response there either. "Perhaps something is occurring in Fort Newsark itself."

Rojer scratched under his eyepatch. "I don't like this one bit. Still, nothing we can do now but work our fingers to the bone getting this thing into the air."

The bulk of the construction done, it was time to assemble the Fire Dragon on the launch field. Crude labour golems dragged the three separate stages of the vessel out and helped assemble this blacksmith's puzzle of pieces inside a web of scaffolding. The last few bits and pieces were nailed down inside the capsule and the ridiculously overpowered scrying apparatus was installed inside beside one of the windows, able to show the exterior view to the world.

The team sipped from waterskins and wiped the sweat from their brows, gazing up at the towering structure they had crafted. The Fire Dragon Mark V was finally ready for their mission to the moon, looming even taller and wider than the failed Mark IV.

"Look at that big beauty," Ella marvelled. "I wish we were going with you. What incredible sights you'll see up there!"

Katherine squeezed her hand, sharing her envy.

"Get your personal kit together," Jackan ordered. "Diving suits ready to go. Get those air cylinders in the backpacks refreshed while we run through our safety checks."

They returned to the workshop filled with excitement and anticipation. One last flurry of effort and they would be ready to launch. Years of mind-bending, back-aching labour had finally come to fruition. Guylan carted off the suits, air elemental gems, a backup portable scrying rig, and their supplies of food and water to the capsule, leaving the others to tidy up the mess of a workshop.

"Call Chief Goddard again," Rojer advised.

Jackan nodded, and they sat down at the scrying device, calling out over the aether.

No response.

They exchanged glances. "Something is very wrong," Rojer said. "I can feel something right bad creeping up on–"

Thunk. Thunk. A pair of heavy somethings hit the floor of the workshop and rolled towards the two men, leaving a trail of blood in soot and sawdust.

Katherine and Ella screamed as the severed heads of Borman the smith and his son Anders came to rest beside Jackan's feet, tongueless mouths gaping, sightless eyes staring up at them.

CHAPTER 29

Overseer Lucid entered the workshop, her footsteps printing gore as the mages reeled in horror – all apart from Rojer Glenn. The experienced combat mage slipped into the back of the room and snatched up the staff he had been using earlier. It was no war staff, but any magical tool could kill.

The woman's eyes drained of false colour, deep hazel transforming to ice-blue. Her lips became a cruel, compressed line.

With deliberate and dreadful ceremony, Lucid donned the golden mask of the battlemage who originally brought them here. She held out her hand and a war staff appeared in it. Atop her weapon, a pale blue gem encased in silver filigree flared bright, ready to unleash her fury. She hammered the butt of her weapon down against the ground.

Her voice deepened, all disguise abandoned. "You are filthy traitors," she growled. "And now we have proof."

Ella shook off her fright. "Why did you kill them?" she demanded in a quivering voice. "What did they have to do with any of this?"

The battlemage turned a condemning gaze upon her. "So, the broken little wretch dares speak up to her betters – you must have been given your current position out of a misguided sense of pity, for it was certainly not due to an overabundance of wits. You would have me believe you were not collaborating with Imperial traitors, carrying messages to and from your spymasters in the Empire?"

The mages stared down at the severed heads, doubly shocked and appalled.

"What is this proof you claim to have?" Jackan demanded. "I–"

"Cease your prattle, old man." The battlemage's staff flared and the stench of burning filled the air. "You are condemned by your own documents and actions, and you will hang for your crimes."

Guylan chose that moment to amble in through the doorway. "That's the supplies all loaded in… uh, what is happening here?" Then he spotted the severed heads and gasped.

Lucid turned her head. Her eyes flicked in the direction of the newcomer.

Rojer Glenn seized on that moment of distraction, his staff coming up. Words of deadly power tripped from his tongue.

The one-eyed mage's chest exploded in a welter of blood and bits. His ruined body slammed back into the wall, slumping bonelessly into a puddle of gore and escaping organs.

Blood dripped though the battlemage's fingers, wrapped around a fresh, steaming human heart. She snorted and tossed it aside like a rotten apple. "Fool. Would the rest of you care to provide me with a moment's amusement?"

Katherine and Ella sobbed, staring at the ruin of their colleague. Jackan staggered over to a workbench, shaking and clutching his chest. For his part, Guylan stood like a statue, daring not move a muscle in case she turned on him next.

"You," she said pointing to the young engineer. "Over there with the rest of the garbage." He scurried over, skirting the spreading pools of blood.

"You tried to hide your tracks," Lucid snarled. "Once we had an inkling that you were a pack of craven liars, it was only a matter of time before we cut through your subterfuge. What was your true goal? An exercise in wasting as much of the Unity's war material as possible?"

"I don't know what you are talking about," Jackan replied shakily. "We are building the device we always said we would."

A flick of a finger and a surge of aether sent the old man crashing to his knees in the blood. "Liar, liar," she said, striking him with the butt of her staff. "Windows. Chairs. Diving suits. Air elementals. Food and water."

"Leave him alone," Katherine demanded.

"You dare bark commands at me, girl?" The battlemage stalked over to Katherine and Ella. She leaned in to stare directly into their eyes, close enough to kiss. "Well, well, if it is not the authors of myriad diagrams and calculations on the subject of reaching the moon. You have built the Unity no weapon to carry war golems far behind enemy lines, and you never intended to."

She kicked Ella's wheeled chair over and sent her crashing into stacked supplies. Wooden panels and brass fixings rained down with bruising force.

"Spare yourselves from torture. Who are you working for?" She glanced around the workshop, but the team held their appalled silence. "You will expose every other traitor you have had contact with."

The battlemage stroked a finger down Katherine's cheek. "Perhaps the others will talk once they see what I do to your pretty skin." She stepped back and lifted her staff, the crystal at its tip flaring, eager to unleash deadly power. "Shall I flay you alive? Or perhaps I will melt it off you, piece by piece. Let us start with your face."

A huge surge of aether from outside set every magical sense in the room screaming. A protective shield flickered into existence around the battlemage a heartbeat before one of the castle's guardian golems – a huge lump of nigh-impenetrable animated stone – was flung right through the wall.

The golem slammed into her defensive shield. For all the battlemage's might and magical prowess, she was, in the end, only human, and outweighed a hundred times over. She was torn from her feet and blasted out through the other wall, demolishing the storehouse behind that too. Bits of broken golem scattered across the courtyard as the walls of the building collapsed atop her.

Lucid blasted from the debris, rising up on wings of magic. Her golden mask of station was dented and a trickle of blood wound down from her scalp. Cold eyes widened in surprise. "You?"

Encased in a shimmering golden shield of magic, Whitlaw Goddard strode though the doorway of the workshop. He wore a battlemage's robes of war covered in protective glyphs and clutched a twisted black wyrmwood staff topped with a venomous green shard of crystal. It seemed he had not sold all his precious collection of artefacts to fund their construction project. "Keep your filthy hands off my daughter, you bitch!" He aimed his staff and aether churned. Septic green energy lanced out.

Lucid was knocked back and sent spinning. Her shield deflected the worst of it towards the outer walls. Stout battlement dissolved into sizzling green slime.

"Get to your vessel," The Chief of the Research and Design Workshop ordered his people. "Hurry - there's a small army coming in fast behind me. I will hold this one off as long as I can."

Guylan and Katherine helped Ella out from under the mess of wood and metal and wheeled her from the building as it began to list alarmingly to one side.

Jackan watched them go. Instead of following, he bent to pick up the staff that had fallen from Rojer's slack fingers.

"What are you doing, old man?" Whitlaw snapped, stepping through the hole in the wall to advance on the battlemage.

The engineer snorted and followed him. "Fighting beside my old friend." He concentrated and brought up his own defensive spells.

They didn't have much time for discussion before Lucid rallied, and fire and jagged ice began to fall among them. They blocked or diverted her attacks and lashed out in kind.

The wheeled chair juddered over uneven ground as they rushed across the courtyard towards the launch field, the void-vessel still covered in scaffolding. Behind them, the workshop exploded from a direct spell-strike. Black smoke billowed.

Some of the castle's staff milled about, unsure what was happening. The gates were open and a heavily armoured force pushed through to confront the confused defenders, demanding they lay down their arms and surrender. The warriors who had survived No Man's Land with Jackan and Guylan weren't so keen on that, but they were surrounded and outnumbered, and it wouldn't take the intruders long to cut them down if they had to.

A squad of five men they didn't recognise blocked the mages' path, one an archer with an arrow aimed right at them. They had been lying in wait for anybody heading for the Fire Dragon. "Stop right there, you blasted traitors!"

A ragged man appeared behind them, hands raised and oozing aether. A spell rolled out across the guards. Their eyes glazed over, and they slumped into a snoring pile.

The mage nodded to them. "Andriyan Korolev. Your chief told me to wait for you here. You are the crew of the void-ship, yes?"

Another building blew apart as battle intensified behind them. Wood and stone screamed through the air, trailing smoke and fire. "We are!" Guylan shouted. "Come with us."

They fled from the castle heading for the Fire Dragon, already fuelled and ready to fly. It just needed its three crew members to climb aboard and ignite the alchemical engine.

Guylan nodded to the Imperial mage and pointed to the capsule. "Get Ella and her chair up there."

"Huh?" she frowned up at him, confused.

"Our pilot is dead," the engineer said. "You were a skymage once, and you will be again. Go! Levitate that damn chair up there and fly our ship."

Andriyan grabbed hold of the chair and began pushing her up the spiralling ramps of scaffolding with muscle and magic.

"Good luck up there," Katherine said, her voice flat as she stared back at the castle, where her father was fighting for his life.

Black clouds churned above the battlefield. Guylan flinched as thunder boomed and lightning flashed. Fire twisted up in a pillar, only to be quashed by a deluge of ice. "Gods damn it." He grimaced. "Did you know I am utterly terrified of heights? For all my bravado, I find myself unable to fly high today."

He began jogging back towards the castle to meet his fate head on.

"Where are you going?" Katherine called after him.

He laughed. "Not to cover myself in glory, that's for sure. You go reach the moon. Do it for us. Make all this worth something." He ran towards the fight, leaving Katherine to clamber up the creaking scaffolding.

Aboard the capsule, Ella powered down her levitation runes, ready for the chair to be securely lashed in place. Her eyes widened at the sight of her friend clambering aboard. "Where's Guylan?"

She shook her head. "Not coming."

Ella cursed, looked out at the billowing smoke. "Good hunting, Guylan."

"Where do you need me?" Andriyan asked, surveying the equipment. He seemed oddly familiar with the capsule layout and controls.

Katherine and Ella stared at him questioningly.

He shrugged. "Empire spies very good."

The two women nodded to each other. "Let's do this."

"How are you standing there taking that?" Jackan shouted as Whitlaw deflected another bolt of crackling lightning into the dirt. The ground smoked, turning glassy from the strike.

"Yes, please do tell," battlemage Lucid said in exasperation from mid-air, holding back her next devastating strike. She studied the middle-aged, balding, portly man standing before her, dressed in all the unaccustomed finery of one of her own kind. She could not fathom how this snivelling bureaucrat was able to defy one of the hierarchy's mightiest.

Whitlaw scowled up at her. "What, like it's difficult?"

Needles of ice riveted down from above, shattering on their shields but leaving them diminished for the following strike. Another lightning bolt stabbed down from the churning clouds, aimed not at them but the ground between the two mages. The ground around them exploded. Jackan shuddered and fell, stray arcs of blue-white energy hitting his charred boots.

Whitlaw stood over him, fending off more fire and ice, flinging back stones torn from the castle walls.

"A shame you have to protect that mad old bastard," Lucid shouted over the boom of battle. "He is no combat mage; and you will fall defending him."

Whitlaw gritted his teeth and fought back with everything he had, attack spells twisting out of him with every breath. His well of aether was depleting rapidly, and he knew this was a contest he could not win – but then, he had not come expecting victory in the first place. He had come to see his daughter safe. Or, if not safe, given a chance to flee.

He hissed as a beam of incandescent heat pierced his golden shield and set the sleeve of his robes alight. His skin began to blister, but such was the fury of the battlemage's assault that he couldn't afford the time to pat it out or he would die there and then.

From among the burning buildings, a spear of razor-sharp ice flashed through the air to shatter on Lucid's shield. Another attack followed, forcing their enemy to divert her attention.

Whitlaw helped Jackan to his feet. The old engineer was panting, and his skin was an unhealthy shade of grey. "Thanks, my friend. Whoever that brave soul is has bought us more time for the others to launch."

Lucid hunted the new assailant. A wave of force ripped through the burning building, tossing timbers and stones aside. A familiar figure yelped and dived to the ground to avoid flying debris.

"Guylan?" Jackan marvelled. "He gave up his only chance at glory to come back and help us? Never would have believed it." He coughed, took a deep breath and drew on his magic once more. "Let's give the lad a hand."

The three mages exchanged deadly spells with the battlemage, Whitlaw serving as the bulwark blocking the worst of Lucid's attacks.

"Where is my daughter?" he shouted to Guylan.

The young engineer pointed up, then resumed his spellcasting.

The moon was rising, bright and luminous above the battlefield.

Terror welled up inside the chief. But there was still hope. All he could do was try and hold on long enough for them to escape...

CHAPTER 30

Lightning flashed outside the porthole windows. Glaring detonations of battle magic left bright spots dancing in their vision. The Fire Dragon rocked from the force of the blasts, hindering Katherine and Andriyan as they struggled to don sealed suits and help strap Ella into the pilot's chair.

The ex-skymage yanked a strap tight across her stomach and threaded it through the buckle. In her head, she repeated the mantra *I wasn't supposed to be here… I wasn't supposed to be here…* as if thinking it might somehow change the terrifying reality she had been shoved into. As the battle raged outside, it astonished her that Jackan Grissom, Guylan Bluford, and Whitlaw Goddard were even temporarily able to thwart an enraged battlemage, but somehow, they were keeping that golden-masked calamity away from the ship while the launch sequence ticked down to ignition.

Rojer was dead, and she feared for the lives of her remaining friends outside, but she couldn't spare the time to dwell on it – if she failed to fly this void-ship, then the last three years of blood, sweat, and tears would prove pathetically pointless. The corrupt hierarchs would take their research and twist it into terrible new weapons to further their own power, profit, and degenerate amusements. The good people of this world had to see that there was a better way to use their talents and resources, and the young had to be shown that they could and should dream of better things instead of cowering in the soul-sucking swamp of fear so carefully cultivated for them by their rich and powerful elders. The hierarchs ruled through fear and a social status quo that they thought chiselled in stone – Ella swore an oath there and then to take a hammer to that sorry state of affairs.

Time was running out, and they had none to spare for even the most rudimentary of safety checks. All that was left was hope and a prayer. She pulled on her helmet. "Hurry!" she yelled over the muffled crump and thud of explosions.

Andriyan cursed and clambered into his own launch chair, fumbling with the straps in panicked haste. "Mage Pickering – you are certain you can fly this vehicle, yes?" His eyes were wide and worried as he donned his own helmet.

"Rojer is dead; she is all we have," Katherine shouted as she powered up the unsecured, boosted scrying apparatus. She nodded to her friend. "You can do this, Ella. I have faith in you."

She bloody well hoped she could. Ella swallowed, then checked the levers and controls arrayed in front of her. Three years of hopes, dreams, and grinding hard work had prepared her for this singular moment. Though she felt herself not wholly up to the challenge, it was better to try and reach for the stars than capitulate and crawl off to prison and torture.

Unlike the Mark IV, this vessel's engines could be ignited from within. Andriyan's finger hovered over the big red rune, ready to hurl them into the sky.

Katherine finished calibrating the scrying device. Runes throbbed on its casing as she angled the glass lens to show her face. She leaned into the brass mouthpiece and cleared her throat. "This is the Fire Dragon, a void-vessel launching from Abelin Castle, within the borders of the Unity." She began nervously, but soon hit her stride. "To all who are able to hear and see this message – I beg you to spread the word of this momentous occasion. On board we have Katherine Goddard and Ella Pickering of the Unity's Research and Design Workshop, joined in this expedition by Andriyan Korolev, a research mage of the Ranneas Empire. Together with Guylan Bluford, Jackan Grissom, Rojer Glenn, and my father, Whitlaw Goddard, we have built a vessel to sail across the dark void between worlds." She paused as a massive boom of detonating magic washed over them. "A Unity battlemage is currently trying to stop us from launching, but if we make it, we will be the first mortals to walk upon the surface of the holy moon." She swivelled the lenses to an exterior view through the porthole, displaying the battle raging outside the capsule, and then sank into the third seat, hastily securing herself and donning her helmet.

Before Ella could finish her final safety checks, something slammed into the hull of the Fire Dragon. Fire and lightning bloomed bright outside. The capsule rang like a massive gong, causing the crew to hiss in pain – they thanked the gods they had managed to put their padded helmets on in time. The vessel leaned sideways, metal and wooden structures groaning in complaint. The scaffolding on the outside fell away. Unsecured odds and ends clattered across the floor. The mages dug their fingernails into the leather armrests and screwed their eyes tight, preparing for a fall and praying otherwise. The void-ship threatened to topple, hanging between life and death for a tortured moment before lurching back to true with a resounding thud.

Ella groaned and opened her eyes. "Thank the gods for–"

A shudder rippled through the structure.

Ignition.

They looked to Adriyan, whose hand had accidently slammed down on the launch rune when they'd listed sideways. He stared back, eyes wide. "Oops."

The Fire Dragon burst into alchemical life; its roar deafening.

With the previous disaster in mind, the three mages steeled their nerves as unspeakable forces gathered beneath them – enough heat and fire to turn their bodies to ash in the blink of an eye. Ella stabbed a finger into the control panel and a thread of her aether triggered the levitation runes designed to lighten the load. The sudden shift in weight caused her stomach to lurch.

The Fire Dragon rattled and creaked as it rose into the air, thrust heavenwards by humanity's ingenuity and magical prowess. At first, it was a slow and steady ascent, but the force pushing them back into their chairs swiftly grew until it felt like an anvil pressing down on their chests.

It was a struggle to breathe inside their helmets. Hellish vibrations shook them in their padded chairs, straps straining. Ella's magical senses extended to painful sharpness as she felt for the wind screaming past. Her hands kept a death grip on the control panel, making minor adjustments as they roared towards the heavens.

Somebody screamed. A tiny whine lost in the cacophony. Ella realised it was her. Nausea erupted: she swallowed the searing bile, snarling as she fought to maintain her grip on the levers.

She sensed a change in the air outside, a thinning and lowering of resistance that marked the point of turning. She pulled on a lever and the Fire Dragon began to tip from the vertical. Something cracked off her helmet. Her head throbbed from the impact, but it had saved her skull. Their vehicle groaned as it fought resistance of the air.

Water measures on the inside wall reached the marked lines, indicating a forty-five-degree angle that would turn their vertical launch into an arc. She eased the lever back, sagging into her chair, panting and sweating as she counted to a hundred. She hoped they were on the correct ascent path.

Beyond the windows, darkness began encroaching upon the blue and white. The vibrations lessened, but the pressure on their bodies remained a steady torture.

Ella felt the aether-hungry levitation runes she'd etched into the Fire Dragon fading, their power sources exhausted. The abrupt silence of the first stage burning out was deafening. That terrible pressure on them relented. Ella sucked in a couple of deep breaths and then slapped a hand on the control panel, triggering the next stage of their ascent. The dead weight behind them was ejected to fall back to land.

The second stage exploded into fierce life, punching upwards, jerking the passengers. Her nose smashed into the front of her helmet. She was hammered back into her chair with the taste of blood in her mouth. The roar and the shaking was worse than ever.

Outside, blue and white was devoured by the star-speckled black of the void. Ella swallowed her blood and worked the controls, turning the vessel horizontal. They began building up enough speed to turn their arcing course of ascent into a circle around their world.

After a hundred seconds, she cut off the second stage arcane engines. All weight fled. Straps and hair and objects began to float as if in the throes of a mighty levitation spell.

"We're falling!" Katherine shouted, their ears still ringing. Her hair was loose and starting to envelop her head inside the helmet.

"Not so," Andriyan yelled, unbuckling himself from the seat. "And yet, also, yes – look outside!" He yelped as he floated free, arms and legs flailing until he collided with the wall.

Ella and Katherine freed themselves and managed to grab onto the portholes, staring out into the void between worlds. They hastily removed helmets that impeded their view. Through one porthole, sunshine seared through the glass, unencumbered by cloud. Through the others, land and sea so very far below.

They had achieved orbitus.

After the deafening scream of noise that was the launch, awestruck silence now reigned.

They said nothing.

Did nothing.

Held their breaths and stared, overcome.

They had done it.

They were circling their world in a fragile construction of wood and metal, and it was a sight beyond beauty. An experience beyond words and explanation.

"Home," Katherine gasped, peering out through a halo of dark hair swaying around her head. "I don't know who out there is watching and listening to our progress on this quest, but… that is our Great Mother down there."

An arc of shining blue and white stood proud against the darkness, slowly spinning as the Fire Dragon revolved around it. There was, it seemed, no up and no down.

"That's the Unity," Ella gasped, pointing at a dirty grey speck. "On that tiny peninsula… there's Orialis!"

Katherine pressed her nose up against the glass, peering out. "It's so… small." The mountains were minuscule, and even the Godspire, mightiest of mountains, was but a molehill.

"We all are," Andriyan added. "The Unity and the Empire, both are gnats in the grand scale of things." He sighed at the sight of it spread out before him. "Would that the mighty and powerful could see as we do now. We are mere insects that live upon the body of the Great Mother. It is humbling."

An entirely unexpected emotion welled up inside them. They shared a queer sense of grief as they admired that wondrous orb sailing through the endless sea of black nothingness. The Great Mother was a lonely island of life and light, and their kind were destroying it.

* * *

Jackan lay on the scorched dirt, bloodied and burnt, breath rasping and a hand clamped to his chest over his failing heart. Death was coming for him. He knew it with the detached certainty of an engineer watching a once-reliable device grind to a juddering stop. He lay back, staring up at the pillar of smoke only now starting to dissipate in the wind. Flakes of ash stirred up by the launch drifted down, tasting like victory.

He grinned despite the crushing pain in his chest. They had done it. Those youngsters had only gone and bloody done it. They'd made it out of this accursed place in one piece, and there was no mage in existence that could catch them now. Everything else he now left to them to sort out. He had every faith in Ella and Katherine.

Guylan limped over to his side. The younger engineer was bruised and blistered but miraculously alive. "What's wrong? Where are you hurt?"

Jackan spat blood to the side. "It's my heart. Damn thing's been threatening to give out for the last year or so. A miracle I lasted this long, so it is." He groaned and shook his head. He couldn't feel his left arm, and his chest was squeezed in a vice. "I wish..." he wheezed. "I wish I could have seen what the moon was like."

"Hold on, you grumpy old bastard. We'll get you to a healer."

Jackan sighed.

And then he died.

Guylan shook him, hard, refusing to accept it.

The old man's body was a limp, dead weight. His eyes were wide and unblinking, but peaceful. The vastness above them was the last thing Jackan Grissom had seen.

Guylan looked up to meet Whitlaw Goddard's gaze. He shook his head, lip quivering.

The chief of the Research and Design Workshop nodded and turned back to their foe. He slowly held up his hands and stepped back, letting the shimmering golden shield that surrounded him fade to nothingness. "There is no longer any point in continuing this fight," he stated to the battlemage facing him across the smouldering ruins of the castle's courtyard.

Piercing, hateful eyes stared at him from behind that dented golden mask. Blood flowed like tears down the metal cheeks to stain the collar of her robes. Half-frozen yet charred timbers smoked and cracked, spitting steam and sparks as jagged shards of ice melted in the shimmering heat.

Somewhere, Red Bess screamed in animal panic. Wood and stone exploded as the dragon burst through a weakened wall and lumbered off into the wilds, free of the castle and captivity.

The battlemage glanced in the direction of the dragon's bellow. She cursed, and ribbons of lightning crackled around her war staff. "You have wasted valuable war funds and collaborated with the enemy – what were you thinking, you utter fools? You will all hang for these crimes against the Unity."

Goddard swallowed. "Everything that was done here was done at my express command. My mages followed their orders to the letter."

She hissed, somewhere between a laugh and pain. "You expect me to believe that? I understood that until recently they were hiding it from you, as well."

He shrugged. "Your personal belief is irrelevant. This is my final, official statement on the matter. I accept full and sole responsibility for all actions taken by the team under my oversight."

She shook her head, dislodging flakes of ash and burnt hair. "All for what? To send your own daughter off to die in a metal barrel in the void between worlds?"

Goddard smiled, a thin and brittle, worried thing. "I have faith."

"In the mercy of gods and hierarchs?" she queried. "Unexpected."

"Not that. I have faith in the arcane arts of my people, in their diligence, and in their mathematics. This expedition will succeed. When they return, be sure you are on the right side of history."

She stared at him for a long moment, then looked to the sky, a taint of curiosity flickering across her eyes for a single heartbeat before the ice returned. "Perhaps they will. But your days of freedom are over. Kneel or die."

Whitlaw Goddard and Guylan Bluford knelt, and put their hands behind their backs.

The battlemage flicked a finger. Devoid of any arcane protections, irresistible force slammed the two mages face down in the dirt. Armed men approached through the rubble and laid hands on them. They winced as links of cold iron pulled tight and sizzled shut around their wrists.

"I consign you to The Howling," the battlemage stated, "where you will be put to the question. You will be judged, and you will be sentenced for your many crimes. You will not be treated with kindness, nor will you see the light of day again for the rest of your miserable lives."

CHAPTER 31

Aboard the Fire Dragon, up and down was whichever way you happened to be facing. All three crewmembers felt a gurgling nausea caused by the spinning and bodily confusion brought on by being unnaturally weightless.

"Do you think the others survived?" Katherine asked, her voice trembling. "My father… he has to be alive… Right?"

Ella pushed off the wall and drifted to her friend. Her broken back and numbed legs proved to be far less of an impediment up here, drifting in the void between worlds, which was… well, she wasn't quite sure how to feel about it just yet. "The chief is incredible," she replied. "I had no idea he could go toe to toe with a bloody battlemage! With us safely out of her reach, I'm sure they will have reached some sort of truce."

Katherine shivered. "Father always had the capability; he just had no interest in being one of those killers. He wanted a loving family and a quiet life." Her locket floated up on its chain and she undid the catch, kissing the tiny paintings of her mother and father before stowing it back beneath her suit.

"Your father was an honourable man," the Imperial mage said. "He fought to preserve our lives. Now I must attend to your wellbeing: my breathing, I find it harder. And you?"

Ella took a series of experimental breaths and scowled. "We need to summon the air elemental. We should be getting on with our checks and our work instead of fretting and gawping at the view."

Katherine reached down for the case containing the gems, or she tried to. Instead, she revolved in place and planted her face into the floor.

"I'll get it," Ella said, carefully moving handhold by handhold. She unlatched the case containing the emergency supplies bag and the summoning gems, withdrew one deep blue stone from the velvet cushion and secured the case again. "Catch." She held the gem between two fingers and gave it a gentle push.

The summoning stone drifted into Katherine's waiting hands. She crushed it against the hull and waited for the swirl of elemental air to form before she explained exactly what was needed by going through the same process of inhaling and exhaling that had worked at the bottom of the pond.

Soon, they were breathing cleaner air.

Katherine moved to the scrying device, checking that it was still functional. She adjusted the lenses to centre the view on herself, cleared her throat and spoke into the mouthpiece. "This is the Fire Dragon. For those of you down there on the ground – I really hope you saw that view. It is a life-changing sight for those of us up here in the void. Soon, we will begin our transition to the moon. May the gods grant us safe passage." She returned the scrying apparatus view to that of the luminous blue orb beyond their flimsy wall and turned towards the control panel.

Despite the strangeness of the situation, they managed to rein in the nausea and childlike wonder. The structure of the capsule had to be checked for damage, the arcane runes of protection and utility repowered, and their current location and height above the ground checked using measurements, mathematics, and the view of the world spinning against the darkness beyond the window. Once around the world to pick up speed and ensure the ambient protection runes on the hull were fully recharged, and then they would fire up the thrusters and slingshot from orbitus towards a landing on the moon. The mathematics of the process was solid, but the timing of it was still somewhat of an artform based on their best judgement. It would require Ella's constant monitoring and adjustment.

An hour of toil passed in silence before Ella wiped the sweat from her brow and then stared at the sheen sticking to her hand. She looked up from her work and glanced at her fellow mages, both visibly sweating.

Ella surveyed the capsule and the searing sunshine that poured in though one of the portholes hotter than noonday sun on a summer's day. "Is it just me," she asked. "Or is it getting uncomfortably hot in here?"

"I think we had better summon ice to cool us down," Katherine advised. "That or we will roast to death. It is not like there is any shade or a breeze up here."

Andriyan worked his magic and began what would become a constant aether-draining battle between sun and ice, heat and cold as the world turned beneath them.

Ella was forced to pause in her toil, her gaze fixed on the window as the line of night spread across the globe revolving below them. "Nightfall," she sighed. "Never could I have imagined all this." She shook off her awe and began activating the sequence to transition from orbitus to the moon. The capsule began to shake as force runes on the exterior stirred into life, orientating their vessel towards the plotted path of travel. The stars drifted past and the world disappeared from the portholes, replaced with a silvery luminescence cast by the home of the gods.

The sunlight searing through their windows was replaced by a deeper darkness as they passed into the shadow cast by their world. Ella began counting, her finger poised over the activation button for the thrusters. The last dregs of the second stage would propel them to the moon; then, the hideously expensive dragon heart provided by their collaborators in the Empire would power the potent spellforms propelling them to the moon and back.

Katherine flew over to Ella. She glanced warily at Andriyan and leaned into whisper in her ear. "I need to pee."

Ella frowned. "Use the bucket. That's what it's for."

Eyebrows raised. "The bucket? Here?"

It took Ella a few moments to figure out what was wrong with that plan, her eyes tracking bits of dust and a stray bit of leather strap floating past. Up here, things floated. The contents of a toilet bucket would not stay put. She pulled a face.

"And there we are!" her friend chuckled. "We really did not think this part through well enough."

"Shit," Ella groaned.

Katherine's eyes grew wide. "That does not bear thinking about. I'll just have to hold it until we can come up with something less horrific than an open bucket – and then we shall never, ever speak of it again." She moved off, muttering and leaving Ella to work the controls.

"Ready to activate the thrusters," Ella said. "We'll start off nice and easy, then slowly ramp it up."

Andriyan fed the elementals some of his aether to keep them cleansing the air, and topped up the spells drained from maintaining the interior temperature. He got back into his seat and paused, buckles half-fastened. Something felt… wrong. His eyes glazed as he looked inwards, studying the aether well inside him. A strangled choke escaped his throat. His eyes widened, filled with panic.

"My aether!" he croaked. "It does not refill."

Katherine turned to him, all thoughts of bodily waste forgotten. "What? That cannot–" She too looked within herself and discovered the terrifying truth. Their wells of magic were not refilling. The only conclusion was that there was no ambient aether out here in the void for their bodies to absorb. Which meant…

Nausea bubbled up Katherine's throat.

Most of the arcane runes that strengthened the structure of the Fire Dragon and protected its vitals from the deadly forces in play were recharged by the ambient aether that permeated the fabric of their world, present in everything: every single bird, blade of grass, rock and sea and gust of wind. It was inconceivable that there was a place in all of creation devoid of the life-giving grace of the gods! Until now. Those protective runes had already been depleted by their initial launch into orbitus… meaning this capsule was currently little more than a fragile basket of wood and metal nailed to magical bombs.

She spun towards Ella, a warning on her lips–

Ella's finger stabbed down on the activation control. The second stage roared back into life, punching them back into their seats as their trajectory changed, heading towards the moon.

A groan of complaint rippled through the capsule.

Behind them, metal shrieked and tore free.

An explosion slammed them forward – the remaining fuel in the second stage had detonated, a catastrophic failure. The force of a sudden spin held them there as their transition thrusters on the capsule engaged without command.

Glittering metal and fragments of wood looped past the portholes as the ship's aether ran amok. Faulty thrusters span their capsule faster and faster, the shearing stress beginning to tear the Fire Dragon apart…

Madīnat-al-Salām: House of Wisdom

Far to the east of the war-ravaged border between two enormous – and enormously depleted – military and magical powers, the philosopher-priest and renowned scholar Nasir al-Shatir entered the Speaking Room of the House of Wisdom, dressed in the finest of silken robes, his white beard long and oiled, and his arms laden down with scrolls of mathematical formulae.

He paused, scanning the stone benches where students and scholars should have sat, eager to receive his knowledge. Instead, one dazed scholar of the House stood waiting for him, fingers and lips twitching in agitation.

Nasir raised an eyebrow. "Is something amiss?"

The scholar's mouth opened and closed, his tongue barren of worthwhile words. "Come," he said instead. "You must see. There is a most powerful scrying being cast across the world." The man did not wait for his esteemed guest's response and instead hurried away.

Nasir sighed and set down his scrolls. His sandalled feet trod these hallowed halls in search of answers. He found his missing students uncharacteristically silent, crowded around the three platforms in the scrying room, each crystal sphere displaying the same image of a dark-haired foreign woman inside some sort of small cabin – a sea-going ship of some kind? On her tongue was the guttural language of the far-flung Unity, a desolate land of corrupt magic and murderous, greedy savages.

"What is this?" Nasir queried.

He was unused to being shushed, and was mightily taken aback by the chorus of vehement glares that met his interruption.

"For those of you down there on the ground," the woman said, "I really hope you can see this view."

The crystal ball flipped back to show the view of metal and wooden walls – the outside of their ship, perhaps? Nasir stiffened at the sight of a shining globe hanging in the darkness beyond the walls of this vessel. The shapes of the landmasses matched the very best work of the cartographer's guild. It took him a moment to accept the truth of his own eyes. Seeing was believing, as the sages said, but understanding required effort.

"How can this be?" he croaked, watching and listening as events unfolded.

A ripple of discussion made its way through the rapt crowd. Scholars discussing the possibilities and the revelations, and others simply awestruck by the sight of their world from the void.

Nasir al-Shatir watched aghast as horror unfolded and an explosion ripped through part of the vessel.

Unity:
Orialis, Senate chamber of
Hierarch Grubman-Lordrach IV

Grubman-Lordrach IV sat on his gilt throne, surrounded by battlemages and noble politicians whose trained faces were every bit as expressionless as the masked mages that guarded their lives. At least, they were the majority of the time; today, their eyes were bulging and their jaws gaping as they stared at the massive scrying ball on its marble and velvet plinth. He himself watched, unblinking, as those treacherous mages he had funded cast the Unity's knowledge and skills across the world, their scrycast utterly insecure and entirely unsanctioned.

His fingernails dug into the armrests as he fought to contain his wrath. All his coin and rare resources, and this was how those wretches repaid his largesse? A fucking flight of suicidal vanity? He could have built an army of siege golems, a mobile fortress fuelled by blood and magic that was almost impervious to harm, or he could have funded a dozen other projects that would have delivered him the glory he had sought in warfare.

Instead he had... *this*... this folly, this unutterable mess. And his name was inextricably tied to it. At best, he would be regarded as a dupe, at worst, a credulous imbecile not to be trusted with anything more than a drinks order. Already, he could feel the weight of the nobles' gazes on his back. Weighing him. Considering if they should switch their attentions and allegiance to another more worthy hierarch. Perhaps even wondering if he, too, was in league with agents of the hated Empire.

He was going to hang all involved. Those mages if they survived their voyage. That fat, balding Chief of the Research and Design Workshop in charge of them. Their gods-accursed cart horses that brought them the supplies to build their bloody contraption!

He watched, seething, as the traitor mages stared out at the world revolving below them, a jewel in the void. The beauty of the view and the achievements in arcane engineering were lost on him; he gained nothing from any of it.

The hierarch was far from upset when the accident occurred. Quite the opposite. He yearned to see the traitors torn apart, betrayed as he had been.

While the others had their attention diverted heavenwards, his thoughts were consumed seeking some way to recover his tainted reputation. How to twist all of this to his advantage...

Üskü:
Rose Palace

Osman the Great, Seventh Grand Vizir of Üskü, frowned at the luminous crystal ball that graced his study. He cast off his voluminous robes and settled onto the plush bed, which creaked under his perfumed bulk.

"What heathen nonsense is this?" he muttered, deactivating the scrying device and rolling over to await this evening's oiled bed warmer.

"As if anybody in their right mind would believe such blatantly false images. Touching the void... heading for the Silver Palace... hah! What nonsense."

Ranneas Empire: Pyotrgraad, Guild Hall of the First

Komissar Taeban Tereshkova was halfway through her report on current Imperial research efforts and reports on the Unity's own developments when a scribe dared to interrupt the meeting of the general staff, chief marshals, and senior komissars. The woman did not knock at the door and instead burst straight in, the guards stationed there meant to stop just such an unwelcome occurrence nowhere to be seen.

The scribe held a portable scrying apparatus box in her arms, which she deposited on the large circular table in the centre of the room. She ignored the protests of her superiors as she folded down the sides and activated the device. She stood to attention and saluted. "An unsecured scrycast from the Unity has been picked up. It is..." Her words failed her. "You must see."

Tereshkova winced as the view of the confined interior of a vessel came into view, with their world glowing luminous and beautiful beyond a small circular window. A very familiar face lurked in the background: Andriyan. Those mad mages had done it. Their Fire Dragon had succeeded in touching the void... with a little help. What she had not bargained on was that they would be casting their scrying out across the world here and now, the worst of all possible times and places – the plan had been for them to launch a few days from now, once she was secure in her secret refuge in the countryside, using a very carefully crafted false identity that she had built up and solidified over years in case it were ever to be required. A wise move of hers, if now rendered entirely pointless by whatever disaster had forced them to launch early.

The mighty of the Ranneas Empire clustered round the table, staring at the scene unfolding before them. It took a while to understand what they saw, and even longer to believe it. One by one, their expressions changed from annoyance to puzzlement to amazement.

"The sheer power it must have taken to launch such a vessel beyond the sky," Marshal Artemyev of the skymage wing mused, shaking his head. "How the Unity have done this..." He tutted in annoyance.

Her direct superior, Secretary Nikolayev stiffened and turned a wary eye on her. "Is that... Soldier Andriyan Korolev I see among the crew?"

All eyes focused on her. She felt sweat bead on her brow. She had not put enough contingencies in place for her involvement to be uncovered in such a blatant, public manner while she was still in the heart of Imperial power. There were no good options left.

"We have infiltrated the Unity's research workshop," she lied while her mind frantically tried to spin a web of lies strong enough to entrap their trust.

"I have seen no report of that operation," Nikolayev said. His eyes narrowed. "I noted your requisition of a dragon heart a month previous. Tell me, Komissar, where is that potent item now?"

The explosion in the crystal ball turned their eyes once more upon the scrycast. It bought her time.

Time enough to flee the room before they could lay hands upon her. She envisioned her attempt would be spectacularly unsuccessful, but she was not one to give up without trying to the fullness of her ability. She ran, and a few moments later, the chamber behind her erupted into roars of outrage.

CHAPTER 32

Katherine had only moments before death claimed them all.

There was no time to figure out a solution.

She launched herself at the control panel and slapped her left palm down on the activation plate, praying the gods would grant mercy.

Without hesitation, she poured her raw aether into it, bypassing all safety protocols and protections to link herself directly to the vessel. She *willed* the structure to hold together, pitting her paltry power against the ravening, uncontrolled forces threatening to tear it apart.

The remnants of the second stage were ejected. Metal snapped shut and sealed airtight. Control lines restricting aether flow re-established themselves. She gasped and shook with strain as protective runes in the hull flickered into life, drinking up her aether like dry sponges, and when that proved insufficient, it began to devour her very lifeforce. The capsule's death-spin slowed. Ceased. She screamed as the remaining transition thrusters on the capsule steadied, propelling them back onto a trajectory headed for the moon.

Perhaps a battlemage, with their vast aether wells and preternatural resilience, might have managed to endure it. But Katherine was no battlemage. She held on as long as she could.

Her will faltered. Her power failed, and the remaining transition thrusters imploded under the strain.

The blowback struck like lightning. Aether from the dragon heart flooded up the pathways that led right back to her. Lines of fire jumped from the control panels and seared up her forearm, eating charred holes right through her smoking flesh. She couldn't stop it… couldn't…

Somebody yanked her back from the control panel, breaking the link between mage and ship.

She floated, dazed, smoking and shaking. Her body was numb, but some distant, horrified part of her knew that wouldn't last.

Hands tugged and pulled at her suit, peeling back the sleeve to expose charred and blistered skin. The material crumbled to grey ash in their fingers, as did the very flesh beneath, puffing off into the air as an expanding cloud.

Somebody was speaking, but she couldn't make out the words.

Ash was in her eyes. She reached up to rub them with her right hand, but there was nothing there but a smoking stump of blackened meat where her elbow had been. That didn't make any sense…

The tingling came first. Pinpricks, pins and needles proliferating. That pain escalated, hot needles blooming into fiery knives digging into her flesh. Up and up towards screaming torment, and further still until she writhed in intolerable agony. The gods, cruelty incarnate, had denied her the blessed relief of unconsciousness.

"Gods have mercy. Hold her!" Ella yelled as her friend thrashed and howled.

Andriyan tried to pin Katherine down – a more difficult task than it seemed without the leverage of one's own weight. The best he could do was try and prevent her from hurting herself further. Droplets of blood misted the air, congealing with the cloud of ash: a smog of Katherine's torment.

Ella searched through the debris for the emergency supplies bag, tossing aside ointments and bandages in search of something stronger. They had been stocked with a couple of healing crystals for emergencies, though they had been meant to heal minor wounds, not injuries of this extent.

She pulled free two swirling red and yellow gems and shoved a healing gem into the smoking stump of an arm. Complex arrays of magical working unfolded and burrowed into the wound.

Katherine spasmed as her tortured flesh drank in the magic. Fluids and blood flowing from the wound slowed, but still oozed. Dead, black scabs flaked off to reveal a growing flush of fresh pink beneath. It was nowhere near enough, and did not touch the sides of her agony.

"Again!" Andriyan demanded.

The second dose sealed it up into a puckered mess of red and pink scar tissue with a nub of blackened bone protruding. It was a horrific wound they were in no way equipped to deal with. They had, at least, stopped the massive blood loss. There was absolutely nothing more they could do about it so far from the attention of proper healers – and at this point, simply turning around was impossible.

Katherine sagged, boneless and unmoving. Her tears formed a shimmering film across her eyes instead of rolling down her cheeks. Her breathing came harsh and rasping – but it came. With luck, she might survive. So long as no infection took root...

"What do we do now?" the Imperial mage asked, his chest heaving. "Many of our thrusters are gone."

Ella shuddered with fear and relief. She sucked in air and let it out slow and steady. "We maintain course using the landing runes inscribed on the hull – and we pray they are enough to get us back on course. Instead of landing, we enter orbitus around the moon, and then we must slingshot around it and use all our remaining power to make an immediate return and seek medical assistance.

"No," Katherine gasped, a strand of blood from a bitten lip twisting from her mouth like a glistening snake. "Don't you dare."

They gawped at her.

Katherine's face was pale and etched with agony. She turned red, watery eyes upon them, but a flicker of stubborn determination showed in her gaze. "I will not cause the failure of this mission."

"Failure?" Ella snarled. "You bloody well saved our hides there! You... your arm... I... I'm sorry."

Her friend's hair waved like a nest of snakes as she wiped the sheen of tears away with her remaining sleeve. "If we return without landing in the Garden of the Gods... do you...

think any of us will escape the wrath of the hierarchs?" Her lips twisted in pain as she fought to keep her cries contained. "If... *when* we achieve something grand, then we have a chance."

Ella and Andriyan exchanged glances. "She is likely correct in her reasoning," he said. "We must make haste to correct our course. If you are agreed, skymage?"

Katherine coughed a mirthless laugh, trembling and clutching at her stump. "Voidmage. The first of her kind." She moaned, shaking as shock struck her body like a hammer.

The title settled around Ella's shoulders. "Voidmage..." It extinguished her unfortunate life of failures and follies as a skymage and hoisted something far grander in its place.

"Andriyan," Ella snapped. "See to her. I must take readings and correct our course before it is too late." She worried it already was, but there was no point voicing that before she knew for certain. Depending on how bad the damage was, and how far off course that accident had flung them, they might be headed into the deep vastness of the void, to be lost in the darkness forever.

The Imperial mage set about dressing the wound and ensuring the safety and wellbeing of her friend while Ella tried to wrangle her thoughts back into some sort of order.

She lifted a brass measuring device to the porthole windows, looking through the sight and taking a series of measurements to try and calculate their current location, speed, and trajectory. The tool was damaged, making it a laborious business, and she had to fight to keep her mind focused on the task in hand. There would not be time to double-check any of her workings. One mistake and they were all dead.

Andriyan drifted up next to her. "Our colleague is patched up and passed out. I think, perhaps, that is for the best."

Ella nodded.

"How may I help?"

She handed him a measuring string, its length marked by black bands at regular, minute intervals. "Tell me how long the Godspire takes to travel two marks east."

The huge spike of rock pierced the cloud far below, not reaching all the way to the heavens, as had been supposed by mages and scholars since time immemorial. It was an awe-inspiring sight from the ground, but to them, the largest mountain in the world made for a handy visual marker. Andriyan placed the string onto the window and adjusted it. "Measuring."

Twenty heartbeats was less time than Ella had hoped before he spoke again, his voice strained: "Mark."

She scowled and closed her eyes, running through her own measurements, combining everything into a mental image of their course moonwards. She imagined their initial projected course as if she had thrown a stone up into the air: the arc as the Fire Dragon rose and began to fall, the ignition of their thrusters that widened that arc into orbitus, and then their ill-fated attempt to launch themselves at the moon.

If the Godspire was *there*… taking twenty heartbeats to move two marks east, then the capsule would be *here*, travelling… She imagined the arc as it aimed for the moon, and missed, heading off into the vast nothing.

It was not a comforting conclusion, but their predicament was not quite so desperate as she had feared. The transition thrusters were gone, but they still had the landing runes to provide propellant force. Would that be enough? They were not designed for such sustained use, but there was still a chance.

Some of the more delicate controls were blackened and broken, but the basic manoeuvring levers still seemed operational. Metal was, after all, far more durable than human flesh.

To regain their original course, or close to it, she would have to first rotate the capsule and then increase their thrust in a slightly different direction. And to do that, they would need to dangerously strain the landing runes – so much so that a landing on the moon might then prove disastrous. Even if they succeeded in that, it was unlikely they could take off again. But a theoretical death was preferable to a certain one.

She manipulated the controls, pulling levers in small, steady increments. The capsule groaned and revolved. She had to strap herself into the pilot's chair to keep from drifting away from the controls.

Andriyan latched onto her chair, looking grim. "We are – how you say – deep in the ass? Or can something be done?"

She didn't have time to look at him. "Gods willing, we might survive. I need you to take more readings as I put everything we have left into this. Let us pray this dragon of ours has enough fire left in its belly." She explained what had to be done and he returned to his position at the window, the measuring string pressed against it. Thanks to the dragon heart, the ship had more than enough aether – the problem was the transition engines were wrecked, and the arrays of runes meant for use in landing were not designed to channel the power required to get them back on course. But that was all they had.

Ella swallowed and activated them. She was gently pushed back into her chair, the force of their acceleration far from that initial dread pressure of launching from the dirt into the heavens.

"Mark."

She tried to gain a sense of how much damage was being done to their arcane engines. Katherine had given everything she had to power the protection runes and restrain the out-of-control aether, but it had been an impossible task. The ship was barely hanging together.

"Mark."

"Switch to the moon," she said, powering down the landing runes to prevent them burning out. Weightlessness returned to them, hair and debris drifting aimlessly. All they could do for now was wait until their approach coincided with her rough mathematics of the time and place to resume thrust.

Andriyan switched sides to gaze at the silver-grey bulk of the moon outside the window. He paused at the sight of the home of the gods, but only for a moment – from here, it appeared more dull grey than shining silver, and its face was pockmarked like a diseased peasant's. Not the divine view he had been expecting. The measuring string was up and held taut as they coasted through the void, the moon growing ever larger beyond the glass.

Over the next twenty-four hours, he took careful measurements and verbally related them back to her as the capsule coasted towards their destination. They took shifts, one sleeping and one always keeping watch over Katherine and the controls. Had they been forced to rely upon heavy physical fuel and alchemical power alone, it would have taken three days of travel to get there, but everything was quicker and faster and lighter with magic.

Finally, the time had come. Katherine was tended to and made secure, then Ella powered the landing runes back up and tensed as a slight weight returned – the love of the moon, pulling them in. It was a disconcerting feeling, to miss your own weight. She watched and prayed the runes held out long enough to reach land.

The capsule shuddered. Through the controls, she felt one of the five arrays of force runes burn out. She swallowed and cut the aether supply to it off, hoping that the others were made of sterner stuff.

Her heart thudded as she counted each interminable moment, each one taking them further from certain death and closer to a most doubtful salvation.

A second array fizzled and failed.

Then the third flickered and died.

Only two left.

Ella's suit felt hot. Her hands poised over the controls were slick with sweat.

"Mark," Andriyan stated. "We have reached position."

She blinked, stunned. She hastily powered down the thrusters – they were back on course to land on the moon!

"You have done it, voidmage," the Imperial soldier said, offering a shaky grin. "Now, all we must concern ourselves with is landing without becoming an egg thrown at a wall."

Two arrays of runes left to act as landing thrusters.

She shuddered and looked to Katherine. Her wounded friend hung motionless, strapped in securely and unaware of the peril. That was probably for the best, she thought.

Ella swallowed and wiped her hands on her robes.

She would get them down safely.

They had not come all this way to fail.

Delicate silver spires and a blush of green appeared on the horizon as they hurtled towards the rocky surface, and a meeting with the gods they worshipped.

"Beginning landing procedures," she said. "Helmets on, and hold on tight."

Andriyan slid into the seat beside her and readied Katherine and then himself for the descent.

Ella secured her helmet, pulled a lever, and began their final descent.

CHAPTER 33

Ella grabbed the controls with both hands. The pull towards the pockmarked grey surface was far less than back home, and it required less power to slow their descent. She adjusted the landing arrays and prayed to the gods as levitation runes flickered off and back on, perilously close to burnout.

The capsule rattled and lurched but held together, a speck of light in the darkness fighting the fundamental forces of a universe intent on smearing its occupants across the surface of the moon. With only two working arrays, Ella had to focus all her concentration and skills on keeping their descent steady – a single lapse could flip them head over tail, and they would hit the surface with no way to slow down.

"Steady," she growled. "Steady..."

Andriyan's breath rasped as he sat rigid in his chair, eyes screwed tight. He muttered prayers to the gods in a language more guttural than Imperial standard.

Ella had no time to indulge her curiosity about his homeland. Her hands darted about the controls, constantly adjusting and compensating.

She reached inside and drew up her aether, extending her skymage – voidmage – senses beyond the confines of the capsule, mentally grasping towards the surface, waiting for the feel of something solid.

There!

She diverted more power to the landing arrays and felt the sudden pressure of weight building as it slowed their descent. "Prepare for landing!"

The Imperial mage turned the hand crank to lower the landing legs, ready to touch down on the surface.

Ella glanced at the floor, scowling. "Should've put a stinking window down there, too." All she had to judge the distance was her magic, and her aether well was far from the largest. She stretched her senses as far as she could, head pounding with the strain of splitting her attention in multiple directions.

The capsule lurched sideways.

Another array had failed.

She pulled a lever, and in the nick of time, managed to compensate.

The ground came up faster than she'd have liked.

"Brace for impact," she yelled, blasting power into the sole remaining landing array.

The capsule shuddered, slowing hard.

The last array failed, and then they fell.

The impact was… softer than she'd expected: a jarring thump and then a hissing of sand and gravel against the hull as the legs and their ropes and pulleys absorbed much of the force.

Ella sat there, chest heaving, staring out at the billowing cloud of dust kicked up by their landing.

A strangled gasp emerged from her throat. "We did it. We're alive!"

The Fire Dragon was on the surface of the moon, where the gods themselves walked. She looked across to Katherine, still unconscious and unaware.

"Congratulations," Andriyan said, faceplate open and wiping a grimy sleeve across his brow. "And a heartfelt thank you."

They sat there until their hearts slowed, their breathing came easier, and they were able to wrap their heads around the fact that they were still alive.

Ella grimaced as she pulled her sweaty helmet off and tested the pull of the moon on her body. Weak as it was, it would still pose a problem to her mobility. She hauled herself to the window and gazed through the cloud of grey dust kicked up by their landing.

They had arrived on another world. "Look," she said, "there, in the distance. Silver spires and golden domes… It's real, and it's right over there."

He sighed with awe. "The Silver Palace. Do you… ah, believe the gods will resent our intrusion?"

"At this point," she replied. "I don't much care. Without assistance, I don't reckon we'll make it back home anyway." She nodded to the scrying apparatus. "Show them what's out there."

Andriyan adjusted the lenses to focus on the view beyond the window, where the dust was slowly settling to reveal a city of gleaming silver and gold, towers and domes and pyramids looming like mountains – more riches than hierarchs and empires could ever dream of owning. More than mankind possessed all together. He increased the power of the cast until the device began to hum and crackle, then leaned in close to the brass mouthpiece. "People of the world, may I introduce to you the first ever viewing of the Silver Palace, the very home of the gods themselves."

The arcane apparatus captured the view and cast their unsecured message back, far and far, through black void and white cloud, gusting wind and city smog, to scrying stations all across the globe and the awestruck mortals clustered around them.

Madīnat-al-Salām:
House of Wisdom

The scholars of the House of Wisdom had been struck silent for the first time in living memory. Not since the aftermath of the dancing plague of fifty years past had such quiet reigned in the hallowed halls of learning, discussion, and debate.

They stared at images from so far away that it defied belief, trying and failing to fit it all into the comfortable little boxes arranged just-so inside their minds. Their worldview had been shaken to its core, and these learned men and women were beginning to realise that all of their vaunted knowledge and learning was as a pebble before a mountain.

In the absence of discussion, the sudden scratching of stylus across slate set off a cacophony of scribery. Each among them struggled to capture the weight of this moment in prose and poetry. One or two scurried out to fetch pots of paint and powder and hurried back to set up wooden donkey-frames bearing the stretched canvas of what was sure to be their next masterpiece.

Nasir al-Shatir abstained from such efforts and instead committed the moment to memory. It was one he would never forget, and he was resolved to experience all it had to offer, emotionally and intellectually. World-changing events such as this came once in, perhaps, many lifetimes. It was his privilege to live through such a one that did not involve plague, war, drought, or natural disaster. Through sheer ingenuity, these mad barbarian mages had traversed the heavens and landed their ramshackle little vessel upon the moon. Such audacity to even conceive of such a plan! Such bravery – or stupidity – to dare trespass upon the domain of the gods.

Whatever their rough origins, Nasir could not help but praise that daring crew. They had been the first, but he was certain others would now seek to follow, and perhaps even travel beyond. Humanity was nothing if not a motley collection of inventive and curious creatures.

Bells and horns rang out across the bustling city streets of Madīnat-al-Salām, summoning all to the many leafy gathering places and temples that graced the greatest city in the world. Word of this momentous event was spreading fast.

His fellows had succumbed to a mania, their thoughts fizzing with life. With new ideas and a new way to look upon the world – indeed, all existence. Knowledge built upon knowledge: this was a well-known saying in the House of Wisdom. But ideas, ah, Nasir knew ideas could explode and ignite the future.

He watched and he listened, immersed in this most sacred of moments. He would not miss a single image or word of what was to come.

Unity:
Fort Newsark

The entire fort had ground to a halt, the industry of war abandoned in favour of marvelling at what their wayward colleagues had achieved, and at what terrible cost.

Every scry-capable device in the fortress was surrounded by mages and warriors, scribes and servants. Whispers of concern and conspiracy were rampant, and all knew that in an age of war, this entire project had to be unsanctioned – there was no possibility that those coin-counting, mud-minded hierarchs would have allowed it.

Wilfred Berkhoff rubbed shoulders with a grizzled janitor called… Jim? A man that reeked of rotgut booze. The man was ashen faced as he stared at the images coming in from the moon.

"Are you well?" the summoner asked.

Jim shook his head. "I know those girls. Good folks. They deserve better."

It was a sentiment Wilfred could only agree with. They were all so young, and as for that poor Goddard girl… he shook his head. A huge latent talent as a summoner, and such a kind temperament, too. However much that git Jeffrozon the Black Wind of Pain and Suffering claimed otherwise, the little imp would fly into a red rage when he heard about the accident that had taken her arm, and possibly her life.

A diamond formation of golden-masked battlemages marched through the fort, barking orders to disperse and shut down all scrying devices. For once, their imperious arrogance fizzled in the face of events of such magnitude. The entire army ignored them. One of those mighty mages swung his war staff and clubbed a warrior to the ground, then raised it in threat to the man's comrades. A hundred pairs of unfriendly eyes turned baleful gazes upon the battlemage, who hesitated, weighing up the number of iron-clad, armed warriors and trained mages staring right back at him. He hesitated too long; whatever fear the lower ranks had of him melted away, and they returned to their viewing.

Wilfred shook his head and huffed. He could see those mighty mages' own eyes drawn to the events happening on the moon; even they could not restrain their curiosity.

Wilfred toyed with the many talismans and religious icons hanging around his neck. "Come on, girls. Find a way to get back home to us safe and sound."

Ranneas Empire: Border Province, Fort the Third

"Nyet! This cannot be…" Kapitan Dushkin said, his pipe falling from his lips. The clay stem snapped on his boot and began sinking into the sucking muck of the trench, present even inside the spell-fortified command bunker.

"My eyes as witness, that is Andriyan Korolev," his soldier said. "I was part of his retrieval unit bringing back the wreckage of the accursed Unity's latest weapon." He paused, puzzled by a sudden suspicion. "If weapon it was…"

An arcane spell detonated a hundred paces away, showering the trenches with muck. The barrage was sporadic, petering out, as if those in charge of the Unity weapons were otherwise occupied. Kapitan Dushkin knew exactly why – on their side of this pointless skirmish, the Unity gunner-mages were themselves distracted by the unsecured global scrycast burning through the ranks.

Kapitan Dushkin adjusted his helmet strap. "Why is he on board a Unity vessel? Is he a traitor? Where is the advantage to the enemy in having a soldier of the Ranneas Empire on their crew?"

The soldier shrugged. "Perhaps mages from both sides have gone rogue."

Such talk did not lead to a long life in the Empire.

The bombardment on both sides ceased as the mages on the vessel prepared to venture forth onto the surface of the moon.

"They go to seek the gods," Dushkin said in awe, all thoughts of war and treachery forgotten.

In the cramped confines of the capsule, Ella found it difficult to haul herself over to check on Katherine. Her overall weight might be less, but her arms still did all the work.

Andriyan had his fingers pressed to her friend's throat. "The heart, it is strong like horse. With care, she may survive."

Ella sighed, a stream of tension fleeing her. "Then you must go out there to seek aid from the gods. Ask for aid, and ask them why they allow this accursed war between our peoples to continue."

"Are you trained healer?" he asked. "Have you enough aether left to keep the air elementals fed and make breathable air?"

She froze.

"Nyet to both," he realised. "All Imperial mages are trained to assist as battlefield healers, and I have not expended so much of my aether. Therefore, logic dictates that I must be the one to stay and keep your friend alive. As an engineer, I will also make what repairs can be made. You must undertake the last stage of this quest alone." He nodded to her wheeled chair, securely strapped to the wall. "The levitation arrays on your chair, they are still powered?"

She dragged herself over and checked for damage. Her heart sank at the state of her beautiful chair. The brass wheels were twisted and unusable from stray objects crashing into them, but the runes painstakingly carved into the metal frame were still intact, and the tiny crystals retained sufficient aether for a protracted sojourn. As Jackan had taught her, she had to adapt. Her mind took the chair apart and reassembled it into crude crutches. She would make it work.

It didn't take long to find the tools necessary to take the wheels off the chair and form two crude metal crutches from parts of the frame, hosting levitation runes and gems. She was as ready as she would ever be.

Andriyan nodded grimly. "Make your ancestors proud."

They slung the portable scrying apparatus on a cord around her neck and tested it. Whatever it saw and heard was transmitted to the more powerful version aboard the Fire Dragon; at the flip of a toggle, Andriyan could scrycast her explorations back to the world they had left behind.

He helped secure her helmet. She fumbled at the backpack, with gloved fingers thick as thumbs, and activated the air filtration arrays inside – it wouldn't last nearly as long as a properly fed air elemental, but it would afford her several hours. Time enough to reach the Silver Palace. Probably.

She slid the faceplate down and sealed it, then they raised wards to keep precious air inside the capsule.

"Luck of the gods go with you," he said, his voice muffled by her helmet.

She signalled her readiness to Andriyan, wishing that Katherine was awake and coming with her. She took a deep, steadying breath of canned air that smelled of metal and leather, opened the hatch, and then set forth on her crutches.

To her relief, no jets of air escaped her suit, nor did noxious gases seep in.

Ella Pickering ventured out onto the surface of the moon.

CHAPTER 34

Ella activated the levitation runes in her crutches and grimly held on as she dropped to the surface, falling about three times slower than normal – a bizarre experience.

Her soft impact raised another cloud of fine grey dust in the dry, lifeless air – if air it was. The makeshift crutches held up well, not sinking too deep into alien soil.

"The first mage on the moon," she said softly, her voice full of wonder. "The first human, really…" The weight of the moment stunned her into silence.

As dust lazily settled around her, she examined the magnificent desolation of moonscape they currently inhabited. The ground was more like a pockmarked plain of powdery sand studded with darker boulders. The fabled Garden of the Gods, except it didn't much look like any kind of garden to her. It was an exceedingly dull, parched desert. The place appeared dead, save for a lone visiting mage. It was incredible to see a sky so black, sparkling with a million more stars than she was used to. An entire river of them wound across the expanse above, and unlike the 'Garden', it was breathtaking in its beauty. She hadn't realised that the untwinkling stars came in shades of red, yellow, blue, and green, as well as the white sparks of light that she was accustomed to.

In the distance, she could just about glimpse silver towers, and… were her eyes deceiving her or was that a hint of greenery? She turned for a better look and winced at the sight of the sun: a blinding orb that left blue lights flashing in her vision. Averting her eyes, she made a mental note that these crude suits needed some sort of stained-glass filter… then laughed at the realisation the others really had made her into an engineer. Her laughter was excessive, almost manic.

She fought down rising panic with deep, calming breaths, and double-checked that her scrying rig was fully operational. The world had to see this. That was the entire point of the last three years of her life.

"Hello, world," she said, peering into the crystal. "Shall we go to see our gods?" Not that any listeners could hear her rasping voice inside the suit. But at least people would be able to see everything she did.

A thought struck her: if they were fortunate enough to make it back, she should take some kind of proof that they really had visited this place. She leaned over and buried her gloved hand in the soft dust and sand, lifting it and watching the unhurried trickle through her fingers. It was scant proof, but it was all she had, so she stuffed handfuls into the utility pockets and pouches of her suit.

With that done, Ella Pickering gritted her teeth and set to walking on her crutches, heading for the Silver Palace. "One small step at a time," she muttered. The feet of the crutches threatened to sink into the shifting surface, but a thread of aether fed into the levitation runes kept her moving forward, feeling so light that she ended up bouncing across the dusty surface. If the feet had been wider, more like those snowshoes the far northerners wore... there was the engineer talking again!

There was an exultation in such freedom of movement, her body so light that she could hop through the air like a grasshopper despite her broken back and useless legs. Here, she almost felt whole again.

"Focus, Ella," she muttered. There was no telling what dangers might lurk in this new world she found herself in, but her heart sang.

She constantly scanned the route ahead, plotting a flat but winding route that skirted the largest craters. It reminded her of the images she had seen of No Man's Land: like a war had been fought here, spell-craters everywhere. War, here? In the very home of the gods?

The thought sent a thrill of fear up her spine. She licked her lips and travelled on towards the city. Her faceplate began to fog up from the moisture in her breath: there was no way to wipe the inside. Another design flaw they had never considered.

The city was far, and her remaining aether would swiftly drain – as she pondered decreased visibility and how long her air might last, she decided that getting there was more important than her remaining aether reserves. In this place, her weight was negligible, and if there was any wind at all she might be able to convince it to carry her a fair distance before her power failed. Flight was in the realm of great mages, and she was nowhere near that powerful, but in this place… she reckoned she might be able to achieve it.

A trickle of sweat wound down her forehead and down her nose. Her right eye stung, but there was nothing to be done but try and blink it away.

She drew aether up from her well and – huh – noticed there was more of it than there had been. She paused, staring deep into herself.

Her stomach lurched and hope flared.

Unlike the void between worlds, there was aether here on the moon. Her well of magic was refilling, albeit far slower than back home. A sixth of the speed, in fact: precisely matching the lesser pull of the moon's love on her body. She filed that intriguing fact away for later research.

The implications were clear: many of the arcane runes built into the Fire Dragon relied on ambient aether for power, and those that had been depleted by the launch into the void would be charging again. It would, she hoped, keep their vessel together for the return voyage, assuming they could devise a way to repair the landing arrays and launch themselves back into the void.

She laughed, a surge of tension draining away. If only she could tell Andriyan that. Ella paused, considering the powdery ground and the scrying apparatus watching everything. Leaning over, she dragged her gloved finger through the dust: "Aether present on moon. Magic recharging." She made sure the lens was pointing right at her message, long enough for her colleague to see it.

She could not afford to linger for long. Her suit was hot and clammy, and sweat had soaked right through her undergarments. The faceplate was badly fogged by a sheen of moisture.

She had to reach the Silver Palace as fast as humanly possible.

The way ahead was an uneven expanse of rock and dust riddled with craters and boulders. Her chair, with its narrow wheels, would have been useless here anyway. She limped forward on her crutches and set the levitation runes to maximum, then tried to use her power to command what passed for wind in this place and found it an ordeal – there was so little of it that it felt a little like searching for sheep in the sea.

She leapt up and out over the grey expanse, the weakling wind carrying her further than she could ever manage with muscle alone. Ella repeated the process, making a series of great hops that rapidly carried her towards the Silver Palace. It was hard and draining work, but the ground blurred beneath her as she travelled, covering an astounding distance in good time.

The Fire Dragon was a dot on the horizon behind her, almost lost in the pockmarked face of the moon. Ahead, the delicate, soaring towers and gleaming domes loomed ever closer. The green of verdant growth began to crowd the bases of those massive edifices. Where there was vegetation, surely there would also be air, and perhaps other life.

The Silver Palace was becoming more real by the moment, no longer a misty legend in her mind.

The gleaming silver spires that reached towards the void were deceptively delicate, elegant lattices that, despite their titanic size, seemed far too fragile to hold their own weight. Those lofty spires topped a bewildering array of shining buildings of all shapes and sizes, no two alike: some bore columned frontages, their material etched with designs she was too far away to decipher. Others were smooth and organic, and one or two were unsettlingly jagged and sharp, like a pile of broken glass. Unsupported walkways linked the upper floors of a few of those buildings like strands of spiderweb. None of them looked in any way practical to her human eye, but then, these were the homes of the gods…

Other, squatter, buildings were topped with smooth and shining domes made all of one piece. Each covered an area as large as an entire town. Colossal doorways like fortress walls invited her curiosity to explore the treasure-strewn caverns that might lie beyond their threshold. Gigantic statues flanked every doorway, animal-headed guardians entirely too lifelike for Ella's comfort. She felt like an insect intruding somewhere she had no right to be. There was something unnatural about the place beyond the obvious, a feeling that she could not quite put her finger on.

It took her a few hops closer to realise that the enormous structures were sparkling clean, like an army of servants obsessed with spit and polish crawled over them day and night. It would take an army, given the vastness of even one of these godly constructions. And there was nothing moving at all. No gods. No people. No birds, come to that…

Ella swallowed her awe and fear and turned her gaze on the vegetation. At least that was something she could comprehend. A line cut across the barren moonscape: on one side only death, and on the other, verdant life. Trees and bushes and wide swathes of green grass, immaculately kept with strips and spirals of bright flowerbeds.

She moved closer, stopping before she reached a smooth white stone pathway that led straight as a dagger deep into the Silver Palace. The gardens extended off to either side, vast and neat and green. Somebody or something was clearly acting as gardener here, snipping off dead flowers and wilted leaves, trimming the grass until each blade was of uniform length. The plants were nothing special, all common species.

The Garden of the Gods was… disappointing, if Ella was being honest. It was immaculate in its neatness, so perfect in its form that it seemed designed by a cabal of aged engineers rather than by an artist who understood the untidy bounds of the human soul. It was a glass smile devoid of life, of warmth. There was no magic here, no surprise or joy to be found in wandering and exploration. It was pretty, but that was all.

She scanned the expanse of garden ahead of her. Nothing. Not even a wind to cause the trees and grass to sway and whisper. The whole place was all sorts of wrong.

Onwards! She took a series of deep breaths and then propelled herself over the threshold, soaring above the white stone path. She passed the borderline and entered into the domain of the gods.

Sudden weight grabbed her in its fist. Her levitation runes were snuffed out by an unknown power. She was yanked to the ground, a brutal impact that bent her crutches.

She hit the path shoulder first.

Jarring pain as her arm dislocated.

Her faceplate slammed into stone, a sun of cracks exploding through glass. The coppery taste of blood in her mouth and the snap of metal as the tube pumping air into her helmet ruptured.

Stunned, spinning off across the grass, limbs flailing.

A tree, looming close.

She hit it. Blacked out.

Ella woke to the hiss of air, torn leather, and snapped metal flapping. She wheezed for breath. Nothing but stale air from inside the suit entered her lungs. Her precious, clean air was gushing out into the garden from the broken pipe.

Then the nausea erupted, bile gurgling up her throat. Unescapable. Inevitable. She knew with cold certainty that she was about to die choking on her own vomit, drowned inside the helmet.

One arm hung useless, and with the shaky, clumsy fingers of the other, she fumbled for the catches at her neckplate, trying to free herself before –

Too late.

Vomit erupted, splattering her faceplate, acidic gunk filling her mouth and clogging her nose.

She gagged, holding her breath, still fighting the helmet.

Crack.

Hiss.

The helmet lifted free.

Filth spewed out onto the grass. Ella was frantic to get it out and get the helmet back on before she suffocated… before she…

A fit of coughing racked her, chest convulsing. Every new bruise throbbed.

She instinctively gasped for air between retches.

And air there was. This place was different from the barren expanse beyond the city border.

Ella wiped her gloved hand across her nose and mouth, and then took an experimental breath. Fresh and fragrant, if chilly. It seemed she wasn't going to die here, gasping for breath or drowning on her own vomit.

She sat on the grass, breathing deeply, feeling mightily glad to still be alive despite the aching of her battered body – but that feeling was nothing new.

Her crutches were destroyed, and the gems somehow entirely drained of their magic. She was stuck here with one working arm, the homes of the glorious gods themselves within sight and yet unreachable.

The scrying apparatus on her chest was intact and still whirring away, unaffected by whatever power had seized her and dashed her to the ground. A witness to her downfall. She scanned the lens across the scene for all the world to see.

"Welcome to the Garden of the Gods," she rasped, spitting blood and bile.

She considered the path down to those gleaming, cyclopean constructions, finding it galling that she had come so far only to fail at the final step. The bitter taste of defeat was worse than her vomit.

Her skyship accident had left her broken and drowning in despair, mired in a sucking black pit she had not seen any way out of. Working with Jackan had dragged her back into the light of a life worth living, and this newest setback would not stop her.

Ella used her one good arm to painstakingly drag her battered body to the nearest tree trunk, where she readied her dislocated shoulder. She took a deep breath, then rammed it into the trunk, crying out in pain as it popped back into its socket.

Filled with trepidation, she flexed her hand. The pain was immense. All she cared about was that her body allowed her to keep going.

"We've not come this far to give up," she yelled to whoever might be listening. "We came here to meet our gods and ask them why they allow this accursed war between Unity and Empire to consume all our lives. I refuse to give up now."

She gritted her teeth and began to crawl.

CHAPTER 35

No breeze cooled Ella's sweaty brow, and her thirst was as acute as her pain. She searched in vain for any sign of a pond or fountain to slake her thirst and wash away the foul taste in her mouth. She peered suspiciously up at the riot of stars in the black sky above, searching for the merest hint of a rain cloud. This was the home of the gods, after all, and she had no comprehension of what was possible here.

The gardens were eerily still. With her helmet destroyed, she realised just how unsettling this place was. It smelled of nothing at all: not cut grass, soil, nor flowering plant. No wind, no chirp and call of birds, nor buzzing of flies or bees going about their business. There was not a guard or servant in sight. Just Ella, the rattle and scuff of her dragging herself and her equipment down the path, and the panting wheeze of her labour.

The Silver Palace was misnamed: it was a city composed of many individual buildings and not a single majestic palace where the gods dwelt in harmony. Off to her right, a columned temple of solid gold that had to belong to Gildanas, god of abundance, faced the gigantic, gnarled trunk of unnatural oak emblematic of Greensidhe, the god of nature. Farther on, a palace made of blue-white ice and myriad faceted peaks about which lightning crackled and arced was surely the abode of Perunuk, The Thunderer.

Slowly, so painstakingly slowly, she crawled towards the nearest building: a vast and asymmetric structure of silvery metal that was all flat planes, hard lines, acute angles and shimmering mirrored surfaces, as much an assemblage of bizarre, spiky artwork as it was a building. There was something about the place that evoked a nebulous sense of dread in her. If this was the home of a god, she had no idea which.

The enormous doorway was flanked with what she could only describe as giant metal humanoid skeletons with ribs like tree trunks and canid skulls larger than siege golems. They depicted beings with an extra pair of arms and octopus limbs on their back. Their jaws bore too many sharp teeth and the eye sockets glowed a dim, baleful red. But to her immeasurable relief, the statues – if statues they were – showed no sign of reacting to her presence.

"I really hope you can all see this," she yelled back at the mouthpiece of the scrying apparatus. "I've dragged this heavy kit all this way, and I would hate for that to be pointless." Somehow, knowing that people might be watching – even if only dozens – made her feel less alone and vulnerable. She cherished the sense of human connection in this cold and empty place.

Her pain was forgotten as she pulled herself to the colossal shimmering door, crafted of what substance she could not tell. Nothing found in nature. She raised a gloved hand, ready to knock, and then she made the mistake of glancing up at the metal giants flanking the portal. The seemed to have shifted by an infinitesimal amount, and red light blazed in their eyes. Superstitious dread rolled over her in waves and she hesitated, hand frozen, sweat beading on her brow.

The scrying apparatus was still showing the world everything. *Pull yourself together, Ella,* she chided. *You are no coward.*

She pounded on the door.

Her knock was a dull thud on thick metal, not the hollow booming she had somehow expected.

"Hello?" she shouted, knocking with all her might. "Great gods, are you home?"

She waited for some kind of answer, racking her mind for any hint of how she should even talk to a god, and what formalities should be observed.

There was no sign that the gods heard her call.

Ella knocked again, fist bouncing off the slab of metal.

"Hello? Is anybody here?"

A strange whisper of aether set her senses tingling, trying to track the source. She swallowed and slowly looked up.

The grinding of metal bones set the hairs rising on the back of her neck. She met the gaze of one of the inhuman metal giants guarding the doorway, its skull turning to regard her. Eyes blazing like furnaces, entirely unfriendly.

Her voice quivered like a reed on a windy day. "Um, hello? I mean no harm or disrespect, your, uh, Divine Majesties."

The metal skull stared at her, gaze burning. The fires flickered and dimmed, and it ground back into position. It was the first sign of life in this place and, praise the gods, it hadn't stamped on her like she was a wayward bug.

She waited some more, but nothing else seemed to happen.

Thoroughly confused, she lifted her hand once more, ready to knock and keep on at it.

But something answered.

The doors swung wide, making not a whisper of sound. The light from the garden didn't penetrate far. Beyond, there was only cavernous, silver-columned darkness, the crackle of arcane energies and the rhythmic thud of distant machinery beating like a titanic heart. Huge, skeletal humanoid figures lined every wall, forming a hall of metal bones and macabre, grinning canid skulls. This place was more tomb than temple.

From the deeper darkness, a hundred glowing eyes blinked into life, coming directly for her. Ella licked her lips and sat as straight as she could, raking fingers through tangled hair in a desperate attempt to make herself presentable for a meeting with one of her gods.

Something slid from the darkness and into the light.

It was no god.

A nightmare construct came for her, composed of shifting angles and slicing hooks, whirling knives and dripping needles. And eyes. Far too many gleaming glass eyes.

Ella screamed and drew up the last of her aether as the monstrous thing's razor-lined limbs reached for her, drill-tips whining.

Two armoured guards dragged a battered and bloodied Whitlaw Goddard across the battle-scorched courtyard of Abelin Castle and dumped him into a prison wagon beside Guylan Bluford. The young engineer's eyes were bruised and swollen, his lips caked in crusted blood. Their hands and feet were bound with styxsteel, rendering their aether useless. The door was slammed shut and chains rattled, locking them in.

The wagon lurched into motion, heading first for Fort Newsark, and then onwards to imprisonment and torture in the dank depths of The Howling. Whitlaw was too drained to feel any worse than he already did. If anything, this trip would be the best his remaining life had to offer.

"Is that you, Chief?" the young engineer gasped. "Are you… well?"

Whitlaw groaned. "I am alive, with all my parts bruised but intact." He didn't voice what he added mentally: *for now*. "What of Jackan?"

With enormous effort, Guylan shuffled up into a sitting position, staring through the bars at the roaring bonfire that was their workshop in Abelin Castle. Their work had gone up in flames during the conflict. All those papers and diagrams, their journals full of notes and masses of calculations and discoveries…

"They tossed his body into the blaze," he snarled, dripping venom from mashed lips. "Right on top of Rojer Glenn. Like they were refuse."

Whitlaw sagged against the bars, feeling old and beaten. "Those men deserved better, but perhaps their deaths could be considered a kindness, all told. They did not suffer for long."

Guylan shuddered, dully staring at the flames as the wagon thumped along the track. When at last the castle was obscured by rock and trees, he turned and peered at his superior through swollen eyelids. "What will they do with us?"

He regarded the young engineer who had been in his charge. The man's dashing good looks and keen mind were crumpled and soiled, his very life hanging in the balance. Whitlaw felt a deep responsibility here.

"Nothing worth thinking about," he answered. "I'm sorry – I should have realised what you were doing and stopped you all from making such a grave mistake."

"It was no mistake," Guylan snapped. "We knew exactly what we were doing, and we did it despite the consequences."

The chief groaned, uncomfortable in more ways than one. "What reason could possibly justify throwing away your life like this?"

"Glory, at first. Can you imagine being the first mage on the moon? My name would have been remembered for all time for that grand deed." Guylan lapsed into introspective silence for a while before answering further. "Then there was the war. The endless stream of corpses awaiting burial, and the mutilated and the mad that wished they had been so lucky. The horrifying weapons and the mages that made them. That includes me. You. Ella. Katherine. Jackan and Rojer. We all had a hand in continuing this atrocity. That was made clear to me when we retrieved Jackan's device from No Man's Land, and then that latest battle..." He peered at his shackled hands. "There is blood on our hands, and this mad quest was a fresh breeze in an abattoir."

The wagon lurched, causing Whitlaw's shoulder to slam into the bars. "I understand that feeling only too well. It is something I have struggled with all my life. That is partly why I set my mind to research rather than pursuing the role of a sanctioned battlemage." His gaze swept the young man sharing his prison wagon. That boy had no real idea of the depravities the hierarchs were capable of, and he did not have the heart to rip away all hope.

"How..." Whitlaw's voice gave out. He cleared his throat and tried again. "How was Katherine doing, there at the end?"

"Don't worry," Guylan said, attempting a smile and regretting it with a wince and a groan. "She is clever, brave, and eminently capable of dealing with whatever this world has to throw at her."

"This world?" Whitlaw scowled at the thought. "At the moment, I am far more concerned with what happens on another. We have not a single shred of an idea what awaits them up there."

"That is one reason we had to go," the engineer countered. "Up there, beyond this ball of rock, sea, and soil, is something humanity knows nothing about. We have so many questions without answers, and so many questions we don't even know to ask. By now, perhaps we have at least a handful more answers. And the entire world will share them with us."

Chief Goddard chewed on his lower lip, deep in thought.

If all had gone to plan, mages around the world were now watching that transmission. He still had true friends and allies among the bureaucrats and merchant classes of the Unity, and even a few that played the deadly game of politics. They would help him if they could, so long as it did not put their own heads in the noose. He just had to provide them a lever against the hierarchs and a damn good reason to pull it.

The chances of any of them escaping this were low, but he did have one last hand of cards left to play. He just needed to survive long enough to use it.

CHAPTER 36

Ella threw a wall of howling wind at the nightmare construct coming at her. It was a hasty and aether-hungry spell, but she didn't care about being subtle.

The thing lurched sideways, screeching in a voice of grinding gears and scraping metal, razor-limbs clashing against a silver pillar, severing what seemed to be tubes beneath the surface. Veins carrying steam ruptured in a scalding cloud.

For a single moment, she thought she might survive.

Then the sepulchral walls came alive. Giant skeletal statues woke and lifted heavy feet, stepping forth from their niches and into the light. Dozens. Hundreds. Too many to count, too many to see in the narrow band of light shining through the doorway – just their red eyes burning in the cavernous darkness of the building as they marched towards her, their footsteps shaking the floor. The two guarding the doorway thumped down either side of her.

There was no possibility of escape. A deep breath and a promise to put up a good fight was all Ella could do.

"I won't die easily," she promised the whirling, shifting thing of blades in front of her.

It paused, limbs whirling and lashing. Its hundred eyes seemed to bore holes right through her soul. The construct facing her was different to all the rest, but looked thrice as deadly.

The ground thundered as the giants marched towards her. She was dead for daring to intrude. Ella waited for a messy death. The noise was deafening, terror overwhelming. She curled up, covered her ears and screamed. But they marched right over her, titanic strides passing directly over her head, then descending like falling mountains.

Two by two, the giants came, marching past like she was an ant unworthy of their notice. At either side, they turned in opposite directions and headed for the gardens. She blinked as the last two left the chamber. "Wha?"

She was left gawping at the single death machine in front of her that – for the moment – didn't seem overly interested in the death part.

It screeched at her, unintelligible.

Then its voice changed, softened, flitting from one language to another – some were manifestly not human, but others she vaguely recognised. She might even have heard one or two on the lips of traders from afar.

"Wait!" she held up a hand. "I know that last one – it was spoken by a visiting scholar from Madīnat-al-Salām." She licked cracked lips. "Do you... do you also speak the language of the Unity?"

Metal clicked and reconfigured. Drill-tips whirred, and blades snicked open and closed, open and closed with neck-severing force.

"Language confirmed," it said in a smooth and flawless Orialis accent. "Region of origin: Unity. Technology advancement level: first-tier human. Social advancement rating: third-tier human. Global ranking: second-tier civilisation."

Second-tier civilisation? What was out there that surpassed the Unity? Who... no, *what* were first? She filed her questions away and focused on a far more pressing issue. "Are you going to kill me?"

The construct ceased all movement. Something whined inside and an acrid burning smell filled the previously scentless air.

"Living human," it said. "Aether-conductive biology confirmed. Substantial structural damage. Designation: mage." Every eye focused on her with soul-shrivelling intensity. "Your existence is an unprecedented error."

She hoped that it was an error that did not required immediate correction. "My name is Ella Pickering," she said. "Are you a god?"

"I am the Caretaker," it replied.

"A servant of the gods?"

"The servant – the Caretaker," it corrected. "I am tasked with the repair and maintenance of this worldsite. Query: you are alive and embodied. Which genelab did you escape from?"

This construct had to be the one in charge of maintaining the Silver Palace, she realised, eyeing all the razor-sharp blades and tools attached to it. Which meant it was the next best thing to a god, and should probably be treated as such if she wanted to keep her hide intact. "Um. I didn't escape anything, Lord Caretaker, I flew here aboard our vessel. We came to meet the gods."

It hummed with thought. "Termination query submitted by Ella Pickering: answer is negative." It floated past her and out into the garden, deadly blades precisely snipping off errant blades of grass that had dared grow too fast. The debris floated skywards and burned to ash beneath its burning gaze. It then turned that gaze on the pristine white path she had travelled along, and rays of scorching heat scoured away all trace of blood and sweat and scuff marks. "You will accompany."

Ella and her scrying apparatus were lifted into the air, the touch of its levitation as soft as cloud. She couldn't sense any aether used – levitation without aether was… well, magic to her. If there was a wide-ranging field of this strange power in use, she theorised that might also explain why the runes on her crutches had failed so catastrophically mid-air.

The giant metal skeletons were spreading out across the gardens, plucking and snipping, pruning and spraying. Ella realised, with faint surprise, that they were the labourers of the gods, and that the nightmare thing in front of her was probably the head gardener keeping this place trimmed, shiny, and polished. The sinister giants were merely fancy golems under its control, if not a part of some strange whole, like a queen bee and its drones. This Caretaker was an independent, intelligent construct created by divine hands, and undoubtedly more powerful than anything she had ever seen.

It paused. "Query: your vessel contains two additional living humans. Error. Error. Do you wish them to remain intact?"

"Yes, please, and thank you," she replied, her voice strained by dark thoughts. "They are my friends."

A flood of aether seared her mind. The scrying apparatus squealed and began to smoke. "No!" she cried as it shattered into smoking parts, its delicate enchantments unable to withstand such power. Her link to those back home, whomever and wherever they might be, had been severed.

The world ripped open in a momentary flash of rainbow light.

A forest of lightning struck the path and the Fire Dragon blinked into existence in front of her, its scarred and scorched hull creaking as it settled under its own weight. A startled face appeared at the porthole: Andriyan, his eyes wide and his mouth open, staring at Ella floating in the air without a helmet, in a garden, next to a terrifying gardening construct that looked like a war golem created by an insane god.

She offered a sick smile as the pain in her skull abated and motioned for the hatch to be opened.

The door cracked open and he warily peered out at her from behind the curtain of wardings designed to keep their air from escaping.

The construct hummed. With a flick of a blade, those protections failed, the aether powering it vanished. Andriyan stood, stunned and fearful, as the mixing air mussed up his hair.

"Don't be afraid," she said, mentally adding *for now*. "How is Katherine?"

"Awakening," The Caretaker answered for him. "Her open wounds have been healed, but her physical form is too damaged from aether-overload to survive full repair."

The Imperial mage swallowed his fear. "Is this..."

Ella shook her head. "Better help Katherine out here. We have a lot to discuss."

She might be awake and aware, but her friend was far from well. Katherine was pale from blood loss, and her dark hair was wet with sweat. Her arm now ended at the elbow, a barely healed stump. Despite her pain and confusion, she took in with unvarnished awe the fact that they had landed on the moon and were breathing alien air. Andriyan offered support as her knees buckled.

Katherine spotted Ella floating there and staggered over, using her sole hand to grab onto the thick diving suit. She eyed the Caretaker and licked cracked lips. "Are you well?"

That was the first thing she thought to ask? Ella mused. Not about the gods and not about the moon. About her. Love for this treasure of a woman surged up inside. "I could use a drink," she replied. "But that can wait. Let me catch you up… ah, could you please set me down?"

The Caretaker did as she asked, a soft, considered descent to the grass as if she were something brittle. The three mages sat on the grass facing the Caretaker. Ella and Katherine were latched onto each other, locked arm in arm and resolved to never let go as she explained what had occurred since the terrible accident.

"May I ask, Lord Caretaker," Katherine said. "Where are the gods?"

Its blades whirled far too close, making them cringe. Their unease went unnoticed by the construct, or perhaps it simply did not care.

"Departed," it replied.

"Dead?" Katherine gasped. "It cannot be! How?"

"Negative. Departed. Moved on. Travelled to the location of Worldsite 712."

It took them a moment to process.

Andriyan cleared his throat. "For clarity, our gods no longer live here in the Silver Palace? They have gone elsewhere."

"Correct. Worldsite 711 is currently hosting no players."

The three mages sat in silence, trying to digest such a heavy meal of information. Ella broke the silence. "It feels a little like discovering I've become an orphan all over again. My father abandoned me like rubbish, and I'll never forgive him for that. And now our fucking gods have done the same. I have to ask, Caretaker, what exactly did you mean by 'players'?"

"The great game," it stated. "The game of life: Creation. Evolution. War. And in ninety percent of worldsites, planetary destruction."

The Imperial mage's shoulders slumped. "We were nothing but a game to the gods, one they became bored of."

Unexpectedly, Katherine laughed. "I guess we got the answer we came here for. Centuries of religious turmoil and warfare waged in the names of our gods, and they were not even here to see it! What a joke we all are – oh, how they would have laughed if they had known! The Unity and the

Ranneas Empire, both squabbling like foolish children." She chuckled, but it had a strained black edge of anger to it. "It has all been pointless."

"Has it?" Ella countered. "Not all religions support the war – many do good work. And it brought us here to learn the truth. When we return, we can tell everybody that..." her voice trailed off as she looked over the battered void-ship they had arrived in.

"You must depart," the Caretaker stated. "This is no place for living mortals."

The two women exchanged worried glances. "If the gods are gone," Katherine asked, "is there still an afterlife for the souls of the dead?"

The Caretaker was silent for a worryingly long time. "Affirmative. Current status: broken. Awaiting repair."

They opened their mouths to ask more searching questions, but spikes and blades rippled outwards in apparent agitation. "Error. Living humans. Errors must be corrected."

Ella swallowed, hastily offering it an option other than pest extermination. "Caretaker, are you able to repair the vessel we arrived in?"

The Fire Dragon groaned, shifting as torn metal flowed back into place, enchanted wood regrew, and arcane runes and thrusters knit themselves back into perfect alignment and flared with newfound power. Ella's broken crutches slammed into the ground beside her, metal bending back into shape with squeals and pops, the levitation runes flickering into fitful life – now operational, under the Caretaker's sufferance.

"Leave," it demanded. "Now."

Andriyan and Katherine left with all haste before it changed its mind, scrambling back through the hatch and readying for launch.

Ella paused, fingers ready to activate the enchantments on her chair to carry her up and in. She couldn't help but ask a question. "Are you lonely?" she asked. "You've been on your own up here for a long, long time."

"I repair and I maintain," the Caretaker said, its surface rippling in increased agitation. "That is what I am. There is no lonely."

She nodded gravely. "Maybe so, but I wager there are some things even you cannot fix on your own. Like our gods-damned afterlife."

It didn't answer, but she thought that set it thinking.

She took a chance. "I don't suppose you could fix my spine?"

"Yes."

Hope surged. "Will you?"

"There is a seventy-five percent chance you would not survive the repair. Do you wish to proceed?"

She sighed. "No, I don't think I will. Goodbye, Caretaker." She commanded her crutches to float up and into the Fire Dragon.

The inside of the capsule thrummed with stored power. The command console had been reconstructed, and their vessel was cleaner that it had been before they left home. It no longer smelled of charred flesh and sweat.

Ella glanced back as Andriyan began closing the hatch.

The Caretaker, despite its inhuman demeanour, and for all that it said otherwise, looked like a lonely silver sentinel, the last guardian of a dead city. She could not help but pity it.

She waved goodbye.

After a moment's delay, a reluctant silver limb lifted in reply.

CHAPTER 37

Andriyan hastily secured the hatch in place.

"Let us leave before that vile construct flays us alive," he said, helping Ella and Katherine into their seats and tying down the crutches. This time he wasn't about to leave anything loose to fly about the capsule.

Ella quickly chugged a waterskin, lukewarm water soothing her parched throat. She ran her fingers over the console, senses feeling for problems in the rune arrays and arcane protections. The aether flowed strong and well through undamaged systems. If anything, every part of their ship felt better constructed than before – though there was also a brand-new lever on the far right with *To be pulled when landing* in the most exquisite script she had ever seen etched into the metal. It could only be a parting gift from the Caretaker – the construct could have shredded them to a fine red mist any time it chose, had it wanted them dead, so it wasn't likely to be a trick or trap.

"Hurry up," Andriyan snarled, buckling himself in. "Let us leave this accursed place of despair and disappointment."

The shiny new addition to her console was banished to the back of her mind as she began launch checks and proceedings; diverting power to the protective runes and the thrusters that would carry them up into orbitus around the moon.

Securely strapped in and with nothing to do, Katherine gazed on the bare stump of her arm. "I want to go home," she said in a quivering voice. "I want my father." She stifled a sob, sniffed, and wiped her face, then put on a more stoic front and steadfastly stared out the window.

Ella nodded grimly. They had to believe for all their sakes that the chief was safe and well. She hoped all her friends were. Their only mission now was to return home intact to see them, and to face a most uncertain fate. A far-fetched fantasy of returning to a hero's welcome flitted through her mind's eye. She snorted and shook her head. She had never been that lucky, and she couldn't imagine the Unity would ever be magnanimous to those who had used its war materials for their own ends.

There was no telling how many people had watched their scrycast, or if it had worked at all across such an enormous distance through the void. Enough, she hoped, for the story of their quest to spread and get mages thinking of making something more useful with magic than the next deadly weapon. With some luck, she might have a chance to tell their extraordinary story before the hierarchs had her flung into prison. What would be would be, but it still reeked like a cesspit.

The Fire Dragon rumbled as power began to build in its belly.

"Prepare for ascent," she said. The others gave nods of readiness, Andriyan's hand resting on the hand crank to retract the ship's legs. He began to pray to Perunuk – but quickly shuddered and stopped himself.

She eased up the power and the repaired thrusters flared into life. Scorched grass billowed up past the windows as they rose on pillars of force. Ella winced, knowing that she was destroying part of the Garden of the Gods so meticulously maintained since the dawn of human history.

The silver spires and golden domes of the Silver Palace sank out of sight as they accelerated, a soft hand pushing them back into their seats as the moon sought to recall them to its dusty embrace. It was a gentle affair when compared to escaping the pull of their own world, and it was not long at all before Ella tilted the vessel and ramped up power to the thrusters, transitioning them into circular orbitus around the moon.

From there, they raised the landing legs, cut off the thrusters, and waited for the ship to slingshot around to a precise point before setting the power back to maximum, laying in a course to the shining blue and white orb that seemed so very small and insignificant at this distance.

The capsule shook as it changed course to escape the moon's pull entirely and transfer them back into the Great Mother's warm embrace. There was little joy and wonder in the journey home. Katherine was worried, hurting and reliving the accident that had taken her arm. Andriyan again began to pray... and then spiralled down into religious trauma, his beliefs upended and his faith laid waste. Ella, concerned about the reception waiting for them, at least had work to keep her mind occupied.

They flew through the void in silence, the sands of time draining fast as they grew closer to the motherworld. A constant series of measurements and course adjustments sent them sailing into orbitus, the cloud and sea so far below whipping past at unbelievable speeds. She turned the vessel and began thrusting in the opposite direction, turning that circle around the world into a downwards arc that would, she hoped, land them somewhere inside the Unity's borders. Nobody had ever tried to do this before, so everything was theory and best guess. And nothing *ever* went wrong when people tried to put theoretical planning into practice...

Ella gave thanks to the ironclad rules of mathematics; while experimental, the team's calculations had served them well so far. A lot of course corrections to keep them on track were solely down to her, and should they have the chance to do it all over again, she would do so many things differently. A few years' additional research would make for a more precise and safer journey, requiring much less aether... if they lived to engage that research.

The shaking began when they hit the cloak of air surrounding the world, a slight tremor swiftly growing to bone-jarring turbulence that strained their restraints. They plummeted through the thickening air. The rattle and squeal of metal and wood joined the roar of re-entry until they could barely hear each other yelling. A ruddy orange glow began building on the outer hull, hungry tongues of flame flickering up past the windows as the interior heat level rose at pace. The protections worked into the hull were being rapidly drained of power.

Katherine stretched to peer out of the window. "We are coming in too fast!"

"Activating levitation runes and landing arrays," Ella shouted over the din, fingers flying across the console.

Aether flowed to the arcane engines, trying to counteract the descent. The capsule shuddered, groaning under the strain as she put in all the power the aether pathways could take. The rune arrays flashed bright in her mind, overburdened and barely holding together. An acrid stench of burning filtered through the flooring as the heat crept higher. It was not enough. They had made a lethal misjudgement in the power needed to manage the descent of something so heavy. Were it a sinking skyship, they would have been tossing everything out of the hatch to lighten the load.

The strange silver lever that had been installed to the side of her control panel called to her. *To be pulled when landing.* Almost as if the Caretaker had examined their shoddy human construction and realised that they were going to burn up and fly face-first into a mountain.

"Do something!" Andriyan yelled, eyes closed, hands in a death grip tight on the arms of his chair.

So she did the only thing there was left to do. She pulled the lever.

There was a thunk and a hiss from the hull, and an immediate slowing of their descent that shoved them deep into their cushioned seats. The burden on the levitation arrays lessened.

"What was that?" Ella asked, extracting herself form the padding.

Katherine peered out of the porthole. "Wings," she cried. "We have wings!"

Four huge, wide and billowing wings of a slick red fabric extended out from the hull, slowly widening to catch the wind like sails on a boat.

"Magic and mundane engineering," Ella said. "We cannot do it with just one, not with our current knowledge. Old Jackan will have a fit when I tell him all of this, and I wager he'll want to dive right back into designing the next void-ship."

White cloud whipped past the windows, wind buffeting them, rain streaking the glass. Rain – how glorious it was to see rain. The hull sizzled, the cooling air inside the capsule a most welcome feeling.

"Any idea where we might be?" Katherine asked. "I can't see much out there."

Ella shrugged in response. "We came in much faster than I'd thought, so we are likely somewhere over the eastern side of the Unity."

"Horse pee-hole!" Andriyan growled. "That puts us near border with righteous Ranneas Empire. Can only hope neither side launches spells at us when landing."

The capsule lurched sideways, caught by a crosswind. They hunkered down and hoped for the best, Ella trying to balance their descent so they didn't flip over.

The ground, when they caught sight of it, arrived with dizzying speed.

"Brace for impact!" Ella shouted.

Andriyan lowered the ships legs, ready to touch the dirt.

She gritted her teeth and hit the final landing control, the one that would overload and burn out the levitation arrays in one final effort.

Stomachs lurched as the descent slowed to a walking pace, the Fire Dragon settling down on the mighty waves of force erupting from its belly.

The crump of explosive spells and whoosh of projectiles announced the arrival of an unfriendly reception force somewhere below. The bastards were trying to shoot them out of the sky.

"Come on, Fire Dragon, come on," Katherine muttered. "Hang on just a little more. Hold. Hold. We are almost home."

Their arcane engineering lasted until the landing legs hit the dirt. Intricate etched arrays flared and fizzled, the delicate aether pathways burnt out. The capsule groaned as ropes and pulleys took its weight.

Something gave way beneath one of the legs, a boulder shifting. The Fire Dragon fell. They screamed as metal and wood crashed home with a crack like thunder. A rocky outcrop pierced the metal hull, a shard of stone jutting halfway through the capsule, just shy of impaling Ella's shoulder.

Their ship shuddered and settled, dirt and gravel pattering down with dull metal tings.

"Katherine?" Ella's voice was muffled and weak to her ears.

Her friend coughed in response. "Dusty but alive."

She sagged in her chair, grateful to be in one piece. "That was far too close. Andriyan? You alive?"

"Bruised, but well," Andriyan replied. "Very glad to be home. Let us leave before–"

The hatch exploded outwards, ripped from its hinges by mighty magic. Sunlight seared their eyes as they craned to see who had come for them. Was it a rescue? Doubtful. Silhouettes of armed men and mages. A Ranneas Empire battalion? Or a Unity border patrol?

It was neither.

It was a sodding Unity battlemage leading a full-blown war party, the man's crimson robes tinkling with icicles from an enemy spell and his golden mask scratched and dented from battle. He reached up and removed the mask to reveal a middle-aged, exhausted man behind that fearsome title. His eyes were wide and staring. "The voidmages," he gasped. "It is all true."

Behind him a gaggle of younger combat mages and mailed warriors crowded the hatch, awe stamped across soot-streaked faces.

Ella groaned and turned to her friend. "I guess somebody saw our scrycast, then."

"We all did," the battlemage said. Staring at the Imperial mage in their midst. "Which is why you did not get obliterated landing smack in the middle of a battlefield, once we realised what this vessel was. It is also why we are currently enjoying a ceasefire with the enemy."

From outside, warriors growled and gripped their weapons. "Move aside!" an imperious, heavily accented voice commanded.

The battlemage donned his mask of station and turned to confront the representative of the Ranneas Empire, his russet uniform bound with inscribed gold plates and shoulder stars donating high rank. "This vessel and all aboard belong to the Empire," the intruder stated, drooping moustache quivering with outrage.

"Horseshit," the battlemage replied.

"This is Empire land, slave of the hierarchs."

"We are clearly under Unity jurisdiction."

"This vessel landed closer to our side of the contested lands."

"The ship is a Unity-funded project."

"Constructed using our stolen dragon heart! The Treaty of Krasno dictates that we have priority."

"There is no precedent for…"

The crew of the Fire Dragon looked at each other in despair as the two high-ranking mages launched into a fearsome back-and-forth over treaties and technicalities. It seemed they had landed themselves right at the heart of a full-on diplomatic incident.

"Hah!" The Imperial mage cast a sneering eye around the ramshackle capsule. "You fling your words at me as if you believe this bucket of rust could carry mages to the moon. I suspect this is a vessel built for spying. Why, I... I..." his eyes widened, staring at the crew. The Unity battlemage followed suit, gawping at them.

"Ella," Katherine said. "You are leaking moondust."

She glanced down and witnessed snakes of it seeping from her suit pockets. It coalesced into silver ribbons in the air before streaming off towards the hatch and heading back up to the heavens where it had come from.

A strangled choke emerged from the imperial mage's throat. "Catch it!"

Mages cast their spells, attempting to capture and contain the dust, but their workings slid off moondust like it wasn't even there. The material taken from the domain of the gods utterly ignored the spells of those mighty magic users. They could only watch in astonishment and horror. For all their might and learning, they had been rendered impotent.

One of the Unity guards stepped up and used his helmet to scoop the last of it from the air. "You wanted this, yeah?" The mages gritted their teeth and ordered a box brought forth to contain his catch.

"Still believe that we did not reach the moon?" Andriyan snapped, weathering the glare of his superiors.

Whatever happened with Andriyan and the Imperials, Ella was now convinced that her own hierarchs would make them pay dearly for what they had done. Their vengeance would be terrible.

CHAPTER 38

A month and a half later.
The Howling prison fortress.

"Hold your tongue," Komissar Taeban hissed through the crack in the wall. "Somebody is coming."

Whitlaw Goddard fell silent, listening as boots approached, then stopped outside of his black and mouldering cell. A key rattled in the lock and the iron door squealed open. He squinted against the sudden light and the hulking silhouettes.

The head jailor spat on him. "Bring this stinking traitor."

He was almost too exhausted and broken down to feel fear. Almost. Death was not the terrifying prospect it once was, not when all he had to look forward to was slow starvation and more torture.

Rough hands dragged him out of the darkness. He tried to struggle, or at least to make a token attempt if this was to be his execution. They were none too careful hauling him down the hallway. He glanced at the door of the next cell, wondering about the occupant he had grown to know so well. He should have liked to meet her properly at least once before the end.

They paused outside the washroom. "Clean this wretch up."

Relief washed though him, accompanied by a sickening sense of gratitude. This would not be the day he died. Instead, this was the day he had been planning for.

The washroom contained a crackling fire, its warmth a gift from the gods. Here, they could heat stones for a hot bath. But that was for the jailers, and the wealthy imprisoned. The likes of him got cold well water, when they got anything at all.

They ripped soiled sackcloth from his back and tossed the rags into the fireplace. Fingers like iron dug into his matted hair and dunked him headfirst into a barrel of icy water. He gasped in shock, hauled back up coughing and spluttering, then down for another go, this time held longer until his feet began to kick. They loved that bit, roaring with laughter as they dragged him back up into the light. The weeping sores on his manacled wrists sizzled in pain as they yanked his hands up high and fastened them to an iron hook overhead.

He dangled there, barely on tiptoes, as rough-handed guards took scouring brush and hard soap to every bit of him, sloughing off dirt and grime and a layer of skin.

As bruised and battered as he was, he did not cry out at the poor treatment. Instead, in his head he went over the words he had rehearsed and refined over the last month of confinement, with aid from the woman in the next cell – his only solace in this hellish place. He'd managed to hold on throughout the torture and interrogations to finally reach this meeting with a hierarch. He suspected he knew exactly which arrogant prick it would be.

Whitlaw stayed very still as they took a razor to his head and face, scraping away matted hair. That, at least, was a relief. A sour-faced healer trudged in and gave him a cursory inspection: they didn't much care if he was in pain, infected, or ill, so long as he didn't die from it before their masters decided his fate.

One more dunk in the water to wash off the debris and soap scum, and then he was ordered to dress himself in a new set of rags. The rough sackcloth rasped against his skin, but at least it was clean and smelled strongly of lavender – likely an attempt to mask the stink of prison from refined nostrils.

"That'll have to do," the head jailer said, eyeing him critically. "Take this thing upstairs."

They passed Empire officials and priests of Perunuk in the hallway, here to torture Komissar Taeban. This collaboration of sworn enemies was an unprecedented thing, both great nations united in hatred of the rogue mages that dared to go meet the gods.

He was shoved and prodded up spiralling steps and along a hallway to reach a sumptuously appointed dining room laid out for a special occasion. The table was heaving with slabs of juicy beef in thick brown gravy, glazed pork ribs, and ripe fruit… actual fruit! His last meal, perhaps. For weeks, all he'd had was stale bread and water, with some thin porridge every third day. His mouth watered as the scents overwhelmed him. A place had been set, directly across the table from the man that had sent for him.

Hierarch Grubman-Lordrach IV was sat at the far end of the table, flanked by two impassive battlemages, one of whom could have been Lucid beneath the mask and robes. The man's greased lips sucked the marrow from a beef bone, which he carelessly tossed aside. Today, his face was sombre, devoid of the usual painted shading and embellishments the great and the good of the capital habitually wore.

The hierarch waved the prison guards away, the door closing behind them. He leaned back in his chair, toying with one end of his thin, waxed moustache as cold, hard eyes bore a hole through Whitlaw. "Sit."

Whitlaw sat, chains rattling.

"Eat. Drink."

With his hands bound, it was an exceedingly messy affair. His hunger made a beast of him: guzzling sweet, juiced apples, barely chewing and wolfing tender meat down before they took it away from him. The hierarch watched, his face impassive but undoubtedly taking satisfaction in the sorry state of the man who had wronged him.

"Enough."

Whitlaw froze, the urge to rip and tear and devour and drink warring with the fear of what they would do to him if he didn't. He shuddered and sat back, forcing his hands into his lap.

"I am going to have you all hanged," the hierarch said, as calmly as if he were saying he was going out for a stroll.

"No," Whitlaw replied, wiping the grease from his mouth. The game had begun and the dice were rolling, bouncing here and there, their faces yet to be determined. "I don't believe you will. That is not in your best interests."

A perfectly plucked eyebrow quirked upwards. "Whatever gives you the idea that a second-rate mage like you knows what is best for a hierarch?"

The Chief of the Research and Design Workshop was not a post that came with great power and prestige. It was a role more to do with balancing the books and personnel than politics, but as with any bureaucracy, you also had to have a deft hand in managing the demands of the arrogant arseholes at the top. The lowly bureaucrats toiling away in the mud knew how things worked better than their superiors.

"You are not angry at the loss of war materials," Whitlaw stated. "Nor the deceptions involved. What aggrieves you, is that we made you look bad in the eyes of your peers and the people. Your name is now a byword for 'feckless dupe'." The prison's guards had made that last bit clear as day, chortling about it on many an occasion.

The corners of the hierarch's mouth tightened. He remained silent.

The fragrant feast in front of the chief was a constant distraction after a month and a half of bare subsistence. "Instead of being a mere dupe," he added. "You should instead be seen as a paragon of the Unity. A hero to the people, your name burning bright through the ages."

Whatever Grubman-Lordrach IV had expected Whitlaw to say, it was not that. "A hero?" he scoffed. "You must also believe me to be a feckless dupe."

He had taken from the man, and now Whitlaw knew he had to give it back threefold. "Not in the slightest, hierarch. It can be done; with the use of specific levers that I have in my power to command."

The hierarch pursed his lips, eyes slitted like a serpent studying his prey. "Go on."

Whitlaw Goddard told him everything.

The hierarch smiled, a sickening sight when they were talking about his execution. "This may very well work," he mused. "You will of course have to be executed in public, but your daughter, yes. We can make of her an unwitting dupe."

"The other mages, too," Whitlaw said. "It costs you nothing to spare them."

Grubman-Lordrach IV tapped a manicured nail against his lips. "Whyever should I do that?"

"Because I would proclaim you a visionary hero with my last words," Whitlaw said, every word regretfully forced out.

"You must also appear to be a magnanimous statesman for that to work. Do you really want the bards to sing tales of the hierarch that hauled a young woman from her wheeled chair to string her up on the gallows?"

The hierarch's eye twitched and his lip curled. He did not like that thought. No, not at all.

"It is far easier to blame one high-ranking Unity mage and one Imperial collaborator than a whole group of your own underlings," Whitlaw added. "Especially after the great deed they have achieved. Alive and well, they will be of use to you, and their glory will be reflected onto yourself if you choose to embrace them while condemning me for my many crimes."

The hierarch's eye burned with greed. "Yes, this will work very well, indeed." He turned to one of his battlemages. "Make it happen."

After weeks of isolation, the cell doors swung open and a jailer removed Katherine's manacles before escorting her down winding hallways into a reception room, where Ella and Guylan awaited her, sat at a table littered with hot food and cold ale.

The sight of them alive and intact broke her. She launched herself in a frenzy of one-armed hugging, weeping unashamedly as they all tried to talk over one another in their relief and eagerness to reconnect. The jailer left them to it, slinking off muttering.

All three of them were bruised, hungry, and hurting in body and in mind, but that was to be expected after a month in the depths of The Howling. Once their greetings were over, Guylan stepped back, his face grim as he took in Katherine's missing arm.

She turned away, unable to face his scrutiny. Despite weeks alone with nothing to do but dwell on the last three years, she had not yet come to terms with the loss.

He licked his lips and shifted from foot to foot. "How did it happen?"

"Aether overload," Ella answered, reaching out to squeeze Katherine's leg.

A shudder rippled up his spine.

"The protective runes were drained, and thrusters broke lose," Ella explained. "She held the ship together and saved us."

He nodded, not wanting to delve into more unwelcome depths. "What of Andriyan?"

"Alive, last we saw of him," Ella said. "I suspect the Empire has him captive."

Ella craned her neck and listened to check if anybody else was approaching their room. "Where is Jackan? I've so much to tell him. Is he..." She spotted Guylan's stricken expression. "Oh." She closed her eyes for a moment, fighting back the tears. "The battlemage?"

He shook his head. "A heart attack, of all things. The old fool had been hiding his symptoms from us for the last year. He did get to see you launch towards the stars, though. He took great pride in that, at the end."

They took seats and sat in solemn silence for a while. "Tell me your story," Guylan asked. "I pray it was worth it."

"I wouldn't bother praying," Ella snapped, then launched into her tale.

He listened, held rapt by the journey he had been meant to make, the accident, and the fraught landing, and then he was horrified by what they found – or did not, in this case – in the Silver Palace.

"Gone," he spluttered. "Just... gone." He laughed, but it was a hollow shade of a thing. "Then there is nothing to be done but move on in the light of knowledge." He picked up an eating knife and turned it over in his hands.

"Our situation has changed," he said. "We are not under guard, and we have been given food, drink, and knives. I suggest we take advantage before they change their minds."

It was a good while before another entered the room.

A crimson-clad battlemage entered alone, not that she needed anyone to guard her from the likes of them. The woman removed her mask.

"Overseer Lucid," Guylan snarled, rising to his feet with an eating knife in hand.

A flick of a gloved finger sent him back into his seat, wincing as his tailbone hit wood. "Eaten your fill? Good. We need you to appear hale and healthy for the execution."

"Ours?" Ella croaked.

She shook her head.

"Andriyan?" Katherine ventured.

"Alive, sentenced to ten years in a hard labour camp." She tossed a brass locket into Katherine's lap.

It was her father's. She opened it to see her mother's fine features. The blood drained from her face, and what little strength she had leeched from her body. "Where is he?"

"Don't be fools," Lucid advised. "Somebody has to pay for this ungodly mess. And your father, my dear, has brokered a deal to save your hides."

A scream erupted from Katherine as she struggled to rise, fighting the battlemage's magic holding her seated.

"Enough!"

The crack and pain of an unseen slap set Katherine swaying and blinking in shock.

"All of you will publicly condemn your father, and your superior," she said.

"Never!" Ella snarled.

"You have no power here. Nor political capital at your disposal. All you can do is waste his final efforts and hang by his side until you are dead. Knowing the hierarchs, they will hang you first and make him watch. Is that what you desire?"

The battlemage stared at Katherine. "He wants you to survive. If you love him, you will ensure that he gets his last wish."

"I need to see him," she demanded.

"Impossible. To try would be to die. What will happen now is that you will be washed and groomed, and then you will sign declarations of condemnation that will be copied and distributed to every city, every town, and every gods-forsaken farm shack in the Unity. Are we clear?"

They reluctantly nodded, too drained and too shocked to fight.

"Good." She turned to leave, then paused in the doorway and looked back. "In all my years," she said, "I have never come across mages that gave me so much trouble. And troubled I am, because what you have accomplished together is incredible. It is a world-changing event, for good or for ill. I cannot condone how you achieved it, but for ingenuity and the deed itself, I can only commend you."

The joy of their reunion now tasted like ashes. Katherine Goddard, Ella Pickering, and Guylan Bluford slumped in dejected silence.

The chief was going to die, and they were powerless to prevent it.

Katherine began to weep, broken.

A week later, surrounded by armed guards and battlemages, the three mages sat watching the farce of justice play out before a baying crowd of priests and politicians.

Whitlaw Goddard was dragged out and fitted for the noose, then Taeban Tereshkova marched out for the same treatment. Katherine stiffened as her father's gaze found her, and she tried to hold it together, for him. Her hand clutched her father's locket on its chain around her neck.

Katherine flinched as Ella's fingers clutched her arm and held on tight. She relaxed and took strength from her friend's unwavering support, enough not to cry during her father's last moments, enough to try and communicate that she was strong, and she had support enough to see her through these dark times.

The words and accusations were a blur to her as terror bubbled up towards the dreadful, inevitable conclusion. She gritted her teeth and clamped her lips shut, shaking as that dreadful moment finally arrived. The hooded executioner kicked the stools out from beneath the prisoners and left her father to dangle there. Her shriek of horror came out as a muffled moan, and Ella and Guylan held her tight to stop her flinging herself at the guards. She was forced to watch, her cheeks running hot and wet.

It took an age of torment for her father to stop kicking, to fall limp and sway in the breeze. He was now beyond all pain, and the bastards could do nothing more to him. The priests and politicians cheered, but she noted that many of the mages and common folk watched in sullen, simmering silence.

The nausea and dread faded, burned away by the heat of her rising fury. She turned her eyes upon Hierarch Grubman-Lordrach IV, who sat there smug and joking atop his gaudy golden throne. "I am going to destroy him," she whispered.

"And we are going to help you," Guylan replied.

Katherine bit her lip bloody. "I can summon up a few allies to aid us. I have a disreputable little friend who I'm sure will be most eager to help."

Ella squeezed her friend's hand. "We went to the moon together – how hard can it be to start a revolution down here on the ground? And one day, when times are better, we'll go back to the stars and build such wonders as to make Jackan, Rojer, Taeban, and your father proud." Her gaze shifted to the hierarch. "But first, him."

The hierarch shivered and shifted on his throne, a sudden chill breeze making him most uncomfortable...

As powerful as he was, he had no inkling that in three years' time, a mob of commoners would tear him from the silken sheets of his country mansion and nail him to his own front door with rusty spikes – the first gilded leech to fall before the Citizen's Revolt and its one-armed leader.

ACKNOWLEDGEMENTS

This book marks a bit of a departure in tone for me: a little less swords and sorcery and a little more about building really cool things. Accepted wisdom suggests that authors should stick to their lane and keep writing the same sort of thing, but ah well, consider me an adventurer. I'm writing what I want to write and hopefully taking readers along for a wild ride of the imagination.

First Mage On The Moon is one of these ideas that's been bubbling away at the back of my mind for years..."What if wizards tried to build a rocketship to go to the moon. Without the modern scientific method, how would magicians explain gravity? What about oxygen? And would their magic even work off-planet?" Much like the alchemists of old, magic-users by their very nature would be curious creatures, so it's not all fireballs and fancy pointy hats however much you want to force them into conflicts.

As much as I love fantasy as a genre, I have always been fascinated by anything to do with space and the engineering that makes space travel possible. So I decided to brew up something that combines two of the things I love and hope it energises and enthrals you as much as it did me when I was writing it.

My thanks go first to Natasha for all her support and help, and to my family, then all the excellent staff at Angry Robot Books, my agent Ed Wilson and the team at Johnson & Alcock, Jörg Asselborn and Alice Coleman for the incredible cover, the stalwart writers at GSFWC and ESFF and all my other writing pals who share the ups and downs of writing and publishing. Truly, I have met some magnificent people along this madcap journey as an author, including many of those unsung heroes who review and post about books online and help keep the spark of awareness alive for authors that are not huge and widely-known names.

And finally, my heartfelt thanks go to you, the reader.

ABOUT THE AUTHOR

Cameron Johnston is the British Fantasy Award and Dragon Awards nominated author of dark fantasy novels *The Traitor God, God of Broken Things, The Maleficent Seven* and *The Last Shield*. He is a swordsman, a gamer, and an enthusiast of archaeology, history and mythology. He loves exploring ancient sites and camping out under the stars by a roaring fire.